HOW TO MAKE A MILLI ✔ **KU-514-847**
– pounds, of course. Even Jake Sullivan couldn't make *that* many girls. Admittedly, he has a damn good try.

Anyhow, come his twenty-ninth birthday Jake's got his million. Come his thirtieth, he's doing three years in Pentonville gaol.

Is our boy downhearted? Not on your life. While you're around, and me, and people like us, the Jake Sullivans of this world are *never* going to be downhearted.

And . . . ponder this – he's going to be out and around and among us again any day now.

The Rise and Fall of Jake Sullivan is an ebullient read. 'The great contemporary themes of sex, power and money are slickly introduced.' (*Sunday Telegraph*)

Also by Hunter Davies in Panther Books

Here We Go, Round the Mulberry Bush
The Other Half

Hunter Davies

The Rise and Fall of Jake Sullivan

Panther

Granada Publishing Limited
Published in 1971 by Panther Books Limited
Park Street, St. Albans, Hertfordshire
Reprinted 1973

First published by Weidenfeld & Nicolson Limited 1970
Copyright © Hunter Davies 1970
Made and printed in Great Britain at
The Philips Park Press, Manchester
Set in Intertype Times

The Rise and Fall of Jake Sullivan

Part One

Chapter One

I could have gone to the pub with the rest of the office but they got into such rounds it was like ordering for a regiment. I should have gone, to keep in with Bennet, but he was always surrounded by so many people keeping in with him that I could never get within forelock touching distance.

I had two fried eggs on toast and a cup of tea in a caff. The previous day I'd had a three hour lunch at the Dorchester to launch something or other. I'd had mountains of caviar, which was awful, drunk too much brandy, which I don't like, and pocketed six free cigars, just in case I ever take up smoking. I came out of the caff still smelling of fried eggs. That's one thing about going to the Dorchester. You don't mind if people come up and smell you afterwards.

I walked round for a bit, but not too much. I didn't want to bump into any of the gangs staggering back and forward to the pub. It was one thing to have lunch on your own in a caff, but there was no need to flaunt it. I had gone with them when I'd joined the office the previous month, but I never seemed to have anything to say. I thought of a lot of smart remarks, but never got them out. It was the summer of 1961. I felt very 1960. January 1960 at that.

I hadn't had a thing in the paper yet and I could feel this was going to be another waste of time. Bennet had no doubt been conned by his public relation friends once again. On our sort of paper, assistant editors like Bennet relied a lot on public relation men. This latest bloke was supposed to be some sort of American whizz kid, which was Bennet's new word of the moment, lifted from Time magazine. He was very rich, very brilliant and successful, but Bennet couldn't quite remember his name, thanks to the stupor brought on by the lunch his contact had given him. Bennet never had lunch with PRs. They were always contacts. All I was given was a surname and an address.

It was 400 Piccadilly. I went several times round Piccadilly

Circus, admiring all the au pairs sitting round the fountain showing off their legs. No one had told me Piccadilly was a street as well as a Circus. In the end I had to run, by which time my drip dry shirt was wringing and my Italian style suit, bought in Market Street, Manchester, was all creased. This was another thing which made me feel so dated. Butcher striped shirts had come in but I didn't even know where to buy them.

Sullivan House was all glass and pine wood. I struggled for the handle of a likely looking piece of glass but it opened before I'd touched it.

'Tom Graham,' I said. 'Of the Sunday News. Mr. Sullivan is expecting me.'

'Oh, is he,' said a commissionaire, making a great show of getting his spectacles out and looking for lists. He grabbed what he wanted from inside a racing paper.

'How do you spell Graham?'

I'd never been asked that before. Every second person in Cumberland is called Graham. He was showing off that he could read and write.

'Oh,' he said. 'Here it is. You are expected. Five minutes late as well. Come this way ... sir.' The sir was a very late addition. He took me round deep carpeted corridors full of debby secretaries carrying papers. He'd said it was the top floor, yet the lift had been right beside his desk. Perhaps I was being shown out sharpish. The Sunday News was that sort of paper. Somebody smarter perhaps had arrived and wanted to interview the chairman, like the Dandy or the Beano.

He pressed a button on a blank wall and the wall opened to reveal a lift. The chairman's own personal lift, he explained. For Mr. Sullivan and important customers.

It was like something out of Versailles. All gilt and polished wood and ornate decorations. I put my collar straight in a mirror and felt under my arms to see if my drip dry had dried, gave my nose a quick pick and tried to rub my shoes on the deep pile to give them a polish.

The lift stopped and I got out into an even more ornate reception room, with originals everywhere. You could tell they were originals. All the signatures were so thick you could have picked them off and set them up in type. A tall blonde girl, with long heavily lacquered hair swept up at the ends, was sitting at an antique reception desk. She looked completely unoriginal. She'd been cut out from a picture in The Tatler, where she'd been photographed enjoying a joke at a debs' party. Super, she said when I gave my name. Super. She'd buzz the chairman's secretary right away.

The chairman's secretary appeared almost immediately and beckoned me to follow her, without speaking. She looked more real. She had intelligent hair, sensitive legs and a quiet walk. She took me through several more reception rooms, full of things to be admired for their good taste. I wanted to say something sensitive and quiet to her, but I could only mumble on about the nice pictures, original originals were they. She disappeared and I was left standing by a statue, feeling I was being observed from all angles. She reappeared at a far doorway and waved at me to come into the next room.

It was the board room, high and long and oak panelled with a rectangular table arranged with eight places, each with paper, pens, glasses of water and worry beads. I said there must be a mistake. I hadn't come to attend a meeting. I'd better wait outside. She said sit down, firmly but politely. She pointed to a chair and desk in the corner, then went out.

A very tall, chinless public school looking chap of about thirty-five waddled in, pushing back his flaxen hair. He went round the table, rearranging the names at each place, then he sat down near the top. A discreet-looking young man in a white cut-away collar and black suit came in and sat in the opposite chair, leaving one between them for the chairman. He said Hello, Jeremy to the first one, looked across the room at me and smiled, then he folded his arms and sat staring into space, still half smiling.

Five other people soon joined them, all much older and greyer except one who looked even younger than me but was very smart and cocky-looking. Then the girl who had shown me in came back and sat at a side table near me, with her notebook ready. I wanted to ask her if perhaps the Prime Minister had got held up in the traffic, but she was busy looking at her notes. The room had a dignified and reverential silence. They must have mistaken me for someone else. I'd be found out, they'd ring the editor and I'd be back on the first banana boat to Manchester.

'Maggie,' said Jeremy, very irritably and peevishly, 'who is this *person*?' Maggie, the girl at the side table who had shown me in, smiled back, giving nothing away. I wished she'd answered. I would like to have known who I was and why I was there.

Jeremy looked round for support in his effort to make me crawl away, but no one caught his eye. The very young smart-alec was filing his nails, but half under the table so the others couldn't see him. The grey middle-aged men had their impeccable faces on, basking back in the glow of their corporate success.

The chairman, Mr. Sullivan, entered. He wore fashionably tight black trousers, a tight black cashmere polo neck and soft black slip-on shoes. He had a crew cut, dark glasses, and he came on clicking his fingers. Bennet had told me the chairman's name was Sullivan, possibly James Sullivan or it might be Joe. He couldn't remember. It was Jake. Jake Sullivan.

'I take it you've all read these boring minutes,' he said, shoving away his papers.

There was a stuttering of Yes, Yes, Yes, Yes, followed by two self conscious Ayes and a bout of required coughing. The company secretary gently pushed Jake's papers back to him, proffering at the same time his Parker Sixty-One. Jake violently refused them.

'I signed that bloody thing yesterday. Do you think I've got nothing better to do than wait for you lot to make up your feeble minds?'

'Quite so, quite so,' said the secretary, flatly, as if that was the reply he would have given whatever Jake had said.

'Right, the cash flow problem,' said Jake. He moved his chair back and put his feet on the table. Everyone studied their papers. 'Are we agreed we go to those bloody merchant bankers? Are we? Come on. I want to hear your lousy opinions.'

It was strange to hear Jake again, and even stranger to see him. I still felt shocked. Jake Sullivan of Sullivan House. It was amazing.

'I feel I must inform the board,' began a grey, pedantic middle-aged voice, 'that I consider that the problem is not as acute as perhaps the chairman believes it to be. The board might be interested to hear that according to my department's statistical analysis, which in the interests of company democracy I might take this chance to distribute amongst you . . .'

'Christ on a crutch,' said Jake. 'No! It's not a bloody Salvation Army meeting.'

The voice smiled, coughed and went on to enumerate certain points as Jake sighed, groaned and studied his watch.

'Moving away from legal considerations,' jumped in another voice, 'I'm afraid I can't accept your premisses . . .'

As the voices drooled on, Jake took his left shoe off, put it to his nose, sniffed, then put it back on again.

'It's my personal opinion,' began another, 'that as our company has always been concerned primarily with direct erections and not with the take-over of other . . .'

Jake raised his eyebrows, in mock disgust at such language, then returned to his shoes.

'I concede that there is some substance in your argument, but as the chairman has previously pointed out, I venture to suggest that there are certain aspects of the present situation that perhaps all of us, gentlemen, are not fully aware of, namely . . .'

'Shut up! For Chrissake,' shouted Jake. 'What are you all on about? I've never heard such crap in all my life.' Jake glared round at all of them. 'Right, the motion is carried. We go for more cash. OK? Thank you, gentlefuckingmen.

'Next, I want a resolution about the take-over. You've got it into your tiny little mind, have you Jeremy? That's what I want the money for. I mean *we* want the money for. The Board. What a laugh.'

'Might I suggest, chairman, that it might be in order to . . .'

'Nothing is in order, unless I say so,' said Jake, getting up from the table. 'Right, I'll give you dozy lot of buggers half an hour to get rid of your piss and wind. Just keep it to yourselves, that's all. I only want the resolution. Tom. This way.'

He led me through a door into a large sitting room decorated entirely in black and white. The walls, the ceiling and the carpets were white. The leather chairs, the leather couches and the curtains were black. On the walls were enormous abstract paintings, all in black and white.

'You haven't changed,' he said, throwing himself down on a couch. I thought he was referring to my clothes. I buttoned my jacket up in case my shirt was still advertising Joe's caff.

'Yeh,' I muttered, not knowing what to say. 'I like your

colour scheme ... I mean lack of colour scheme.' I always tried to start interviews by talking about people's surroundings rather than about them. It sort of eases them in.

'There's no apartheid in this apartment,' said Jake. 'But I like a bit of colour now and again. Rita? Rita, where are you? Come here, I want you.'

His American accent had gone and he was shouting for Rita, in broad Carlisle.

At the far end of the room a coloured girl appeared, carrying drinks. She wore very high-heeled shoes which she toppled on, trying hard to balance the drinks.

'What do you think, then, Tom? The only trouble is if I fancy a Chink next or a Nip or a Red Indian, I'll have to change the decor. Can't have any clashes. Rita, you're dripping all over me Axminster.'

'No I'm not, Jakey,' said Rita in broad cockney. 'I've been ever so careful with the drinks.'

'I don't mean the drinks, darling. Come here and give us a kiss.' Rita bent over and kissed him. 'Don't bend that way in front of guests. How many times have I told you. You don't want to put him off his State Management Brown Ale. Right, you can go now Rita. You'll be exciting my yokel friend. Go on. Get back on your back. I'll need you later.'

Jake took off his spectacles and passed me a bottle of Brown Ale. It was State Management, which meant it must have come from Carlisle, the only area in England where the drink is nationalized.

'How's your lousy job, then, son?' said Jake.

'Well, you know, sometimes it's OK, sometimes ...'

'There you go. You can't give a fucking straight answer. That university made you worse. Everything has to be modified, hasn't it, with reservations thrown in at every comma. Life doesn't have reservations. It's just people like you who create them, turning living into coitus interruptus.'

'Oh, aye,' I said, smiling.

'I got that from Reader's Digest,' said Jake. 'I thought you'd like it. I don't. I'm sending for my money back. How much have you got in the bank?'

'As a matter of fact ...'

'Give a straight bloody answer!' said Jake. 'Don't piss on like that. As a matter of fact you've got an overdraft of £25.

You won't catch that up for two months, on your chicken shit income.'

'Money isn't everything,' I said and immediately regretted it.

'Of course it isn't. Only fools think it is, such as ninety-nine per cent of the population who haven't got enough and think their worries would go if they had. That's why you *need* money, to show how unimportant it is.'

'Did you get that from Reader's Digest?'

'No, the back of a Christmas cracker. Rita? Some more drinks.'

'Lovely face,' I said as Rita reappeared. I felt I had to say something, as she was obviously being paraded for my benefit. I couldn't think of anything suitably obscene, not that I would have come out with it anyway.

'You're trying hard,' said Jake. 'She could be yours, for two Shredded Wheat tops and some Green Shield Stamps. It's about time I traded her in. Some people have muzak in their chairman's suite, others have iced water. I have cunt on tap. Just for the chairman's use. But stick around, son.'

'Well, I better ask you a few questions, if you don't mind . . .' I said, getting out my notebook.

'Put that away. Rita might think it's some new kinky toy. Relax. Don't try to prove anything. Be yourself. That's why I wanted to see you. I was watching you in the lift and you were like a frenetic idiot.'

Jake pressed a button. The lights went out, the curtains closed and on the wall was projected a film of me standing nervously in front of the commissionaire and then going into the lift. I could see I was standing all hunched and cross-legged as I put my tie straight and picked my nose.

'It saves me a lot of money,' said Jake. 'I've got the upper hand from the word go. I know whether people scratch their balls when they're on their own or smell under their arms. And of course I tell them. And with me zoom lens I can go right up close and read any documents they're reading.'

He pressed the button again and the film finished.

'Dairy Maid Fresh Orange Juice on a Stick will now be on sale in all parts of the cinema. Rita? She hasn't nicked off again has she? I think she's got a rubber truncheon back there. Did you hear the one about the two women who got into bed and one said, "I want to be frank with you" and the other one said "No, I want to be Frank tonight." '

I smiled. I knew it was a dirty-joke, but I knew I wouldn't be able to work it out till the next day.

'What do you think then, Tommy lad?'

'What do you want me to think?' I said.

'I want to see you open your mouth and just say something. Natural, like, without all this education fucking you up.'

'It is a bit vulgar, isn't it,' I said gesturing round at the room. 'You're obviously overcompensating for something. You're not impotent, are you?'

'Rita? Come over here. My friend with the straw sticking out of his arse wants to see something . . .'

'No, no, no. I believe you. There's no need to show off. But you can't help doing it, can you, even though you're a million-aire and only twelve.'

'I like that. Only twelve. So when are you going to join me?'

'I didn't know you were coming apart.' I was becoming a bit more confident, but still wary. 'Shall I interview you now or when you've finished your exercises?'

'I don't want to appear in your shitty newspaper.'

'It's a good newspaper, actually, in that it does fairly well what it sets out to do, given that . . .'

'Actually, eh?' said Jake, mocking me. 'I like to hear loyalty. I suppose if you were on the Cumberland News you'd say the same.'

'Well, I think I'd better be going . . .'

'Personal assistant, what do you think? Four thousand a year, plus expenses? And you can have luncheon vouchers thrown in, or Rita . . .'

I got up and started towards the door. I didn't want to go for one minute. I wanted to stay on and perhaps see what he was really like, but I felt it was some trick to humiliate me. He'd have some smart reply the minute I appeared eager.

'Meanwhile, back at the ranch . . .' said Jake, pushing past me and into the board room. I followed slowly, trying to slide along the wall unobtrusively.

'Right, you lazy lot of buggers. Hands off heads. Hands on cocks. That resolution, OK? Good. By the way, Jeremy, you did get that stuff from Companies House?'

Jeremy was looking round at me, very suspiciously.

'Don't take any notice of him, Chinless. He's just come out of the bogs. He won first prize in the Cumberland News Spot the Ball competition. The first prize was to see me. All righty, let's go.'

Jake was doing his American stunt again, clapping his hands and jumping around. 'Right, who owns all the shares, then, Jeremy?'

'Well as a matter of fact, Jake . . .'

'As a matter of fact nothing,' shouted Jake. 'You get bloody slower every day. You wouldn't think he was a public school boy. So busy buggering each other they haven't time for sums. Bloody public schools. Did you go round yesterday when I telt you?'

'Well as a matter of fact, I was rather tied up all day yesterday. I just haven't had time to work it out . . .'

'Who were you working it out with last night, you great slob?'

'Last night?' said Jeremy. 'I can't remember as far back as last night. What.'

He was hoping Jake would smile at this. He opened his mouth wide, tilted his head at an angle and gave several adenoidal ha ha ha ha's, just to show how witty he thought it was.

'I don't know why I took him on,' said Jake, looking round at everyone except Jeremy. 'I thought I'd have fun, bossing round a big cunt from a public school. Bloody stupid, wasn't I? He's not even a good bloody estate agent. What do you think I should do with him?'

Jake paused, knowing no one would say anything. He still hadn't looked at Jeremy. Suddenly he jumped on the table, ran across it and had Jeremy by the scruff of the neck. The other directors busied themselves with their papers and pencils, trying hard to look the other way.

'You bastard,' said Jake. 'There's only one rule I insist on in this bloody company. And you know it. Keep your cock out of the pay roll. OK?'

Jake gave Jeremy one last thump, this time in the balls, then propelled him towards the door. Jeremy was shouting about his lawyer and witnesses and damages.

'Get out. You're fired. No more public school assistants for me.'

Jake was looking across at me, winking.

'Now Michael,' continued Jake. 'As we're all in such amicable agreement, when do you think we should make our formal offer?'

The meeting at last got down to some serious work. I started to move towards the door, expecting Jake to shout out some obscenity, just when I was half way across. I got safely to the door without anyone taking any notice of me.

'Don't forget what I said Tommy lad,' said Jake, very quietly, as I opened the door. 'I'll expect you on Monday morning, or else. We Cumberland lads should stick together.'

I went out without turning round. I'd had enough of his vulgarity and B picture melodrama.

'You Welsh bastard.'

Chapter Two

I'm not a Welsh bastard. In fact I'm probably more Cumberland than he is. My Dad was a fitter, born and bred in Thwaite, but his firm in Carlisle laid him off when I was about six and we all moved to South Wales. He died when I was twelve. He came home one day from work, took his bike clips off, put his bike away, cleaned his bait box out and dropped dead of a heart attack. Me Mum decided to come home to Thwaite. She'd never liked the Welsh.

Thwaite is about ten miles outside Carlisle, a little forgotten farming village on the edge of Cumberland Fells where nothing ever happens and even a nothing like Willie Sullivan, Jake's father, could feel he was a sophisticated townie. He hadn't intended to come to Thwaite. He'd come over the Scottish border from Dumfries to a dance at the County Hall in Carlisle. He'd taken Lilly Clapperton home on his motor bike. The bike broke down in Thwaite and he never went home. Lilly ignored him for months, but he persisted. He took a job looking after the books for Armstrongs, Thwaite's only builders, as he was always good with figures. In the end Lilly had a choice between the usual beetroot faced farm labourers, which was the only talent around, or Willie Sullivan, that dashing white-collar worker with the motor bike who was so good with figures.

She shouldn't really have fallen, of course, not a lass with her principles. Willie was a foreigner. He was born in Scotland and had a soft Dumfriesshire accent. Even worse, with a name like Sullivan, further back he was probably Irish. Lilly disapproved of all foreigners. Irish, Jews, Blacks, Yellows, Italians, people with red hair, people with long hair and anyone else in any way different from her. They should all go back to their own countries. She was furious when she read in her *Daily Express* about foreigners who not only had the indecency to settle in England but then had the effrontery to turn round and dare to *criticize* England. Lilly Sullivan had quite a good war. She had all those nasty Germans and Japs to hate.

But she was a good mother. She told them that, so it must be true. She never told lies. She never did anything silly, like gossiping, or losing things. She always made ends meet. She bought nothing on the never-never. She didn't ill-treat them, put dirty clothes on them, or run bills up at the Co-op. She always had meals ready on time and never left them in the house on their own. Unlike some people she could mention. She was strict and unemotional and very suspicious of the world. Suspicious in the sense that she could see through everything. Nobody could fool her. She suspected other people's kindness, so she never accepted any. She was as suspicious of little do-gooders and busybodies in the village as she was of big national events. That Battle of Britain. Just the Government's latest publicity stunt.

Her logic just missed being logical and she held on to it stubbornly, whatever the facts and however she contradicted herself. She was so obtuse in some of her pronouncements that it was impossible to knock them down. I'd called at her house one day after I'd done some little job for the Scouts Bob-a-Job week. She had to sign my card, to prove I'd done the work. She said she wouldn't sign. I'd have to sign it myself. That was how Hitler got control of the people.

Willie on the other hand never had any opinions, one way

or the other, though he could chunter on for hours, out of the corner of his mouth, without committing himself either way. She usually slapped him down, especially when he wanted to behave, as she put it, like a beast. She was having none of that.

She was quite proud, secretly, of Willie's job. Armstrongs started expanding, thanks to the post-war housing boom. With a bit of his wife's determination, Willie could have gone with it. He did, in one sense. Instead of working from a corner of Fred Armstrong's room, which was where he'd started when they'd just been a jobbing builder's, he moved to a large site office in the middle of a Carlisle council housing estate. But inside this office, William had become more pathetic than ever. He huddled in a corner with masses of impressive-looking charts and graphs and time sheets, all of them yellowing at the edges. He was officially time keeper, but no one really knew what that meant. He shared the office with Mr. Omerod, a real eager beaver who was the site's general foreman. He whizzed round, organizing the world. The minute he was out, the young labourers would come in to ask Willie if he would help them fill in their pools coupons with his log tables, or could he work out their paternity orders on his slide rule. As Willie was huffing and puffing through his acres of papers, another labourer would be nailing a dead fish under his stool, or digging a hole behind him, or balancing buckets of water on the door.

He never had tantrums or raged at them when he found out. He just pitied them. They were the post-war flotsam, he said. They'd never seen service. They didn't know what discipline was. Willie Sullivan had never seen service either, but as the war retreated he imagined he had. The army didn't take him because of his chest, not that he wanted the army. He got a Home Guard job helping to guard a naval establishment on the Cumberland coast at which he spent most of the war, which was lucky for him. He missed the birth of his first son Jake.

This happened on 7 November 1940, the second winter of the war. Lilly said it was typical. Just the sort of stupid thing Willie would do. She blamed him for Jake, and the war. As all men were beasts, she'd desperately wanted a girl. Jake didn't stop screaming from the minute he was born. He wanted continual attention, drinks, carries, cuddles, pee-pees and then drinks again. He never slept all night till he was well over four, and neither did Lilly. He was hell, from the minute he was born, as she continually told everyone. She didn't beat him or scream back. You didn't show emotions of that sort. You had to go through it, just as you have to grit your teeth and get through life.

Willie was well out of it, hiding away on the Solway coast. Trust him. He did come home at weekends and Lilly was so tired and exhausted she fell again. It was another boy, born in 1942. He was called Cedric and right from the beginning he was completely different. He just lay back and got fat and gurgled and cooed. He slept like an angel and with his golden curls looked like one. He was so little trouble, so placid and content, that you could easily think he wasn't there. Lilly loved him from the day he slipped out, his little eyes closed. Jake had to be hoiked out, with forceps, and he came out glaring around, screaming at the world.

Lilly told these details to everyone who cared to listen. When we came back to Thwaite we moved in across the road from her in Solway Terrace. She was still going on about it, as if we'd never been away.

Jake wasn't very quick at speaking. At two-and-a-half he was still grunting. He thought he was being perfectly clear and he went into tantrums when no one could understand him. These tantrums continued until he was four. Whenever he didn't get what he wanted, he lay on the floor and had convulsions. If he was slapped for doing something, like putting his fingers in an electric plug, he cried, then went back and did it again. The only way was to forcibly pick him up, put him in a room and lock him in.

Lilly never went along with Jake. She was determined to win, to keep him down and in his place. And she did. When Cedric came along she knew she was right. That was how little boys should be. Seen and not heard.

Jake couldn't get to school quick enough. For the first year, he was the brightest, most eager kid in the place, rushing around, wanting to do everything, answer every question and help the teacher at every turn. But Miss Steel was an old dried up spinster who disliked that sort of neurotic energy and irritating eagerness. She wanted children to sit still when they were told, put their hands on their heads and shut up. Jake could never sit still, or shut up. So she beat him down. His brand of enthusiasm annoyed a lot of teachers, irrationally almost. They knew it wasn't wicked, but it got on their nerves. They stood him in the corner, threw him out of the room, anything to get peace.

When I left Thwaite at six Jake was predominantly still bright and eager. When I came back at twelve to join him at Thwaite Secondary Modern, he'd given up trying. He was against them. All the teachers at the Primary School had doubtless reacted like Miss Steel. Very soon most teachers had genuine grounds for not liking him.

Thwaite Secondary Modern was simply the Primary School with another couple of classes knocked on. For decades it had all just been the village school, but the 1944 Education Act had split it into Primary, up to eleven, and Secondary Modern, up to fifteen. Most kids went straight on. Very few from Thwaite ever passed the Eleven Plus and went into Carlisle to the Grammar School. I never sat the Eleven Plus, with moving around so much and my mother being so little clued up about the education system. Neither did Jake. They said he couldn't. He was too bad. So when he moved to the Secondary Modern next door, his reputation preceded him.

Jake could only coerce idiots like Basil and Roy to be friends. He'd fought everyone from the beginning, trying to be the gang leader, but he ended up on his own, as he was so nasty even to his friends. He tried to make a virtue of this, maintaining he preferred to be a lone wolf. He said he didn't need mates. He spurned any advances from masters as well as boys. He disbelieved everything they told him. He said they were stupid. How could they teach him anything when they were all so thick? He thought I was the thickest person he'd ever come across for doing homework. He'd failed to get much reaction out of me physically, even by thumping me in the playground, so he tried to beat me mentally . . .

'Come on, I'm waiting for you,' he shouted between the cracks of our kitchen door. I was inside at the kitchen table. Our house was like his, two up and two down. My mother was in the living room, watching telly. With my Dad suddenly dying she'd come into a bit of money and we had the first telly in Solway Terrace. We also owned our house. It only cost about £300, but it was ours. We and the Sullivans were the only owners in the street. White-collar Willie had always had a good job of course.

'I said I'm waiting.'

'Shuttup, man. I'm busy.'

'You bloody swot,' came the hoarse whisper through the door. I went to the door and whispered back at him. I didn't want my mother to come through. I wasn't supposed to play with Jake Sullivan.

'Me Mam'll hear you,' I whispered. 'I'll see you tomorrow.'

'You're doing them sums, aren't you?'

Jake said this as if he was conducting the Spanish Inquisition. If I admitted so dastardly an action, that was the end.

'No, I'm sticking in me stamps. I'll give you some swaps if you go away.'

'Liar. I can see your 'tic book. I'm just going to come in, and I'll tell your Mam you asked me to.'

'No, don't. Be a pal. Give us half an hour, eh.'

If Lilly Sullivan had known that other kids weren't supposed to associate with Jake, she would have sued them all. Despite everything, she was fiercely proud. She might run Jake down, but no one else was allowed to. Her house was the cleanest and neatest in the street, if you overlooked Willie's motor bike which he kept under a greasy tarpaulin in the front hall. Our house was always untidy and disorganized, though it wasn't dirty and smelly, like the Patricks'. The Patricks lived opposite and had about eleven kids. Mrs. Sullivan's perpetual shout, which I seemed to hear throughout my childhood, was 'KEEP ON YOUR OWN SIDE!' She hated everything about the Patricks. They were Catholics, of course.

'Come and play in the lotties,' said Jake. The lotties meant the allotments, little gardens set up during the war so that ordinary households could produce extra vegetables. Now they were a wilderness, but ideal places for people like Jake to grab little girls and pull their knickers down.

'No, I don't like the lotties. They stink.'

'So do you,' said Jake wittily. I crept nearer the kitchen door and tried to slam it, but Jake had got his foot in.

'Ha ha ha, that got you. You better come out now.'

I could see through a crack that he was picking his nose and chewing it. He was staring vacantly across our back yard towards the lotties, in a sort of trance. He wasn't at all in a panic for me to come out. He didn't expect me to. He was going through the motions. He just wanted to keep me back. I stood silently behind the door.

'What you doing now?' hissed Jake. 'Playing pocket billiards? I can see you. Where are you?'

I was watching him through a crack. It was like looking through binoculars with the edges blurred but the centre very clear. He was still looking vacant but he now had his legs apart, pissing against our kitchen door. My mother would have hysterics.

'Your door's bloody filthy,' said Jake. 'Don't you ever clean things in your house? I'm gonna have a shit now. Got any paper?'

The conversation was getting nowhere. Jake knew I was hiding behind the door, even though I hadn't answered. I got down on the floor and slid towards the living room. Me Mam was up close at the telly, examining Gilbert Harding's hairline. Someone in the Co-op had told her he wore a wig. I got behind the couch and managed to creep round and out of the front door without her noticing. In the background, even above the noise of the telly, I could hear Jake kicking on the door with his boots and demanding paper.

My mother became aware of the noise at last. She switched the telly down and took her glasses off so she could hear better. Jake's noise was now ear splitting. He was sure I'd be forced to come out, just to keep him quiet. My mother threw open the door so quickly that Jake fell over, his pants half off. He jumped up at once and flew across the yard and onto the wall.

'If I ever see you in our yard once more, Jake Sullivan, I'm going to the po''ce. Do you hear?'

'Tom said I had to wait for him.'

'Don't tell lies. He's not even in.'

'He is!' protested Jake. 'He's in the kitchen. We were just chatting. What's wrong with chatting, Missus. It's a queer do when you can't even chat . . .'

'Get off that wall. I've never heard such lies in all my life. You'll come to a bad end, my lad.'

'Oh drop dead, you stupid old bitch,' said Jake, dropping over the wall and off into the wilderness of the lotties.

I remember this non-incident because everyone always believed Jake told lies, yet they always believed me. I kept out of his way for days, convinced he would beat me up, but he never said anything. Just gave me a Dinkie. I was overwhelmed. 'It's brand new,' he said, going off to sit in the lavs and miss the English period. 'I nicked it from Woolies yesterday.' I felt my hands tainted with holding stolen property. I was scared to take it home, in case there was a police raid. I went and threw it in the River Eden.

Jake often played truant for the whole day, going into Carlisle to see what he could take from Woolworths, then he'd have his tea in the Citadel Station. He'd queue up, stuff his pockets with Walls pies, and when he came to pay say he only had a cup of tea. He thought it was a great joke. It was getting away with the stealing which amused him, not the desire for objects. He gave all the Dinkies away and hardly ate any of the pies. He didn't do it often. Just when the whim took him. I thought it was terrible.

I thought his attitude to school work was even worse. He was far cleverer than me at things like arithmetic, but he just didn't care. There were lots of lads in the class like this. It was a Secondary Modern and therefore nobody was supposed to be academic, but I knew for a fact that half a dozen were brighter and quicker than me. I couldn't get over the fact that they were content to do nothing and end up farm labourers like their dads, or at the best as minor clerks in Carlisle. By just a bit of effort and a couple of GCEs, they could get out of that sort of life for ever. The school had started to put a few boys in for O levels, easy ones like Art and Technical Drawing and Scripture, but it was a start.

'You're mad,' I said to Jake when we were about fifteen and it had been decided I and three other lads would take five subjects. 'You don't want to stay here all your life. You wanna get out.'

'What? And become a phony jerk like that lot?'

He meant the teachers. We were walking to school and he was getting out a battered packet of cigarettes, flaunting it so some master would see him. 'What's wrong with being a labourer? You can get a start on £10 a week, more with overtime. Teachers don't make that for years. And you don't have any responsibilities. You just do what you like. I don't know why you want to go on with this stupid lot for another five years. You must be mad. I want some money, quick.'

He wasn't really all that interested in money. From Primary School days he'd had a flourishing little business buying and selling Dandies and Beanos. This had now developed into Hank Jansens and other books. He even wrote a dirty book himself, all in schoolboy handwriting, full of huge erections, massive breasts and white thighs. It involved people we all knew, like masters, the vicar, and the local squire figure, Sir Featherstone-Caldew. He rented it out at a penny a read and made a lot of money. But it was all just a game, to show he could do it, to get some sort of popularity and power. He'd spend all the money on cigarettes and never save it. He was lighting up his cigarette with what looked like a piece of printed blue paper.

'Yeh, it's half a fiver,' said Jake. 'The other half's inside Robson's desk. The bastard had it locked inside a tin box.'

'What were you doing in his desk?'

'Shitting all over it, what do you think?' Jake blew out some smoke rings, showing off like mad. 'I broke in last night. I'll probably have a look round the staff room tonight. Do you fancy it?'

I didn't say anything. I felt scared with the knowledge of him being a thief. I didn't want to be seen walking with him, but I couldn't disappear now. We were almost at school. Jake was jumped on by two masters and searched the minute we got into the playground. There was no sign of half a five pound note, which the clever masters felt would be the incriminating evidence.

'Get off me, you buggers,' screamed Jake, lashing out at them. 'I'll have my solicitors on to you.'

We had this long serious lecture in the assembly hall, asking if anyone had any clues about the break-in. The village constable came round. We were meant to realize the end of the world had come with this most heinous crime. They all knew it was Jake, but no one could prove it. They even got on to Cedric, who was twelve and in the second form. He was the most popular boy in the school, huge and fat with a red face and curly yellow straw hair, easy-going and everyone's buffoon. He was goalie for the school team, at only twelve, which made him world famous and therefore very popular. He said, no, he didn't know what Jake had been doing last night. Doing his homework, wasn't he? He was asked how he knew that. He said Jake had told him.

Jake was useless at all sports, which infuriated him. He couldn't run or swim or catch a ball or swing a bat. Cedric, for all his size, could do everything. Jake took up things like weightlifting, which gave him an excuse for picking up kids and throwing them, or kicking in classroom doors to try his strength. Then overnight he dropped it and took up girls. He maintained he got it first when he was fourteen. He'd taken the day off and gone to the fair in Carlisle, helping on the dodgems.

'I had this fight with a drunken soldier,' he told us next day in the school bogs. 'He tried to get on without paying. I grabbed him by the balls till the police came.'

'You are brave,' I said sarcastically.

'Do you want to be thumped?' said Jake. 'About midnight the woman in charge said come back to her caravan and help her with her takings. She meant help with her knickers. She was lying there with them half off. I said it's your big night, darling. Leg over, chaw, and I was away. She said she'd never had it as good since the Festival of Britain.'

That was Jake's story anyway. A few days later he was expelled from school. It was nothing to do with his alleged seduction or even the robbery. He was caught masturbating in the school lavatories. He only had a few weeks to go before he left school, but the headmaster said he had to leave immediately. The head didn't tell Mr. and Mrs. Sullivan the real reason. He said it was for 'continual disobedience'. Jake had no such inhibitions.

'Tossed out for tossing off,' he told everyone. 'They were just jealous when they saw what I could do. That was the real reason, you know. When I get into Who's Who that's what I'll put down. "Education – kicked out for wanking."'

Chapter Three

I did get a bit in the paper at last, about a friend of a friend of the Royal Family starting a mushroom farm. They lapped up anything remotely royal, but at least our trivia was harmless, compared with the other gossip columns of the day. But once I'd got going I managed to stake my claim to the few perks that were around, such as good expenses and free tickets for theatres and night clubs, if you can call that a perk.

I didn't even think of turning up at Jake's office to ask for the job. Antonia would have had hysterics if I'd contemplated it, but even I realized it was a half-baked offer, thrown out as a grand gesture. I was doing a crummy job but at least I had a job on a London paper at twenty-one. Big deal.

'Listen, I'm not going to come all that way just to go to a boring place like that,' said Antonia on the phone.

'It won't be boring. And if it is, it'll be a giggle.'

'I don't want to go. And anyway, I've nothing to wear.'

This meant that she'd agreed, so I got my uncle's evening suit which was so baggy in the trousers and so short in the jacket that I looked like Charlie Chaplin, but it was evening dress. The ticket, addressed in flowing PR handwriting to Robert McPherson, Esq. had stipulated formal dress. Antonia came up on an earlier bus than usual, carrying her gown in an Ellison and Cavell bag. She moaned about her dress and said she hated such phony places and meeting horrible people and how did she look. I had been going to tell her right away the bad news, that Ronald McPherson, Esq. had had the sack that morning. But I decided not to. Better to keep my fears to myself.

The editor got all these posh invitations, as editor, naturally. When he couldn't go to more than six a night he let some of the underlings have some. Most of the underlings lived out in Penge and Cockfosters and Theydon Bois and other fictional places and couldn't be let out at short notice. I'd got this invitation after I'd been hanging around the lavatory smiling at Mr. McPherson. Now that he'd gone the way of all editors and been replaced by Bennet, perhaps they wouldn't even let me in at the door.

26

We went straight into the Club, no bother, and were led to our seat at the back. When I got used to the semi-darkness I made out the familiar figure of Blacker, one of our drunken subs. He was in his ordinary suit, only it looked scruffier and more stained than usual. He seemed to be with someone who looked as if she'd just come from behind a barrow. At another table I saw an idiot secretary from the women's department. Her partner was Fred – our copy boy. And here was me, dressed for a silent film, and Antonia in her first long evening dress.

The waiters were flurrying round the big nobs grouped at the front round the stage. These were obviously the famous night club big spenders. They must keep all the free guests, like me, well out of the way. On close inspection, I was quite glad. Each seemed to be about sixty, very small and fat and bald, with beady eyes, a big cigar, a shiny suit and patent leather shoes. Each had a tarty girl whose breasts drooped towards her partner's bald head as she leaned across the table, looking adoringly, but straight over his shiny mohair shoulder trying to see something better, such as a sugar daddy under fifty-nine and over five feet tall.

None of them talked to each other. Her face had a painted smile which speaking would ruin. His face was a death mask which he knew, so what was there to smile about The only noise was coming from one table in the middle. I nudged Antonia the minute I noticed. She refused to look.

'It is, honest. Quick, look now.'

'If you look again,' she said, 'I'm going. And if you so much as wave at him or try to catch his attention, I'll never speak to you again.'

I waded into the shrimp cocktail and steak and tried not to look round. I hadn't had the confidence to go to a proper London restaurant up till then. I'd existed in Manchester on Chinese meals because they were so cheap and so English. On the few occasions I'd taken Antonia into the West End we'd ended up eating Chinese, usually the Universal. London Chinese food was a bit more exotic, but I could still find easy things like sweet and sour. We always intended to branch out. We'd start off walking round Soho, looking for places with menus outside, pressing our noses against the windows like Orphan Annies. But when posh people came out and went Ha Ha Ha very loudly, we moved on. It always looked so exciting inside. I felt like a kid coming down from the dark bed-room and peeping at the grown-ups and all their noise and light, then creeping back again in case they found out. This is an analogy I must have got out of Sunny Stories. My Mam and Dad never spoke to each other and they couldn't have any lights on as it was the black-out.

There was a loud screaming from Jake's table and I had to turn round this time. Two busty girls, more common but more lively than the painted ladies, had jumped up on their chairs and were shouting and waving. They were obviously having a great time at Jake's table. Jake himself was rocking back in his chair, giving a huge grin and showing off his gleaming teeth. People at other tables were looking on admiringly, wish-ing they could have such fun with that nice clean-looking young man. I knew from the size of Jake's grin that he must have come out with some really awful obscenity, hissing it through his teeth. His face always looked its best when he was doing his worst.

Jake's teeth were his best feature. There must have been a lot of vitamins in those Cumberland tatie pot dinners. His complexion wasn't very good though not as bad as it was at school. He still had adolescent spots but most of the protuber-ances had gone leaving only scarred craters. These pock marks were quite attractive. He gave an impression of cleanness. His crew cut added to this, and so did his heavy horn rimmed spectacles. He never wore these when I used to know him and I wasn't sure if they were a gimmick to make himself more distinguished. I did ask over that drink in the chairman's suite and he'd said he was myopic with only three weeks left before he went totally blind. I said how sorry I was. Then later he said he kept spare birth pills in one corner, a midget transistor tape recorder in the other, and he'd had no glass in them since he got them. I'd leaned over to have a closer look and he'd kneed me in the crutch. There was a loud shout behind me from one of the young men at his table. There goes another inquisitive bugger.

Jake was wearing a red tuxedo. This alone made him stand out, even without all his jumping about. He wore it with a white polo neck silk pullover. This was his own idea, long before they'd come in, and it was one of his few combinations which came off. On his feet he was wearing white gym shoes.

In theory they matched his polo neck, but they spoiled the whole impression. In 1961 nobody wore unusual or way-out clothes at smart places. When Jake's ensemble failed, he looked even more ludicrous and out of place.

'What do you think of the jacket?' I said to Antonia, draining my glass for the third time, waiting for the waiters to drag themselves away from ogling all the fun at Jake's table.

'It's fine,' said Antonia. 'It's not too short at all.'

'I mean Jake's.'

I expected her to refuse to look, but she turned quickly round. As she did so the lights dimmed, getting ready for whatever we were getting ready for. Across the tables I could hear Jake singing the ABC Minors' Song – 'We are the boys and girls well known as', which we used to sing every Saturday morning at the Lonsdale cinema in Carlisle.

It was the first night of two American comedians whose names I've forgotten and never knew anyway. All the painted faces clapped hysterically when they came on. From Jake's table all that could be heard was loud booing. During a sentimental ballad Jake belched and when a girl singer ended by thanking everyone, very sincerely, for being a lovely audience, Jake let out his loudest farts.

'That's the last free place I'm coming to,' I said, realizing at last that we weren't going to get any more free wine.

'I hate you for bringing me here,' said Antonia.

'Thanks,' I said. 'I like to see people enjoying themselves.'

'You're grunting,' she said. 'That means you must think he's turning your way. I'm warning you.'

'Oh wrap up. What an old misery guts you are.'

I decided to go all silent and sullen, just to let her see she had managed to spoil my evening. A hand grabbed the back of my shoulder.

'Come on, Tom, let's get out of this fucking place.'

I held on to Antonia, despite her struggles, and we both followed Jake and his giggling cronies outside. He stood on the kerb, put his fingers in his mouth and whistled. A white Rolls Royce drew up immediately and we all got in. We drove down Piccadilly and up Park Lane at sixty miles an hour with Elvis Presley records being played at full volume on a record player built into the cocktail cabinet. Antonia had withdrawn her hand and was refusing to be touched.

'What do you think of the club, then, Tom?' shouted Jake.

'Very nice,' I said.

'You must be bloody mad,' said Jake.

'He is,' said Antonia. 'He is also a creep. He tries to get in with everyone by saying what he thinks they want to hear. He hasn't an opinion of his own.'

'I meant it was very nice to see such a place,' I began lamely. 'Just to see what they're like . . .'

'Oh shuttup,' said Antonia.

I was furious with her for showing me up. She was being extra vicious, attacking me in public. I didn't know why.

'What did you think, then, Missus?' said Jake.

'I thought it was the nastiest place I'd ever been in,' said Antonia.

'All night clubs are like that. And I've been to them all.'

'Then you must be hard up.' People didn't say such things to Jake, not to his face. All his cronies turned to stare at Antonia, puckering their flabby mouths, expectantly.

'I am,' said Jake, laughing. 'But I know it. All the millions I've got, yet I spend my evenings at those terrible places. But I have a good time when I'm there. I save up my best farts, especially.'

'We heard you,' said Antonia. 'Rather childish, I thought.'

'I'm a childish bloke, that's one of the secrets of my success. Those bald bastards are so old they're dead. They drag them out from coffins every evening, dust their cocks and stick cigars in their arse holes. Those big titted girls are made of plastic. They get blown up every day then let down in the evening. Only the drunks ever try to fuck them. Ever fucked a piece of saggy plastic, Sammy?'

'All the time,' said Sammy. This was the young sharp looking crony I'd first seen at the board meeting. He was combing his hair in the cocktail cabinet mirror, not listening to the conversation.

'In the old days,' continued Jake, looking round to see that everyone was listening. 'Sammy, leave your goddam hair or I'll throw you out the window. It used to take centuries to make a million. You knocked your guts out making raincoats or corsets like those blokes back there. Then when you're sixty you're too fat to enjoy yourself. You can only get girls by paying for them. You can't get a hard on 'cos you haven't the energy. You can't eat for ulcers. You can't smile because you know you're gonna drop dead any minute with a heart attack. What's the use of having money at sixty? Now today, children, you can make it young. That's our welfare state for you. You can have a ball, a real gas, and still be only thirteen, like me.'

'At pathetic night clubs?' said Antonia.

'Where else can I go to waste my money? It's just like pubs, but I can't go there any more.'

'Because you're too famous,' said Antonia.

'That's it. Autographs later.'

'Why have you got to waste your money?' said Antonia. 'Why can't you give it to charity?'

'Who's your friend, Tommy lad? I thought your Mam was still in Thwaite. Were you invited in this limousine or did you crawl under the floor boards when no one was looking, eh?'

The other friends began a quick conversation, hurriedly drowning any reply from Antonia, asking Jake insane questions about his new flat, complimenting him on his Rolls and thanking him profusely for being so awful to them. Jake was singing 'Heartbreak Hotel' and not listening.

His flat was a penthouse suite at the top of a modern block at the back of Park Lane. A tall stately butler opened the door the second we got out of the lift. He looked as if he'd just stepped off a bottle of Rose's Lime Juice. Jake pushed past him and we all followed.

'Jones, we'll have some champagne. And if Princess Margaret or Lord Snowdon call, tell them to get stuffed. We're busy. OK?'

'Certainly, sir.'

'No, forget the champagne. Here's ten bob. Take the Rolls and go and get eight fish suppers, with plenty of salt and vinegar.'

'I want a saltbeef sandwich,' said Sammy.

'You mean *could* I have a salt beef sandwich. These cockneys. No bloody manners. Tom, come and see round the rest of the pad.'

He beckoned to Antonia. She didn't move, except for a slight shudder as she caught sight of a larger than life painting in oils of Jake, the face so creamy and tanned it looked like an advert for Ambre Solaire. The only other paintings were reproduction Tretchikoff. I followed Jake into the hall where he pointed proudly to a large gilt framed picture which contained his press cuttings. I waded on through white fitted carpet so thick and fluffy you needed snow shoes to get across. There was gold and gilt and walnut dripping everywhere. Each of the bedrooms was like some show house bedroom out of the Ideal Home Exhibition, luxurious bad taste department. Jake's bedroom contained a circular bed with a built-in TV and cocktail cabinet. There were switches to operate the blinds, the TV, the bedroom doors and front door intercom and a switch to move the bed round, up, down and sideways.

'Cost £5,000, that bed,' said Jake. 'I got fed up playing with Meccano.'

There were six TV sets in the house. The kitchen was enormous, with enough equipment to cook banquets. The only thing edible which could be seen was a tin of Nescafé and a packet of Kelloggs Corn Flakes. They looked rather forlorn, beside the spit roasts and ultra-violet grills.

It was the bar which probably got the first prize for vulgarity. He'd converted a whole room, installing a row of lights at the foot of the wall like footlights. Above, as if on the stage, were painted a row of naked Can-Can girls. Jake switched the lights on, to give me the full effect. The footlights were trained to shine only on their crutches, which they did with such an intense glare you had to shield your eyes.

'Yeh, it's a grand place you've got,' I said. 'I bet they'd love it in Thwaite.'

I was enjoying walking round with him chatting. I'd been unable to get a word in for Antonia in the car. I'd have something to say to her when I got her home.

'You missed a treat,' Jake said to Antonia back in the main room. 'But I suppose you can always wait for the film. Have a pathetic chocolate.'

He produced a circular box which was three feet in diameter and contained enough fancy wrappings to decorate Regent Street at Christmas. Antonia gave another little shudder and turned away.

'You're a Muslim are you, Tony?' he said to Antonia. 'Never eat black meat on August Bank Wednesdays. See if you like this record.' He pressed a button and in the wonders of full stereo the room was suddenly filled with an American voice describing in great detail the sexual act. It went on and on, giving positions, advice, peculiarities and unusual methods, all in the same flat monotones.

'He's a doctor, you know,' said Jake. 'I just got the record from the States. Good, isn't it? He's a doctor, you know.'

'You said,' said Antonia, flatly.

Jones came back with the fish and chips and Antonia refused to have any. I was getting really fed up with her. She might hate him, but she didn't need to make it so obvious. I was amazed at Jake for caring and trying to get in with her. The cronies came to what they thought was the rescue again, chatting animatedly about take-over bids and stocks and shares and development plans. I realized I didn't really know what Jake did. He must do something, to have a board room, six TV sets and the closeups of dancing girls. Sullivan House hadn't shown any signs of production, but then London offices were all show. No one ever actually produces anything in London.

'To get back to what you were saying, Tony,' said Jake, turning on Antonia, still waiting for her to object to being called Tony. 'What sort of charity do you recommend?'

'What? Please yourself. I don't care.'

'Typical of the younger generation. They don't care. When I was still at school like you I cared passionately.'

He waited for her to rise to this one, but she didn't. He must have been finding out about her.

'Well I just might give to charity,' continued Jake. 'It's either that or make a huge pile of pound notes, cart them all up Skiddaw and set fire to them. Or on the other hand, I might give it to some really deserving charity, like Save the Blind Dogs, or Homes for Aged Sex Maniacs. When I've done this next huge deal, I'll let you know how I feel.'

He was waiting for me, or at the best Antonia, to ask him what this huge deal was. Antonia looked round, then stood up.

'What time is it, Tom?' she said and without waiting for an answer moved to the door. 'We must go. Thanks for a super evening.'

I didn't say anything all the way to the bus station. I'd waited for her to apologize. As she didn't, I thought I'd let my silence show what I thought of her behaviour. If I started criticizing, it would lead to an argument. It was the early hours of the morning and I was too tired for that. She said she was too tired for anything. She was getting the first bus back.

'There's no need to be like this,' I said, despite vowing I wouldn't say it. 'I think he's a fascinating bloke.'

'You're easily fascinated.'

'You don't even know him.'

'I don't want to.'

'He wants me to work for him.'

'You're mad enough to agree. You like anyone who's nice to you. Like a little obedient poodle.'

'Shall I come with you?'

'No. And you needn't wait. Get home to bed. Don't let your fascinations keep you awake. Thanks for a lousy evening.'

She got on the bus. I waved as it left the station. She stared straight ahead and I regretted waving. It was somehow demeaning and weak. Like an obedient poodle.

Chapter Four

I was on the first bus to Carlisle, wearing my oldest jeans and dirtiest shirt and carrying the bait box which my dad had been carrying that fateful day. I'd bought the Daily Mirror, to try to look like a real working man. It was six o'clock in the morning and I'd never been up so early in my life. It was like entering a new planet. There were people I'd never seen before, yet they'd been coming in on this first bus every day of their working lives. They were mainly elderly labourers, sitting clutching their bait boxes, depressed, tired, resigned and very thin. They looked silently out of the windows into their past.

'Lend's half a dollar till Friday' said Jake, suddenly leaning over my seat and shouting in my ear. 'Go on, don't be a tight twat all your life.'

I got half a crown and gave it to him. He grabbed it without replying then went round the rest of the bus trying to borrow more. He was on the back seat with a couple of other young labourers. The only noise came from them. When he'd borrowed about ten bob he came back and started reading out bits from the Daily Mirror, putting in obscenities and the word fuck every second word. I laughed. The old men sat silent and motionless.

'What do you think of this, then?' Jake said to one old bloke, pushing a picture of a girl in a bikini under his nose. 'Do you fancy it? Go on, I'll hold your false teeth while you have a go.'

'She's very nice,' said the old man at last, slowly and carefully.

'Well she's a bloke, do you know that? It's always a bloke, the same one as well. He just puts on a different wig and different tits every day.' Jake was wise to all newspapers. He got it from his mother, though she probably hadn't told him that one.

He then went through in detail, for the benefit of his mates and the rest of the bus, the girls he'd laid over the weekend, where, when and how. His mates intermittently laughed and shouted, making the only break in the gloom. Jake did little drawings on the wet windows, when he needed to explain the exact details about some girl. As we got nearer Carlisle, the sun came out and the windows dried. Some skilled workers, bricklayers in clean brown overalls and electricians in blue, got on and sat up erect and proud, reading their Daily Expresses. Then we were joined by some early morning office workers, young girls who sat at the front doing their makeup, well out of the way of Jake at the back. They'd heard his comments every day and took no notice when he shouted at them. 'Morning, darlings. You get it last night, then?'

You wouldn't have thought Jake was going to work. He had on his best black drape jacket which came down to his knees and made any movement, least of all digging holes, very difficult. His shoes were black suede with crepe soles about six inches thick. His trousers were so tight he often wore them to bed as he couldn't get them off when he came home drunk. Under his long jacket you couldn't see how creased they were. He had a white shirt with a heavy medal at the neck and a long black lace hanging down. His Tony Curtis hairstyle was so long and piled so high it took a jar of Vaseline a week to keep it in place. At eighteen, Jake was the biggest Teddy Boy in Cumberland. That didn't mean much, but as he stood at Carlisle Town Hall on a Saturday night, swinging his bicycle chain and kicking the railings, he frightened most people. He never actually got into many fights. He just made the right noises.

He had no other clothes so he had to go to work as he was, much to the disgust of Mr. Ormerod, the foreman. Even if he had, he would still have worn his ordinary clothes. His mates were just the same. Work wasn't serious. It was just a laugh, so why dress up for it.

Jake had worked at several places after he'd left school, but he'd had the sack from them all. He'd refused to go to Armstrongs at first, because his Dad was there, but in the end there was nowhere else left. It was thanks to Willie that I was being taken on as well, just on a day to day basis, during the Christmas holidays. I'd been too late in applying for the Post Office. I was now in the sixth form at the Grammar school, having moved on from Thwaite.

Immediately Jake got into the workmen's hut on the site he shouted at old Ted to hurry up and get the boiler ready. Then he and the other young labourers, all in their Teddy Boy gear, stood around drinking tea out of their tin mugs and shouting at the fifteen-year-old apprentices, asking them about their sex life. When Willie Sullivan blew his whistle, they all booed and groaned. 'Let's have you, you lazy lot of buggers,' said Jake, suddenly rushing to the entrance of the hut, showing enormous enthusiasm. He clapped his hands and rushed round, making sure Mr. Omerod could see him. The apprentices scurried past. The old labourers, with their worn clothes and worn faces, plodded out, ignoring him. They'd seen these cocky young labourers many times before, who thought it was all a game and didn't care, till one day they'd have a screaming family and screaming wife to look after and it became vital to keep their job, however rotten. Then they'd wish they'd got an apprenticeship.

'Morning Mr. Omerod,' shouted Jake, already half down a manhole, digging like mad. Mr. Omerod had come out of our hut, making sure no one was lurking inside. 'Lovely morning,

Mr. Omerod. How's the kids, Mr. Omerod? And that lovely wife of yours, eh?'

Mr. Omerod didn't answer. He gave me a shovel and told me to start work beside Jake. Bill the ganger would look after me. I started and in ten minutes my back was in agony. The old men who'd started slowly were still at it, digging away patiently without looking up. Their nobbly narrow arms were like slow motion pistons. My hands were almost bleeding and I looked at my watch, convinced it must be dinner time. It was only eight o'clock. Jake had disappeared. I heard a hissing noise from the hut and he was beckoning me over. I went to see what he wanted.

Inside Jake was going round all the old men's bait boxes, seeing if they had anything he fancied, and shouting at old Ted to keep that boiler going. Two of his mates were moving a bench round a box in the far corner. I was scared Mr. Omerod would be in any minute. I excused myself, saying I was going to the lavatory.

'Then piss off, then,' said Jake. 'We don't want you. Fucking students. All the same. Give us them cards, Joe. I'm bloody banker.'

At about eleven Mr. Omerod took me off the gang and said I now had to help the tiler. There was a machine, luckily, a long conveyor belt which took tiles up onto the top scaffolding. Me and the tiler's regular labourer, Norman, had to keep loading it so that the tiler and his apprentice on the roof could work non-stop.

'You a student, then?' Norman grunted, without looking at me. He was about forty, very muscular with hair all over his face and a thick wide leather belt round his middle.

'Sort of,' I said, wishing I could have made a smarter reply.

'Got a girl, then?' he said five minutes later, leering at me.

'Not on me,' I said. His expression didn't change. He was handing me some more tiles. I was out of breath with rushing back and forward to the machine.

'I put my hand across this morning and I felt her hair. It was all tough like. Ever felt hair?'

'Felt her what?' I said. Norman was giving me the creeps. He had a glazed expression which he wouldn't take off me.

'She soon woke up,' continued Norman. 'She knew what I

wanted. So I had it, like, know what I mean? Instead of break-fast.'

'I'd rather have Sugar Puffs.'

'Have you had it yourself, know what I mean, like?'

This was all he was after, my puny experiences. I wondered if Jake would be like that at forty. The tiler shouted at me from the roof, telling me to get some nails from the stores, so I got away from Norman.

At lunch time I felt a real man of the world, all dirty and tired and sweaty. Jake was standing in front of the boiler, all clean and polished, filing his nails. He'd probably been there half the morning. He was shouting at Michael, one of the apprentices, without looking at him, asking if he'd got it or did she have her rags up. When he'd finished on his nails, he handed me the file.

'There's a little door at the back of the machine. Open it with this file. The screw will come out dead easy. Then put the file between the rollers. OK? You don't want to do any more work this aftie, do you.'

I was grateful for his kind attention, but I was a bit worried. I ate my Spam sandwiches, trying to decide whether it was better to fall foul of Mr. Omerod or cross Jake. The problem was solved when Jake walked back to the tiles with me after lunch, took the file and put it in the machine himself.

'Never work hard at something you don't enjoy,' said Jake on the bus home. 'Only daft fuckers do that, like them lot.' He was nodding at all the old men on the seats in front of us, staring out of the window with the same expressions they'd started the day with. 'They're scared stiff of life.'

'Most people don't enjoy their work,' I said, 'but they've still got to earn a living doing something.' I wanted to go on and say that if only he'd done a bit more work at school, he needn't have become a labourer, but I was very conscious of still being a sixth former and trying hard not to throw it around in any way.

'I know and it's fucking unfair,' said Jake. 'But they won't beat me.'

'How?'

'The minute I stop enjoying it, I'm off.'

'You're enjoying it?'

'Yeh, course. Got some good mates on that site. It's a good laugh. Just like school really.'

'But you hated school, Jake.'

'Who told you that? I hated the masters, but school was smashing. It was one long laugh trying to beat them. It's the same now, trying to break that git Omerod. It's good pay as well. Much better than being an apprentice. And it puts in the day. What more do you want? You little know-all cuntface, eh?'

I said it sounded great, the way he described it. He had the right attitude, but what would he do when he didn't enjoy it any more?

'Don't you worry, my old son. I won't waste my time on that lot. The minute I get fed up, I'm away.'

Unfortunately for Jake, they got fed up with him first. The following Friday Jake clocked on at the right time then couldn't be found all day long. Mr. Omerod at last tracked him down inside the loft of an almost completed council house. He'd boarded himself in with a firkin of Nutbrown, a transistor, five stolen bait boxes and an eighteen year old conductress from the Ribble bus company. Mr. Omerod couldn't believe his eyes when he stuck his head through the trap door. 'What are you doing here?'

'I am on a split shift,' simpered the conductress. Jake laughed so much he rolled over and almost fell through the trap door. Mr. Omerod gave him his cards and said, Get.

For the first week, Jake stayed in bed every day till five o'clock. Lilly and Willie screamed at him, saying if only he was like Cedric. Cedric had just started his first job as an apprentice at Armstrongs. He was learning to be a plasterer. Lilly and Willie were very thrilled. Jake poured scorn on it all the time. He said they gave the plasterer's jobs to mental defectives because in a few years time it would be all plastic walls and plastic ceilings and nobody would want plasterers. He must be mental anyway, making only £3 a week when Jake was making £13. This argument soon fell to pieces, once Jake was out of work and making nothing a week.

I don't know how long he was jobless because I went back to school in another week when the new term began. I didn't hear anything about him till the following summer. I decided to go on the buses during the vacation instead of labouring. I needed some money before starting university. I had to go on a course to Preston to learn what to do. I didn't realize being a conductor was such an intellectual job. They even had final exams and a passing out parade. On my break, during the first day back in Carlisle, I was sitting in the canteen having a sausage sandwich when Jake came in, dressed in his conductor's uniform. He had his arm round a big busted blonde conductress called Gloria. I knew who Gloria was, though I'd never spoken to her. It had been the big thing in the sixth form at the Grammar school to fancy Gloria.

'Christ, it's Graham the Wank,' said Jake. 'They haven't taken you on, have they?'

'I didn't know you were a conductor,' I said.

'I'm not, I'm an inspector, so watch it.'

Jake bought fried egg sandwiches all round and sat down, his arm still round Gloria but this time he'd got it inside the buttons of her tunic. She jumped up, saying she should have been at the Town Hall three minutes ago.

'Lovely fat arse,' said Jake as Gloria waddled out. Her uniform was very worn and shiny and tight fitting. Her leather belts holding her money bag and machine cut into her diagonally across her front, making her breasts stick out even more. The lads at school were always imagining her naked, but I said she was sexier in her uniform. I'd seen her off duty once in a flared skirt and a cardigan and she looked nothing. That was when I began to think I might have kinky tendencies, fancying Gloria in her uniform, though the word kinky hadn't come in yet in that sense. Jake was telling me how long he'd been laying her. Whether he was or not, he would have been telling me, just to show what a man of the world he was.

'On the top deck between bus stops?' I asked.

'You're coming on, cuntface,' said Jake. 'But don't push it.'

Gloria's husband was on the buses as a driver. She always managed to be on a different shift from him so that she could take Jake back to her place in the afternoons.

'We got into the bedroom yesterday and the bugger was already there, sound asleep. He'd had his shift changed.'

'What did you do?'

'Well I wasn't going to get into bed with him, was I. He isn't even pretty. Whoops!'

Jake did a little camp dance round the canteen, to every-one's amusement.

'*You're* coming on,' I said.

'Where, where?' said Jake, in mock horror. Then he sat down beside me. 'I bet that university's full of homos. Tell us about it then? What's it like?'

'You wouldn't fancy them,' I said. I didn't want to say I hadn't actually started yet.

'But I fancy that, though. Wow! Hello sexy.'

He was shouting at Beryl, the area manager's secretary, who was tip-toeing on her incredibly high heels through the canteen, looking very snooty. She was trying to get past as quickly as possible before she picked up any of the heavy clouds of fried eggs, stale money, smoke and sweaty uniforms which hung permanently over the canteen. Most of all, she didn't want louts like Jake to intercept her.

'I say Beryl, darling,' said Jake, putting on a posh voice. 'How about a spot of lunch, what?'

Beryl wasn't at all posh but she tried hard and felt herself a definite cut above any conductress. She knew all the duty rosters before anyone else and used to give out hints, just to lord it over everyone. She had a cold salad and a glass of milk on her own at Binns, the local department store, and would never be seen having lunch in the canteen. I thought she was a boring jumped up nothing. Jake said he bet she was a real goer.

'About time I had a bit of class,' he said, watching her scurry out. Beryl wore twinsets and a string of Woolworths pearls, which was presumably what Jake meant by class. Admittedly she did look fresh. Her twin sets were in pale colours, white, light blue or pink and always spotless. Her rosebud pink lipstick looked fresh on and she used exotic things like eye shadow and mascara. She must have been in and out of the ladies' lavs like a yo-yo to keep herself so well turned out. She certainly stood out. I agreed with Jake that she didn't look bad. He was very pleased. 'But only in comparison with all the other slags,' I said. 'Look at them, they come on duty like pit ponies who've never seen fresh air for decades. And the ones that have heard that make-up's been invented dip their faces in it and come on looking like whores. Or Gloria.'

You've got to be quick to be a good conductor, taking and giving money, setting the machine correctly and watching the stops and fare stages, all at the same time. Jake was quicker than anyone else; brilliant at counting out the money in the evening, which all the conductors hated. While everyone else was still checking their tickets sold against their money taken, and filling in their books, Jake had handed in everything, absolutely correctly, and was gone. For the first three days when I started, I was so worried about all the things I had to remember that I couldn't sleep.

My money was always out, to my disadvantage, until Jake gave me some tips on how to balance it in my favour.

'OK, so you think you're down. Right, you've got a full bus. They've all just got on and they're only going to the Town Hall. You don't take any fares, you just stand on the platform as they rush off. Most of the buggers won't pay, as they'll be trying to nick off sharpish, but a lot will – the idiots who want to pay to show off how honest they are. You take their sixpennies, punch a ticket, but in all the rush you can't give the ticket to them. You just throw it on the ground.'

'How does that help?'

'You're just punching *penny* tickets, aren't you? Who's going to issue sixpenny tickets when no one's looking at them? You'll never get anywhere, you won't.'

'And where do you want to get, Jake?'

'Not that joke again. I've told you. When something turns up, I'll be off again. Hey Beryl! Hello darling, how about a bit?'

'Do you mind,' said Beryl, coming out of the door of her office. We were walking down the corridor into the canteen. Jake was jubilant at having forced a reply out of her. All the young conductors were always trying to make Beryl, but she slapped them down sharpish, especially Jake. She turned up her nose higher and clack-clacked off so fast in her high heels it looked as if she was in a stilts race. Jake smacked his lips. I laughed and said she looked ridiculous. 'But I suppose if you've spent your life on a building site, you think anyone who's clean must be the Queen Mother.' I expected a big thump for that one, but he was too busy making a sucking noise after Beryl. It was just a game, anyway, this fancying a bit of so called class. The next week he started laying a cracker packer from Carrs biscuit works. She was married, but her husband was a long distance lorry driver.

Jake was so seldom at home, with laying Gloria and the

cracker packer, that I heard before he did that his Dad had collapsed. He fell off his desk stool and lay there. Everyone thought it was another joke. Someone must have sawn through the stool leg, or some such silly trap. But Willie didn't get up and they took him to hospital. It was only a minor coronary and he was soon recovering. Lilly was furious. She said he'd done it just to frighten her.

'I don't know how he had a heart attack,' said Jake. 'Never knew he had a heart. Just a big lump of jelly.'

'Oh, he's not a bad bloke,' I said.

'Give over. No one would miss him if he died. But he won't. He's one of those long living ghouls. He'll creak on forever, putting in the days, putting in the weeks, putting in his life. The whole thing's a farce. I read some fucker going on about the dignity of labour the other day. There isn't any. They're all beaten down.'

'You sound like a Communist.'

'They're beaten down even more. In a few years' time, things might be a bit better. With all this automation, there won't be enough jobs to go round. Do you know what they're gonna do? At birth half the population will be put on a pension straight away. They'll buy the things which the other half of the population produce. What do you think of that, then?'

'Who told you all this?'

'Aldus Fucksley or whatever he's called. I was reading something about him the other day. Ever heard of him, then?'

'Huxley. Oh yeh. Everyone's heard of him.'

Jake grabbed my arm and twisted it back. I shouldn't have mocked him. I was genuinely surprised that he'd been doing any reading at all. I'd never seen him read anything, except Hank Jansens at Thwaite Secondary Modern. He twisted my arm further and further back until I cried out for him to stop.

'You bighead. Any more of your lip and I'll really plate you. Lend's a quid till tomorrow and I'll let go.'

I nodded that I would and he stopped. Despite his good money on the buses, with running Gloria and the cracker packer, he was very hard up. When he had it, he was very generous, sharing it all round – I will say that for him. I remembered an uncle once gave him five bob. He took me and another lad into Carlisle on the Saturday morning to the ABC minors, paid us in and bought us goodies in the middle of the film. In return, I had to watch out for the attendant and her torch while he had his arm up some girl during the Adventures of Lassie.

We were walking out of the bus station together, on the way home. I said wasn't he going anywhere? Man of the world and all that. He said Gloria's husband and Mr. cracker packer were both at home. Give us me quid back then, I said. He'd just borrowed it out of habit.

'Something might turn up, he said. As he said so Beryl came out of another exit. She didn't see us. Jake grabbed me and we both followed her. She was in her walking-out clothes, which meant a different pair of high heels, dark blue this time and even higher than her indoor ones. She had on a trim blue raincoat and carried her long tightly furled walking-out umbrella which had never seen action in its life. It was an accessory, just as her long gloves were. She pulled them over her well manicured, pink varnished fingers. This was something else she had over the conductresses. Their hands were ingrained with the dirt of years of handling money and their nails looked as if rats had got at them. Beryl's hair, which was auburn and neat and always in good condition, was about the only head of female hair one ever saw. The conductresses wore either headscarves or rollers.

Beryl was walking fast, despite the high heels. She looked even smaller outside, threading in and out of the crowds. In the office she looked quite big. She was in fact just five feet, but she had a sort of pocket-size curvaciousness. In a few years she'd probably go dumpy, but just now she was very carefully held in with her Middle X or Big W girdles. She was very neat and fastidious in all her movements. I'd been talking to her in the office that day – she talked to me, being a student and nearer her class – and she'd suddenly said, 'Oh, what a mucky pup I am.' I didn't know what she was talking about. There was a great rustling of stiff petticoats and coy crossing of legs and she discovered an invisible speck of dust on the hem of her dress. She'd just come from a holiday on the Costa Brava, which she was dying to tell everyone about. As she didn't speak to the conductors, she had to tell me. I'd forgotten to tell Jake. I told him now and he nearly collapsed. He had no idea where the Costa Brava was, except it wasn't near Silloth, but he knew it was big deal. He was banging into

passers-by, going on and on about how could a common secretary afford such a holiday?

'Everybody can afford them these days,' I said. 'I thought
you said she wasn't common? That was the big attraction. I
think she's completely common.'

'I think you fancy her yourself, the way you're always on at
her. Well just watch it, eh. Or I'll really fucking murder you.'

He was dead serious. I still couldn't see what he saw in this
perfectly ordinary little shorthand typist. I said I was fed up
and was going home on my own if he was going to mess
around. He said hold on, let's follow her round this corner. I
hoped she wasn't meeting a boy friend. I wasn't in the mood
for one of Jake's scenes.

Beryl was fumbling in her shiny black handbag for a key. I
thought we must be getting near her place. Then she stepped
off the kerb and into a car, an old but highly polished Morris
Minor. She drove off with a roar. This time Jake really couldn't
get over it. He lay against a wall and said fucking hell, well
fucking hell. I couldn't be bothered waiting for him. I got
the bus to Thwaite on my own.

That night Jake did go home, as Gloria and the cracker
packer were otherwise engaged. He opened the door and went
in shouting for his Mam as usual. When she appeared he said,
'Is me Dad dead yet, and if not why not?' His mother threw
him out. He came round to our house. I was on a late shift or
I would never have got rid of him. My mother still hated him
and wouldn't have him around, though now he was grown up,
or supposed to be, it was harder to stop him coming to the door.

His mother refused to have him back in the house. She'd
had enough of him. He decided he'd get himself a little bachelor flat. He'd read about them in Men Only. It would cost a bit
of money, but if he gave up Gloria and the cracker packer,
he'd be able to save a bit more. Something posh, as was fitting
for such a smart bus conductor about town, who had his eyes
on the superior Beryl.

Our day off was the same that week so he dragged me to see
a block of flats he'd seen advertised in the Cumberland News.
He probably felt I was more presentable than he was, though
that's the last thing he would have admitted.

It turned out to be a conversion. All the same, it had been
well done up with a brand new façade of glass and concrete.

The front door had one of those intercoms you speak through – the height of smart, for Carlisle in 1958.

'Hey, what does the postman do with these little holes? Shove his cock through them? They spend all this money doing the block up and they economize on the letter boxes.'

I told him what they were and he said he knew all the time. A tall thin public school type took us up to show us the last vacant flat. Jake was very impressed. It wasn't much really, just one poky room, bathroom and kitchen, but it was all new and sparkling, in a formica sort of way. The public school bloke was showing us everything very haughtily, but carefully adding Sir on to every sentence. You never knew who had money these days, even a Teddy Boy and a spotty-faced youth in a school scarf.

'Look, fuck the Sir bit, eh,' said Jake to the bloke. 'How much do you want?'

'Well, Sir, counting the rates and full central heating and hot water, it comes to exactly £350 a year.'

'I want to know how much a *week*, cuntface.'

'Let me see. Just under £7 a week, Sir. But many of our clients prefer to buy a seven year lease which would come to just £2,000. This is the last flat, I might add, Sir . . .'

'Seven pounds a week! Come on Tom, before I thump this git.'

Jake swore all the way down the stairs. His maximum wage was £14 a week, with overtime, so paying half for a flat was ridiculous.

Outside there was a bricklayer finishing off a bit of pointing. Jake recognized him as a brickie from Armstrongs. He asked him who he was working for now and was told Johnstones. Jake said he might have guessed.

'He always was a con man,' said Jake, turning to me. 'He used to nick so much lead from every firm he worked for that they had to lay off the plumbers. They couldn't keep them working.'

'Mr. Johnstone's in the next street on another job,' said the bricklayer. 'He might give you a start, Jake. I know he's looking for labourers.'

'Get stuffed,' said Jake.

We were going back that way. As we came past a house being done up Jake went in to look for Johnstone.

'Hey Johnty, you old cunt,' shouted Jake. 'What fettle?'

Johnstone was directing some men working on the stairs. He didn't look down at Jake.

'You wanna get rid of that slob round the corner,' said Jake. 'I wouldn't take a flat from him if he was giving them away.'

'Who you talking about?' said Johnstone irritably, measuring up a wall. Jake explained we'd been round looking at his other property.

'He's from the estate agent. Nothing to do with me. If you want a start, come back on Monday. I'm busy now. Right, Charlie, two coats on there will be enough. And put some more water in that emulsion when you're tel't.'

Johnstone pushed down the stairs past us and walked out to his Consul. He pulled up the collar of his sheepskin jacket to ward off the sight of Jake. Jake didn't take the hint but dashed round the car, pushing me in the back and jumping in the front beside Johnstone.

'Thanks Johnty, old lad. The Town Hall will be grand.'

'You cheeky git,' said Johnty, accelerating fast and trying to frighten us.

'You still fancy Gloria, then?' said Jake.

'You what,' said Johnstone. His little pig eyes began to look human. 'That big titted lass on the buses?'

'That's right. You always said she'd make a smashing sow. She doesn't half, Johnty lad. A real goer, I can tell you. Her husband's on nights this week. Want her address?'

'Yeh,' said Johnty, swerving to avoid going over Eden Bridges. Jake told him Gloria's address. He wrote it down with one hand as he was driving up Lowther Street.

'Thanks, lad. I will give you a start. See me tomorrow, eh.'

'Give over. I'm looking for a flat, not a job. And I don't want something shitty like yours. I want a bit more class, know what I mean? Got anything else on the go?'

'Is he on nights all week?'

'All week. You'll be lined up there all right. How much did you pay for that place, then, Johnty lad?'

'What? Oh, two thousand. It was in a bad state, though.' Johnstone was hardly concentrating on Jake and his questions. His mind was half away, riping open the buttons on Gloria's shiny sexy sweaty tunic.

'What did it take you to do it up?' said Jake, casually, as if he was just making polite chat.

'About the same again.'

'So you spent four thousand altogether?'

'I will have done. I've paid for nowt so far.'

'And you've got four flats, have you?' Johnty nodded his head. 'So it costs four thousand and you get eight thousand back by selling them on seven year leases?'

'A bit more. The ground flat is two and a half thou. It's got the garden.'

'Jesus Christ! It's money for jam. Stop the car. I'm getting out.'

'Don't mess around. I want you to show me her house. What time does he leave?'

'Who told you about it?'

'About what?'

'Converting.'

'Everybody's doing it. You can't go wrong. Do you think I should go back for me Yankee car, Jake? She might prefer something a bit flashy.'

'I said stop the car. It's giving me a headache.'

Jake started to open the door. The car was still moving so Johnty was forced to stop, though he didn't want to.

'Heh, Jake,' shouted Johnty. 'I've just realized I haven't got any . . .'

We couldn't hear the rest. Jake was striding up an alleyway with me following. I'd no idea what was going on. I can never understand figures when people start throwing them around. I need it all written down. It's the same when people start spelling out words aloud. My brain never works quick enough to take them in. Jake was like a computer when it came to grasping things quickly, especially anything involving numbers.

We'd arranged to go to the pictures, after we'd looked at the flat. But Jake was now marching off in the direction of the river. He was in a world of his own. Every time I started to ask what he was thinking about, he said shurrup, man.

'You know what,' he said at length. 'You don't *need* any money at all.'

I thought he was talking about the pictures. I said he hadn't to worry, I'd pay him in, though I'd already loaned him that quid.

'No, no, you daft git. You can make money without having any money. This is what's been fucking me up all along.'

'Oh aye,' I said, looking at my watch and working out that we'd already missed a Mister Magoo.

'You buy a house which costs two thousand, but you only need pay a little bit down. OK? Converting costs another two thousand, but if you don't pay for that till you've sold the whole lot, for a cool fucking eight thousand, then you've made four thousand, in your hand, without having had any money!'

'And there's a Bugs Bunny. We've missed that now, thanks to you.'

'It's ridiculous! I always knew it, even without knowing it. My stupid old git of a father hasn't made eight thou in twenty years of work, yet old cuntface Johnty can make that over-night. I was right. The whole thing's a fucking farce. Now I've got proof. What's the point of working when people can make it like that, without working? Answer me that?'

'We'll just have to have some chips instead.'

'Bloody hell. And if you enjoy your lousy job, that's just as pointless. Christ, what have I been doing all these years? Not only do you not need any money to get going, you don't even have to do any work. You just become an in-between man, playing at sums. With one hand you buy something with money you haven't got. With the other hand you grab all the real money while some fucker does all the work. There should be a law against it.'

'There probably is,' I said. 'Come on, here's a bus.' We'd been walking for miles, getting nowhere, except further away from Carlisle. 'Come on. It's too late now. We've had it.'

'We've all had it, boyo. We've all been taken for a great fucking ride. But not me.'

It was dark when we walked down Solway Terrace. Jake didn't want me to leave him because I'd been there when the heavens had opened on the road to Damascus. He wanted me to listen to him, even though I wasn't interested. He said come and have some supper at his place. I said he'd been chucked out. He said that didn't matter. They'd be asleep. I wanted to get home. My mother would have taken her liquid paraffin by now and gone to bed.

There was silence in Jake's house as I crept in behind Jake. Lilly appeared like a ghost and said that Jake's father was dead.

'Does that mean there's no supper?'

His mother saw us to the door and closed and bolted it after us. I said how terrible. He needn't have said that. But there was no use coming to our house. Me Mam was in bed. I'd see him tomorrow. Tarrawell. Jake kept on walking down Solway Terrace, on his own. He disappeared into the fields muttering about at last, at last, something had turned up.

Chapter Five

I was sitting in the office one Tuesday about half past one and it was like a graveyard. Tuesday is the first day of the Sunday paper week and you'd expect it to be all bustle, especially in Fleet Street, the heart of the Empire and all that. Fred the office boy was also there sitting in the news editor's chair drawing naked women on the office memo pad. The pad was covered with circular soggy brown tea cup stains, as if someone had been doing a potato cut pattern. Fred was fitting in the nudes so that he could use pairs of tea cup rings as gigantic breasts. He'd go far, that lad.

I had a ticket for a free lunch at the Connaught Rooms. If it had been the Connaught Hotel or the Savoy and the unveiling of a new sexy film star, I would have gone. But the Connaught Rooms and the launching of a new deodorant was well down in the second eleven of free dos. I was getting very blasé, after three months before the mast. Or should I go across the road and play shove ha'penny? I'd said I would, when I was finished what I was doing. I was actually doing nothing. I'd rung a few people, but they'd all gone for lunch about eleven o'clock. There was even less point in the pub these days now that Bennet didn't go. He ate in the directors' dining room, since he'd been made editor. I'd dreaded him being editor, but it turned out he quite liked me. At least I was getting a few bigger features to do, instead of being legman on the gossip column.

'Is that Tom Graham?' said a voice on the phone, just as I was giving up lunch as a bad job and deciding to write my expenses and my letter home instead. 'This is Michael.'

I didn't know a Michael, but I said oh yes, hello. Journalists can't afford to hang up. It might have been Prince Michael.

'Michael Stein,' said the voice.

'From Carlisle?' I asked, hesitantly.

'From Sullivan and Co.' he said. 'I've got a table booked at Wheelers. See you there in ten minutes, OK?'

I rushed out, screamed for a taxi and jumped in. I didn't fool about with getting buses anymore, oh my word no. Wheelers, I said, settling down to read the midday Standard which I'd pinched from the news desk. 'Which one?' said the driver. I was back to square one. I hadn't realized there was more than one Wheelers. I spluttered on, trying to get him to tell me how many there were without appearing too much of a hick. He said forget it. It would be Old Compton Street.

At that ridiculous board meeting I'd hardly glanced at the bloke called Michael who seemed to be Jake's right hand man, though I'd noticed he was very smooth, genuinely smooth and cultured, compared with Jake. It was obviously the Michael Stein from Carlisle. He seemed completely out of place with Jake, but then he'd been out of place in Carlisle. He'd been the local little rich boy, who'd gone to public school and Oxford then for some reason had come back to Carlisle to be articled as a solicitor. I'd known who he was, but that was about all. I'd never met him in Carlisle. I couldn't imagine how he'd got mixed up with Jake.

He was sitting on the first floor at a corner table. The waiter was pouring him out a glass of the house chablis. He wore the usual sparkling white shirt, cut-away collar and discreet pin-stripe suit. His dark hair was neatly parted and beautifully brushed, as if his mother had just done it for him. He was tall and thin and very clean. He smiled at me over his half glasses, the sort Sir Alec Douglas Home was wearing. It was Michael's only apparent affectation. The rest of him seemed to be an identikit picture of the successful London upper class professional man, fresh out of his club.

He half rose, taking off his spectacles and putting them in an inside pocket which must have been so inside that it made no crease in his waisted jacket. 'How nice of you to come,

Tom. Do sit down.' He offered his hand. It was cold and white.

I sat down and he studied the long shiny menu. He said the oysters were a bit small but I'd find their fish soup very pleasant. Then sole, of course. He could recommend the Mornay. He ordered unobtrusively for both of us before I'd realized, pushed the menu away and looked at me.

'Tell me about yourself.' This is the sort of question which gives the impression someone is fascinated by you, but it's only asked because the person can't think of anything else to say. I blurted on about my job and doing student journalism at university and how my mother really wanted me to be a teacher. He said yes and no and nodded at the right moments, but I somehow felt vulnerable.

'Now tell me, why do you want to join Sullivan and Co?'

'But I don't,' I said, on the defensive for some reason. The way he'd put the question had forced me to deny it. 'Who said I did?'

'I see,' he said, pausing, not answering my question. 'You're probably making the right decision. Working with Jake Sullivan is, how should I put it, rather hellish. How's the soup?'

'I can imagine.'

'You can't, that's the danger. You think he's amusing and outrageous and refreshing. That's how he often looks from the outside. He's genuinely very nasty. He likes destroying people, especially ones he likes. And he's rather fond of you.'

'That's nice,' I said.

'You see he's got romantic notions about Thwaite, and his boyhood.'

'Haven't we all.'

I wanted to hear how Jake had got where he was. What had happened since his boyhood and why he should now be interested in me, a crummy journalist on a crummy paper. But Michael began again to say that Jake wasn't nice. He was obsessed by how awful Jake was. I knew that already and was bored hearing it. I could get all that sort of thing at home from Antonia.

'Why don't you leave him?' I asked. 'If he's so awful.'

'I can't. These things happen.'

I presumed he meant because they were such close business partners, so I saw it as a chance to ask about Jake's business. I didn't get very far. Michael seemed too bored by it, or perhaps he didn't want to tell me. All he wanted to do was make it clear I wouldn't like working for Jake. It was 1961. A young man like me could do well in lots of firms.

We went downstairs and he tried to help me on with my raincoat. I didn't want to put it on. It looked quite clean and presentable held inside out. It had once been off-white and the smart thing for young journalists in Manchester. Now it was just a grotty grey. Outside in Old Compton Street, as we were passing all the bare breasts and jackbooted thighs, Michael tried again. He was wearing a very well-cut black overcoat which was slightly too long for him. He got my raincoat on this time and carefully helped me to get my arms in as if I was a spastic. He was so considerate about it, as if he was used to doing such little services, that I felt embarrassed. He was older than me, so much smarter and cleverer, that it seemed incongruous. I couldn't get the raincoat incident out of my head. He insisted on walking with me for a little bit, saying we were both going the same way, which we weren't. I tried to chat him up again on his first meeting Jake.

'Meeting Jake? Oh yes, how it all began,' he said, slightly stepping sideways so that he could look at me. He was one of these people who have to look at you, and you at him, when they're talking. Walking and talking at the same time was agony for him. 'I first saw him at the El Ole. That was one of the places I used to go, for my sins.'

'That's funny,' I said. 'That was the last place I saw Jake, before I lost contact with him.'

The El Ole was one of Carlisle's first modern coffee bars – now closed. They were a bit late getting that far North, but when they arrived they had all the regulation bamboo awnings, rubber plants, gurgling Espresso coffee machines, empty chianti bottles, arty but inefficient lighting and arty and in-efficient waitresses who tried hard to look too good for the El Ole, which wasn't very difficult. They were mostly failed art students, or pretending to be, who didn't wear uniform, unless you call white make-up and long matted yellow hair a uni-form. They could never remember the orders and when they did get it right they could never find you, what with all those rubber plants and matted yellow hair to fight their way through.

Everybody went on about how phony it was, how pretentious and, most of all, how bloody expensive. Everybody went there. There was nowhere else, except lorry drivers' caffs or cadaverous tea rooms with old ladies huddling in the corner. In the evening it was full of students, especially in the vacation, spinning out a coffee for two hours. At tea time you got the smarter salesmen, with their A.40's full of samples and bright tweed county caps pulled down at a jaunty angle. They'd be chatting each other up, finding out whose wife they could spend the night with instead of driving home to their own. At lunch time you'd get the young men about town, those whose dads had little businesses which they were working in, or at least passing the time in. They could afford the El Ole's ridiculously expensive sit-up-at-the-bar snacks. They'd talk about rugby or fast cars or parties for hours, anything instead of going back to the shop. The morning, that was when the up and coming con men came into their own.

They usually sauntered in about ten, having popped into their offices to say hello and tell everyone about this important client they had to see. Then they'd sit in the El Ole for up to two hours, or longer if they did have a real client who might be fool enough to buy them lunch.

None of them had dads with shops. They were living on their wits. They'd got to grammar school but had left at sixteen with small O levels and big ideas. They wanted money fast and unlike Jake had no intention of doing any hard work, even for a laugh. After all, they had gone to grammar school. They'd picked up a little bit of middle class veneer, mixing with those professional people's kids. I've often wondered if Jake had gone to grammar school if he would have acquired any polish, or if he'd gone on to university if he would have picked up any restraint. Just as well he didn't. It takes a very clever person to survive being educated.

Anyway, these lads were all up to date with their Italian-style suits and pointed shoes. At fifteen they'd had the best Teddy Boy haircuts in the grammar school but now they affected public school haircuts, grown rather long, but very neat with a high parting. They'd sit up at the bar of the El Ole, cracking their fingers. When they thought no one was looking they squeezed their spots. Over their shoulders they'd order another Espresso from Cynthia, the dopiest waitress of all whose job it was to wrestle with the Espresso machine.

They were all estate agents. That's what they called themselves. The property boom had begun in Cumberland, though in a very quiet way compared with the South. A few new estate agents had opened who were trying hard to compete with the old established family firms. One or two took on sharp-looking lads from grammar school at sixteen who were far too sharp to think about night school or correspondence courses and acquiring proper qualifications. They didn't get paid much and they were officially only clerks, which of course they denied. What they were good at was chatting up the slow-witted on the telephone and talking the nervous into a supposed fabulous buy. For their part, they were always looking for a likely opening, knowing that by the time they were twenty there would be some even sharper sixteen-year-old lads around at half the money. They knew who owned what, how much it cost, how much it was really worth, what was up and coming and what was dead, but dead. They were always working out ways of getting in the backdoor and getting the business away for their own firm. And if they could manage it, for themselves. Their main aim in life was a bit on the side. Money as well as sex. It was the money which Jake Sullivan wanted to hear about.

They ignored Jake, this out of work bus conductor with his greasy Teddy Boy haircut. Despite lashing out on a short-jacketed 1958 Italian-style suit, he wore it with his old lace tie and brothel creeper shoes. He still looked what he was, a country yob trying hard to be a tough Teddy Boy townie.

He'd left the buses the week after the meeting with Johnty, the conversion expert. He walked into the office of Mr. Foster, the area manager, jammed his money bag down over Foster's ears and said he was going. Beryl was in the room at the time, which was why he'd gone in. She walked out as soon as she saw a scene coming.

Jake was then left homeless and jobless. For a few days he hung around transport cafés, standing hunched over the juke box, defying anyone else to play it. He bullied drivers into letting him sleep in their cabins. Then he came into town and sat in the corner of Bruciani's fish and chip shop, terrorizing people into buying him chips. At nights he slept in a Salvation Army hostel. He'd been walking round the estate agents one day, thinking about Johnty and staring at the lists and prices in their windows, when he noticed all the young sharp lads going into this coffee bar. He'd felt at home in the workmen's caffs. Peering through the bamboo of the El Ole made him feel aggressively inferior.

One day he felt more aggressive than inferior, marched in boldly, so he thought, and sat down in a corner, determined to give a mouthful to anyone who asked him to leave. He was drumming his fingers on the table, nervously, when Cynthia had come round, wiping the tables. That's a nice tune, she said. Jake noticed how filthy his finger nails were, compared with the smart lads at the bar. He put his hand in his pocket, knocking over the three foot long menu. When he picked that up he put his elbow through a piece of bamboo awning and a bunch of plastic grapes fell with a crash on the floor. Cynthia laughed gaily. The lads nudged each other. Cynthia beamed through her glasses like Dilly Dream then bent down and cheerfully scrabbled on the floor, searching for the grapes.

'Never mind, never mind,' said Jake, hissing angrily at her for drawing even more attention to him. Cynthia was very tall and thin and her flared, starched skirt, however fashionable, looked ridiculous on her. She bobbed up from under the table like Alice in Wonderland, smiling idiotically.

'Well here I am,' she cooed. 'Bingo! And isn't it a lovely morning. What is your pleasure, kind sir?'

Someone had once told Cynthia that what was so refreshing about her was that she was always a little ray of sunshine. This was when she was eight years old and four foot high. Now at twenty-two and six foot, it was about time she stopped shining. She probably knew inside that if she ever did, that would be that. But she must never admit to herself she was so enormous and so plain. She must concentrate on her gaiety and her feet. She also had lovely feet. Not just some one, but *everyone* had told her that. She had two wardrobes containing fifty-five pairs of shoes; each Friday she bought another pair, prettier and more frivolous than the ones before.

She thought Jake was a scream. She laughed at him even more the next day. She was always nice to him. Being half blind she didn't notice how scruffy he was, compared with the sharp boys at the bar.

I was on the buses for the rest of the vacation. Just before term started I had a morning off. I went into the El Ole and was surprised to find Jake. I couldn't understand how he was living. I'd heard he hadn't a job or any money and was just hanging around the El Ole all day. I ordered him a coffee. He knocked it straight back and nodded to Cynthia.

'Get lost,' I said, thinking he meant another coffee.

'Cyn,' he said, over his shoulder like the lads did. 'What's for supper?'

'I was thinking about sausages, Jake,' she simpered, breathlessly through her hair. 'Would that be all right, my sweetie pie?'

'It'll do,' said Jake. 'But don't let it happen again.'

'You couldn't possibly get them on your way home, could you, Jake? If I gave you the money in your little handy pandy?'

'What do you think I am? Meals on Wheels?'

'And a Tutie Fruitie Pie, my little cuddle bunch.'

'OK, then. Give us the dosh.' Jake held his hand over his shoulder and Cyn put some money in it, giving it a little squeeze. He got up, all nonchalant, and went out.

When the rest of the lads found out what had happened, right under their very noses, their estimation of Jake soared. Not one of them had found out that Cynthia had a bit of money of her own, and her own flat. Her parents, who lived down in West Cumberland, thought she was still at art college, which she'd been thrown out of after one term. She'd previously been thrown out of the technical college, where they'd also been subsidizing her. Jake had it made. Free digs, free food, free lays and free coffees all day at the El Ole, as long as the manageress wasn't around. Having ignored Jake in the corner, the lads were soon all over him, lapping up his stories about hard times but easy lays. He told so many of them about Gloria that it must have been standing room only at her place.

One afternoon he walked into the bus station, knowing it was Foster's day off. He sat himself in Beryl's office, boasting about how well he was doing, about how he had his own little business and own little flat, why didn't she come round and see it some evening, eh?

'It's just a peed a terre,' he said. 'You know, for peeing in when I'm in town.'

Beryl didn't like vulgarity and said she was going to call an inspector. She did. Jake was thrown out.

Another afternoon Jake was going past this old three-storey

Victorian house in Warwick Road when the door opened and a coffin was brought out. Jake took his flat cap off and went up to the door to help them out. He watched them get into the hearse, then he reopened the door, which he hadn't closed, and went round the house. It was in a terrible condition, all scruffy and smelly. The coffin had contained the last occupant who'd been crouching alone in her room as the whole family died off one by one. The house turned out to be in good condition, apart from the smell. He went on the roof, looked at the basement, measured the garden and by the time the family solicitor had got back from the cemetery, Jake had his offer in – £2,000, take it or leave it.

'This bloody solicitor said he couldn't possibly discuss it. Nothing could be done until the last will and testicles, puberty and probate and all that shit had been proved. And anyway, I hadn't an appointment.'

By talking to neighbours in the street Jake found out who was the next of kin. He rang each of them, in his best voice, saying he had made this handsome offer to the solicitor. He knew the solicitor would want to put it into the hands of an agent, but if they accepted his offer now they'd save agent's fees and have it all cleared up very quickly. He was a very busy man and he'd want a quick decision. It turned out they'd been dreading the bother of having to look after the house and were grateful to get shot of it so easily.

He told the solicitor it was all arranged, apologizing for going behind his back. He said he was a family friend, which was how he knew the executors. He asked the solicitor if he would handle the conveyancing of the house for him. He'd intended not to use a solicitor, having heard from the lads what a con they were, but it was a method of keeping the solicitor happy.

Jake's next step was to get three builders to put in estimates for converting the property. He chose one at £1,500 and told him he could start in two weeks' time.

The solicitor was a fairly slow doddery old boy but he was soon asking for Jake's ten per cent, as a deposit to seal the offer being accepted, that's if Mr. Sullivan's surveyor had reported to Mr. Sullivan's satisfaction, and Mr. Sullivan's mortgage had been arranged.

Surveyor? Jake said he hadn't worked in the building trade

all his life to need some public school jerk of a surveyor to tell him a good house when he saw one. And as for getting a mortgage, he would be paying in full, in cash. His accountant would be dealing with that. Expect the cheque in the post any day. That's why he employed an accountant, for Christ's sake.

Jake told me all the plans the next time I saw him in the El Ole, presuming I'd be too stupid, or too loyal, to let them out so any of the sharp lads could jump in. He didn't seem worried about getting the money, as his scheme was so fool-proof. All he wanted me to do was work out an advert to put in the Cumberland News.

'Six luxury flatlets, at only fifteen hundred each for a seven year lease. It's a bloody bargain.'

'I couldn't write it better than that, Jake.'

'You educated cunts, it's all you're any good for, bloody words. Come on, stop fucking around, get your biro out.'

'What's a flatlet?'

'You what? Do you sit and wank all day long at that school? The money we taxpayers waste on schmucks like you.'

'What's a schmuck?'

'Give over. I'd be better getting Cyn to do it, if she could read and write. You'll be wanting to know the laws of conveyancing next. I can't give away all my secrets, you know.'

He did seem to have picked up a lot, just by hanging around the smart agents.

'That sounds a lot of money, Jake,' I said. 'Six flatlets at fifteen hundred each ... That's nine thousand ... Jake, it's nine thousand pounds!'

'Listen, Einstein, I'll do the sums, you just get your little mind to work on some good selling words.'

'How about "beautifully appointed" or "architect designed"?' I said. 'You have got an architect, haven't you?'

'Nine thousand isn't much, you know,' said Jake, drumming with his fingers on the table to show he was thinking. 'I wonder if I can put the prices up a bit. It's gonna cost me all of four thou to buy them, do them up and that. That's only a profit of five thou, Tommy lad. And it'll take eight weeks.'

'A lifetime.'

'That's the quickest the builders can do. I've got a completion clause if they start fucking me around. OK, don't ask me, you ignorant sod. That means *they* pay me five quid a week for every flatlet unfinished after eight weeks. Nobody messes me around, my word no.'

I finished the ad and it suddenly struck me that not only did the well appointed luxury flatlets not exist yet, Jake didn't own them. Wouldn't it be better if he bought the house first? And anyway, what was he going to buy it with?

'Stick around, kid. Have another coffee. Cyn, another capuchino for my educated friend here.'

'Oh Jake, I can't. That's the fourth one you've had this morning. Caroline's watching me.'

'Fuck Caroline,' said Jake. Cynthia giggled.

Caroline was the very superior middle-aged manageress. She was coming over towards us. I made a great show of paying for the coffees so that she wouldn't hang over us like a vulture. We were only half way through the coffees when Jake jumped up and said let's go.

'Don't touch those coffees,' Jake shouted to Caroline. 'I've spat in them.' As we were going out the door he said to me, very loudly, that he was putting in a take-over bid next week. And the first thing he'd do would be to sack the management. Caroline could be seen through the steamed up window holding a tea towel at arm's length and wiping the chair which Jake had been sitting on.

'What's the hurry?' I said as we rushed along Scotch Street.

'They're open in five minutes,' said Jake. 'Come on.'

It was only five to ten. I said he was raving. They didn't open till eleven, and anyway I didn't feel like a drink.

'The bank, you daft git. I've got an appointment with the manager at ten fifteen.'

We had bags of time so we stood at the Town Hall. We were able to see the corner of Bank Street and watch them opening. Jake combed his hair and polished his shoes with the backs of his trouser legs. He looked almost nervous. I said so, half expecting a thump.

'Well I am. Nervous with excitement. No, guilt. Yeh, I almost feel guilty. Five thousand profit, in my hand, for nothing. It's ridiculous. Look at that bloke cleaning out the steps of the lavs. I bet he wouldn't know what a five pound note was if he met it in his porridge. I'll have so many I'll be shitting them. It's all wrong.'

'It does sound wrong to me, Jake.'

'Of course it is. People shouldn't be able to make it as easy as that.'

'Then don't do it.'

'You what? And let some other cunt get away with it? I'm not cheating anyone. I'm helping the Government's housing problem. If someone's in there stuffing themselves, then Jakey boy's getting in there as well, fighting to get to the top of the shit heap.'

'Why?'

'Like fucking Everest, because it's there. I can't stand here all day arguing the toss with the likes of you. Out of the way. Let Rockefeller get moving. My tie straight? See you in the Ole in half an hour. Order me a Jag, if you've nothing else to do.'

I was on at eleven and didn't really have much time, but the Ole was on my way to the bus station so I thought I'd wait for a bit.

'Morning,' said Jake, marching into the manager's office and sitting down, without waiting to be asked. The manager was at his desk with an undermanager hovering behind, passing papers for him to sign. Jake leaned over and picked up a wooden plaque which said 'J. F. C. Klein'.

'So that's how you spell your name, eh? Jewish, is it?'

The manager went on signing papers.

'Look, come on, Kleen or Kline or whatever. I haven't all day. Ten fifteen, you said. There are other bank managers, you know. They'd be very grateful for my business. I'll expect a half per cent below your usual rate, of course. Two thousand over eight weeks at six and a half per cent will come to twenty pounds in interest, so you won't be doing too badly....'

Mr. Klein nodded, signalling that his deputy could now withdraw, which he did backwards, smiling and nodding like a mandarin. Mr. Klein slowly cleared his desk while Jake chuntered on. Then he pulled a sheet of clean paper from a drawer, placed it in front of him and unscrewed the top of his Parker 51.

'Yes,' he said clearing his throat and staring at a wodge of crepe which was coming off Jake's shoe. 'What can I do for you, hmm?'

'What do you mean? I told you all about it on the phone yesterday. Where do you want me to sign?'

'You probably told Mr. Bickerstaffe. No, no, no, Mr₁ Heathersgill. He was in attendance yesterday.'

Mr. Klein was now staring at the clock on the wall and checking his watch. Jake was forced to start at the beginning and explain his scheme, which he did breathlessly, tumbling it all out. Mr. Klein didn't listen. When Jake finished he asked him curtly what securities he had. Jake said, eh, you what?

'I mean, Mr. Sullivan, how much money have you got of your own? I understand you are not a member of our bank. Which bank have you got your money in?'

'I haven't got any bloody money. What do you think I'm doing here!'

'Then what other securities have you?'

Jake went into how completely fool-proof his scheme was. He didn't need securities because nothing could go wrong. He'd pay him back without fail in eight weeks.

'Ring the solicitor, if you don't believe me. Contact the builder. He's ready to start next week. If you're so bloody thick, ask them. Don't just take my word, if that's what's worrying you. Read the Cumberland News on Friday and you'll see the ad.'

'The what, Mr. Sullivan? You're advertising this scheme of yours before you even own the house? That is rather premature, not to mention highly immoral and probably illegal. Mr. Bickerstaffe, get me the Cumberland News advertising manager on the telephone. You do realize, Mr. Sullivan, that if you sell something you don't own you could go to prison?'

'Christ, is this a bank or a Sunday School? I know what I'm doing, even if you bloody don't. Look, do I get the two thousand quid or do I go elsewhere?'

'Certainly not,' said Mr. Klein, rising to his feet. As he did so two other officials entered from a side door. 'I don't even *know* you.'

'Don't be so stupid, what's that got to do with it? OK, OK. Make it just £200 for the deposit. Please yourself, if you don't want to make money. I don't care ... Just £200. Please ...'

Jake was advancing backwards as they got nearer him.

'I don't know you,' continued Mr. Klein, 'and what's more I don't like what you've told me about yourself and your preposterous plans. Not one bit. Good morning Mr. Sullivan.'

Caroline was now advancing on Jake as well. He'd come

back in such a temper, red in the face and white in the eyes that Cynthia immediately gave him a coffee. He was now a bit calmer, having told us about his encounter with the bank manager, but still shaking.

'That's it,' said Caroline. 'Both of you. Out. I'll pay you till the end of the week, Cynthia, then that's it. And as for you, Jake Sullivan, if you set foot in this establishment again I'll call the police.'

Until the board meeting, that, as I said, was the last time I'd seen Jake Sullivan.

Chapter Six

We were on top of a layer of a souffle sort of fluffy grey cloud where it's impossible to tell where the air ends and the sea begins, unless of course you crash. Then you know. It was the first time I'd been on a plane and I was scared stiff. There was this sexy hostess, dressed up like a Bunny for some reason, who kept on bending over me, dangling her cleavage as if to say your safety cord is down there, put your hand in and pull. She'd been dishing out champagne and savouries all the way from London and I felt like going to sleep. But I was scared.

Not only was it my first plane trip, it was my first free trip. I'd had free noshes until they were coming out of my ears, in the six months since I'd been in London, but never actually been anywhere. Bennet was always going on facility trips and inaugural flights, meant for the air correspondent, but I'd never gone anywhere. I'd got this trip off my own bat, so I thought, till I came back to the office and Bennet was all knowing leers. He'd already heard about it and tried to pretend he'd engineered it for me, which of course he hadn't. Certainly I could go, he said. I could get a feature out of it, give me bags of time to really get to know the chappie. Perhaps do a news story as well.

There was a gap in the clouds and I could see some genuine sea-looking sea. It must be the Solway. I felt quite excited. I turned to Michael beside me, but he was deep in some sort of magazine. He'd hardly spoken since we left London, except to say it was the most ridiculous idea he'd ever heard of, but typical. He'd got through the New Statesman, the Spectator and the Listener, ignoring all the cleavages which had been suspended in front of him. Goodness knows what the lads at the back had been getting through. There had been two sexy hostesses when we'd started off, but I hadn't seen one of them since Watford. I'd heard Jake, though, all the time. He and Sammy, his assistant, and a bloke called Ron, whose face I vaguely recognized, had been shouting obscenities at the two girls all the way. There had been lots of scuffles and screams, but I hadn't turned round. It was like being back on the first workers' bus to town all over again. Michael and I were the old men.

'Hold on to your cocks, lads,' shouted Jake. 'Chastity belts on girls. Here we are.'

We landed at Crosby aerodrome so smoothly and comfortably I hadn't realized we were down. It was just a ten seater plane, beautifully finished and appointed, with a bar, a little cinema and a dining table. Jake had two planes. The ashtrays were full in the other one, so he'd said, which was a pity as he'd got some blue films rigged up. Never mind, we'll get two nice hostesses.

'You couple of stuck-up shits,' said Jake as we were getting off. 'Have you been pulling each other off all the time? Never mind Tom, on the way back it'll be your turn. I won't tell Antonia. She's probably having it off with some old Etonian anyway. That's all they do at that place, isn't that right Ron?'

'That's all I did,' said Ron in a broad Liverpool accent. 'It was the only thing worth doing.'

There was a fleet of chauffeur driven Rollses waiting. I found myself in one with Michael and Ron. I tried to chat up Michael, but didn't get anywhere. He was very cold and distant and seemed annoyed with me, perhaps because he'd warned off Jake. So I got talking to Ron, at least I got listening to his monologue. He wasn't interested in me, but he didn't mind giving his views on everyone, most of all himself. I soon realized who he was, the wonder boy of Fleet Street. He was operating as a free lance after a brilliant career at Cambridge, where he'd done all the right things, like the Labour Party, the Union and Varsity. He'd been one of the first of the new working class lads who'd cashed in on being working class, grinding down all the Etonians by the crudeness and nastiness of his wit. All the debby Girton girls had wandered round in his wake saying Ron, darling Ron, did you really live in a council house? Please tell us more about your father. Is he really a docker? Oh, how marvellous. I'd hated Ron without ever having met him. These lads who make a stir at Oxford or Cambridge have it easy. Everybody in London is listening to their noise. You might be the biggest thing to hit Durham since the Venerable Bede, but nobody outside Durham knows or cares.

I was annoyed most of all to realize who he was. Jake had promised it was an exclusive story, the bastard. It had originally been a personal thing. He'd come round to my flat, uninvited, saying that he wanted Antonia and me to come in his plane on Friday. He was a bit disappointed when I said Antonia had exams. He said he'd speak to her teacher, that would do the trick. I said I couldn't come either. I had a job to do. Then he changed tack and said, OK, if I was being all shitty, he'd *make* it into a job, then I'd have to come, as it was such a brilliant story. He'd speak to my half-witted editor.

I still didn't know what the story was, though if I'd had a camera on the plane I could have made a fortune from the News of the World. First of all he said he was meeting Fidel Castro at Silloth and they were going to march on Whitehall. Then he said he was being made the new Bishop of Carlisle and the raveup was at the Cathedral, bring your own reefers. No, he said, it was really just a short flight, they'd turn right round after they'd bombed Caldew Castle to the ground. This was where the Featherstone-Caldews lived, the local nobs whom Jake had always hated.

'Stop asking fucking silly questions. It's September 3rd, isn't it? So, what goes on September 3rd, baby boy?'

With all the talking, or listening, to Ron I'd got lost. I knew we were now near Thwaite, but I didn't recognize this new estate of bright-looking colourful houses. I hadn't been back since my mother died. I could hear a band in the distance. Then we entered a street which was thick with banners, streamers and people. I recognized a lot of them. They were mostly gaping at the decorations. When our fleet of Rollses arrived they all rushed round as if they'd never seen cars before.

'Christ, who are all these aborigines?' said Ron.

'Well, there's Bobby Blacket from the Tarn Inn,' I said. 'There's the Cummersdales, and that's Arthur Blenerhasset from Lanwathby, and the Forsters, the Armstrongs, the Grahams, the Lowthers and that looks like the Patricks from Solway Terrace....'

Jake led our little party, a busty hostess on each arm, through the crowds to a little bungalow which was covered completely in flowers and streamers. There didn't appear to be anyone in it, as far as I could see, but trestles and tables had been set up outside and a huge buffet was being laid out, waiters bustling round opening bottles. There were two photographers from local papers, rushing round like idiots. Jake was giving them his biggest toothy grin. He stood outside the house, waving and giving the V sign and flexing his right arm and cuddling the girls.

There was a sudden burst of cheering from the end of the street as the crowds parted to let someone through. A plane which had been circling overhead let out a monster balloon which said 'Happy Birthday Mam from Jake'. I remembered then that 3 September was Lilly's birthday, the same as my mother's. The other birthday coincidence in our families was that Jake and I shared the same birthday.

There was another burst of cheering. The bottles had been opened and a line of butlers and waitresses, all in uniform, marched out into the crowd, distributing glasses of champagne. Everyone rushed forward to get their free drink, ignoring Mrs. Sullivan who had managed to get through the crowds and up to the gate of her house, looking very dazed. She looked much older and more worn than I remembered her. She looked even tireder when she saw Jake.

'What's happening?' she shouted at him, becoming furious just at the sight of him. 'What's going on?'

'It's Rentaflunk, Mam. Don't worry. You just ring up, tell them how many, and they do the rest. Much better than a ham salad in the Co-op tea rooms, don't you think Mam? It's not cheap, mind.' There were a couple of local reporters hanging on to his elbow. One looked about thirteen and had a big blue note book which said Shorthand. 'Yeh, must have cost the best part of £200, just for the eats and drinks.' He waited till the reporters got it down. 'But what the hell, Mam. It's your birthday, isn't it? Have some champers.'

'I don't want any of that filthy stuff,' said Lilly. 'All I want is everyone to go home. At once!' She banged her little umbrella and swung her string shopping bag. People near her laughed, thinking she was being funny, which infuriated her even more. 'Go away!'   ,

Wasn't she proud of her son, what a good lad, we were all proud of him, he was so famous, she must be thrilled, what did it feel like, had he always been good, oh come on, Mrs. Sullivan, just a few words, please.

'I'll give you a few words all right. I said, go away! Right, well I'm going then. I'll never forgive you for this, Jake.'

Jake couldn't believe she wasn't pleased. He was still laughing and joking with the reporters who were calling him Jake after every third word, as they always do with people who are known to be a bit of a card.

The photographers were lining up to take another picture. You can hardly tell when London photographers are taking pictures because it happens so silently and quickly. But these blokes were still on plate cameras, which take hours to load and are used whether it's a hound trail, Carlisle United or a visiting celebrity. They were very flustered with all the rush and bustle. They would really have liked to have got Jake up against a wall and said smile, taken two shots, then gone home.

I saw Ron pull out a Nikon and aim it at the crowds round Jake, standing back to get in the girls, the local photographers and Jake's Mum. He must have taken a hundred shots while the locals were getting their first ready.

Jake wet his lips, preparing to kiss his mother for the benefit of the press. He had his arms out, in slow motion, so they wouldn't miss it. As he did so, Daft Jimmy staggered into them, slobbering all over Jake's suit as the flash bulbs went.

Every village has a Daft Jimmy and ours actually was called Jimmy, Jimmy Fairbairn. He was harmless enough, though you had to know him. A new bread delivery man once crashed into a wall when Daft Jimmy ran after him, shouting and slobbering at the mouth. All Jimmy wanted to do was to tell him Carlisle United's score. Jimmy's life revolved round United.

Somebody would tell him how they'd got on of a Saturday and for the following seven days he'd go round shouting it at everyone. He was very friendly, good with kids and would run messages for everyone. His parents had never put him away nor had they dressed him like an idiot in childish clothes as many people do. He always wore a dark three piece suit and had an old fashioned pearl tiepin in his tie which he was very proud of.

'What fettle then, Jimmy,' said Jake, bending down to pick up Jimmy who'd slipped after he'd crashed into Jake's arms. 'How are the lads doing?'

'Ugh, ugh ugh. They want Ivor Broadis back, ugh ugh ugh.'

'Ivor Broadis? You're raving, Jimmy. He can't play marbles. Did you hear I'm making a take-over bid? When I get control, I won't forget you, Jimmy. Still got your boots?'

Jimmy grunted with the excitement and started to tell Jake something else, probably last week's half time score. Jake suddenly realized his mother had gone, running up the street. He pushed Jimmy away and went after her.

'Ugh ugh ugh. Ah do Mrs. Lowther's messages noo, you know, ugh ugh ugh. Jake . . .' shouted Jimmy, staggering after Jake.

Jake caught up with his mother, caught her by the arm and forced her to stop.

'Don't be so daft, Mam. It's all for you. Really. I thought you'd like it. I know I haven't done much, and I owe you a lot. I really do, you know. Oh, Mam. Come on.'

'Let go of me. I don't want any of it. I've never been so embarrassed in all my life. All these folk watching. Who invited them all?'

'Oh Mam.'

'Don't "Oh Mam" me. Get out of the way.'

Daft Jimmy had caught up with Jake by now. A couple of flunkeys, seeing the famous host, rushed up with a tray of champagne glasses. Jake took one and gave it to Daft Jimmy.

'Don't be so stupid, Jake,' said his mother, as Jimmy drained it in one go. 'You know what'll happen. . . .'

'Well, it's your birthday. I want everyone to have a good time, even Jimmy. Centre forwards always have a little sup before a big match, gives that extra sparkle, doesn't it, Jimmy?'

Jake gave the bottle to Jimmy. His mother grabbed it from his trembling hands and threw it all over Jake. The bottle smashed to the ground, the champagne oozed out amongst the broken bits of glass, its sparkle deflating like a burst balloon. Jake looked deflated as well. He'd kept up his jokes and grins, convinced he'd made this terrific selfless gesture of goodwill to his mother. She'd be bound to come round in the end, enjoy herself and be grateful to Jake, her successful son.

Lilly disappeared from sight. Jake made no attempt this time to chase her. He noticed a local photographer at his elbow, putting his plate away. He grabbed his camera and smashed the photograph to the ground. The photographer was protesting, saying it was the best shot and no one else had got it. Jake took out his wallet and shoved a ten pound note in his face then stormed off.

This scene had happened away from the house and the main festivities. The crowd was still shouting and drinking like mad. Jake barged through them and into his Rolls and was gone before most people realized. I couldn't see the car I'd come in. We were all booked into the Crown and Mitre Hotel in Carlisle for the night, so there was no hurry. I wanted to talk to Lilly, if I could. She'd always disliked Jake, but I wanted to know why it had turned to hate.

'Ugh ugh ugh, Tom.' Daft Jimmy had now caught sight of me and was brandishing a piece of paper. 'Can you get his autograph ugh ugh?'

Jake had three terrible months after the failure of his first deal. The bank manager had pressed him so flat with his thumb, like a nasty little insect, that for days Jake went around literally quivering with rage. He didn't dare go home to his mother, after what he'd said the evening his father died, but he still had Cynthia's bed to lie on. Cynthia lay with him most of the time, which she enjoyed but he didn't. He wanted her to go out and get another job sharpish. She had a little money from her parents, but it wasn't enough for two.

Jake at last took a job as a long distance lorry driver. He'd driven tractors in the fields, dumpers on the building site, but I'd never seen him with a car. I don't know how he'd learned. According to Michael, he'd got the job with a forged licence.

Michael began to meet him around this time at the El Ole, so he told me when we walked back from Wheelers after that lunch. Jake had a little bit of money now he was in work and started going again to the El Ole to spend it, taking care that Caroline wasn't around. The smooth lads had heard about his fiasco with the bank manager and pissed themselves laughing at him, behind his back. One of them had told Jake, with great delight, what had happened to his house. Johnstone had bought it in the end, for £500 less than Jake was going to pay. He was putting in eight flatlets, not six, and giving Gloria one, for free. Jake hit him in the stomach, sending him flying across a table. After that he sat in a corner on his own.

'He looked so out of place,' said Michael. 'With his Teddy Boy hair cut, his jeans and his leather jerkin. This is what he wore for driving the lorry. He often left his lorry outside, just to annoy everyone. He gave off this sort of glow, like a pugilist, waiting in a corner, shadow boxing, ready to jump up and lash out as soon as the bell went. I couldn't take my eyes off him. I bought him a coffee, just to find out who he was.'

The smooth lads at the bar were surprised to see this. They'd been trying to chat up the famous Michael Stein for ages. They didn't like him as they considered him stuck up and snooty, but they knew his Dad was loaded, so that was enough. His Dad owned a very successful woollen mill just outside the city which had been started by his grandfather, who'd come across with the Huguenots or some of that lot, and had been churning over quietly for about a century. Michael's father had turned it into a huge business, buying up other local mills and concentrating on high class tweeds which he sold to all the best couturiers in London. He had desperately wanted Michael to come into the business after Balliol, but he'd refused. Michael said he wanted to be a poet. His father said he'd get nothing from him in that case. If he got a proper profession, then he'd help him. To please his invalid mother, Michael decided to come back to Carlisle, sacrifice three years of his life and be articled. This had been a big sacrifice in many ways because he'd got into some local scandal a few years previously as a teenager. It had gone to court, he'd been Mr. X and the details had never come out. The smart lads at the bar said it had been a couple of paternity orders which his

Dad had settled. They'd wished they had wealthy dads to settle their orders.

Jake was particularly rude to Michael, hating his effortless confidence, but nobody else was talking to him, or buying him coffees. At first he told him to fuck off. Michael smiled and sat down beside him. Jake said OK, a large capuchino. Jake thought he'd found a sucker and gave a V sign behind Michael's back to the lads at the bar. But after that he made sure he always came in around eleven, which was when Michael usually came.

Jake boasted non stop to Michael about this huge deal he'd nearly pulled off, but he'd been cheated at the last minute by Johnstone. He said he was suing him. Michael asked him which firm, as he was a solicitor. Jake said it was a London firm and he wouldn't know it. He wasn't going to deal with any shitty Carlisle firm.

Michael thought Jake was very amusing. He genuinely thought the deal had sounded good and told him so. But he also said he thought the property boom was fading and Jake would do better to be a middle man, such as an agent. You always made money then, no matter which side won. Jake said he was raving. The boom hadn't really started yet. The big money was to be made as a developer, and he only wanted to make the big money. He'd nearly had five thousand in his hand overnight, so why waste time getting a mingy three per cent as an estate agent?

'Well I must go,' said Michael. 'I'm due in court in ten minutes. We're representing a builder who's gone bust.'

'Well that's bloody soft. How does he pay you?'

'Legal aid. People like us get paid whatever happens, as I told you. It's no use having these big ideas Jake, if you can't . . .'

'Fuck off.'

Cynthia at last got another job, in the Housing Department of the County Council, so Jake gave up lorry driving at once. Michael had helped Cynthia to get the job, by putting a word in the right place, but he didn't tell Jake.

Jake knew from the beginning that Michael must be loaded, with that posh voice and those clothes, but he didn't immediately touch him for a loan. He thought, just as the boys at the bar had thought, that it was only a fad for Michael who would soon drop him. He had enough pride not to lay himself open to another humiliating refusal. But when Michael seemed genuinely interested in his ideas he asked him for two grand for two months at seven per cent, the full bank rate of interest. Michael told him honestly that he was sorry, he hadn't got it. His father wouldn't let him have any, till he was qualified.

'You're no good then, are you?' said Jake.

'Apparently not.'

'You've just been wasting my fucking time.'

'If you say so.'

'Well buy me some lunch then, make yourself useful.'

But Michael hadn't been wasting time. For all Jake's shouting, he had begun privately to agree with Michael that he was presenting himself all wrong and that it probably was best to give up the big ideas and go for something easier, like an estate agent. With Jake's flair for figures, he could easily do it. And all the Vaseline on his hair, was it really necessary? If Jake combed his hair down, like the other lads, Michael said he would get him a job in a new agency, as an assistant at ten pounds a week. Jake shouted and said who did Michael think he was. He was already getting twice that on the lorries. Michael tactfully didn't add that Jake hadn't actually driven a lorry for almost a month, since Cynthia started work.

'OK, just to please you, I will. But do us a favour, stop humming that fucking rubbish.'

'It's Potato Heads Blues, Louis Armstrong and the Hot Five. Don't you like it?' Michael was very keen to get Jake interested in traditional jazz, but had completely failed.

'It's crap. All jazz is crap, just like Shakespeare and opera and ballet. It never gets anywhere. People just pretend it's bloody marvellous. They make me sick. But it won't last. I bet you in ten years' time nobody's interested in trad jazz. Elvis now, he'll never be forgotten.'

'Of course he will,' said Michael. 'His music is crude and primitive and completely ephemeral.'

'You what?'

'It won't last,' explained Michael.

'Who wants it to last. You want it crude and primitive and *now*. Like money. I want it this minute to enjoy, not when I'm sixty, or even thirty.'

'But of course, Jake. You shall. I'll write to Santa Claus today.'

'Get stuffed.'

Jake didn't do very well in the estate agent's office. He did clean himself up a bit, but he hadn't got the right degree of subservience to insinuate himself with prospective sellers and he certainly didn't instil confidence in prospective buyers. As an in-between he was distrusted by both sides. Watching all the chances going to waste, all the properties being underdeveloped, made him more dissatisfied. But there seemed no way of getting any capital together. That was all he needed in life, to get him really started. There was nobody who would loan him it and he couldn't save on his £10 a week. He thought of holding up a bank, or breaking into the Co-op. He'd once planned as a boy how he could break into the Post Office at Thwaite. He'd found a disused manhole at the back, but they blocked it up the day he planned to go through it.

He got the bus out to Thwaite one afternoon when Michael was taking his final examinations. The office was very slack, Cynthia was at work and there was no one to buy him coffee. He found himself, without realizing it, walking to Solway Terrace and into his front door.

'Hey Lill,' he shouted, barging in and sitting down in his Dad's old chair. 'Got any tea? I'm starving.'

'What are you doing here?'

'Waiting for me tea, you haven't gone blind in your old age, have you?'

'You'll get nothing here, my lad, and take your feet off of that pouffe.'

'Where's his motor bike, then,' said Jake, getting up and putting the kettle on. 'Still got this lousy cooker. And I can smell that lav. You wanna get out of this dump. Do you want some tea, mater? Cup of lovely tea, darling, made by your loving son, hmm?'

'No thank you. I can make it myself.'

'Come on then, where've you hidden it?' Jake went round looking in cupboards and turning out drawers.

'If you mean your Dad's bike, Cedric got it.'

'That fat lay-about. I could have got £25 for that bike. Who's the eldest son anyway? I'll have my solicitor on to you. Dad always said I could have it.'

'He's doing very well now, Jake,' said his mother, smiling.

'Haven't the worms eaten him yet?'

73

'I'm talking about Cedric.'

'As usual.'

'He's at Spadeadam, you know, yon rocket place. Takes him only forty minutes on the bike. Do you know how much he gets?'

'Amaze me.'

'Twenty five pounds a week! That's almost twice what your Dad got all his life. He has done well, our Cedric.'

'Bloody marvellous. He'll be getting his MBE next, or has he got it and you haven't told me?'

'Don't try to be funny, Jake. If you'd stuck in like Cedric you could have done as well. That Tom Graham. He was in the same class as you, wasn't he. You could have gone to university. If only you'd . . .'

'Oh give over Mam, you're giving me a headache. I've mashed the tea, do you want a cup . . .?'

'All right then.'

Three weeks later he went back to see his mother, rushing in, shouting that she need no longer have that lousy kitchen and smelly outside lav. She'd have a bathroom for the first time, two bedrooms and underfloor central heating, so how about that?

'I'll hope you'll take your words back, Mum,' said Jake. 'You can't say I'll never be any good to anyone now.'

'What are you blathering about?'

'This, have a look at the photograph. See, a fabulous bungalow. You know, no upstairs. Just what you always wanted.'

'It does look lovely, Jake. It's so white and clean. But here, I don't want your photograph . . .'

'Keep it. It's yours.'

'I've no time for games. Come on, out of my way.'

'Mam! It's yours. Honest. Cross me heart. Mother's death – no I didn't mean that. I mean it really is yours. Listen. I'm telling the absolute truth. Three weeks today you move in, OK? They're finishing off the paintwork and laying the lawn.'

'How can it be mine. Stop being so stupid.'

'Listen, you sell this dump and get a lovely new house. Easy.'

'Don't be so ridiculous. You couldn't buy one room of that bungalow for the price you'd get for this place.'

'Don't you worry about that, Mam. I'll make up the difference. I'm in the business, aren't I?'

'What business?'

'You know. I'm an estate agent. I told you last time. I've advertised this place in last week's Sunday Times. Bijou cottage in choicest Lake District. Genuine Cumberland woodworm in all rooms.'

'Oh, Jake, you shouldn't have said that . . .'

'Oh give over, Mam, that's what you do these days. Roy Brooks does it all the time. You make it funny and people start panting. I've had twenty-seven replies and I'm putting the price up every day.'

'I don't know, I'm sure. The whole world is mad these days . . .'

'Just sign here, Mam, so we can get rid of this dump and get the new one. Don't worry. Yes, sign here as well. Honest. If you don't move into that house in three weeks' time, then, well I don't know what. I'll join the Rechabites. It's true. Thanks Mum, you're a darling.'

Jake was as good as his word. Lilly did move into the new house, that very one she'd seen, in three weeks' time. Jake helped her to move and carried her over the threshold with great giggles. He took her round proudly and she oohed and aahed.

'See the lawn? Solway turf, you can't beat it. That's the same stuff they have at Wimbledon. Do you know when they unrolled it little Solway shrimps started jumping out.'

'Ooh, it's lovely Jake. Much better than all this foreign muck they're always boasting about.'

On the mantelpiece in the living room Lilly picked up a booklet which said at the top, Cumberland County Council. Jake grabbed it from her.

'I didn't want you to see that, Mam. It's the rates book. I'll look after them. I don't want you to have any expenses at all.'

'Oh, Jake, I can do that. I want to be independent. I've got my little cleaning job which keeps me going. I can easily afford the rates, after all you've done.'

'Mother, I said don't worry about anything.'

So she didn't, even when a month later she got a rates bill. She decided to pay it herself as it wasn't much, to show Jake she wasn't depending on him too much. Then she got a demand for rent. She soon told them what she thought of that, treating her like a council house tenant. This was a private house. They said no it wasn't. And if the rent wasn't paid in two months' time, she'd be out.

It was the worst trick Jake had ever played on her, she said. Selling her house, keeping the money for himself and moving her into a council house. But she had signed the papers, giving Jake the house. She couldn't do anything about it now. She decided never to have any contact with him again. And she didn't, until he threw that ridiculous party for her, expecting everything to be forgiven and forgotten.

It was plain sailing after that, once he had a bit of capital. Jake soon found a large detached Victorian mansion in Stanwix, Carlisle's snob area, overlooking the river. They wanted £6,000, but Jake offered £5,000 for a quick sale. He pulled out £500 in fivers, taking them from his wallet with a lot of flashing and boasting, to cover the ten per cent deposit. He'd made £1,000 from Lilly's house, so he still had another £500. He'd put this in the Building Society, just to impress them. He easily got his mortgage. He was more presentable this time and he had a steady job – he told them he'd been there three years and was earning £1,500. He'd already got a girl in the office to type out the reference he'd written for himself. And he had another two references if they wanted. They could contact the County Housing Office, who would send a reference. Cynthia, who worked in this office, had already arranged that, just as she'd arranged for Lilly Sullivan to jump the housing list and get a house on the council's most modern estate. Then there was Michael Stein, the solicitor, yes, a member of that family, the son actually, great friend of mine. He would give a reference. Jake's mortgage, £4,500 at 6 per cent over twenty years, was a formality.

Michael looked after the legal side, on his own, not from his firm, as he was now qualified. Jake asked him to come in on the deal, as a partner, but he said no. He'd just give all the help he could, as a friend.

Jake felt he didn't need a lot of help. He'd been over and over such a scheme a thousand times in his head since he'd first met Johnstone. He'd raced ahead far too quickly that first time, when the bank manager brought him up short. Now he took it very carefully.

The house was converted into six executive style flats, all with central heating. The top one was called a penthouse and the ground one was the garden apartment. He took care not to advertise in the Cumberland News before everything was legally his and the flats were as good as completed. He got three times as many applicants as he had flats. Michael did the interviewing at his office, while Jake worked away in the wings, screaming at the builders in a language they understood. He'd chosen the second cheapest of five estimates which was £4,000. They were ready on the dot and for the four middle flats he got £2,000 each, and for the penthouse and garden flat £3,000 each. The total, all in cash, which he got in his hand was £14,000. His actual cash expenditure came in all to £4,500 – £500 deposit, £4,000 to the builder. He had a £4,500 mortgage to pay up, but he still owned the whole property as he'd sold the flats on twenty-one year leases.

He'd ended up with the deeds of a valuable house to flash around as extra security when needed and £8,500 in the bank to float the next property development. He'd made, in clear profit on the deal, the £5,000 magical figure he'd set his heart on. It was all done legitimately and cleanly and above board with everyone very happy, except Jake. He was furious with himself.

'I've wasted three months of my life,' he told Michael. 'I could have done all this the first time, instead of messing around doing stupid things, like lorry driving, or hanging around that lousy coffee bar, and that stupid git Cynthia.

'Right, we've no time to waste now. Let's go.'

Chapter Seven

I did a news story about Jake and his ridiculous party, but it
never appeared. I found it difficult to do because I knew so
much about him. The more you know, the harder it is to write
anything. This is probably true about most things. You can be
so bogged down by knowledge that you are inhibited from
trying anything.

I'd done the story very lightly, describing all the country
characters and their comments confronted by this twenty-two-
year-old brash millionaire from London. I hadn't mentioned
the scene with his mother. I felt that was unfair. Or was I
scared of Jake?

The story was all set up in print on the Friday evening, which
is when most pages of a Sunday newspaper are ready. Everyone was very pleased. On Saturday there was a huge piece in
Photonews in the *Daily Express*. They concentrated completely on Jake's encounter with his mother. They had the
picture of Lilly, looking absolutely furious, throwing the
champagne at Jake. It was a very nasty, micky-taking story,
but a great read. They referred to Jake all the time as the
'self-styled youngest millionaire in the country' which must
have had him furious.

My story was chucked out completely, even from the early
Northern editions. I hadn't got an exclusive after all, as they'd
thought, and most of all I hadn't got the best part of the story.
'What do you mean, you were trying to be fair?' shouted Bennet. 'If you're going to try to be fair all the time you might as
well give up being a journalist. Every story is unfair to someone.'

I crept out of the office on Saturday at five o'clock, just as
the real panic was beginning. It was only on Saturday evening
that it began to look like a real newspaper office, with scores
of extra subs brought in and middle-aged copy boys I'd never
seen before rushing around with piles of green agency stories.
The gossip column had gone to press, so my job was over,
though I worried all the way to Paddington about whether I
should have stayed on and given a hand.

Antonia was at Oxford Station waiting for me, standing outside beneath the 'Welcome to Oxford, the Home of Pressed Steel' sign. We went to a party where she talked animatedly to some very superior Christ Church blokes with floppy yellow hair and floppy white hands who didn't look at me I sat in a corner, feeling out of it.

I'd met Antonia at Durham when I'd been the smart under-graduate know-all running Palatinate, the student newspaper, and she'd been only eighteen and still at school. I was baby stealing, and from a vicarage at that, though being a vicar's daughter around Durham was as common as being a coal miner. When she went on to win an open scholarship to Oxford and I left to be a journalist in Manchester, I thought that would be it. I felt this most of all when I visited her in Oxford, me a provincial university bloke on a crummy newspaper while she was surrounded by the cream of the nation's youth, all future prime ministers.

'You are stupid,' she said, back in her room in Winchester Road. 'I hate those sort of people, you know it.'

'You didn't look it. You were all animated and talking non-stop.'

'I had to, as you wouldn't speak.'

'Well.'

'Now don't go all sullen.'

'I'm fed up.'

'Great, that's all we want. I told you not to get mixed up with him. You might have known he was lying and that there would be another journalist there. He's just taking advantage of your softness and stupidity. He wants a friend to push around, so he's nice to you and you're flattered, until someone else comes around. You're just lowering yourself.'

'I'm not.'

'OK, you're not. Let's drop the subject. You've talked about it non-stop. It bores me to tears.'

'And you bore me.'

'Fine. You might as well go then. You've done nothing but moan since you arrived.'

'OK, if that's how you feel. I'll go.'

I went into her bedroom, got my pyjamas and shaving tackle and left, slamming the door. I stood outside for a bit, hoping she'd come after me. I watched the lights go out, then I heard her landlady locking up for the night. I caught a slow train to London. It stopped at every station and took all night to get there. It was all Jake Sullivan's fault.

He rang me on Tuesday, all very remote and businesslike, and said that if I was still doing that feature he could spare me an hour to finish off the interview. I hadn't started it yet, with the news story fiasco. I rushed round at once. I must have no pride.

They gave it two pages, covering the whole centre page spread. It was pretty topical, with the Express having devoted so much space to Jake earlier in the week and starting popular interest in him. Up till then, there had been mainly just odd little paragraphs.

It was a good piece because Jake answered the questions absolutely truthfully, as no one had done before. Asked about his education he said he was expelled at fifteen for wanking. That word hadn't a chance of getting in, but after great internal rows and arguments, 'masturbation' was used, for the first time ever in the paper. You'd have thought they'd got pictures of the Virgin Birth the way they went on. Jake lashed out at all politicians, churchmen and the aristocracy. He swore all the time and the pages had to be covered with asterisks. He said any yob could make a million. He was the biggest yob he knew, so it must be true. They were amazed in the office that I'd got him to say such things about himself. He loved women, he said, so much so that he tried to love a different one every night. He'd no intention of getting married, not when there were still twenty-five million women in Britain he hadn't yet got to know intimately. At the end he said the woman he loved most of all was his mother and he could never forgive himself for being such a bad son. This bit of slush went down very well, appealing to our sort of readers, making him almost likeable after all the terrible things he'd said. 'Britain's most eligible bachelor?' was how the subs put one of the cross-headings.

Jake rang to say what a brilliant piece it was. He had some literary agent on, asking him to do his memoirs, and offers to go on telly, all of which he was turning down. I said he was mad. 'That was a favour for you, sonny boy. I haven't time for all that newspaper shit.'

On Wednesday I got a solicitor's letter. Their client wanted a complete retraction and apology and her position made quite clear and God knows what else. The editor was furious with me, having believed all Jake's rubbish. Didn't I know he was married?

I said I'd just presumed he wasn't, the way he'd been talking.

'Never presume anything,' said Bennet. 'If this costs us money, you've had it. We might get away with an apology, dressed up as a new story. The solicitor says the wife, Mrs. Beryl Sullivan, has been married to him for three years. She did an enormous amount for him when he first started, which he also doesn't acknowledge. You've been taken for a real ride, haven't you. Go on, get out of my sight.'

'Hello beautiful.'

'Do you mind.'

'Not at all,' said Jake. 'Not when I'm walking with you.'

'You're not.'

He was walking after her, not with her, threading in and out the Saturday morning crowds in Scotch Street. Beryl was doing her mother's shopping, carrying a huge straw fisherman's basket, just to prove she'd been to Spain for her holidays. She went into the market. When she felt the apples, making sure they were fresh, Jake's hand came from behind, put back what she'd picked up and found even crisper ones which he placed in her bag. When she got potatoes he made the woman wrap them in newspaper and told her not to put her dirty stuff in the lady's lovely bag, made in Hong Kong.

'It was not,' said Beryl. 'I got it . . .'

Then she remembered she was ignoring Jake. She closed her bag tight, sealed her lips, and tot-totted off, keeping her legs tight together as well, just in case. She picked up a Carlisle Journal. Jake paid for it and put a bar of Cadbury's Dairy Milk chocolate in her bag, closing it firmly. He put his finger over his mouth and signalled that no one had to talk. He walked beside her up Castle Street, on tip-toe, doing exaggerated grimaces and pretending to be quiet and invisible.

They were going past a new looking shop window when Jake pushed her into the doorway and grabbed her by the hand.

'Quick, Jock, Snowy. In this doorway, quick. No one will see us here,' said Jake, humming the Dick Barton signature tune. 'Pum pu pu pum, pum, pu pu pum. . . .'

'Do you mind.'

'Didn't they teach you any other words at that convent?'

'How did you know I went to a convent?'

'Because I've been passionate about you since you were eight. You looked fantastic in your blue gym slip, your white socks and Clarks sandals.'

'What lies.'

'OK, your Co-op sandals.'

'Look, would you mind leaving go. I can't stand here all day.'

'Why not. You're outside the smartest office in Carlisle.'

He took Beryl by the arm and let her walk a couple of steps onto the pavement. She looked up and saw a large pinewood sign which said 'Sullivan and Co.' Jake was breathing on his knuckles and rubbing them on his lapels. Then he opened the door and stretched out an arm expansively.

'Come in, my dear. Have a cup of coffee. I think the board meeting has finished.'

Beryl went in, slowly, looking round, expecting a trap. A very busty girl with bleached yellow hair jumped up, pulled her skirt down over her knees. She wore it short, for 1958, which meant that if she wasn't careful, her bare knees could be seen.

'Good morning, Mr. Sullivan. Mr. Stein has been looking for you.'

'Good morning, Marlene. Tell him I'm in conference. I want you to pop down the street and get two coffees, very hot, all right, my dear? If you see the bishop coming this way, tell him not now, I've got an important client. Now, madam, what sort of house . . .'

Marlene minced out, waggling her bottom. Beryl looked round the office. On first sight it did look smart and clean, but she could see that the fitted carpet was second-hand and the Woolworth's formica on Marlene's desk was peeling off. There was a row of neat looking folders behind her on a shelf but she could tell by the look of them they were empty. The walls were panelled in very yellow-looking pine. She could see from some bad joins in a corner that it was wallpaper. You couldn't pull the wool over Beryl's eyes, as her father was always saying. She was so neat and meticulous herself that she could spot any shoddiness a mile off. But all the same, she was very impressed. The last she'd heard of Jake was that he was on the dole. She'd never believed for one minute he'd start his own business.

'I don't want a house,' said Beryl. Her legs as well as her mind had been wandering. She put them together, placed her straw bag on her knee and her walking out umbrella on top. Now she was on guard.

'Of course you don't,' said Jake. 'I didn't want to embarrass you in front of the staff. You wouldn't want to look the sort of girl who walks into a strange bloke's office for no reason at all.'

'That was considerate,' said Beryl, still looking round.

'Actually, I was considering myself most of all. Marlene's crazy for me, naturally enough. If she thought I'd got a girl friend she'd probably commit suicide. She's not all that bright, but she's well developed. She's only eleven you know.'

'I think I'd better be going. It was very kind of you to let me see, but . . .'

'Sit down, woman. Have you got ants in your knickers or something?'

Marlene came back with two coffees. Beryl took a sup of hers and made a face, looked at Marlene, then looked over her shoulder, condemning Marlene as an idiot once and for all, without speaking to her.

Jake had only been in the office a week and hiring Marlene had been the first thing he had done. Michael said it was stupid. Jake said if people like builders saw a sexy girl through the window they'd be rushing to get in. He'd worked on a building site. He knew the mentality. Michael said that if other people looked through the window and saw Mr. Builder sitting with a sexy girl of fifteen Mrs. Builder would soon find out and that would be that. Jake didn't understand small town mentality.

It was two months since Jake's first deal. He'd got several other old properties being converted or being bought and needed an office of his own. Michael had decided to come in with him. He was leaving his firm anyway, now he'd qualified. Nothing else amusing had turned up. He thought he'd help Jake for a few months, for fun, till he got bored, or Jake went bust and went back to labouring.

'Marlene, pop your head in that boardroom,' said Jake. 'See if that meeting is still on.'

Marlene walked across the room with a glazed expression on her face. She opened the other door and looked into a pile of empty fruit boxes and a battered sofa. She turned to Jake with her mouth open, waiting for the next instructions.

'Don't just stand there, you stupid git. They'll be wanting you to take down the minutes. Go on in.'

This was another thing Michael thought was ridiculous, pretending they had a huge staff and suites of other offices. He said in Carlisle it was best to do the opposite. It was only in London where show counted.

'What do you think, then?' said Jake when Marlene had at last closed the door behind her.

'I think that's the broom cupboard,' said Beryl. 'It was when this place was Robson's fruit shop.'

'It *was*. I built a back addition, so there clever clogs. Sit down!' Beryl was going to have a look, but sat down when Jake shouted at her.

'Why do you have to show off all the time?' she said. 'And be so loud mouthed.'

'I can't help it. I've got an inferiority complex. It's OK for you with your Morris Minor and your holidays in Hong Kong. I've got fifteen younger brothers and sisters to support and me mother on the streets and me Dad in prison.'

'That was terrible about your father, Jake. So sudden. Had he been ill at all?'

'How did you know about that?'

'Because I've hated you since you were eighteen. You looked awful in your bus conductor's uniform and Teddy Boy haircut.'

Jake lay on the floor and laughed and thought she was the cleverest girl he'd ever met. Cynthia never made a joke in her life. He picked up the telephone, rang for a taxi and took Beryl out to lunch at the Fantail's restaurant at Wetheral. He forgot completely about Marlene in the broom cupboard. If it hadn't been for Michael, popping in at four o'clock to show a young builder the office, she would probably have spent the weekend there.

They went to the pictures in the evening. Afterwards, he brought Beryl back to Cynthia's flat for coffee. Cynthia had gone to see her parents for the weekend in Workington. He got the Top Ten on Radio Luxembourg, forcing Beryl to sit on the bed beside him, saying don't be silly, it was the best way to listen, just close your eyes and lie back in the dark. Beryl kept her eyes wide open and one hand over the side of the bed holding tight on to the handle of her walking-out umbrella. When the last strains of Number One had finished, Connie Francis singing 'Stupid Cupid,' Jake put his arm across the bed and laid it on her right breast. She catapulted it straight back. Jake lay for a bit, smiling, then he put his hand on her leg. She hit it so hard with the umbrella that he jumped up and screamed. He lay down again, pretending to be asleep, then rolled over quickly and threw his whole body over her, pinning her down on the bed. She burst into tears.

'I said I'm sorry,' said Jake, running after her down the street.

'I knew that was all you wanted me for,' said Beryl, still sobbing. Her hankie was black with her mascara.

'But I didn't do anything.'

'You tried. You're just a beast. Like everyone else.'

'I know. I don't know what came over me. Christ, I must be bloody stupid. The first nice girl I've ever met and I go and do that. Honest, Beryl. I know you won't believe me, but I'm fucking sorry.'

'Stop that,' shouted Beryl, stamping her little foot and choking through her sobs.

'What?' said Jake, holding his hands up, to show he wasn't touching her.

'That language.'

'I really am,' said Jake, amazed, not knowing what was going on. 'I'll never fucking do it again.'

'If you use that word once more . . .'

Jake stopped, blinked and considered. He had to think carefully over the words he'd been using. Like everyone else on the building site, he'd used fuck every third word, as an adjective, a noun, a verb and even as a comma. It was meaningless and he never thought twice about it. He walked Beryl home the rest of the way in silence. He couldn't think of anything to say without swearing.

Beryl took a lot of winning round again, but Jake was determined to do it. She seemed to him to have such personality and class. Then again no girl had ever refused him before, so Beryl was a challenge. No bloke had ever tried a second go at Beryl, once she's rapped their groping hands with her brolly.

She was determined to save her precious jewel for the nuptial bed. Evelyn Home was right. They wouldn't respect you otherwise. But Jake had apologized and come back. He'd done it sincerely. She felt he'd revealed a bit of his real self to her. She could see some good in him. Jake was her challenge, to carry on and mould him along the right and proper lines.

She'd also realized he was handsome. He'd looked really common on the buses, with his nasty greasy hair. It had accentuated his sticking-out ears and large brow. In his dark suit, with his hair combed neatly forward and parted, she'd hardly recognized him that day he'd barged into her office. And of course she'd been wrong about him being a no-good. He couldn't be a no-good to be able to run his own business.

They got married three months later, on 5 November 1958, fireworks night. It was a register office marriage. Beryl brought along a girl friend and Jake had Michael as his witness. Jake didn't invite his mother and Beryl's parents refused to come. They'd invited Jake home once for high tea at their semi-detached house. Jake had never been in a semi before. He'd been genuinely impressed and looking forward to seeing what French windows were. They'd disliked him on sight. He told her father he must be stupid to have worked for thirty years as a clerk in the Civil Service. He could come and work for him for twice the salary. Jake thought he was doing him a big favour.

The day after they were married, Beryl went to the office of Sullivan and Co., sacked the stupid Marlene and moved in. She wanted to keep an eye on Jake.

Michael had no head for figures. His job was looking after the legal side and being nice to prospective buyers. Jake had a head for figures, but it was all in his head. He had no experience of putting it down. He'd never worked in an office or seen people write things down before. Beryl soon reorganized the whole office. She'd run the bus company's complicated time tables and work shifts for five years, so looking after an office staff of two was a dawdle. She discovered almost at once that they were in danger of running into a cash fluidity problem. By financing six houses at once, Jake was tying up all their money at the same time. If anything went wrong, such as a house not being ready in time or a delay in selling the flats when they were ready, they wouldn't have enough cash to run the office and pay the existing mortgages. When Jake saw all the figures written down, he agreed to take things more carefully. He was very proud of Beryl and was always boasting about her to Michael.

All three of them worked very hard, putting in twelve hours a day. Jake and Michael took twenty pounds a week each. Beryl got nothing. After all, she was married to the managing director. She loved these early months, when they were so dependent on her. She even agreed that they should sleep in the office for a week while Jake ostensibly looked for a luxury flat. He'd had some difficulty keeping Beryl away from Cynthia's flat. He was still living there up till the week before he married Beryl. Jake never discussed what happened, but apparently Cynthia left Carlisle a week after Jake got married and never returned. Jake took over her flat, explaining to Beryl that he'd decided after all to keep his old place on because of the romantic associations. Beryl now laughed at her own prissiness that first night on the bed. She was avid for bed.

Michael couldn't decide who was winning. He felt it had to go one way, Jake giving in and becoming a conventional semi-detached husband, or Beryl turning into a female yob. At the moment both sides seemed to have won a few points. He thought about inviting them home to dinner, but Jake had never once asked about his home life or where he lived. Now that Beryl was desperately running Jake's life for him, there seemed even less point. He got on well with Beryl. She was always on at Jake to keep his suit clean, like Michael's, and polish his shoes, like Michael's. She'd been thrilled with Michael's wedding present, a set of crystal wine glasses, sent from Harrods in London. They'd never been used. Jake refused to have any of that foreign shit with his meals. He'd always drunk tea with his dinner and wasn't going to change now. The only other presents were two identical pairs of wooden salad servers, Empire made, both from Binns. One was from Madge, Beryl's best friend, and the other from Cedric, Jake's brother.

Sullivan and Co.'s biggest running problem was builders. This was Jake's province, as Michael looked after customers. Jake said just leave him to kick their arses, he knew how to handle these fuckers. Language, language, said Beryl, automatically. Jake's swearing and threatening worked, in that the conversions were usually ready in time, but there was always trouble afterwards. The little builders Jake was using just weren't up to such things as central heating. He'd force them to use chip board instead of bricks for interior partitions to cut costs, but when the radiators leaked, walls below started warping. He refused on principle to employ Armstrongs, who were the largest local builders. His object was to ruin them, not help them.

Jake was useless in the resultant rows. The builders would give him a mouthful back, rightly blaming him. Swearing at tenants, telling them all walls warped at first in new luxury flats, didn't help either. Michael wasn't much better. He was too polite and ineffectual. Beryl was the best. She was firm but forceful, calming everyone down and satisfying both sides.

In six months they'd bought and converted, or were in the process of converting, ten properties. Jake asked Beryl to work out their profits so far, as she was so clever. She said it was pointless because there was so much money still to come in and so much to go out, any figure would be unreliable. Who wants to be reliable, said Jake. On paper, then, said Beryl, their clear profit would be about £20,000 when the present houses were sold. To celebrate, Beryl bought a new fitted carpet for the office and Michael bought a magnum of champagne to start the office's drinks cabinet. Jake said how bourgeois, which was his new word, picked up from Michael. He agreed at last to try the champagne. He drank about half, saying all the way through that it tasted like the Dandelion and Burdock he used to make in the lotties, then he was sick all over the Cyril Lord carpet.

His celebration was to expand even further. Despite the protests of Michael and Beryl he bought their first country property. They'd stuck to the city so far, mainly in Stanwix, the safest residential area. Jake was reading out the Cumberland News one Friday when he started shouting at the low prices. 'Listen to this near Ullswater – paddocks, servants' wing, five farm cottages, ten acres and the house itself which is enormous, all for only fucking ten thousand pounds.'

'Language, language,' said Michael, imitating Beryl.

'You can't go wrong,' said Jake. 'If you knocked the whole lot down you could build a council estate.'

'Have you heard about your mother recently, Jake?' said Beryl, quietly but cattily, imitating Michael.

'Shut up, Fatso,' said Jake to Beryl.

'Is he talking to you Michael?' said Beryl. 'Cheek.'

Beryl had put a lot of weight on, but it wasn't worrying her. She was so happy. They all were. It was office jokes all the time.

'Ten acres!' said Jake, standing up and walking round. 'We could put up twenty semi-detached, with semi-detached garages, for twenty semi-detached families. We could make twenty thousand pounds on one deal.'

Michael and Beryl both groaned. They hadn't realized he was so serious. They acknowledged it was Jake's flair and imagination and enthusiasm which found and created the properties. They did all the donkey work, tying up the ends which Jake forgot about. They were just as important, they maintained, so they felt justified in trying to keep Jake in his place.

'Let's stick to what we're doing, Jake,' said Michael. 'We know Carlisle. We don't know the country.'

'Think big, laddy, think big. There might be oil in them thar fells, then you'd be sorry. Pass us that map, fatty. If you lot don't want to make twenty thousand, I do.'

'It would cost fifty thousand just to finance that sort of new scheme, then you'd never sell them, stuck out there. The builders would make all the profits.'

'OK, clever guts,' said Jake. 'Then I'll buy a building firm.'

'Don't pass him the map, Beryl. Pass him the Monopoly money.'

Over lunch the next day, Jake bought a building firm. All his whims and intuitions had come off so far, so he couldn't see why this one shouldn't. He'd gone for a pint and a pie at the Board Inn across the road and met Steve, a bloke he'd once laboured with at Armstrongs. Steve had a sheepskin jacket on and a Jaguar outside and was boasting about his own firm and how well it was doing. If only he had a bit more capital he could make a bomb. He was turning down work all the time. A pint and a pie for my sheepskin friend here, said Jake, and how much would you like, two thousand, three thousand, five thousand?

Jake went to see Steve's office and books, just to show he

didn't work completely on whims, and bought a half share in the firm for three thousand pounds. He didn't tell Michael and Beryl, not at first anyway.

'OK, I agree with you yellow bastards,' said Jake back at the office. 'We'll stick to what we can do. I'm buying that property, but we'll convert it into luxury holiday apartments, not into a new estate.'

They groaned. Jake bought the house for eight thousand pounds and they groaned even more. Nothing made him more eager to make a huge profit than buying a bargain. To save travelling costs, he said he would erect tents on the site for the labourers, so they would be right on the job.

'You're raving,' said Michael, imitating Jake. 'How are you going to get labourers to sleep in tents?'

'Listen kid, who's been the labourer, you or me? You public school jerk, just wrap up, eh. When I was a labourer, I slept anywhere.'

'Yes, and I've seen some of the people you've slept with.'

'Watch it, sexless,' said Jake.

Steve was all for the tent idea. He started working out how many they'd need, how much stores and cooking equipment. It would be expensive. They'd probably need about five hundred pounds to set it up, could Sullivan and Co. stand it? You're in the Big League now, said Jake. That's just petty cash. See Beryl.

This led to the first big row. Beryl was naturally furious that Jake hadn't told her he'd taken over Steve's firm. She looked after the books so meticulously that something going through without her knowledge ruined everything. But most of all it was humiliating. Jake had humiliated her in front of Steve.

Michael was much more stoical. Jake came back from the site one day to say he was putting in a swimming pool. As it was Ullswater, not the Mediterranean, wouldn't an ice rink be more suitable? Yes, said Jake, Steve could probably do that as well. Then Steve came up with porterage which Jake thought was great. He couldn't wait to put it in the Cumberland News advert. Nobody would have heard of the word so they'd be ringing up, just to see what it was.

Beryl started being sick in the mornings and Jake said there was no need to be like that, just because he'd humiliated her. She'd have to put up with a lot more of that before she was through. She was four months pregnant and hadn't realized. Jake said Christ, don't bother me with trivialities, not when he had a big deal going through. There was some money left in the petty cash. Get an abortion. They could put it down on the company's accounts, taking out contacts.

He meant it. He couldn't afford to have half his staff laid up, not at this time. He'd always hated children, and if it wasn't a boy, then she knew what she could do with it. Beryl cried tears into her stencils.

Jake drove at eighty miles an hour in Michael's Rover to Penrith. He'd always scorned the Rover, saying it was a typical middle-aged man's car, but he needed a bit of room. He'd decided to go down to the site, see how things were going, then take Steve into Keswick. He could do with a night's booze and a couple of girls. He hadn't had a break in six months.

There was no sign of Steve, or the tents, or the stores or any of the materials when Jake got to Ullswater. He met a couple of labourers wandering around who said that Steve had come with three lorries the day before and taken everything to a new site. There was no new site. Steve had completely disappeared.

Jake came back to the office and told Michael and Beryl. He lay on the carpet and roared and laughed at their long faces. 'It's just money,' said Jake. 'We made it easy, we lost it easy. But when I get that bastard, I'll have him by the short hairs.'

Steve had cheated them out of about four thousand pounds altogether. Michael said they should sell off the house quickly and not lose any more. He was quite pleased in one way. He thought it would put an end to Jake's ideas of moving further afield. With the baby coming along, perhaps he'd settle down in Carlisle now.

They advertised the Ullswater house but the highest offer was five thousand pounds which Jake said was ridiculous. They'd just keep it. He'd think of something and if he didn't, the land at least would be going up in price

Jake sat around the office for a week, not apparently thinking of anything. Two houses became ready, but half of each was lying empty, unsold. Michael said put the prices down, now the market was slowing up. Jake said put them up, make people think they were better than the others. Nothing happened.

'What's happened,' said Michael, 'is that we've supplied the needs of the few dozen executives who happen to find themselves in Carlisle, poor souls, and want modern accommodation. It was a crying need. You had a brilliant idea, Jake. But we can't keep expanding at the same rate for ever. This is a small town. We've got to pedal a bit more slowly now, waiting for new people to arrive. They will, they will, don't worry.'

'Have you done?' said Jake. 'You should have been a fucking vicar.'

'I did think about it.'

'Well now's your chance. You're useless here. Beryl, ring the station. I want to know the next train to Euston.'

'You've got Lowther coming to see you in ten minutes.'

'Fuck Lowther.'

'He's worried about the sewage. He thinks it'll need a new main drain . . .'

'The station, woman! Christ, stop twitting on. Thank you. Listen, you lot. I've no intention of standing still, even if we can make a bit of money. That's the same as going backwards. We're going to go on at the same rate as we've been doing these last six months. I'm not stopping now. You two can do what you like. Have you got those times, woman?'

The next London train was the Royal Scot at midday, which was in half an hour's time. Jake said he would catch that. Before Beryl could start protesting, Jake gave her some more instructions.

'Shuttup and listen. I want you to ring every estate agent in the West End and say the managing director of Sullivan and Co. will be passing through London on the way to Monte Carlo tomorrow and he's looking for a *pied à terre*. You want a list of all their West End properties. OK?'

'The West End, Jake . . .'

'I don't know where it is. It's up to you to find it. That's what you're paid for. It's where all those cockneys live, isn't it? Christ, it's like talking to the wall.'

'The cockneys live in the East End, as a matter of fact,' said Michael. 'No one lives in the West End these days. One lives in Chelsea, or Kensington, or Knightsbridge, or Hampstead . . .'

'Don't bother me now with all that crap. Tell Moany Face here. Are you listening? I'll ring you here at nine tomorrow morning and I want you to read out to me a list of agents and properties, all right?'

'How do I find the names of agents, Jake . . .?'

'God give me strength. Ask the Bishop here. He's the know-all in this place. And I also want a list of builders.'

'But Jake . . .'

'Ring the trade directories, you stupid bitch. Right, is that all? Put the bloody lights off when you leave. Some bugger left them on last night.'

'Can't you wait till next week, Jake?' said Beryl mournfully. 'What's all the hurry?'

'While we're pissing around here playing marbles, Charlie Clore's buying up half London. That's what's the hurry.'

Jake went out, slamming the door behind him. Beryl and Michael sat silently for about five minutes, staring at each other blankly. Michael said he was going for a walk round the cathedral. See if there were any openings. Beryl managed a small smile. She watched him cross the road, then she was sick all over her Remington Rand typewriter.

Part Two

Chapter Eight

Jake had never been further south than Penrith when he got on the London train that day in 1959. For that matter he'd never been any further north than Dumfries, where his father came from, but that didn't matter. No one goes north to make their fortune.

Once when he was seven he'd set off to go to London. He'd stormed out with a red handkerchief over his shoulder, saying he was never coming back, ever. They'd all be sorry, he shouted. Cedric stood at the door and cried. His mother didn't turn but continued quietly peeling the potatoes. 'You be back at twelve o'clock,' she said, 'or you'll be sorry. It's tatie pot for dinner.'

Jake got a lift just outside Penrith. The man said yes, he'd take Jake wherever he wanted to go, what a lovely red handkerchief, let me feel it. They were in the middle of Penrith when the man's hand strayed from the handkerchief onto Jake's bare knee and started slowly feeling up inside his trousers. Jake didn't understand what was going on, but he didn't like it. At the traffic lights in the centre of the town, he opened the car door and jumped out. He hitch hiked a lift back to Thwaite and got home in time for his tatie pot, just as his mother was putting it out ready for him.

Jake remembered this incident as his train passed through Penrith. He knew now what it had all been about. He must have half-known at the time to have retained it in his subconscious all those years. He knew about the subconscious. It was all described in his Reader's Digest which he'd bought on Carlisle station.

He was wishing he'd bought a first class ticket. He'd thought about it but he had been a bit worried that he wouldn't know what you did in a first class compartment. For the same reason he'd decided not to go for lunch in the restaurant car. Instead he went for a beer and a sandwich in the stand-up buffet. He was about the only one able to stand up. It was full of drunken Scotsmen reeling back and forward, clutching plastic cups full of lukewarm McKewan's Export. He hoped none of them bumped against him, forcing him to fight them.

All he knew about London he'd gathered from newspapers, TV and Michael. Michael had been an officer at Chelsea Barracks during his National Service and seemed to have spent most of his Oxford years at London parties. Jake wished he'd asked Michael for some directions, or a street map, quietly, of course, when Beryl wasn't watching. He always pretended in front of Beryl that he took no notice of Michael.

The further south he travelled, the more apprehensive he became. He kept telling himself it was ridiculous. Wasn't he running his own firm and making a lot of money? Christ, his stupid old father had even been to London. If *he* could manage it, anyone could. His father had boasted about it for years, until his mother let out that it had only been a day trip with the working men's club. They'd all had a good time seeing the sights, except Willie. He'd just walked round Euston all day till it was time to get the train back.

That had been back in 1935, centuries ago. Now in 1959 Northern accents and people were in, so they said, ever since *Room at the Top*, Albert Finney and all that. But that meant the Yorkshire and Lancashire North. To someone from Carlisle, Yorkshire and Lancashire were in the deep South. He'd never heard of anyone from Carlisle going to London and living to tell the tale. He did once know a labourer who'd gone, but he'd never been seen since. Then there was a girl from Wigton who'd got herself in the family way and gone to London. She hadn't been heard of for three years till a Carlisle United Supporters Club outing had spotted her in Soho with a Blackie. That was another thing. He'd never seen a coloured bloke before. He looked out of the window, suspiciously. A station sign flashed past saying Watford. He put his hand in his inside pocket and transferred his wallet to the front pocket of his trousers for extra safety.

He did have a cheque book, somewhere. Beryl had insisted that as managing director of Sullivan and Co. he should have one. Mr. Foster had had two. He'd had such trouble going to the bank one day to get out some money, his *own* money. He'd put Pay Self and crossed it and they'd said he should have put Pay Cash and crossed himself, or something fucking stupid. Anyway, he'd thrown the cheque book at them and never used one again. He paid people like Beryl and Michael to look after such trivialities.

He had fifty pounds in cash, but he didn't want to count it, not on a train when anyone might see. Beryl had given him it the other day when he went down to see Steve. That would be enough for the Savory Hotel, or whatever that dump was Michael always went on about.

The train arrived on platform one three minutes late. Jake was nearly knocked over in the rush down the platform. He half expected big banners saying Welcome Jake Sullivan. Somebody surely must know who he was. At the worst, there must be someone *he* knew, which at least would prove he existed and had arrived. He stared round for a familiar face. Carlisle, that big city, full of people he knew, was only three hundred miles straight up that line. Someone else must have trickled down, apart from himself. But no. Perhaps Carlisle didn't exist any more, now that he'd left it behind.

He passed a pub doorway, full of people sitting up silently at the bar, all marooned like himself. They looked scruffy and beaten. He watched an Irish barman pour out a Guinness, shove it over the counter, then scurry into a corner without talking, as if he didn't want to get mixed up with all the débris. Jake half hoped a drunk would stagger out, so he could thump him and give himself an identity. He realized he'd never been on his own in a strange place before. It needed other people to bring out his aggressiveness. Left to himself, he day-dreamed sloppy thoughts, just like anyone else.

He came to a piece of garden. He could tell it must be a garden because there was a fence round it and a defeated looking tree crouching in the middle. Amidst the old news-papers and fluttering rubbish were sprawled the remnants of healthy-looking middle-aged men, unshaven, with nothing else to clutch onto in life except their paper carrier bags. They might have been waiting for the gas chamber trucks.

Only a newspaper moved and he saw that it said Newcastle Journal. He noticed another, torn in half, which said Glasgow Bull and another saying Cork Examiner. His eyes were pulled to a carrier bag which said Binns, Carlisle. This was as far as they'd got, all these fortune hunters. How could he do better than this lot? There were ten million Londoners who'd all got in first, who knew their way around and had pulled up the drawbridge on the rest. I'll remember all this, thought Jake, when I'm a millionaire. I'll come back in me Rolls and throw fivers out of the window at them, you sentimental fucker, you.

'Taxi,' he shouted boldly, waiting for the roar of London's mighty traffic to grind to a halt.

'Ver to, mate?' said the driver.

'Eh, just the centre of the town.'

'Look, don't mess abaht. I'm on my vay home. Vich centre?' said the driver, in Broad East European cockney.

'The centre of London City, you know, so I can walk round Chelsea and Knightsbridge and Kensington . . .'

'You vanna get back to the bog mate, that's vot you vanna do,' said the driver, accelerating away.

Half an hour later Jake almost fell down the steps of Holborn tube station. He found a map which said You Are Here but he didn't know where Here was. He went up and down the escalator three times, examining all the adverts for corsets. Perhaps he'd wandered into a sewer, not a tube. From nowhere, a surge of people suddenly engulfed him, hurtling off the escalator and carrying him into a tube, where he sat petrified for several stations. He worked out he was heading for some place called Cockfosters, which must be near Carlisle, judging by the length of blue on the map. He changed trains and came back, getting off at Leicester Square.

He blinked at all the lights and colours and noise. Then he was swept along by another moving pavement of people, this time all singing and shouting, a fairground crowd in search of a fair. He took refuge in a plastic restaurant, quickly, as if he was worried someone would sweep it up before he'd tasted their Sensational Egg Wonder and Bacon Barbecues. A red hot plate was banged in front of him before he'd even realized he'd ordered. Then before he could take his first bite, the plastic waitress was back, ripping off his bill like a nasty entrail. In the middle of the plate was a small metal dish containing a rubbery piece of congealed egg and bacon rind. He wasn't sure whether he was expected to eat from the dish, or empty it on the plate. The bill said fifteen and six. It must be a mistake. He got twice as much egg as that for half a crown in Carlisle.

'Hey, darling,' he shouted after the waitress. He'd heard

somewhere that everyone in London was darling. 'You've made a mistake, darling.'

'Get lost, eh,' said the waitress, in broad Carlisle. 'Fifteen and six, you can read, can't you?'

'Heh, are you from Carlisle?' said Jake, smiling.

'Get lost. Oscar! You're wanted.' She beckoned to a desk in a corner. From behind it a huge African in a dinner jacket emerged and moved towards Jake. At the doorway, two Chinamen, both in dinner jackets, were now watching Jake, their hands suspiciously in their pockets. Jake put a quid on the table, took two mouthfuls of the egg, and left. Perhaps he should go into catering, that's where the money was, not property.

He spent the next two hours wandering round Soho without knowing it. He'd been convinced his first night in the capital of the Empire would end in some glamorous, exciting, sordid, dangerous, hilarious, frightening adventure. Instead he ended up at a bed and breakfast place off Russell Square. At one in the morning, when nothing had happened, he asked a policeman the way to the Savory Hotel, or perhaps it was the Savoy. The policeman, in a broad Glasgow accent, told him to be on his way, son.

He was directed by a Pakistani to Russell Square and had picked on the place because it said 'Northern Hospitality' over the front entrance. If he was going to be mean and do it on the cheap, instead of going to a luxury hotel, he might as well have a place which was homely and familiar where they would understand his accent. He went inside where two seedy blokes grabbed his money, gave him a key and went back to talking Italian, which he didn't think was very homely. Every member of the staff turned out to be Italian. Northern Italian, of course.

His room was the size of a cupboard. He couldn't sleep for the noise of the Northern Italians shouting at each other all night long. He looked out of the window at the heavy red glow of the London night, thinking that if the end of the world came now, nobody would know where he was. But he would show these fucking Londoners. Londoners? What was he thinking about? He hadn't seen one all night. His mother was right. The place was full of fucking foreigners. He needn't have come South of Penrith after all.

Chapter Nine

Jake woke up at six thirty on his first morning in London and didn't know where he was. There seemed to be a fight going on in the corridor outside. Then he remembered it must be the Northern Italians talking to each other. He thought about storming out naked and threatening to thump them, but they probably wouldn't have reacted. He wished he had a badge, or a famous face, or three legs or something which would make people notice him. He was Carlisle's smartest young con man, didn't they realize. But he knew that even with three legs he still wouldn't have registered. He was yet another object shovelling through their life, anonymous, unimportant, whose face wasn't worth taking in because there would be no need ever to recall it. Tonight another grey face, equally nothing, would take its place. He tried to remember when he'd last been up at six thirty. It must have been on the building sites. Christ, that was centuries ago. He might as well get up now.

The first estate agency Beryl told him about on the phone was in Piccadilly. He hung up briskly, showing he was already a fast moving cockney, and went to see it.

The office was all panelled walls, stone arches and highly polished floors. There seemed no sign of life, then Jake saw a movement in a row of what looked like ornate confessional boxes. In each, sitting up on a high carved stool, was an identical horn-rimmed, striped-suited, high-collared statue. What time's mass? said Jake. I beg your pardon, sir. Jake gave his name and said he was expected. I beg your pardon, sir? Jake explained again. Terribly sorry, they had no recollection of a lady ringing and saying the managing director of Sullivan and Co. was coming. Had he a card? Not at this time of morning, mate. A visiting card? No, everyone in Carlisle knows me. Carlisle? That was in Wales, wasn't it, sir? Just give us your list, said Jake, and stuff the sermons or I'll plate you. Three assistant bishops rose from the boxes and advanced towards Jake, brushing non-existent specks from their non-existent frock coats. The first bishop was standing holding the front door, saying how terribly sorry he was that they couldn't help. Good morning.

'You bloody idiot,' said Jake on the telephone. 'Why did you send me to that sort of place? I don't know why I employ you . . .'

'How was I to know?' bleated Beryl. 'When are you coming home?'

'There's the bloody pips. Get some more addresses ready while I put some money in.'

'Michael says go out and buy the Evening Standard . . .'

'Tell Michael to go and stuff himself. How can I buy a bloody evening paper. It's only ten o'clock in the morning. You lot wouldn't last one minute in London. . . .'

To Jake's surprise, there was an Evening Standard paper seller outside the phone booth. He was also selling the Star and the Evening News. Jake could see the headlines about Macmillan and Never Having Had it So Good. Jake waited his turn then asked the paper seller if it was yesterday's Evening Standard. The man was giving out papers and taking in money like a croupier, dealing over, round, and under Jake, ignoring him completely. Jake decided to wait this time and catch him on his next turn. He saw a Playboy magazine and idly turned over the pages, looking for the nudes. There was a loud crack and Jake jumped in the air, shouting and holding his hand. The newspaper seller had brought down a wooden hammer right on Jake's furtive fingers. 'Now fuck off, eh,' said the man, out of the corner of his mouth, still throwing out papers and catching the money.

Jake moved on to another stall. He bought a paper without commenting. He looked at the date and it was that day's after all. It seemed to be all written by Scotsmen, at least they all had Scottish names – Alexander Walker, Ramsden Greig, Jeremy Campbell. They must be doing well, all these Jocks. From that moment, Jake became Scottish. That had been the trouble in that Piccadilly estate agency. Nobody had understood what he was talking about. He'd be from the Gorbals and have a really broad Glasgow accent. It would suit him much better. He'd never believed himself that he'd been brought up on the soft Cumberland fells. It just wasn't him.

The next agency was off the King's Road and was all smooth young lads in tight cavalry twill trousers and chukka boots. They had their feet up on pinewood desks and were talking like adding machines into two telephones at a time. A girl in a beehive hair style slinked up and asked him what he wanted. Jake had never seen this hair style before and wanted to put his hand in it for birds' nests or lift it off and blow on her bald pate.

Jake came on strong, in broad but clear Scots, banging on the counter and shouting what he wanted. She let him rant on, about all the property he owned in the Gorbals and what it was like in Barlinnie, then she asked very quietly what price of house he was interested in. All prices, said Jake. Of course, she said, with no trace of sarcasm. She brought out their lists. Jake studied them noisily. The girl watched him smiling. He was from Glasgow was he? Jake muttered aye. Did he wear blue or green? Even on the building site, in his role as the biggest working class yob around, Jake's blind spot had been football. He just couldn't work up any interest in it.

'Well, thanks very much, then,' said Jake, ignoring her question and preparing to go. She picked up the lists before he could take them and said she would like to have his address and phone number.

He didn't have a Glasgow address to give, unless he made up one. But what the hell. Who cared if he contradicted himself. They probably just asked addresses to keep track of people, in case they came to a private deal with the owner and cut out the agent. But he still had his mother's suspiciousness of giving away such intimate details, in case Hitler found out.

'Fair dos, then,' said Jake. 'Give us yours. I also want to ken whether you wear pink or yellow knickers.'

'You work fast, you Scotsmen,' she said.

'You haven't seen anything yet,' said Jake.

'But I'd love to,' she said, writing down her address and phone number for him. Jake gave her the Russell Square hotel address and number. He didn't expect it to be so easy. His first try and he was away. A London Cynthia would be ideal, a nice place to stay and a nice head of hair to stick his hand up.

The lists were long and comprehensive and they all gave prices. Carlisle lists didn't disclose the prices. You had to ask for them specially. The best sounding ones seemed to be in Kensington. He jumped into a taxi like a professional and commanded it to go to Kensington Church Street as if he'd been there every day of his life.

He spent the morning looking round the area, going from

street to street, keeping the same taxi to save time. He was amazed how some houses had been done up yet next door there would be one so beat up it looked as if a bomb had hit it. He measured doorways with his eyes, seeing how they could be divided or expanded, estimated depths of basements, looked for fan lights on roofs and concealed side entrances. By two o'clock he'd eliminated thirteen and found two which were promising. He rang the agency, said he wanted one of their laddies, quick, with keys.

The best looking of the two had three storeys, an attic and a basement, which would be five proper storeys when he'd finished digging out soil from the front and putting a new roof on top. The price was ten thousand pounds which he thought was ridiculous, considering the condition, but it was London and he'd have to adjust his values. The one next door had been done up after a fashion. Even Jake realized that alternate blue and yellow stripes was hideous. He knocked at the door. After a lot of scuffling, it was opened by two West Indians. One walked past him quickly without speaking. The other lit a cigarette and watched him.

'You've got a smashing house,' said Jake. 'I was just admiring it. Did you do it yourself or did David Hicks paint it for you?'

'What do you say, man?'

'Is it yours?'

'It might be.'

'It must have cost you all of ten thou,' said Jake.

'It didn't cost me nuthing,' said the man. 'But I did hear she paid five thou. Come on in. See the amenities, man.'

'No thanks. See you.'

The agency laddie was called Eric and was about eighteen with a sharp cockney face and no interest in anything except combing his hair. The minute he let Jake into the house, he went searching for a window to look at himself in. Jake had a wander then came back to chat up Eric and find out how busy the firm was and the names of the main people. Eric said houses were coming in and going out at such a rate that no one had any idea what was going on.

Jake rang from the public phone box at the end of the road. He said he'd offer six thousand pounds in cash, as it was in such fucking awful condition. He couldn't hang around much longer in case it fell down on top of him. Ridiculous, said the man, that was 40 per cent less than the asking price. Thirty per cent less, said Jake, lying. He said Mr. Grosse had told him he could have it for nine thousand pounds only yesterday.

Mr. Grosse, he knew from Eric, was a partner who'd flown to Dublin that morning on holiday. Impossible, said the man. Are you calling me a liar? No, no, said the man. Just as well, continued Jake, or he'd transfer to Mr. Borg, the head of the firm, whom he usually dealt with.

Jake cupped his hands and pretended to be shouting into another phone. 'Tell Glasgow to get stuffed. I can't wait any longer while they make up their minds.' He carried on a few other imaginary conversations, then came back to the man. 'I can't waste any more time with you. You do know about the brothel do you? Crowds of coloured buggers going in and out all day. Right next door. Ask that stupid mongol boy of yours, Eric. He saw them as well. What's that? You'll have to discuss it. I can't wait. Ring me back in fifteen minutes at this number, if I'm still here.'

Jake gave the number and hung up. Then he rang TIM and left the receiver off the hook. He stood outside the phone booth, reading his Standard, telling anyone who tried to use the phone that it was out of order. After sixteen minutes, he replaced the receiver and immediately they came straight through. The very lowest offer was seven thousand pounds. Jake said OK. As a big favour, he'd take it.

He rang three builders whose address Beryl had given him on the phone. He said he had a five storey property in the best part of Kensington he wanted converting, central heating, ten luxury flatlets, no crap work, come round immediately and give him an estimate. Two said straight away that they weren't interested. They had too much work without bothering about those sorts of jobs. The third, who were very superior, said they might consider it, but they couldn't give an estimate for five weeks and they couldn't possibly do the work before the spring. And anyway, they didn't accept enquiries on the phone. He'd have to write, giving full details. Get fucked, said Jake.

He blamed Beryl. She'd got the big posh con men. He wanted some small building firm which he could boss around. But perhaps there was so much work going in London that you couldn't boss any of them? He got another taxi and started touring the area again, jumping out and knocking on the door of every house which had been done up. He ooed and ahhed about their marvellous house, a lovely job, such taste, such ingenuity, he couldn't possibly ask how much and who was their builder? After initial bewilderment, they became very agitated. The word 'builder' had had a Pavlovian effect on them. They'd sue him if they ever saw their builder again, not that they expected to as he'd disappeared leaving every job half finished.

Only one person was prepared to recommend the builder they'd used, though they said he was an idiot, a twister, a liar and a cheat. His men were useless and he had no idea what he was doing. He was also Irish and illiterate. Apart from that, yes, they could just recommend him. He was so cheap. Jake said he sounded perfect. Many thanks.

The address he got for J. P. Ryan seemed to be a derelict house. The paint had all peeled, the pointing had fallen away so much that you could put your hands between the bricks. There was no glass in any of the windows. The front door was boarded with a sheet of corrugated iron. Jake checked the address. It was right, so he pushed open a side door. It fell with a crash and two huge Alsatians knocked him to the ground and started trying to rip his arms off. 'Oh, look at them,' said an Irish voice. 'Aren't they just loving you noow.' She was huge and fat and wearing an apron. She said she was Mrs. Ryan. J.P. would be home soon. Come on in and have a cup of tea.

The back of the house was in slightly better condition. The garden was piled high with rubble, old lavatories and baths and sinks, but there were some rooms with proper windows. She led him into a large kitchen. The atmosphere was hot and fetid. In the middle was a large stove with several large black simmering pots. Around the walls were wooden benches, the sort Jake remembered from the labourers' huts. Under the benches were three dogs, four cats and three hens. On a bare orange box was the largest television he'd ever seen.

J.P. arrived about seven o'clock, puffing and panting, followed by eight Irish labourers who looked as if they'd just come off a chain gang. J.P. pushed his wife aside as she tried to stop him coming in, dripping wet, but she made the eight labourers take off their boots before entering. Their bare feet seemed to be as dirty and wet as the boots they'd taken off. They left steaming wet footprints on the stone flags as they dragged themselves to the benches. They sat down, like monster orphans in the workhouse, while Mrs. Ryan went round them dishing out a plateful each from one of the bubbling pots.

Jake couldn't understand a word they said to each other. Their accents were so broad and their mouths so full. Jake tried to talk to J.P., to tell him what he wanted, but J.P. pushed him aside. He wasn't all that tall, but he had a bull-like bulging chest and close-cropped white hair. He wore a cheap plastic leather jerkin, miles too small for him, a fairisle pullover which looked as if it had come from a children's rummage sale, very baggy green flannels, a battered trilby and a lethal-looking leather buckled belt. He was as scruffy and dirty as his workmen, except that he wore brand new brown shoes, not boots, and a tie. The discriminating could tell from these signs that he must be the gaffer.

'Chrisssst Almighty,' he said to Jake, his mouth bulging. 'Let a man get at his meat. Mrs. Ryan, will you give that eejit some sopper at once now and stop him blathering.' Jake took a plateful. He'hadn't eaten all day.

When the labourers had finished they all lay back on the bench where they'd been sitting, closed their eyes and snored heavily. After half an hour, they got up and one by one went to the kitchen sink, stuck their heads under the cold tap and swilled themselves. They got their boots on again with a lot of joking and belching. They were now all ready to go out for the night. They looked no cleaner than when they'd come in, but you could tell they'd been near a tap by the water dripping down from their soaking hair. They gave their hair a quick comb at the doorway, just to perfect their toilet, and said they were off to Camden Town.

'Grand looking lads,' said Jake, to make conversation.

'They are that,' said J.P., lying back on a battered couch, picking his teeth with a knitting needle like Desperate Dan. 'And as healthy as the day is long. By Christ yes.'

'It's all this healthy work' said Jake.

'Christ Almighty, what are you talking about? This is the unhealthiest town in the whole universe. Sweet Jesus. It's Ireland that's done it. Ireland! You understand. *Ireland!* Mrs. Ryan will tell you herself.'

Mrs. Ryan had sat herself in front of the television and was reading True Romances and telling nobody anything.

'They've never had any of yon fancy medicines in their lives,' continued J.P. 'By Christ no. Every time they were sick, do you know what their mothers gave them? A piece of root to suck. Sore legs, sore backs, sore stomachs. It didn't matter what was wrong. A stick of root out of the bog never failed. By Christ no! I'd never let my lads touch any of that English shit, would we Mrs. Ryan? The whole bloody population's being poisoned with drugs. You're not from the Council, are you?'

Jake said no and began quickly, while he had J.P.'s attention, to explain what he wanted. By Christ, certainly he could do that, said J.P. He'd been doing central heating since before Jake was born. Christ aye. He had the best craftsmen in Ireland, all experts, every God's son of them. Nothing they couldn't do. No bother at all, just as long as he wasn't from the Council. Jake said great. In that case could he possibly look at the house and give an estimate? Next week perhaps?

'Jesus Christ, what are we sitting on our arses for!' said J.P., jumping up and putting on his battered trilby. He'd taken it off and put it beside his plate while he'd been eating, in honour of Mrs. Ryan's cooking. 'There's no time like the present. Christ no. Use all the hours that the Good God sends. Sullivan you're called? You're not from Galway, are you? I thought I could tell from your accent. Christ, you fuckers are everywhere.'

He put his arm round Jake's shoulder, leaving a layer of sawdust on Jake's best Italian suit. He stuck a measuring tape in his pocket and took Jake out to his lorry which was parked half on the pavement at the front of the house, its engine running. He drove all the way to Kensington in the middle of the road with no lights on and never once looked where he was going. He was either facing Jake, telling him about all the bloody Sullivans he'd ever known, or he was hanging out of his window, blaspheming at pedestrians who dared to put one foot in the roadway.

The house was locked, naturally enough. In all J.P.'s enthusiasm, Jake had forgotten it would be. He said that was it. They'd better wait for the morning. Be much better in the light anyway.

'Christ Almighty, who wants light? If I can't look a house over in the dark, then I might as well give up. There's no lights in Ireland, you know. I've built three-storey houses in the pitch black many a time. You don't need light. Electricity, running water, gas, lavatories, people don't know they're living these days.'

J.P. stepped back and holding both his fists in the air like a sledge hammer struck the front door. One of the panels split and he put a beefy hand through, ripped away the guts of the door handle and kicked the door open with his foot. He went round the house as if he owned it, kicking in doors, breaking open cupboards and jumping through floorboards to test them. It was all beautiful, he said, a lovely house, what was wrong with it? Jake said nothing, he just wanted it turned into ten luxury flatlets.

'Ten? Are you making it into the Ritz hotel? Let me see now, a bit of hard board here, and here, and there. You'll get twenty lovely rooms out of this lot. Jesus Christ, people will get lost if they have more than eight feet each. And central heating as well? Are you trying to molly coddle them?'

Jake had never met a builder who tried to save him money. It had always been the opposite. He began to suspect that J.P. had never installed central heating before. At the slightest suggestion of this, J.P. almost had a fit. Jake apologized and said it was a joke.

He tried to persuade Jake against putting in more bathrooms. That lavatory in the back garden was enough, what more did they want? Jake said he wanted a narrow back addition, three storeys high, which would contain three extra bathrooms. They could make the rest on the landings. J.P. argued but gave in. Jake asked if he would look after sending the plans for the new addition to the Council.

'Council? What are you bloody blathering about? They'll just mess you around. It'll cost you twice as much and take twice as long. They'll make you put in three feet founds when nine inches is quite sufficient.'

'But nine inches will probably fall down,' sake Jake.

'Christ Almighty. How long did you say you were letting them for, seven years? Well, Bejesus. This will last seven years. What more do you want? Do you know what the boogers did to me the other day? I did a lovely addition for an old lady, just covering in an alley between two walls. They made her pull the bloody thing down, just because she hadn't told them! Spite, that's all it was.'

Jake decided to look after the planning permission himself. He'd be able to make sure then he applied for a grant to cover half the costs of installing bathrooms and lavatories. J.P. said he didn't know anything about that. He had nothing to do with any authorities. Income tax, Insurance, Stamps, he couldn't be harished with all them people.

'If you listen to them boogers, they'll have you filling in forms and sticking in stamps all bloody day.'

Jake was all for cutting corners, but he thought J.P. was taking it a bit far. There was so much money around, there was no need to avoid the law, in fact you could use it to your advantage, if you read it the right way. J.P. said he didn't read anything. He wasn't worried about them catching up with him. He'd never filled in a form in his life so how were they going to get on to him, eh? Once you filled in one, that was it.

'But what about your lads?' said Jake. 'I know they're healthy, but what if one falls ill? He won't get any sick money, will he?'

'Bejesus! What do you think Mrs. Ryan's for? She's a mother to them, so she is. And if they're ill more than a couple of days, then bejesus, we put them on the boat home, so we do.'

They had a look in the basement where Jake could smell damp. J.P. said he should see a doctor. He'd never smelt a dryer basement in his life. In the attic, Jake saw a bit of wood-worm. Woodworm? J.P. said. These floors were better than Buckingham Palace.

There was a crowd of angry neighbours outside, gathered around J.P.'s lorry. It was parked on the pavement, stopping them getting past, and the noise of the engine had woken every child in the street. The vibrations had even brought pictures off a wall, said a furious officer class bloke with a curly moustache. He demanded to know J.P.'s full name and address, at once.

'You're bloody lucky to have walls,' said J.P., jumping into his lorry and driving straight towards him down the pavement, scattering the crowd. Jake just managed to scramble on the back.

'What about the estimate, then?' said Jake, as they drove

through Kensington. J.P. reacted as if Jake had cast doubts on his parentage. At first he didn't know what Jake was talking about. He never went in for such things. Christ no. Jake persisted and at last J.P. started emptying his pockets, scattering razor blades, six inch nails, lumps of lead, electric plugs, ball cocks, taps, copper piping and a blow lamp. J.P. obviously didn't have stores. He kept everything in his pockets.

He threw two bundles of scrap paper at Jake. They were sodden and smelt of moths. The blow lamp must have been leaking. One set of scraps had the heading 'To Work Done' written in a schoolboy scrawl on the back of exercise paper. The other said 'Estimate'.

'Give us the estimates,' said J.P. 'I'll do the bugger for you now, as you're in such a hurry.'

He had both hands off the steering wheel. Jake said no, no, don't worry. He could write it out at home, at his leisure.

'You write it in yourself,' said J.P. 'You're the educated one.'

Jake had never been called educated in his life. It must be his Italian suit which had done it.

'Make it seven thousand,' said J.P. 'That should do it.' Jake had expected double. He couldn't have got all that work done for seven thousand pounds in Carlisle, and things were supposed to be twice as expensive in London. If he sold the ten flats at £3,000 each, he could clear a profit of around £15,000. He'd have to keep a very close eye on J.P., which would probably be a full time job. But it wouldn't be a bad profit, for a start.

They pulled up outside a pub as Jake was still doing his mental arithmetic. J.P. jumped out, leaving the engine on as usual, telling Jake to follow him. They searched round the drunken Irish bodies on the pavement and at last found the eight which were J.P.'s. Jake helped to drag them to the gutter then pile them one by one on the back of the lorry.

Back at the house, the ones who came round were given another dish of stew by Mrs. Ryan, the others were left to sleep it off. Jake took another plateful then said he must be going, could he use the phone. He rang the number the girl at the estate agency had given him. A severe Scottish voice replied at once – 'Church of Scotland Hostel for Young Ladies. What do you want, it's verrry, verrry late.'

That was it. He'd spend the night with J.P. No one would

notice another body stretched out on the floor. J.P. came back in, his flies half open, as Jake was on the phone. He'd been out in the garden relieving himself.

'It's for you,' said Jake, handing J.P. the phone. 'Some women complaining about you leaving your engine running.'

Jake fell asleep, with J.P.'s blasphemies still ringing in his ears.

Chapter Ten

'What's your name, little girl?'

'Funny,' she said, standing at the doorway, looking me over very superciliously. She had a singsong Southern accent, the sort they'd laugh at if she ever went back to Cumberland.

'You're a big girl for two,' I said. An au pair had opened the door when I'd first arrived, and led me into a drawing room where I was now sitting, looking at the framed vintage cars and old maps of Carlisle. She looked at me, considering carefully. Her mother had been talking for two hours, mainly about the early Carlisle days of Sullivan and Co. She'd started off weepily and ended up all faint again at the memory of Jake leaving her pregnant and going off to London. I presumed she'd gone to her bedroom for a cry.

The minute I'd stepped into the house it had all come out like a floodgate. She'd remembered me from the old days when I was a bus conductor and just thought I was a passing friend. I hadn't yet managed to get in that I was the bloke she was suing. She'd obviously not taken in the name Tom Graham at the bottom of the article, or if she had she hadn't associated it with me. There was no reason why she should have done. I had to tell her soon because I'd come to plead with her. If the action went through, I was for the push. I wondered if she'd hit me, call the police or set the au pair on me. The au pair looked like an Olympic discus thrower who'd come across for a free sex change on the National Health.

I got up and walked round the room, followed by Funny's

eyes. I looked out of the window onto a back patio. The whole garden had been laid out in brightly coloured marble and must have cost a fortune. In the distance I could see rows of gnomes glistening in the lawn.

Jake hadn't contacted her for three months, so she said, after he went off to London in 1959. She had to go down herself in the end and make a scene. Halfway through the ranting and raging the waters had broken. She'd been rushed to hospital where the baby was born, after a twenty-four-hour labour. Jake had been forced to bring her down to London after that, even though it had been a girl.

The house was a semi-detached in Pinner. No wonder Jake didn't go near it now, but it had thrilled him in the early days. There was a golf course near the house, which she agreed gave the impression of countryside and they called the house Skiddaw, just to complete the sylvan setting.

Jake enjoyed the idea of himself as a family man, going home on the tube to Pinner to his wife and family. He had very little money at first and had been amazed how much he'd had to pay for Skiddaw; he thought he must be in the stockbroker belt at least – almost £5,000 which had taken all his spare cash as the rest was tied up in getting his first London deal off the ground. He bought himself a bowler and an umbrella which he wore with a polo neck pullover, to annoy everyone else on the tube. When he discovered his next door neighbour wasn't a company director but a foreman joiner and that on the other side was a retired railway driver he was furious. Nothing personal, he was just furious with London and the South for being so far ahead of the North.

As he got a bit more money, he started pouring it into the house; he put in a double garage, three TV's, another bathroom, a back addition, a patio, a bar, had the outside bricks painted alternately red and yellow which resulted in complaints from all the neighbours and covered the front with so much fancy wrought iron and it looked like the inside of Alcatraz, having decided, when the first shock of Skiddaw's ordinariness hit him, to make it different from everyone else's.

He soon discovered Beryl's class was a laugh. She had a Marks and Spencer mind, he said. He'd rather have her in Woolworth's flash than all those discreet self-coloured twin sets. And as for thinking she was intelligent, he must have been mad. It was like being married to a cow. All she ever thought about was the baby and the house.

There was a noise at the yellow panelled double doors at the end of the drawing room, and Ingrid the au pair lumbered through with a trolley piled with goodies followed by Beryl. She'd gone out with raven black hair, now she was blonde. She'd also changed her dress, her pearl necklace and her shoes. Clothes, the great comforter.

Beryl poured tea from a large silver teapot. She had bright orange nail varnish on her fingers. Her toes, which were peeping through her high-heeled open sandals like museum specimens, were also in orange. She seemed smaller and fatter than she used to be. Her face, legs and hands seemed to have got podgier. Her legs were slightly apart and I got the sensation of fat little thighs like ham shanks. I leaned back hurriedly and tucked into a swiss roll, an eclair and a piece of jam sponge. Beryl had already finished two cream cakes and a gateau.

'Fanny,' she shouted. 'Would you like a Carrs Sports Biscuit?'

'Oh. I thought it was Funny.'

'You thought what was funny?' she turned aggressively, closing her legs. She'd stopped chewing.

'No, your daughter. When she told me her name I thought she said Funny, not Fanny.'

'It's literary. One of Jake's stupid ideas. After one of those books he was always reading.'

'Fanny Hill?'

'Something like that,' said Beryl. 'I don't think he ever read any of them. He's always pretending he's fantastically interested in something or someone. But he's just putting it on. He's just a kid, taking up these passions all the time, then dropping them. That's what he did with me.'

'No he didn't,' I said. 'He was sincere about you. Honest.'

'What lies,' she said, turning her head away.

'He was, he used to bore me for hours going on about you.' I smiled, just in case she thought I was criticizing her by using the word boring.

'Really?' she said, wanting to hear more.

'You were all he wanted, you know.'

'Have you seen him then?' she asked. It was a chance to get in my connection with him and explain the newspaper article.

112

'Not really,' I said, back pedalling. 'Just friends have been telling me . . .'

'I don't care anyway. He's only interested in himself. Always has been. Always will be. I could never feel sorry for him, after what he's done to me.'

I sat back, waiting for the invective. Fanny came in and said she would have a biscuit. Beryl grabbed her eagerly and tried to cuddle her, to show me how much she loved her.

'Oh, no kisses today?' said Beryl.

'Yes, I've got a lot today,' said Fanny, cramming a biscuit into her mouth.

'Where did you get them from?'

'The fish.'

'How did the fish give you kisses, Fanny?'

Fanny went on eating. She got to the end, paused, then took a piece of sponge cake. She finished this then looked at her mother as if she was an idiot.

'From their wings, of course.'

Beryl told her not to be so silly. She called for Ingrid to take Fanny away. The minute the doors were closed she got back to Jake, telling me again what a beast he was. She'd never see him for weeks then he'd come home in the middle of the night, half drunk and jump on her, know what I mean? I did know, but it was embarrassing and I looked round for any little ears, or worse, big muscles taking it all in. I didn't want to hear about their sex life, not so much anyway. She would probably have told the milkman or the postman if they had knocked at the door and walked in. She just wanted to tell someone the details about the last time Jake had come to the house, just a year previously.

'Where have you been?' said Beryl, as Jake came through the French windows one evening. 'I haven't seen you for six months.'

'In the garden, where do you think? I've always fancied that gnome with the big red arse.'

'Don't make such a noise. Fanny's just gone to sleep.'

'Where's the sexy au pair? That's what I've come to see. You did get one did you?'

'Yes, she's in Fanny's bedroom.'

'It's like that is it,' said Jake, wandering round looking at all the ornaments and doilies and antimacassars. 'You want to get rid of all this rubbish. Complete crap.'

'You bought them all, Jake.'

'I know. We all make mistakes.' Jake stared at her.

Beryl glared back, but decided not to start a row. She asked if he'd like a cup of tea and he said yes, why did it take so long for her to ask.

'I hear you've moved into new offices, Jake. You are doing well,' she said, pouring him out tea.

'What do you expect me to say to that? Make a speech or sign autographs? You don't care about my work, so shuttup eh. What's on telly?'

'Oh, Jake. You haven't been home for months and all you want to do is watch telly.'

'I don't. I came home for a bit of sex, but you've locked her up. I haven't had a woman for months.'

'What about Maggie?'

'She's my bloody secretary. I can't sleep with her.'

'But you would.'

'Christ, anybody would. She's only twenty-one, and luscious, and clever.'

Beryl, who was twenty-four and becoming fat and slow and knew it, refused to rise to all this. Jake was being deliberately aggressive, trying to pick a row. She poured herself some more tea.

'I said the telly, woman. Put it on. Make yourself useful.'

Beryl didn't move. Jake asked again, then he got up, grabbed her by the arm till she shouted. He put the television on and sat down again. 'That's for nothing. Just wait till I find out you've been doing something.'

Beryl sat all evening on the verge of tears, eating a pile of Crunchie bars and combing her wig. After the Epilogue, Jake switched off the telly and turned to her, smiling.

'Oh, it's nice to be at home in the bosom of one's family again, having an evening of sparkling conversation and delightful home baked foods. Come on, then, where's the supper? I want something cooked, you should know that by now, not all this processed shit.'

Beryl looked at him reproachfully, then she put her head in her hands and sobbed gently.

'Christ, don't tell me. You've got a headache.'

'I have,' said Beryl. 'I can't help it.'

'You can't help anything. But why is it you always have one near bed time, eh? Or you've got a toothache, or you feel tired, or you've got to get up for Fanny? No wonder I haven't come home for a couple of months.'

'Six and a half months.'

'You've got a little book, have you, where you tick it off? Look, don't sit there like a fucking mummy. I've come to tell you something, if you're good. I don't know if I will now, with all this moaning.'

'What Jake?' said Beryl, brightening up.

'How about a cruise, eh? Round the Med or somewhere for a few weeks?'

'That would be lovely, Jake.'

'I saw one advertised for the Bally Ear Ache islands or somewhere, only £1,000 for a month for two. What do you think?'

'What about Fanny?'

'Fuck Fanny. That's what you've got the au pair for, isn't it?'

'She is very good with Fanny, I'll say that . . .'

'There you are. I'll book it then. Three weeks or four?'

'Whatever you can spare, Jake. You're the one who's so busy, so you're always telling me . . .'

'Me? I'm not going. I can't spare three hours, never mind three weeks. You're lucky I came here at all. You're going with your mother.'

'Oh Jake.'

'Don't Oh Jake me. You're always going on about how guilty you feel about your mother since your dad died.'

'I just want to go with you.'

'Nothing would give me greater pleasure, darling. Believe me. But I can't. With this new building I'm run off me feet.'

'Then I'm not going.'

'Christ! What ingratitude. I offer you a fabulous trip of a lifetime, and that old bag as well, all for free, and all you do is moan. I know some women that would give their right testicle for a luxury cruise. Typical, just typical, after all I've bought you . . .'

'Money isn't everything, Jake,' said Beryl. 'It isn't even anything . . .'

'Look at this fabulous house. I've spent thousands on it, just for you.' Jake was walking round again, kicking the walls and the furniture. 'Christ, it gives me the creeps. You never did have any taste. No wonder I only come home in the dark. I wouldn't like anyone to see me in this dump.'

'Stop banging, you'll waken Fanny.'

'You go on about her as if she was a human being. All she does is piss and shit and cry, who cares if she wakes up. They should all be in baby farms till they start school.'

'She is your daughter, Jake.'

'So what? It was an accident of birth, that was all. It's just fucking conceit to pretend you love something, just because you gave birth to it. That's what you do. You're just loving yourself.'

'Don't talk like that Jake.'

'Shall I talk through my ears then, or my nose?'

Jake bounced up and down, doing impressions of talking through his ears and hands and legs. Beryl smiled. He picked up the teapot and started singing through it. He had a conversation with the standard lamp and lay on the floor, listening to the carpet talking. Then he leaned over and gently took Beryl by the arm. She was giggling. He pulled her onto the floor beside him.

'You are awful, Jake. It's all you think about.'

'Let's have a bit, Miss Clapperton. Now we're on the floor, Miss Clapperton. Mr. Foster won't hear, not with that bus conductor's bag over his head . . .'

'You were awful Jake,' said Beryl.

'And I haven't changed, have I?' said Jake.

'No,' said Beryl, sadly.

'I've even got the same underpants on, do you want to see?'

'Not here, Jake.'

'Well where do you fancy? Out in the street, in the garden? I probably should have stayed out there. East West, gnome's best.'

'What are you talking about, Jake?'

'How about it then?'

'I've told you, Jake. I'm not going with my mother.'

'I don't mean that. I mean a bit here on the Cyril Lord. It's supposed to resist stains. I wonder if it works for semen? You never see things advertised as a semen remover, do you? I spent hours as a kid trying to get it off my trousers. I used to ruin all me hankies. They go stiff as boards, have you noticed?

116

And sheets, well, you've had it with sheets. What do you think? I could set you up in a little semen removing business. You're always saying how bored you are.'

'I don't know what you're on about. You get sillier all the time.'

'No wonder, having to talk to myself. I once thought I could talk to you. I must have been raving.'

'There's Fanny. Come on, let me up. I'll have to go. Once she wakens at this time I've had it.'

'And I haven't,' said Jake, rolling over and lying on his back, looking up at the ceiling. Beryl got up, put her clothes straight very carefully and smoothed her hair as if she'd been in a wild orgy.

'Now where have I put the Rose Hip Syrup?' said Beryl.

'That's her name is it? I thought she was Scandinavian. Rosa Hirrup, sounds a good clean Jewish girl that. I fancy it. I can just see her with her large gleaming legs and long sexy teeth. I bet her parents have had them in a wire brace since she's been thirteen. They've probably put a tooth brace on her cunt as well, to make sure no Gentile gets in with his uncircumcised tooth brush ...'

'Ssh, Jake,' said Beryl, searching round.

'I'll just go and have a look at her,' said Jake, getting up and tip toeing loudly to the door. 'Very sexy, these Jewish girls.'

Jake went out. Beryl put the carpet straight where he'd been lying and tidied up the cushions.

'Curiste,' said Jake, returning, putting his hands over his face and groaning. 'She's enormous. It would be like trying to lay the Queen Elizabeth.'

'Ah, here it is,' said Beryl, finding a plastic drinking cup full of purple juice. 'Are you coming, Jake?'

'Doesn't look like it,' said Jake lying on the carpet again. 'I'll just sleep here all the night. My breathing might waken up Fanny, and we wouldn't want that, would we? Nice bit of stuff this. I fitted it myself, didn't I, back in the old days before the revolution. I wonder how soon they'll have fitted people and fitted babies to go with fitted carpets? Fitted wives would be great. I think this one is made for you sir, yes, right size, makes no noise when you walk on her, absorbs everything you give her. She comes in all colours. Very clean, hard wearing and 50 per cent artificial fibre ...'

'Well I'm going. Don't be long, Jake, will you?'

'Don't worry. I'm getting shorter all the time. Going, going, going ...'

He let Beryl leave the room then he got up slowly. He put his jacket on, still repeating 'going, going' to himself. He got to the french windows and slowly let himself out the way he'd come in.

As he closed the windows behind him he stopped muttering and shouted very loudly, 'Gone!'

Beryl didn't see Jake again after that. Michael contacted her, on Jake's behalf, saying he wanted a divorce. He would admit adultery, bestiality, homosexuality, anything she fancied, as long as she gave him a divorce. Beryl refused to discuss it. She was waiting for him to come home.

'But I don't suppose he will now,' said Beryl. She was going faint again, having got rid of all her spleen. Perhaps this would be the time to tell her that it was me she was suing about the newspaper interview.

'What do you think, Tommy?' she said.

'Well, I agree. You've had a terrible time. He's been a real bastard. But I don't see what you gain by refusing a divorce. That's the sort of thing *he* would do, out of nastiness. It's not like you at all. You're too kind. You're also young and pretty. You would get a lot of alimony. You might as well marry again as soon as possible and forget him.'

'Do you really think so?' said Beryl, smiling at me.

I was trying to keep my face straight, coming out with all this foot-in-the-door sob stuff. This was how you got in to see the parents of runaway children when they wouldn't see any other journalists. I felt a real bastard. But I didn't want her to smile back at me. I wasn't going to marry her.

'I do,' I repeated. 'I know it sounds cruel to say all that, but what else is there to do?'

'Perhaps you're right,' said Beryl. 'Do you know I'm suing some terrible newspaper over what Jake told them? Perhaps I'll drop that as well. And give him a divorce. Then I'll be rid of him for ever. Talking to you has helped a lot.'

It was now a parody. I expected her to take her grand-mother's nightdress off and reveal herself as the wolf Jake. But she'd no friends, no one to talk to all day. She just needed some reaction to make her act. She said yes, she really would finish with him completely now.

'I'll go back to Cumberland. I never liked this house, or London. I was never part of it.'

Going, going, gone back.

Chapter Eleven

The first London office of Sullivan and Co. was in Soho next to a strip club. Jake said there couldn't be a better position for a young, upright, thrusting firm. And he knew all the positions.

It had formerly been a little jazz club which had gone bust when rock and roll and teenage singers arrived. It consisted of two dark and dingy semi-basement rooms for which Jake bought a two year lease for £1,500. When he rang Michael in Carlisle to tell the news Michael thought he'd gone mad. Not only was it a ridiculous price for a slum, it was completely short sighted. They'd only just be settling into it when they'd have to find something else. Jake was hardly listening to Michael's objections. He'd gone on to say that this great Irish bloke J.P. was going to do the converting. He was going to open up what little windows there were, clear it all out and divide it with hardboard into three little offices. Michael said this sounded even worse. Then fuck off, said Jake. Get yourself a new job.

Michael came down on the overnight sleeper, first class, took one look at J.P. and his gang and nearly went straight back, he couldn't believe such a person could exist. But J.P. had served Jake's purpose well during his first months in London. That first conversion had been ready on time and nothing had fallen down. Jake had easily sold it for what he was asking and made £15,000 on the deal. He regretted the minute he'd sold the leases that he hadn't asked more. On the strength of it, he bought three more houses, much bigger and in a slightly better part of Kensington. Again, J.P. did them up. Nothing luxurious, or even flash, just cheap efficient flats which groups of girls or minor executives with large families could cram into.

London was so much bigger, so much different and so much more complicated than Carlisle. In those six months Jake had simply stuck to what he'd already done so successfully in Carlisle. The problems were a matter of scale, not degree. He was doing what he knew how to do and with J.P. he had someone who spoke his own language. Buying up an old house, by getting a mortgage or a loan, then modernizing it by putting in a few partitions and adding some bathrooms, then selling the house off in separate units was all comparatively straightforward. After the success of the first house, J.P. was willing to wait till all the units had been sold before he was paid for his conversion work.

J.P. was cheap enough, but one of the scale problems in London was that it cost so much to buy an old property in the first place. With three houses being bought over at around the same time, Jake hadn't much ready cash. He'd always kept away from banks, after that first fiasco in Carlisle, but he now thought he might try a London bank, just to see if they were any more clued up than Carlisle. He'd got started on his own, thanks to getting that bit of capital from his mother's house, and was now succeeding on his own, so he felt more confident of impressing a bank. He'd been fed up for a long time with having to use building societies. They felt they were doing such a huge favour when they agreed to a mortgage. Jake maintained they were more bother than they were worth. All they meant was endless paper work. They insisted on seeing the house, sending in their own surveyors, studying his bank balance and other properties, till Jake was screaming at them with impatience.

He'd been in London five months when one day he walked into his bank, on spec, to ask if they'd put up a bridging loan for three houses he had his eye on. He'd pay it back in three months when he sold the converted flats. In twenty-four hours they said yes. They even offered him more than he wanted, to cover all his other expenses, such as the builder, till he got back his money. They seemed to think the whole deal was absolutely normal. Jake couldn't get over it. With building societies there had also been endless messing around afterwards when he sold the house, paying back or transferring mortgages before he could start on another one. He'd even thought at one time about laying out all his own money on a house, but that was a temporary mental aberration. He knew without knowing it that you never never spend your own money.

Even though he was still on his own in London, Jake soon had so many London houses on the go that he took on other builders, bigger and better and more expensive than J.P. Through one he started to use a sharp young architect who knew the London planning laws backwards. All the arguments about what could or could not be put up and knocked down were from then on looked after by him. The banks made getting finance easy, the architect looked after permissions and the contractors, while Jake went round looking for properties.

As he was on his own, the paper-work soon became a nightmare. At first he'd got the Carlisle office to do as much of it as possible, but working by remote control was very clumsy. It also wasn't very impressive. It was OK on the phone, talking about his architect (as if he owned him completely), referring to his building firms (as if J.P. was Wimpeys), saying he'd have to discuss things with his merchant banker (rather than the Kings Cross branch of the Midland Bank) and constantly boasting about his branches throughout the country (i.e. Carlisle). On the phone, a one-man business can masquerade as anything. But when it came to revealing his whereabouts, pigging in with J.P. and his navvies took a bit of disguising.

He found a London accommodation address, a smart Bond Street address and phone number. It looked very good on headed notepaper, as long as you didn't know that the same address was used by twenty other little firms, all of whom had their mail and messages sent on and hardly knew where Bond Street was.

The next stage was a secretarial agency, farming out work to them on a day to day basis. It was one thing to have poshly headed notepaper, but somebody had to type out the posh sounding words.

The most obvious stage, finding somewhere proper to live, was forced upon him. He intended from the beginning only to sleep at J.P.'s for a couple of nights, till he found something more suitable for a man in his position. But with working twenty-four hours a day, keeping all the balls in the air, racing round the architects, the banks, the estate agents, J.P.'s workmen and looking for new property, he always ended up coming home to Mrs. Ryan's in the small hours of the morning and just dropping. This went on for almost three months. It began to be embarrassing, even Jake felt it, when he'd progressed to bigger, classier builders for most of his jobs, yet he was still coming home to scruffy old J.P.'s to sleep.

It was Beryl, of course, who forced the move, coming down in a fury to find out why he hadn't contacted her. The actual place her waters broke was Jake's posh Bond Street address. She'd managed to track him down there one morning when he'd gone in to pick up his letters.

The move to a semi in Pinner meant that Jake's umbilical cord with his working class roots began to moulder away from then on. This was probably why he'd shacked up at J.P.'s for so long. Despite all the big deals, fast talk and quick money, there was part of him which felt securer with J.P.'s labourers than with West End agents.

He gave J.P. the job of converting the slummy Soho office partly out of sentiment. It was the last job J.P. did for him. Jake didn't think it mattered what sort of job he did, as long as it was quick and cheap. It wouldn't be for long. He hadn't bothered to explain to Michael the advantage of a short two year lease. Michael was too stupid to see the way London property prices were going. If he kept it a year, then moved on to something better, he could easily re-sell it for £1,500, what he'd paid for it in the first place. It would be like having a place rent free for a year.

Michael put his foot down when he saw the job J.P. was making of it. During the six months Jake had been in London, Michael had been very carefully improving their image in Carlisle, cutting down on the number of properties and concentrating on a few very superior ones. He said it was even more important for Sullivan and Co.'s image that the London office should *look* good. He agreed it didn't really matter all that much in Carlisle, but in London looking affluent was the most important thing.

He gave in on J.P. doing all his nasty internal partitions,

but insisted on a tasteful front. He knew a brilliant young designer who could do a beautiful job. When Jake found it wasn't going to cost too much, he agreed. Perhaps it was about time he did look affluent.

Sullivan and Co.'s London office opened on 1 January 1960. J.P. had finished the three little offices well on time, much to Jake's delight and Michael's surprise. He even agreed to the secretary, Maggie, whom Jake had found. She had been the girl who'd done most of Jake's work when he'd been using the secretarial agency. His only remaining objection, and that was a minor one, was that Maggie was to have an office to herself. A 'cubby hole' was what he actually said. He'd thought from the beginning that it was silly when they had little space to divide it up into three such poky little cubby holes. A staff of three with three offices between them was rather overdoing the image.

'Four,' said Jake.

'Three,' said Michael. 'You, me and Maggie. You're not bringing Beryl back are you?'

'Four,' repeated Jake. 'You, me, Maggie and Sammy. You're also wrong about Maggie having her own room. *You'll* be sharing it with her.'

'Who on earth is Sammy?'

'My personal assistant,' said Jake. 'Now go and get lost, eh. You might not have work to do, but I have.'

Sammy was called Sammy Durek but Jake insisted on calling him Sammy Durex. He was eighteen and had previously been a hair stylist, a croupier and before that a gigolo, moving in with anyone, male or female, who would feed him and buy him clothes. Jake had met him on the platform one evening at Tottenham Court tube station when he was waiting for the last tube home to Pinner. Sammy was dressed all in white. He had a fabulous tan and looked straight out of a beach scene from La Dolce Vita. Jake said the last tube had gone to St. Tropez. Sammy said that was funny. He was off to St. Tropez the next morning. Jake didn't believe him, especially when he caught the same tube as he did, all the way to Pinner.

On closer inspection Jake could see Sammy's tan was real. He had the top two buttons of his white towelling Jaeger shirt, bought for him by a friend, open to reveal brown hairs curling over an equally brown chest. His hair was long, well ahead of fashion, in the French style with a high parting. He had three gold rings and a bracelet. Jake couldn't get over his casual opulence. Despite his well groomed, well heeled looks, Sammy wasn't posh, or anyone-for-tennis, as Jake had first imagined. He was broad cockney, with no side and not even any wise guy smartness. He was simply a young smart lad on the make. Jake thought if only he'd been born in London, at the centre of things, he could have been like this at eighteen instead of all scruffy and hick-like. He didn't believe Sammy's stories about his jobs, or did Sammy believe Jake's stories about the money he was making from property. As a mutual calling of each other's bluff, they turned right round and got the last tube back to London. Sammy took him to a club where he'd been a croupier, to prove he knew about gambling, and Jake threw his money around, to prove he had some to throw around.

It was Jake's first night out in the West End. He hadn't had time, or even the inclination, until then. He'd been too busy making money to think of spending it. Going home to Beryl had become a reflex action, something to do when he couldn't phone anyone. Nobody had suggested doing anything else. J.P. wasn't what you'd call an expert on West End night life.

After the gambling club, Sammy took him round three other clubs, all fairly seedy and full of provincial girls straight off the Northern train trying hard to be hostesses. Sammy arranged one each for them, with Jake's money, and they were taken upstairs to an attic flat. When Jake woke up, the girls and Sammy had gone. A week later Jake got a postcard with a French stamp on, from Sammy at St. Tropez.

Sammy moved into the Soho office a week after the others. Michael suspected he'd been looking for something better to turn up, but he didn't say anything. Straight away, Sammy went out of his way to be nice to Michael, asking about his clothes, his tailor, his wine, his poems, all naturally and easily. He genuinely wanted to learn. He wasn't doing it to keep in with him. Michael, being a gentleman, showed no enmity. He was more furious with Jake for having found someone without telling him, especially someone who could give him so little. Why couldn't Jake have got to know some experienced property man, or estate agent, who could be of real use? Jake said Sammy was of use. He'd created all his brilliant schemes for himself. He didn't want some rival to find out about them. All he wanted was an assistant who could be trained to think along the same lines.

The office settled down very quickly, with Maggie and Michael doing all the legal and paper work and Jake and Sammy hunting for properties.

Jake was very close to Sammy, almost to annoy Michael. He encouraged Sammy to be as awful as he was, but not quite. Sammy was always careful never to say the sort of things to Jake which Jake said to others. Jake was now only twenty-one, three years older than Sammy, but he acted as if he'd been in the London property business for twelve years, rather than just over twelve months. He had picked up a lot. He could scan a building and immediately see how it could be converted. He could walk down a street and decide if it would take a year to come up, ten years or never. He was a walking A–Z and could tell by the address if a place was worth going to see. The postal district was usually just enough. He'd take anything in S.W.3 but wouldn't look at S.W.10. He knew that N.W.3 was a natural but N.W.2 a dead loss. In selling flats he'd often put the phone number as the top attraction in the ads, if it was a FLA or a HAM. If it was REN or GLA then he'd omit it.

At the time, in 1960, Chelsea had a different sort of image, thanks to the Chelsea set. The gossip columns made out it was simply the haunt of half-witted debs and chinless wonders. It wasn't the place to attract the new moneyed classes. Jake said it would be, once the creative young working class lads with the real flair and brains, meaning himself, moved in and made it commercially desirable.

He took Sammy on trips round London, spotting property from the tops of buses. They'd go from Trafalgar Square to the World's End with Jake making Sammy look for possibilities. He taught him not to despise Fulham. He said you should always invest in the next door areas, not necessarily to develop immediately, just to wait till it came up. Then you could sell at a big profit without ever doing anything. He said this was what Woolworths did in the thirties, when it moved into the High Streets. It bought up the next door shops, knowing that their own success would bring up the value of everything else. Sammy asked him how he knew this. Jake said stick around. When you've been in this business all your life, you pick up a thing or two.

Jake even picked up an eye for architectural details. This was strange, considering his background in Thwaite. There was no architecture at all in Thwaite. Perhaps this was a help, making it easier to see faded Georgian fronts which Londoners took for granted. He could spot columns which had been bricked over, carved pine mantelpieces which had been varnished black. He went for Regency and even Victorian before Victorian became a selling phrase. He'd call it a 'converted period house' not saying which period.

They'd often jump off on their bus tours when Jake noticed a new For Sale sign up – not for an old property, they always had enough of those, and not for a property already in the hands of a developer. What he was after was a new block put up by the builder himself, trying to branch out as a developer. Jake soon knew all the names and could tell from the board if there was a middleman or not. He'd go in and ask the price of each flat. He'd know at once if it was too high or too low. If it was low, he'd get it down even lower by offering immediate cash for the whole lot. They'd haggle a bit and Jake would say OK, keep it on offer for him for twenty-four hours and he'd let them know. Back at the office, they'd go through the long lists of people wanting flats. If the flats could be sold at a higher price, they'd take the deposits which would more than cover the deposit on the block. If they didn't get a higher price, then he'd just ring up in twenty-four hours and say he didn't want it. It was done mainly to impress Sammy, to show him a fool-proof way of making money without even doing any developing. Jake of course didn't do any of the paper work or finding tenants. He'd just ring Maggie at the office, tell her the price he'd offered and get her to find tenants. That's what he had a staff for, for Chrissake.

There was one racket Jake didn't touch – getting rid of sitting tenants. The Rent Acts had secured the tenancies and the rents of people in unfurnished properties. These people couldn't be evicted, so naturally the prices were very low. A house worth £10,000 would be on the market for £3,000, just because three old ladies were crouching somewhere inside. People like Rachman, the notorious Polish developer of the early sixties, gently encouraged sitting tenants to move, by cutting off electricity and water, moving in sixteen Pakistanis, knocking a few walls down or taking the roof off. Jake thought this was immoral, being a good Socialist, so he said. He was more interested in taking money from other developers or from flash executive types looking for a snob telephone number.

There was so much money around there was no need to do this sort of thing. Prices were going up month by month. 'It was ridiculous,' said Jake. 'I couldn't go wrong. People were pressing money into my hands for flats even before I'd found the houses to convert. Sammy was getting back-handers from people, just to tip them off when a new house was ready. It was like taking goodies from kids. And I was doing a public service, wasn't I? Helping homeless idiots. Christ. But I was really just pissing around in those days, playing with little houses for little people. I hadn't yet discovered where the really big money was.'

By July 1960 the three rooms in the Soho office had expanded. They took over the ground floor and redivided everything into ten even smaller offices. Sullivan and Co. soon had a staff of twelve people. Jake still had his own secretary, Maggie, and his personal assistant, Sammy Durek. Michael now had a secretary and an assistant, a young solicitor. There were two young estate agents, both Jewish and from the East End. They had worked for big Mayfair firms. Jake had brought them in for their contacts – he also let them share in the profits of schemes they initiated. There was a glamorous receptionist who sat in the front office and two other debby-type girls who were employed to do all the extra secretarial work, but most of all to look good and give the right ambience. Ambience was Jake's new word.

To keep an eye on all the young con men and make sure that the debby girls didn't do absolutely nothing all day, Jake took on a middle-aged Scotsman called Jimmy Black. Jake, in his jolly way, insisted on calling him Daft Jimmy which was a reference only Michael got. Jake had met Jimmy in a pub. He was drinking neat whisky and looked every inch a con man with his military appearance, toothbrush moustache and bowler hat. He wasn't. His moustache was real and he'd been thirty years in the army. He'd been paid off as a Regimental Sergeant Major which was why he'd bought a bowler. He had a broad Glasgow accent and saw through Jake's right away, ask- ing if he was from Carlisle, sir.

Jake took him on as office manager. He was very solid and reliable. Jake pretended to despise all the yes-sir, no-sir, but he quite liked having Jimmy report back to him all the office gossip and to carry out any hatcheting.

Michael kept out of any office politics or involvements. He kept himself to himself. All the new people couldn't see what Michael saw in Jake. Jake kept nothing to himself. If he wasn't wandering round, climbing over office partitions and shouting 'He's picking his nose again', he was lying on the floor of his own office, with the door wide open, announcing to the world that he had a hard on, or he felt like a meat pie, or a woman, or both.

Jake spent about a year, working from the Soho office, specializing in converting old houses. By the end of it he'd got it down to such a fine art that he could make money not only without doing any developing, but without having the work of finding tenants either.

He stumbled into this system by chance when he was having lunch with Sammy in a nosh bar round the corner from the office. As part of his Scottish kick, he'd been lunching in bars up to then, drinking chasers – beer and whisky together – and eating Scotch eggs. Jimmy told him that Scotch eggs were about as Scottish as Chinese food was Chinese and that all the tartans on the pub walls were wrong. Jake said fuck off Jimmy, you're fired. Jimmy said yes sir, as you will sir, will that be all sir?

Jake had been at home in pubs with all the beer and swear- ing. When he moved on to the nosh places that Sammy went to they all seemed a bit foreign and exotic. He didn't of course admit to Sammy that he felt a bit out of it, the way he'd done that time in the El Ole in Carlisle. But this time he was able to hide it better, with someone to take him and tell him what was best. Sammy let him boast that he'd been eating sauer- kraut since he could wank. He didn't make any comment when Jake put sugar on it the first time, saying it was the sour- est sauerkraut he'd had for a long time.

Living at home in Pinner had just been like being in Carlisle. Beryl had given him fish and chips, when he'd deigned to come home. When he stopped going home he took a service flat in the King's Road. But he hardly took advantage of the service as he was always working so late at his office. Beryl thought it was other women which was keeping him away but, for that first year, it really was work.

These lunches with Sammy became his only meal of the day. He ate salt beef till it came out of his ears and soused herrings and liver paté till he felt sick. He drank lemon tea all the way through, even with his coffee.

He was boasting loudly to Sammy one day, as usual, that his problem was that he was too good. He had so many fabulous properties he didn't know what to do with them. In particular he was going on about a huge house in Paddington which he'd just got for £15,000 from the Church Commissioners. There had been stories about it being a brothel put around by Jake. He said they needed to be shot, wasting poor people's money. They should be developing it themselves, not letting con men like him make all the money. No wonder the Church had had its day.

A fat foreign looking gentleman at the next table, with a cigarette-stained double-breasted black jacket and unmatching baggy grey trousers, leaned over and said he'd give Jake £20,000 for it.

'Do you think I came up the Clyde on a banana boat?' said Jake, sneering at him in broad Gorbals. 'If I were you, laddie, I'd stick to boot laces.'

The man explained in halting English that no, no, no, he wasn't in boot laces he was in corsets. Jake said that with his fat he should be. He and Sammy both roared at their own wit, but the man went on to explain that he was also in property. He'd heard Jake mention the house yesterday and he'd sent his son along that morning to look at it. Mr. Sullivan had a very lovely property there, if he didn't mind him saying so. Jake was flattered that the man had discovered his name.

'Listen, laddie, when I've finished with yon place, I'll want £50,000 for it, not fucking twenty.'

The man came closer and whispered in Jake's ear that he was willing to buy it now, this minute, for £20,000, before Jake had done any work on it at all.

'All I vant is the contract, Mr. Sullivan. Look here. I give you the 10 per cent deposit right now. All right, Mr. Sullivan?'

The man took out a battered wallet from his pocket and

counted £2,000 in fivers on the table in front of Jake. No one turned round. The other people at the man's table had eye glasses to their eyes, studying lumps of jewellery and passing round paper packages to each other.

The man repeated that all he wanted was Jake to hand him over the contract. He would look after everything else.

Jake had so far paid only his £1,500 deposit which ensured that no one else could buy the house. The contracts were being exchanged and Jake had twenty-eight days in which to pay the rest of the money to the Church Commissioners. That was all that had happened to the house up to then.

'Hold on, hold on, Gunga Din,' said Jake. 'If I'm buying at £15,000 and selling at £20,000, that's a profit of £5,000, right? I've already paid down £1,500 so first of all I want that back from you, laddie, plus my £5,000 profit. Count out £6,500, fatso, and the contract's yours.'

The man pretended he didn't know what Jake was talking about. But he did. He was completely fluent when it came to figures, just like Jake.

'Keep the heed,' said Jake as the man started gesturing that it was too much. 'And don't wave your smelly hands at me. Listen, Shylock. I still owe them £13,500 on the deal, don't I, 90 per cent of £15,000? You pay me £6,500 now, then you have only £13,500 still to pay on the contract. That's £20,000, which is what you said, or are you now backing out, you fucking sassenach?'

The man smiled and said Jake was very clever, but it was only correct that Jake should get his profit now. Sammy said he couldn't understand what they were doing. Jake said he was too slow to catch a fucking cold.

Jake went back to the office, chuffed with himself, told Michael what he'd done and told him to assign over the contract to his fat Jewish friend.

A week later, the man came into the restaurant and sat down again at the table next to Jake and Sammy. Jake asked him which builder he was getting to do the conversion. The man said builder? For why did he want a builder? He'd resold the contract the next day to a Polish friend for £25,000. Jake laughed and bought him and his friends lemon tea all round.

Very soon the nosh bar became a market for changing con-

130

tracts. When anyone knew they'd got a property particularly cheap, they immediately sold the contract to someone else. The same contract would go round and round up to half a dozen times, each time fetching more money, till at last someone decided the ceiling had been reached, for that week anyway, and he would get down to doing the actual developing, still making a large profit on the finished house.

Jake enjoyed the idea of making £5,000 over his 3s 6d plate of salt beef. He also liked the idea of putting one over on all his new Polish, Lebanese, Russian, Hungarian and Israeli friends. They were much more devious than he was. Jake wasn't devious at all. He was all above board. He made no secret of what he was paying and what he would make. They in turn thought this was being *really* devious. He must be concealing some very complicated dealings. And he wasn't Jewish either. So he *must* be very clever.

Jake learned a lot from them. Everything he'd been doing up to then he'd more or less discovered for himself, without knowing there were scores of property developers in London doing exactly the same, and a lot more besides.

This was when Jake decided he was fed up being Scottish. He'd kept it up for a year. From the beginning people had always been saying he couldn't be Scottish, not with that Christian name. He said hadn't they heard of the Jacobites? James the First had had the pet name of Jake which was why his followers became Jacobites. Jake had been a good Scottish name from then on. What a lot of ignorant cunts there were around.

Jake had got his information from Jimmy, though he pretended he'd always known it. It was probably true. Willie Sullivan was Scottish and Jake had been one of his family names.

Now when he became Jewish, his Christian name didn't need any explanations. It was short for Jacob of course. Overnight he was talking about his Bar Mitzvah presents and calling everyone a schmuck. Sullivan was the Anglicized version of Sollivansky, the old Warsaw ghetto name, so he explained. Do I have to tell everyone everything in this place, do I?

Chapter Twelve

I managed to get Jake into the paper a few times, just to lower, or raise, the tone. The fact that the Express had written about him that time made it OK. I did two picture stories about him and his latest girl friend. Getting a lead story and getting a picture was the biggest problem each week. The picture was hardest of all because it held up the whole page. It had to be a girl, aristocratic if possible. After that, in order, came a poli-tician's daughter, a Lloyd's underwriter's daughter, a teenage novelist, a dress designer, a model and lastly a starlet. On Tuesdays we'd dismiss any film company trying to shove some girl's big breasts at us. Our column wasn't going to be tainted by commercialization. On Friday, we were desperately ringing round the film companies, asking for any Daily Mirror reject pin-ups.

When Jake's girl friend was a starlet, I'd save the picture (provided by Jake) until the last minute on Friday, at the height of the usual panic, and everybody would be relieved to get anything. At least there was no film we had to mention. Jake's starlets hadn't actually got into any films yet.

I got a rise from £20 to £30 a week after my run of bril-liant picture stories. Bennet the ediitor went on as if he'd got special permission from the Bank of England. But it was more than the Union minimum at the time, so I was pro-gressing.

One Tuesday I came back from lunch at four thirty to find there were little huddles of people all over the office and in the composing rooms, heads down, whispering, and Heather McTweedy, one of our women's staff who was forty-nine but gushing like a teenager, informed me coldly that we were closing. The rumour had started from El Vinos and was all over Fleet Street by three. Everyone had rushed back to the office, but Bennet had disappeared. The evening papers were ringing up, asking for the latest, but nobody knew anything. Our noble proprietor was skiing in Switzerland. It was late November, the time of the year when papers usually close, just in time to give everyone a jolly Christmas.

There had always been a good atmosphere in the office,

matey and jokey with no bitchiness. I suppose I should have guessed from the turnover of editors that our days were numbered. You can tell a successful paper by the longevity of its editor. But I'd believed all the Proprietor's guff about our vital role in his galaxy.

Now no one was friends. Each person went defensive and secretive. People took to making whispered phone calls in the telephone booths in the corridor. People would rush out, then come back, tense or excited, and we'd all crowd round, hoping for something, then fall back, retreating into our corners and ourselves.

New rumours came every hour. We were being taken over by The News of the World. We were being sold to Woman's Own. It was forgotten in ten minutes when another rumour came out of a hole in the ground, gyrated in the air like a whirlwind, picking up everyone in its path, then moved on to other victims. We got little comfort from the fact that we would be only the latest in a long line of Sunday papers to bite the dust – The Empire News, Sunday Graphic, Sunday Dispatch, all like us household names in their day, but when we packed up nobody would notice and the following month few could believe that such a paper had ever existed. Yet the Sunday News, so I was told, was one of the powers in the land in the 1930s. Queen Mary had loved it.

The final announcement came at six o'clock. We were all in Heather McTweedy's office. She had taken it upon herself all afternoon to be the clearing house for gossip. It was the second story on the BBC six o'clock news. Then the ITN news made it their lead item when they got the Proprietor staggering off his plane at London Airport and making fatuous comments about the tragedy of having too many brilliant eggs in his basket. It was probably the Sunday News' finest hour, getting such national attention. It reunited us all for the evening, as we adjourned to the pub and drank away our sorrows. It turned out to be quite a nice pub and it was a jolly evening. I wished I hadn't been so standoffish and gone in more often. Heather McTweedy got drunk and said she was going on the streets. After all, no one would think that such a beautiful, elegant woman's writer would ever do such a thing – a gay quip in the height of adversity. But her mascara was running, her baggy eyes were hanging down to her blotchy lips and she looked as if she'd already started. A linotype operator, who didn't know who she was, asked how much.

What really united us for that evening was the fact that we'd learned our fate, not from the proprietor or the group's editorial director or even Bennet, but from the radio. Typical, we all said. Disgusting treatment, but what can you expect from that lot? They don't care.

The next day we all trooped in again, and hung around till the proprietor condescended to confirm the news. The rumours then centred round jobs and compensations instead of take-over bids. There were several papers still left in the group, but they were mainly in the North. None of our Fleet Street stars, which everyone considered they were, would contemplate going back to the dreadful provinces. They'd had a long enough struggle to get out of them in the first place. There were endless hypothetical discussions about whether one would go to Wigan as an editor or stay in London as a copy boy. There was a London group office and several London-based magazines, some of them very good, but all with small staffs and no vacancies that anyone could find out about.

As for compensation, the betting ranged from nothing at all, to a month's salary for every year one had worked with the firm. As I'd only been there a year, all the compensation rumours mattered little to me. I said so once to Heather, which was a terrible mistake. She loathed me from then on. By inference I'd flaunted being young, which was unforgivable. At twenty-two I would obviously get a job somewhere, but at forty-nine she didn't have much hope. She started a rumour that I was the only person who was going to be offered a London job, and so everyone hated me. I cleared out my desk, throwing away all the old stories, yellow with age and stained with tea, and the copies of old expense sheets I'd kept in case the income tax people ever came back at me. I took a big wodge of copy paper, some office envelopes, a box of paper clips and an old hand towel which I'd been given when I first arrived. I felt I deserved something after giving them a year of my life. Then I went to Oxford to stay with Antonia, waiting for the call from London which would announce my fate.

She was kind and considerate, saying how awful it was, but I had to cheer up, perhaps it might be for the best. I'd sent out a few begging letters, to other papers, but I had no contacts to ring personally. I knew it would be useless, with so many better qualified journalists already looking for jobs. I thought about PR. A very smooth bloke called Rupert, whose tame Irish peer I'd once written about, rang up to say I could be one of his executives at £30 a week, the same as I was getting now. I said I'd think about it. Antonia said things weren't *that* bad. I should wait and see what the London job was they were going to offer me. It must be on one of the magazines. She was sure I'd like that.

It wasn't a call in the end but a duplicated letter which informed me that they were unable to offer me a job but I would get the magnificent compensation terms of two weeks' pay for every year of service. In my case that meant £60.

I rang Stan, the old chief sub, as he was the only real friend I had. He was surprised I hadn't been offered a job. He said no one else had been – except him. He was almost ashamed of himself and said I hadn't to tell anyone. He was going to take up a job as an assistant in the group's cuttings library. I said he was mad. With his thirty-five years' service, he could get a huge sum in compensation and then get out. He said a lump sum was no good to him. A steady job was what mattered. When I got to fifty, I would agree. I said best of luck, then. He said cheers. I never saw him again.

I'd hardly hung up the phone when Jake rang. I was ringing from the public phone booth in the Banbury Road at the end of North Parade, the nearest one to Antonia's digs. I didn't know how he'd got the phone number or knew I was in Oxford. But I didn't ask him. I was in no mood for his boastings.

'What's it feel like then, Mr. Graduate?' said Jake.

'Get lost,' I said.

'Wish I had all those GCEs and O levels and XYZ levels. If only I'd stuck in at school like you, Tommy lad. What was it you told me that time? Education was the only way to rise out of one's environment. Some pompous shit like that.'

'I'm hanging up if that's all you've rung for.'

'Hold on, got your reporter's pencil ready? I've got the names of some good soup kitchens . . .'

I hung up, waited and the phone rang again. Jake was still pissing himself laughing. He must have a good secretary to have got back again so quickly. She must still be listening.

'Sorry, me old mate. It's just so bloody funny. But I know

what it's like. I've been through it, me old sport. So anyway. Where was I? Oh yes, bring your cards and I'll give you a start. OK? I think three thou for a start. What do you think, Tommy lad?'

'What as?'

'Christ, fucking impudence. I offer this destitute bum a job and he wants to know what as. Maggie, cross him off my Christmas list. What do you think I want you to do? Lick my arse, of course. So what else are you good at?'

I put the phone down, but didn't hang up. I could faintly hear Jake laughing, then shouting for me, saying it was just a joke, for Christ's sake. It wasn't fucking charity. He *wanted* me to join him. But this would be the last time he was going to ask me.

I replaced the receiver and left the telephone box. I went down the road, into Port Meadow and walked along the river. If only the bastard had even told me what he wanted me to do. I didn't really know what *he* did. I didn't believe most of the stories he told me about himself and his property deals. I couldn't understand them either. It seemed unbelievable that such shits as Jake could make a million by property. Surely he would be found out soon. Why wasn't everyone doing it?

I had a drink and a sandwich at The Trout, then continued walking till it was dusk. Antonia had collections all day, so there was nobody to go back to Oxford for. Perhaps I'd have to borrow from Jake, when my £60 ran out. He owed me at least a dozen half dollars, from back in the old days. Not of course that I was seriously considering joining that bastard. I was a journalist after all, not a lackey. A journalist. Not a fucking lackey. And that's swearing.

Chapter Thirteen

A freelance who wants to do well has to be twice as clever and twice as productive as a staffman. I was a complete failure, whatever the reasons. I just couldn't get any conviction in my voice when I rang up diary columns with trivia about famous people. I had a rest over Christmas, naturally, as the papers were so thin. By January 1963, I was also pretty thin, with my £60 gone and no work in sight.

One day Bennet rang up, the one-time editor of the old Sunday News. He'd put his golden handshake into starting his own PR firm. It was doing jolly well, so he said. I said, of course, creeping like mad. I always knew he would do jolly well.

He'd got this new account, a big property consortium, and one of his jobs was to produce a glossy brochure about the post war property business, tracing the history and showing what nice chaps they all were, useful members of the society, who helped the homeless, never beat their wives and were always kind to animals. He'd thought of me, having gone to university and all that and being such a big friend of you know who. He knew I could probably do with the money. Sixty pounds for five thousand words. I said great. How kind.

The brochure was to be circulated to all MPs and other supposedly important people, after they'd been filled up with free lunches and free entertainments and free holidays. I said that if that didn't convince them that property people were lovely human beings, I couldn't see my puny five thousand words doing the trick. Bennet said the brochure was the intellectual part of the campaign. The campaign, I gathered later, was to try to stop the Government slapping any capital gains tax on property. They could cost the property boys millions, which was why they were desperately lashing out so much loot. Bennet got £2,000 for that brochure, the bastard.

I enjoyed doing it because I wanted to know more about the property boom anyway. The first surprising thing I found out was that the rise of Jake Sullivan wasn't at all surprising. He was just one of the many who made it, with little education, no professional training and no one to help him.

Between 1945 and 1963 at least a hundred people in Britain became property millionaires. People like Cotton and Clore passed into British folk lore. There were some, like Jake, who made the headlines for a short time. There were some who never made the headlines, keeping completely in the background. The most successful property millionaire of all was one I'd never heard of, Harry Hyams. Mr. Hyams started out on his own in 1959 and by the mid sixties had a property company worth £60,000,000. Compared with that, Jake Sullivan hardly existed.

War time bombing had knocked down so many of London's buildings, yet the Labour Government's post-war restrictions stopped new buildings going up. The 1947 Town and Country Planning Act and the various new taxes and planning regulations worked so well that speculators were discouraged from speculating. But when the Tories came in, in 1951, and began lifting all the property controls, the flood started overnight. The demand for property had been stemmed for fifteen years. Profits were suddenly immediate, enormous and easy to keep, with no capital gains tax. Jake said fuck the 1947 Act and all that crap. All he had done was realize that there was nothing to stop you making money, without having any money to start with and without doing any work. All that you needed was a telephone. Look at Jack Cotton, said Jake. At the height of his empire he was still running it almost single handed, working from his bedroom at the Dorchester Hotel. He had two single beds. One to sleep on and one where he spread out his important documents.

It all became a bit clearer, if simpler, when Jake explained things. Having no money and doing no work wasn't strictly true, but it wasn't far off it. In Jake's case, as with everyone else, it's the bank which has to have the money, to finance the scheme in the beginning. It's the builder who has to have the men to do the work and the architect who has the experts. Then at the end of it all it's some huge corporation, like an insurance company, with their millions of pounds they desperately want to invest, who take the completed building from you and hand over the cash.

This is the classical situation, though it took Jake quite a while to reach it. I kept going round to see him, long after I'd handed in my glossy five thousand words. I wanted to find out how he personally had made it in London. Purely sociological interest, of course. I still wasn't going to join him. At £60 an article, who needs charity?

At the end of 1960, during his first year in Soho, Jake was still concentrating on houses and flats. He had acquired a much larger staff than he strictly needed. It was partly show, to impress himself with how well he was doing, and partly because of the fact that he was dealing with lots of little units which need more administration than if he'd just had a few big blocks. Coming from outside, with no contacts and no knowledge of London, he'd taken on several people he needn't have done, if he'd known his way around. It was intelligent to hire the two bright young estate agents, and to give them some of the profits for work they brought into the firm, but it was a short term policy. If they were any good, they'd soon want to branch out on their own and keep *all* their profits. There was a much better way of picking the brains of estate agents which would tie them to the firm for a long time, but he didn't discover that till later.

Jake got out of old houses and into large scale property deals by chance, just as he'd got into property by chance in the first place. If he'd known the right people he could have seen how to do it a lot sooner, without having to think it out for himself. Jake was always on his own.

By 1961 Michael was on at Jake to stop spending his lunch hours in scruffy Soho caffs. Jake said he'd learned a lot from the crowd there. Michael agreed, but they were rather scruffy, shady operators. Jake was a much better quality operator than they were. Jake said fuck off, snob. He was just jealous of him spending his lunch hours with Sammy.

This hurt Michael. It wasn't true he resented Jake spending so much time with Sammy. He now rather liked Sammy and had had dinner with him several times, while Jake was working late at the office.

He simply thought that if Jake wanted to be a success, he had to progress all the time, socially, commercially and in every way. That's the way things worked.

'Don't be a fucking hypocrite,' said Jake. 'I'm gonna make a million, but I'm not going to be a fucking social climbing snob like you.'

They were in Jake's office, which meant that the whole building could hear, as the door and windows were all open, as usual. Michael had come in, casually, to ask what Jake was doing for lunch and an argument had flared up from nothing.

'No one is asking you to change,' said Michael. 'Perish the thought. You are being childishly stubborn, as usual. All I am pointing out is that you are stunting your development . . .'

'By wanking,' shouted Jake, breaking in, knowing everyone was listening. 'I've heard that since I was ten. Why don't you try it sexless? Eh? Stop looking away, you public school cunt.'

'It's *you* that's the snob. An inverted snob.'

'Don't be filthy,' said Jake, smiling and jumping up. 'Come on then, Mike, where are we going, you fink? I was coming to ask *you* what you're doing for lunch. So vat are you doing standing there, vasting my time. We could be drinking champagne cocktails with important people in the Savoy Grill. Maggie! Take your finger out and get us a cab, eh.'

They went to the Savile, which was one of Michael's clubs. The following week they went further west to the Burlington, another of Michael's clubs. This was much smaller and more olde worlde than the Savile. The chairs were full of people who looked as if they'd been asleep since the Crimean War. There was only half a dozen people in for lunch, though the dining room was enormous.

'This is my favourite,' said Michael. 'The Savile is a bit competitive. Here you can really forget the rat race.'

It was four o'clock before they realized what time it was. Jake had been very interested in having all the old pictures pointed out to him, the customs of the club explained and the history and scandals of the older members whispered to him. It wasn't till they were walking home that Jake took in the dreadful news. The club had failed in their final drive for new members under the age of thirty, which was what they desperately needed as the average age was sixty-five. The expenses of running, heating, cleaning such a huge old fashioned place, and of paying the large staff, was making it impossible to continue. They would have to close. Each member would get a little share of the proceeds, as by the constitution of the club it was owned by the members, that's if there was anything left when they paid their overdraft and other debts.

Michael was almost in tears but Jake couldn't stop laughing.

He said it was the funniest thing for years. After all Michael's boasting and perhaps making Jake a member, it was going to close as a dead loss.

'Do me a lot of good, you said,' said Jake. 'Just the place for contacts. I'll really get to know all the right people there, eh, when it's a hole in the ground.'

It was this phrase which set Jake thinking. He'd always poured scorn on the Church Commissioners for selling him that house, the one whose contract he'd re-sold at a huge profit. He'd always said they themselves could have done it, if only they'd had the right advice.

'I've decided not to be a bastard all my life,' said Jake when they got back to the office. 'I'm going to help the club to continue. I want you to arrange a meeting with the club committee. You can explain to them my plan, as you're so smooth at social climbing. You can pretend it's your idea.'

It didn't take Michael long because the club jumped at the idea. A joint company was set up, by Jake's firm and the Burlington Club in partnership, to develop the site together. What the club was contributing to this firm was the freehold of the site, which they owned. Jake was to do the rest, which was the easiest thing he'd ever done. With the security of the freehold behind them, it was almost a formality for the joint firm to get a bank to finance the construction of a giant office block. Jake even had to refuse offers of help. Several huge contractors offered to loan him all the money when he approached them about putting up the building. When he said he already had the money, thank you, and at only 1 per cent over the bank rate, they then said couldn't they buy some shares in the joint company from him? This would give him even more cash in his hand. 'Do me a favour eh, just fuck off and get on with the building, eh,' was what he told the chairman of one of the contractors when he personally rang Jake at his office.

Planning permission was easily granted. The Burlington was about the last low level, undeveloped building in that part of London at the time. The plot ratio was agreed at 4 : 1. Plot ratio, a scheme devised by Lord Holford after the war, decides the relationship between the area of the site and the gross floor area of the building to be put over it. Jake's architect was pleased that the LCC had agreed the plans and the ratio without any argument. Then Benny, one of Jake's young estate agents in the office, discovered, through his contacts, that a new building going up next to it had got a ratio of 5 : 1. Jake got rid of his architect right away. He'd done a lot for him, in converting old houses and taking away all the planning worries, but Jake had now no sympathy for him. He was obviously not clued up on large office blocks. Jake knew he was on a winner, even without being courted by the contractor, and he felt he could easily find a better architect. He did. And this one, after a lot of haggling and arguing, got the ratio up to 5.5 : 1.

The area of the building was 50,000 square feet. He got a deal of £5 a square foot from the contractor, which was a reasonable price for 1961 without skimping too much. The total cost of construction, including all fees, came to £300,000.

The offices were let even before they were finished, to a giant American corporation who were looking for prestige offices in London. They agreed on thirty shillings a square foot in rent, which meant an annual rent of £70,000. They didn't get all the building as half of the ground floor became the new accommodation for the Burlington, giving it the smartest and newest club accommodation in London, for which they paid a rent of £5,000, half of which came back to themselves as the joint owner of the whole building.

As the total rent from the building was £75,000 a year, the total *value* of the new site was now £1,000,000. The value of a property is generally assumed to be thirteen times its market rent.

The difference between the cost of the development and its final value was therefore £700,000. Half of this profit belonged to Jake. For a personal stake of only £1,000 – which was all he'd had to put up for his share of the joint firm – he'd made a profit on paper of £350,000.

Everyone was happy. The bank had made a good investment. The American firm was renting a good building, at a rent which a couple of years later seemed ludicrously cheap. The Burlington Club was delighted. They'd had a site converted from running at a loss to being worth a million pounds and bringing in an annual rent of £75,000, half of which was theirs. And they had a brand new club which proved a big attraction to new members. It had cost them nothing, except six months minor discomfiture while they'd camped with another club. They made Jake a life member.

Jake of course was pleased, though he went round saying that the thrill when he'd made his £5,000 profit on his very first deal was much better than the £350,000 he'd just made.

This £350,000 profit was genuine, though it was still on paper. It gave the best possible security for further development. Jake threw a huge champagne party when the deal was finished, for the bank executives, the chairman of the contractors and all the others who'd been involved in the deal. It was a rather vulgar party, so Michael thought. Jake had two strippers performing during the meal. All the executives thought it very amusing. It established Jake as a character.

It was at this party that the bank manager told Jake how to realize a profit on the building tax free and without giving it up. He could put him in touch with an insurance company, one of his clients. They would give him the million pounds in his hand, or at least two thirds of it anyway, as a mortgage on the building. He'd have to pay back the mortgage of course, but he could easily do that out of the rents. But he'd have the million pounds in his hand now, and still own the building.

The first deal of Jake's contained most of the elements of all office developments of the period. It had of course been a joint development with the Burlington. But after this Jake had enough of his own money, contacts and know-how to develop on his own, and keep all the profits at the end. Once he'd discovered how to use the wealth of the insurance companies, he was set.

There were many refinements on the part the insurance company played when it came to handing over the big money. Depending on the current credit squeezes or tax interpretations, the developer could sell rather than mortgage the property to the insurance company, then lease it back from them to rent out any way he liked. The main point was that the insurance company, or some other such big institution, enabled the developer to realize his capital and then move on and do it all again. The insurance companies weren't taking any risks. They rarely put down any money until the building was up and let. In the post war years they had so much money coming in they hardly knew what to do with it. In 1947 British insurance companies had invested a total of £2,500,000,000. By 1963 the total was almost £10,000,000,000. The biggest boom was in life insurance, a particular post-war phenomenon.

Life insurance meant they had long term commitments, so they needed long term investments to put their money in. Property is the best long term investment of all. Putting it in Government stock, as they often did before the war, was like giving it away.

At the other end, the Big Five banks also had a lot of money on deposit which they wanted to hive off as investments, unless the Government temporarily stopped them doing so. But unlike the insurance companies, the banks were taking some risks. They were putting up the initial bridging loans for schemes which were still a glint in the eyes of people like Jake Sullivan. But West End bank managers believed that by investing against real estate, whatever happened to the gradiose schemes, they couldn't lose. Undeveloped sites were jumping up in value every day. If they had to, the site they'd helped the developer to buy could always be sold off at a profit, whatever happened to the developer himself.

Only the developer was taking the big risks. With hindsight, it's easy to see that there were no risks, as property values kept on spiralling up. But they were still basing most of their plans on intuition. There was no certainty, for example, that when they got the buildings up, anybody would want to rent them, or that if they did rent them, rents would not have gone down in the meantime.

'Aren't you worried about the risks?' I asked Jake.

'I don't care about risks. I started with nothing and that's the worst I can end up with, so what's the worry? But there ain't no risks, buddy boy, you bet your sweet arse there ain't. I can't put the buildings up fast enough. So when are you joining?'

I'd dropped in to chat, not to beg work. We successful freelance journalists. I'd wanted to show off some of the information I'd dug out for the brochure, such as the insurance figures. Jake had let me come out with my spiel then said piss off, what a load of cock. Forget the insurance companies and all their boring investments. When you're big like I am, said Jake, everyone runs after you to give you their money. Money and success attracts money and success. That's all there is to it.

Jake made a success of his success. It suited him, always having been a know-all with no modesty or inhibitions. It really started from the moment the Burlington story leaked out among the estate agents and property contact men. Jake was immediately courted and fêted. He began to spend most of his lunch times at the Mirabelle, being treated by people wanting to get a finger in his success. He'd swear at them, twist their arms, insult them and they'd laugh with delight and plead once more for him to take their money. They'd pass on gossip about what other people were doing and which sites were coming up.

'See cunt face,' Jake told Michael as the big offers came in. 'They came to *me*. I didn't have to do any arse creeping. And if I don't like it, they can go and get fucked.'

Jake did like it. Mayfair, millionaires, company chairmen and champagne cocktails in the West End night clubs were a new experience which amused him. He also used it to his own advantage. Now that he'd given up little developments, it was useful to be in the swim, to have an ear to the ground for the big sites coming up. He'd lost his two young estate agents a long time ago, so he did what most developers did to ensure a good flow of sites. He teamed up with an estate agency, allowing them to buy up to a 10 per cent share in new developments. It was a very well established family firm from Mayfair and he took the son and heir onto his board, for a while. This was Jeremy, the bloke I'd seen having his balls pulled at that first board meeting. Even that didn't stop the firm backing Jake. Jake's profits were too huge to worry about Jeremy's testicles.

Jake then went on to sell shares to one big insurance company, up to 40 per cent, which made them even more eager to help his schemes. This meant that Jake took just over half of his ultimate profits, but it made him into a millionaire, in cash. This was when he moved into Sullivan House in Piccadilly, took a luxury penthouse apartment, decided he was now a dynamic American, and the Big Time spending began.

Part Three

Chapter Fourteen

This time the tune being played throughout the board meeting was 'Love Me Do'. Jake still had his American hair style, but was more soberly dressed in a striped blazer, a bow tie and button-down collar. 'No ball games today,' he said curtly. 'My doctor has told me that one good fuck is equal to a five mile walk. That means I walk twenty miles a day, so I don't need the exercise. You sexless fuckers can all drop dead for all I care. Right Jimmy, let's have the gen about those shares we're going to buy.'

Jimmy Black, the ex-army RSM from Glasgow, put on his horn-rimmed spectacles and took out some papers from a folder.

'The shares were last quoted on the Manchester Stock Exchange at 13s 6d each, though there have been no dealings in them for some time. There are 50,000 shares. We could probably get them all for 14s 6d each . . .'

'How much would that be, smoothie?' said Jake, turning to one of his directors.

The smooth director started to mumble the reply, but Jake didn't give him a chance to talk.

'I don't want to know. I pay people to look after such trivia. Come on Sammy,' said Jake springing his trap. 'Leave your cock alone and tell us what you think about the company.'

'A load of crap,' said Sammy, putting on his sunglasses and combing his hair. The other directors watched Sammy, loathing him, willing him to go just too far. Jake smiled to himself, waiting.

'Tell the members of the jury what exactly you mean, honey child,' said Jake. 'They haven't got the benefit of your knowledge.'

'Well, it looked after cemeteries, didn't it?' said Sammy. 'That's why it's called Seacrill Paradise Estates or some such shit. They sold all the plots off forty years ago and have done bugger all since. I can't see why you're bothering, personally, if you ask me.'

'We are asking you, Sammy baby,' said Jake.

'Well they bought a few crummy mills as well, didn't they. But they're all derelict, aren't they, like everything else up there.'

'Yes,' said Jake, smiling. 'It is now a derelict company, but it did some smart property moves in its day, folks. It bought up waste ground all over Lancashire just before the First World War, then when all the millions of bodies were brought home, it carved up the land into thousands of little plots for the poor dead soldiers. Wasn't that just hunky dory.

'But it didn't completely sell off the plots, as our friend Sammy has told us. It charged a ground rent on each of £1 a year as upkeep, which was rather silly. They never put the price up, so they've been up-keeping the plots at a huge loss.'

'I told you it was a lot of crap,' said Sammy butting in and showing off.

'One could say that,' said Jake. 'They've run up tax losses of around £100,000 so far.'

'Diabolical,' said Sammy.

'But they have still got a little bit of money left, haven't they Sammy?'

'I couldn't find none,' said Sammy.

'What about the Somme Trust?'

'I thought that was for the kids' school fees.'

'There are no kids, Sammy child, just a couple of sexygen- arians who now look after the company. Once the Somme Trust is empty, they'll have nothing left. It's got £20,000 in at the moment. Why do you think it's called the Somme, Sammy?'

'Because that's where they put their big sum when they sold the plots.'

'The Battle of the Somme, sweetie pie. The summer of 1916, remember? The British Army suffered half a million casualties.'

'You're quite right, Mr. Sullivan, quite right,' said Jimmy. 'It was a terrible day for the British Army, terrible.'

'Thank you Jimmy. If I want to give you permission to breathe, then I will. Otherwise, shuttup, eh? And I wasn't quite right either. The exact figure, for those dead, wounded, miss- ing or taken prisoner, was 498,054. Maggie, I want that exact figure in the minutes. OK?'

'It does all seem a bit pointless, Jake,' said Michael, breaking in to try and bring the subject to a close. 'I thought we were going to discuss going public? That's what it says on my agenda.'

'Precisely. As I was saying, before I was rudely interrupted, the Seacrill Paradise Estates Company, to give it its full title, has assets of £20,000 in cash, a couple of empty cotton mills and tax losses of £100,000. It's a natural. Jimmy, buy up all the shares today. We should get it for £40,000.'

'Yes sir,' said Jimmy.

'Next time anyone asks you to do something, you do it, Sammy boy. Yes, I'm talking to YOU! You useless twat!' Jake paused and stopped smiling, suddenly lunging across the table at Sammy. Sammy just managed to escape Jake's ball-grabbing hands. He stood in the corner, watching the door and Jake at the same time, ready for a proper escape. Jake laughed loudly, pretending he'd just meant to frighten Sammy, not actually grab him.

'Right,' said Jake, sitting back in his seat and looking round. His gaze fell on Jimmy. 'You've bought those shares, have you?'

'No sir,' said Jimmy. 'Not yet sir. I'm waiting for the meeting to . . .'

'Christ, when I tell you to do something, I mean *now*. Fucking hell, I don't pay you to sit around like a spare prick at a wedding.'

'Sorry, sir,' said Jimmy, getting up.

'This cunt is now fired,' said Jake, nodding towards Sammy on the floor. 'He's done it once too often. My new personal assistant from now is Tom Graham. That's the third form swot sitting over there with the big ears. He'll get three thou a year, with another thou in exes. OK, or do I have to write it down in words of one syllable?'

'No sir. I understand sir.'

'Right, you can all go now, except Michael. I want to talk to him.'

Everyone rushed out. I followed slowly. I wanted to tell Jake to his face that I'd already changed my mind, even before I'd started, but he'd gone into his private suite followed by Michael. I knew he was playing at being a tyrant, showing off, but it was still revolting.

I was met in the corridor by Maggie as controlled and quietly efficient as ever.

'God, isn't it warm?' said Maggie. 'He always has the heating on far too high. I'd love to go skiing now, wouldn't you?'

'I can't ski,' I said, as she led the way into Jake's private lift.

'You can't? Good God, in that neat suit and clean white shirt I thought straight away, there's a guy who can ski, on snow or water. Well, there you go. And here we are.'

We'd arrived in a basement, not the ground floor. She stepped out and I could see it was a private garage. A chauffeur was polishing Jake's white Rolls.

'I'll show you to your car,' said Maggie.

'I haven't got one,' I said.

'Of course you have, silly boy.'

She led me to a brand new Mini Cooper and gave me some keys. I got in the car slowly, and found there were keys already in. I shouted after Maggie.

'Those are the keys to the flat,' she shouted, pointing to the ones in my hand. 'Good God, didn't he tell you about that either? The number's on it. It's in South Street, just round the corner from his place. You lucky feller. OK got it all straight now? Mind how you go.'

I got to the flat and found that my things were already being moved in from my Kilburn pad. Jake was really taking care of everything. He'd said he'd tell me at the board meeting what I was going to do. Now that he had done I wasn't sure I fancied following Sammy as his licensed smart alec. The phone rang and it was Jake.

'Everything OK? Ashtrays aren't full are they? Beds soft enough? Just ask if you want anything, nice girl, nice boy, filthy pictures?'

'No thanks, I'm trying to give them up.'

'I forgot you're a fucking prig. But we'll soon change that. Anyway, I've done my bit. Now it's your turn.'

'You mean as your personal assistant?'

'Not fucking personal assistant. I just said that. No, I've created a brand new appointment for you, the first one ever. If you make a success of it, you could be the founder of a new profession. You could be as important as the first prostitute or the first astronaut.'

'Come on then, what is it?'

'You are my Surprises Assistant. All you have to do is organize surprises for me.'

'What sort?'

'Christ, if they're going to be a surprise, how the fuck do I know what they're going to be? That's your problem, sonny boy.'

'Thanks.'

'You'll have an office. You spend what you like, do what you like, go where you like, as long as you come up with a surprise.'

'What if you don't feel like a surprise?'

'If it's a good enough surprise, mate, of course I'll go for it. There will be two sorts of surprises. The ones you organize and present without me asking. Those will be Surprise Surprises. Then there will be the ones I'll ask for when I've suddenly got a spare hour, or two hours, or a day or a weekend, or whenever I'm bored or fed up. I'll say I feel like a surprise and you'll say let's go. Those will be Request Surprises. OK? I don't want to make *any* decisions. I make fucking decisions all day long. I'll be completely in your hands.'

'But I don't know what sort of things you like.'

'Christ, you grew up with me, didn't you?'

'But I don't know about you *now*.'

'Then stick around, find out.'

'I'll be useless.'

'Then I'll fire you. Simple. That'll be *your* surprise. See you.'

Jake rang off. I couldn't decide if the idea had come into his head that minute and he was trying it out for size by saying it out loud, or if it was a genuine job which he'd thought about for a long time.

That evening Jake took me for dinner at the Mirabelle, his main haunt at the time. He sent the soup back, it wasn't thick enough, he refused the bread, it wasn't warm, he asked for HP sauce, he felt like a sauce sandwich. They hadn't got any. Jake got up and stormed out, throwing fivers all over the place. We went instead to a club near St. James's. He took me up an alley I hadn't noticed before and came to a boarded-up doorway. Jake knocked on it three times, a panel was opened and an eye inspected him, saw it was Jake, and the door was immediately opened.

Inside was all red brocade and satins and gilt, with mirrors on the walls and ceiling reflecting everything like a surrealistic nightmare.

'It's bloody, this place,' said Jake loudly, as a young boy in a striped T-shirt hovered round him. 'We'll have two of your awful steaks. Have those lot eaten?'

Jake nodded his head towards the bar, where two girls were twittering together on high stools drinking orange juice. The boy nodded that they had and started to go over towards them.

'Leave them just now. I don't want them sitting watching me if they're not eating. Put me down for both of them for eleven o'clock, OK? Tell them not to get pissed.'

'Yes sir. Medium done or rare?'

'Are you talking about their fannies or the steaks?'

'The steaks sir,' said the boy.

'Your after-shave is making me feel sick.'

'Sorry sir,' he said. He went off with the order, waggling his bottom inside his too-tight black trousers.

'What's this place?' I said to Jake. 'A brothel?'

'Do you mind, that's against the law. You fucking graduates want everything. Ask Felix what it is, he owns the dump.'

Jake shouted to Felix. A man with a little pointed beard looked round from behind the bar and waved, then disappeared again. I could see through an opening that he was sitting at a switch board.

'I don't know why I come here. What a place,' said Jake, pouring whisky into himself.

I don't know whether it was the drink or the surroundings, but he was becoming more and more irritated and depressed. He was shrugging his shoulders and banging his arms and legs, but not belligerently as he usually did. It was more like petulance. I'd never seen him like this before.

'Why have we come here then?' I asked, regretting saying so, but knowing that I was being pushed into such a question. He wanted me to ask it, so he could jump on me, but really jump on himself.

'Christ, where do you want to go then?' he asked furiously.

I didn't reply. I was a sounding board. He was talking to himself and I needn't have been there. The waiter brought the steak and he cheered up a bit as he said how awful it looked, as lousy as everything else in this place. Having something to react against seemed to take him out of himself. I suppose if you have all the money you want and can do what you like you feel furious when you're not enjoying yourself. I knew that what I should be doing was laughing at him, mocking his ridiculous, petty mood and getting him out of it. Thinking on these lines made me realize I'd already begun to fall into being his assistant.

He looked older than me, which surprised me. I suddenly had a desire to wrestle with him, the way we'd done as lads, when we'd start pummelling each other for no reason, then just as suddenly stop.

He'd stopped banging and was looking at me. I wanted to ask what he was thinking about. Instead I found myself saying that I thought the place was quite nice, the steak was lovely, how was his? The moment was gone. I was back to ineffectual chat and he was back to his loud mouthed self, and his farcical gimmicks. I expected him to press a button and all the background, including us, would disappear and it would turn out that he was just showing a film of us. I must have been drinking quite a bit of whisky.

'Where the fuck's Felix?' Jake shouted. 'I'll have him by the balls when he comes, if he has any.'

Felix did at last appear, all smarm and charm. Jake repeated my question about the brothel to him, despite my protests and assurances that it had been a joke. Felix did huge double takes, pretending to be angry and affronted. Good gracious. If I wasn't Mr. Sullivan's friend, then, good gracious, he didn't know what he'd do.

'What a *shan*,' I said to Jake. 'You needn't have done that.'

'I haven't heard that word for a long time,' said Jake. 'I bet Felix hasn't either. You wouldn't think he came from Penrith, would you?'

'He doesn't look it,' I said.

'He went to the Royal College of Art and now he's got the biggest call-girl racket in London.'

'Well, it follows, doesn't it?' I said. We were now half through a bottle of Nuits St. Georges which Jake had ordered, deliberately mispronouncing it in a way which showed he knew quite well how to pronounce it.

'Did you ever write about him in your lousy gossip column? He did drawings of all the young starlets and famous peers, until he found he made more money by bringing them together in his studio and letting them get on with it.'

Felix was busy back at the switchboard. I asked what he was doing.

'You pay a subscription of £100 a year and when you ring up he provides a girl, or a boy. You have to take what you get if you ring in. If you come here, you can at least have a look at the goods.'

'That seems a lot, £100,' I said.

'That's just the membership, mate. You pay for what you have as well. It comes in as a monthly bill. I put it down as entertainment, like a restaurant bill. Which it is anyway, scampi, steak and a couple of fucks. You can have anything, if you have the money. That's the trouble.'

Jake ordered another bottle of wine. He'd drunk most of the first one.

'Sounds a smashing idea to me,' I said.

'It is, for a fat old millionaire who can only get it by paying for it. I think it should be stopped.'

'Why do you come here?'

'Because it's here. Have some more wine and shut up, you bloody virgin.'

It was just after eleven when we finished. Jake shouted for the two girls who rushed across, gave us each a big kiss and linked our arms. Felix led us to the door, wishing us a good night and telling Jake not to do anything he wouldn't do.

At Park Lane Jones the butler was waiting, ready to usher us in, asking Jake if he felt like anything to eat. He had some chips he could make him. Jake said no, just give the girls some gin.

'The thing is,' said Jake, as we sat down in his drawing room, leaving the girls to wander round, examining the lush furniture. 'I don't seem to be able to pick them up in the streets any more. I went in the tube the other night. I haven't done that for fucking years. I followed this blonde girl, but she told me to get lost. Then I went to Battersea fun fair. I was always a cast at fairs, picking them up like that. Just my type. But I can't get them any more. I like them earthy and filthy, not all antiseptic like these two snotty whores.'

'You probably look too smooth now for girls on fair

grounds,' I said. 'And you probably don't spend long enough chasing them. You're too impatient these days.'

'Don't stand around admiring yourself all night girls,' shouted Jake. 'Get stripped off. I might need you any minute. Jones, some more whisky.'

'Don't you wish you were poor again?' I asked.

'Don't be mad. It's fucking great. It's just that there's no surprise in sex any more. You know you're going to get it, and what it's going to be like, so it's no fun. If only I was kinky, that would be OK. I could dress up in a different suit of rubber each night and have a ball.'

The two girls were now in their underclothes, tittering and trying to hide themselves as if they were modest and retiring.

'Which one do you fancy?' said Jake. 'You can have the choice, as you're the guest. And a virgin. Hear that girls? Treat him gently, eh? You don't want to put him off it for life. Don't worry, I won't tell Antonia.'

'I don't care,' I said, lying. 'Tell who you like.' It all seemed so farcical and unreal.

Jake got up and went across to a book shelf and brought me a copy of Catcher in the Rye. He asked if I'd read it. I said yes, years and years ago. He thumped me but not hard.

'It's great. I didn't know they wrote books like this these days. I want you to get me some more good books like this. I just don't know about them, or films.

'That's all I want really, a few nice surprises. Nothing big, nothing showy like all the toys I've already got. Houses, cars, girls, meals, booze, they're all just toys. I don't get any real surprises these days. I was thinking in bed the other night, lying with one of these twats there, that it was *all* surprises as a kid. Just new daft things, you'd suddenly hit on. You don't seem to get them as a grown up.'

'You're grown up are you?' I said.

'If you're gonna be fucking funny, you can fuck off.'

'Sorry, sir,' I said.

'I don't want much, just a few nice things now and again.'

'But don't you remember as a kid how rotten it could be? You'd discovered something like a new game, then when you went back the next night and tried to recreate it, it was never the same again?'

'Yeah, that's true. Heh, you two sexless cunts. Cover your

fannies up. You can go now. I've gone off of you. Tell Felix to send the bill.'

They both jumped up, acting affronted. I was very disappointed. I'd fancied them, rather than adolescent chat with Jake. I said I was going home as well. I was tired. Jake said if that was how I felt, then go, he didn't care. I could tell he wanted me to stay, but I really was tired. My usual bed time is ten o'clock, half past ten on big nights like New Year's Eve. It was now well after midnight.

Back at the flat I managed to keep awake long enough to make some notes. Under the heading of Surprises, I ruled several columns. I put Sex at the top of one column, then crossed it out. Jake could definitely not be surprised by anything in the sex line. I made two other headings – Educational and Artistic. Then I sub-divided them into Half Hour Surprises, Hour Surprises, Two Hours, Half Day. That was about all I could manage before I fell into bed. I must just have dropped off when Jake rang.

'Wake up, sexless,' he said. 'You missed yourself. I brought them back the minute you left and had both of them with me Ovaltine.'

'Just as well I left,' I said. 'I prefer hot chocolate.'

'I was trying you on this evening.'

'For size. Well try this one,' I said, sighing. 'Aaahh ...'

'Keep your lousy eyes open another minute. I've just discovered something awful.'

'It wasn't Ovaltine?'

'Shuttup, eh. I make the jokes. You laugh. I've just discovered something about me.'

'I might have guessed.'

'The toys are great. I'm enjoying them, really. It's great having a fuck when you feel like it, buying clothes, houses and all that stuff.'

'If you're keeping me awake just to tell me all this, I can get it in Reader's Digest ...'

'But you know what? I like work best. Honest, I'm happiest working. Don't tell anybody, will you? I'm disappointed by myself. It's fucking depressing, that's what it is. Goodnight.'

My office was a cubby hole at the end of Jake's corridor. I didn't have my own secretary but I could use any of Jake's, when they weren't busy. Apart from Maggie, he had three, all middle-aged and frumpish who sat like harridans guarding the entrance to his suite. I was just inside his domain, but not part of it, as the harridans made clear by giving me the chipped Woolworths cups at coffee time instead of the Willow Pattern bone china.

They seemed impervious to the fact that the boss they were guarding was a jumped-up yob, a loud-mouthed lout. They went on as if they had Prince Philip inside, hushing visitors, worrying if there was too much sugar in his tea, discussing how he looked, and always referring to him as Mr. Sullivan. He would burst out when he was bored, fart loudly and walk round making obscene comments, asking Miss Moon, who had close-cropped hair and was the most frumpish looking of all his secretaries, if she was getting enough. They'd all smile and go about their business. Jake hadn't changed. But his success had made others throw a mantle over him. Not of respectability. No one could pretend Jake had that. But an aura of cleverness and power. It said on the headed notepaper that Jake was managing director, so obviously he must be different and cleverer than they. He knew best, was always right and could do what he liked.

His farting, well, that was just one of his little foibles. His shouting and throwing things and banging on the walls, well, at least you knew where you were with Mr. Sullivan. His inquiries about your sex life? Well, some bosses weren't interested in you at all. His tales about his own sex life. They were just Mr. Sullivan's little jokes. You got used to them.

It was now the spring of 1963 and I hadn't done a stroke for months. Jake seemed to have forgotten about me. I knew he was very busy, mainly with Seacrill Paradise company. He was also involved in a couple of take-over bids. He'd just started them. They drove everyone else mad because he'd never tell them what he was up to.

I spent several weeks reading guide books, studying maps

and making long lists which I pinned up on the walls to make myself look busy. I got them all up and it struck me that I was turning myself into a junior Willie Sullivan. I took them all down again.

I rang Antonia lots of times, but she got involved in some boring play and spent most of her time in the arms of some chinless wonder from Christ Church who was supposed to be the new Albert Finney, coming from Christ Church, I ask you. She didn't say she was in his arms of course. She just said I shouldn't spend so much time on phone calls at the firm's expense. It was immoral. Anyway, she must rush for a rehearsal.

At nine o'clock one morning Jake must have remembered me because he called me into his office. I thought it was a joke at first. All I could see were rows of flashing lights. Some were high on tripods and some were on the floor, all in different colours and different intensities, flashing and buzzing like the Big Dipper. He had another set on his desk inside a black box. These were smaller and more discreet and seemed to be going off and on in sequence, humming gently like some scientific instrument. I knew better than to remark on them. I looked around for Jake. He was standing at one window making obscene signals, bending his arm up and down, nodding his head then giving the V sign.

'I thought about getting you to follow Doris home one evening,' said Jake. 'But I think I'll keep her a mystery. Quick, look at that. What a pair. She always sticks them out at nine fifteen, just as she starts work. When I see those tits coming round the curtains again I know it's eleven o'clock and time for tea.'

I looked out of his window. A perfectly ordinary secretary of about forty, admittedly with a huge bust, was waving from an office block opposite. Jake waved back and gave a few more complicated waves.

'She understands everything I signal,' said Jake. 'It's taken almost a year, but now she's almost human. She says she had it last night, but it wasn't much good. He went to sleep so quickly. I wonder how big it was. I've forgotten to ask that.'

Jake started gesturing with his hands, like a fisherman describing the fish that got away. The woman smiled and made saucy faces at him, then turned away.

'She thinks I'm the office boy,' said Jake.

'Aren't you?'

'No, here's the office boy.'

Jimmy Black came in as Jake spoke and said yes sir, was there something sir. Jake produced from a drawer an office memo, written by Jimmy to the firm's accountant, about the Paradise deal. He shoved it into Jimmy's face.

'I told you it was a fucking secret,' said Jake. 'On no account must the name of the firm be written down or mentioned to anyone until everything has been settled, and not even then. Understand?'

'Yes sir. Sorry sir.'

'And don't call me sir.'

'No sir.'

Jimmy was watching the lights and looking very worried. I sat at the back of the office beside the bar. It was a nice bar, long and low and made of pinewood, not like the vulgar one in his flat. Michael had forced Jake to get a decent interior decorator for his office. There was a very low table, also made of pinewood, covered with magazines. I reached out to get one. I knew Jake wanted me to stay, to embarrass me as well. I decided to pretend to read. I picked up a magazine. It was Titbits. Beside it was Reveille, Weekend, and other magazines with half-naked pin-up girls on the front. There was also a pile of American horror comics. Michael had the same low table in his office. On it he always had the Statist, the Economist and the Times Literary Supplement.

Jimmy realized I was there and jumped slightly. Then he turned back to worrying about the lights.

'Go on, fuck off,' said Jake. 'Or I'll set the lights on you.'

The phone rang, the internal one, and Maggie said the Daily Sketch wanted him. Jake said he'd take it. He pressed another switch, put down the phone and the reporter's voice filled the room, coming through a loudspeaker on the desk in front of Jake. The reporter said very breezily congratulations, it was great news. He was speaking quickly in the hope that Jake would go along with him and be talked into a confirmation before he realized. I smiled at the lameness of the attempt.

'What news?' said Jake.

'Oh now, Jake, *you* know what I mean,' said the reporter. He was one of those who call everyone by their Christian name, especially if they are in show business or known to be jokey,

It would just take the Queen to make half a joke and he'd be calling her Liz.

'I don't know what you mean,' said Jake. He looked worried for a minute. I began to think there was a bit of news I'd missed, stuck in my cubby hole, writing out lists.

'Come off it Jake. It's all over Fleet Street,' said the reporter, a bit less breezily now. 'Everyone knows. You might as well give us a quote now and you won't be bothered again, I promise.'

'The only thing that's all over Fleet Street is shit, which is what you're talking now. I'll give you thirty seconds.'

The reporter knew he had a slight whip hand until he revealed the question. Jake would be wanting to know what it was, but if he pushed it too far, he'd be cut off.

'It's about you and your lovely wife to be,' said the reporter. Jake began smiling immediately, obviously relieved. 'She's a lovely girl, Yolande.'

'You what?' said Jake. 'You're raving. I'd rather marry you than marry her.'

'Oh darling,' said the reporter. Jake looked at me and groaned loudly.

'Got a right fucking comedian here,' said Jake. The reporter pulled himself together with a cough, as if he was the top of the bill at the Palladium and had just finished his brilliant act.

'Well, you and her have been seen around the nighteries,' said the reporter. 'And she did have a ring on her finger.'

'You mean some one had his fingers on her ring,' said Jake. The reporter broke into loud dirty laughter.

'Sorry old boy, I had to give you a buzz. We had this idiot ringing in with a tip-off. I didn't believe it personally for a second.' He gave a creepy laugh, apologetically. 'By the bye, if you did decide to pop the jolly old question, you would let us know first, wouldn't you? We've always given you a good show.'

'Like fuck,' said Jake.

'Anyway, many apologies old boy. You know how it is.'

'I *do* know how it is. I fucking do. But you don't. That's why I'm here and you're there. Now fuck off.'

Jake switched the phone off with a crash, then called Maggie. He gave her the names of his executives he wanted to speak to, one by one. He told each in turn that on no account must anyone hear about Paradise. He'd called for Michael, but he couldn't get him. He tried again but his secretary said he was out at a meeting. 'You mean he's not fucking in yet,' said Jake.

I hoped Michael wasn't ill. I was going to his place in the evening. He'd said I could bring Antonia, but I hadn't managed to contact her yet, with her stupid rehearsals.

Jake stormed out of his office, beckoning me to follow. There was a young smooth bloke in Maggie's office, sitting on the side of her desk, flicking through her files. Maggie was typing and ignoring him.

'Out, fish face,' said Jake, grabbing him by the arm and twisting it. 'If I bloody catch you in here again, you've had it.'

'But Jake, Oh, stop it. I've got this brilliant scheme to tell you . . .'

'Well go and write it down, if you can, you illiterate slob.'

Jake let go his arm then aimed a kick at him as he pushed him towards the door. In the next office, where his other secretaries were sitting, there were two other people, also waiting to try and catch Jake. They were both standing with typed memos in their hand, reading them through for the tenth time, trying hard to look busy and important. The minute they heard Jake's door open they were ready to pounce. Jake ignored them, pushing past the jungle of rubber plants and cactus and geraniums which the three old dears surrounded themselves with. Maggie's office was completely stark and clinical by comparison.

'Someone's gonna get lost in this foliage one day,' said Jake. They giggled, except Miss Moon, the one with the Eton crop, who went on typing. 'Looking at these phallic cactuses all day must give you a big thrill, girls. But no more, eh? Miss Moon, if you can keep your sexy fingers still for a minute, I want you to stop Smithson coming through and trying to pester me. OK? I'm relying on you. Next time he comes past, just put your hand out and grab him.'

The two others who were waiting for Jake were now closing in behind him edging for position. They smiled smarmingly as Jake told Miss Moon what to do with Smithson, then Jake suddenly leaned backwards and pretended to grab one of them, showing Miss Moon exactly what he meant. Jake went out and into the corridor, banging into yet another bloke who was hovering outside. He'd only ventured as far as base one, still wondering whether to brave the gauntlet of Miss Moon, then Maggie, then perhaps attempt a final assault on the man himself.

'Oh, oh, Mr. Sullivan. Could you spare me a minute sir, I've got . . .'

'See Michael Stein. I'm busy.'

'He's not in, sir,' said the bloke, smirking.

'Then see anybody. I'm busy.'

Jake went round the corridors, scattering people and barging into rooms marked private, shouting over partitions and going into the ladies' lavatories and combing his hair.

It didn't take long to go round his loving flock. Although the building was Sullivan House, he only had the two top floors. The rest were let, some floors to the estate agency and the insurance company who had shares in his various enterprises.

'Tom!' he shouted for me. 'Come and meet Phyllis, the sexiest girl in the building.'

Jake was lying prostrate across a desk with his face up against the face of a very tall aloof girl. Their eyes were almost touching as Jake tried to outstare her. She was going boss eyed trying to look away and pretend he wasn't there.

'She went to Roedean, you know, Tom. Show him your roads, Phyllis, there's a jolly hockey stick. They're all lesbians at these girls' schools you know. Your job from now on, Tom, is to come in first thing and try to get her on heat. Like this, see. She loves it.'

Jake was holding a yellow marking pencil under her chin, tickling her.

'Do you like butter Phyllis? Butter than anything else?'

Phyllis got to her feet giggling.

'She's a good lass,' said Jake, getting up and slapping her affectionately across the bottom. 'That lovely arse has ridden more ponies than you've had hot dinners.'

The other girls in the room were looking at me. They'd seen Jake go through this routine many times, but I was a new face. I hovered in the doorway, giving a twisted smile, trying to catch their eyes to let them see that I thought Jake was as awful as they must do. But they didn't seem to think so. A bossy looking little old woman of about fifty-five was bustling across the room to Jake, all smiles and bare teeth at seeing him.

'No! No!' shouted Jake. 'Hold on to your pants lads, here she comes! Sexy Sarah!'

Jake was backing to the door, making a great show of holding on to his trousers. 'Watch it, Tom. She'll have them off you. She makes Speedy Gonzales look like a bloody snail. Sorry darling, I must rush. I've got three of them in my office, lying down waiting for me. I'll come back and service you later, OK? Stay bright.'

Jake went back up the corridors singing loudly 'We are the night shite shifters, we shift shite by night.'

A typical morning for Squire Sullivan, who makes it a rule every morning to inspect his estates personally and exchange pleasantries with his serfs.

In his office, Jake picked up a red telephone and dialled a number. He turned on the loudspeaker so I could hear his conversation. It was a bank and he asked for the manager as if he owned it. As he waited, he picked his nose, rolled the contents between his fingers like tobacco and then flicked it across the room.

'Fucking filthy place, London,' he said abstractedly. 'I love it. I never got nowt when I picked my nose in Thwaite. The atmosphere was too clean.'

'Sorry, Mr. Sullivan, I missed the beginning of that,' said a posh but rather nervous voice.

'Oh you're there are you,' said Jake, picking up a letter and reading it. 'You've got your hand out of the cashier's knickers. I've got your lousy letter here. What do you mean by it, eh? After all the business I've given you.'

'But Mr. Sullivan, there's a squeeze on.'

'I don't want to know about your bloody sex life.'

'Ha ha ha,' said the manager.

'Is this refusal final, or is it just a try-on before you put the bloody interest up? I know you banks. Biggest crooks in London.'

'I am afraid it is final, Mr. Sullivan. I'm very sorry. But I'm sure next month when the new trade figures are out the Government will allow us once again to . . .'

'Stop twittering on like an old woman. Just tell me one

thing, eh. Is it your own stupid decision or did you put it up to head office?'

'I've told you Mr. Sullivan. There's nothing would give us greater pleasure than to help you, but it's not our decision. We've been told by the Government to limit loans until . . .'

'Christ, there you go again. I ask a simple question and you give me a bloody lecture. Listen, mate. If this is just your decision then I'm getting on to the chief general manager straight away. Understand? And if it's already been to him, then I'm transferring my account to another bank tomorrow. Right, now pick the bloody bones out of that.'

There was a silence from the other end. The manager could be heard moving some papers. He fidgeted with them, coughed and pressed a buzzer on his desk.

'Leave it with me, Mr. Sullivan. Could you ring me this time tomorrow morning?'

'Like hell. *You* ring me, OK?'

'As you will, Mr. Sullivan . . .'

Jake turned to me and said these banks were all the same. They went on as if it were their own personal money. I began to ask him if he remembered the first bank manager he ever talked to, but he was busy getting ready for a fart. I could tell this because he was half raising his right buttock to let it out. He put his hand down inside his pants to capture some of the odour.

'Smashing smell,' he said.

He dialled another number and spoke to another bank manager. This time he was all soft and wheedling, asking about the manager's health, his kids, his grandchildren. He retired in two years, didn't he? Well, he was still keeping that director-ship lovely and warm. Just between the two of them, of course. No one else would ever know. Yes, he was working on a new scheme. He'd let him know the details as soon as possible and how much he'd want, tomorrow probably.

He rang his architect and screamed when he heard some plot ratio was only 4:5. 'Try them on Schedule Three. Christ, what? You never thought of that? Have I got to do everything myself? That clause is so bloody wide open I could drive the Royal Scot through it, never mind a bloody coach and horses.'

He made an internal call to Smithson. 'Get off your arse and stop moaning. I want you to get me the list of directors of all the companies belonging to Provincial Centres. What? They won't give them to you? Of course they won't. Get yourself round to Companies House this bloody minute before I have to kick you there. I also want the balance sheets, the shareholders and the register of charges. OK? Christ on a crutch. What a fucking staff I've got.'

Jake spent about an hour on the phone altogether, taking more calls and making decisions, giving agreements or telling people to get stuffed. I read four Reveilles, two Titbits and something called Nudie News. He dictated more instructions, plans, memos and answered five letters into a dictaphone, then called for Maggie to come in.

Maggie came in, smiled at me and sat down in front of Jake without looking at him. She put her pencil and pad on her lap, folded her hands in a cathedral and leaned on them, looking out of the window, her chin up in the air. I'd always liked the look of Maggie. I liked them clever, but I knew what happened to people who got mixed up in the pay roll.

'You getting enough then?' said Jake.

'So so,' said Maggie, looking over his shoulder at me, smiling slightly. She knew so much about Jake yet he would never know anything about her.

'Right then, keep taking the pills,' said Jake, half-heartedly.

Jake got his papers together, put them in a pile in front of him and looked at his watch.

'Right, in half an hour I'm going for a one hour surprise with Tommy here, so stop fucking around, eh darling. You can take your knickers down now.'

Jake went straight into a long series of complicated instructions which Maggie took down without moving or looking at him and without having to ask any questions. I moved to get out but he said sit down. I thought desperately of all the one hour surprises I'd got planned, and they all seemed obvious and corny. I'd spent most of the time so far filling up my Surprises list under the heading Places. I'd only just moved on to having two other headings – People and Situations. I'd been going round the office, trying to chat up the people, to find out what they knew about Jake which I didn't.

I found out he knew nothing about London, apart from the night clubs and restaurants, so that was easy enough. I felt there were many places and situations which I could surprise him with. But I hadn't discovered much about the people he knew. I found out a little about Michael, such as that he was a secret poet and had once had a poem in Transatlantic Review, hence Jake's continual joke about it. And that Maggie was on the huge salary of £40 a week, which explained why she took Jake and his language. That was about all.

'Right, that's it, knickers on, chastity belt locked, and don't let that wog take you in with tales about the size of his prowess. Tom, let's go.'

The sun had come out, the first bit of spring-like spring, so I got a taxi and said Lincoln's Inn Fields. I felt safe about this as I'd done it so many times myself during my lunch hours from the Sunday News. We listened to an orator on a soap box on the corner shouting that the Bible was pornographic and should be banned. Jake shouted 'Fuck the Pope' and there was a big cheer from the middle-aged clerks who were standing around in their 1940s-length raincoats. We cut diagonally across the square, through the trees and I told Jake to shut his eyes and open his mouth. I bought two ice cream cornets and shoved one in.

We elbowed our way through the crowds and round the wire netting surrounding the tennis courts and netball pitch. Once Jake caught sight of the girls playing netball, all sweaty and sinuous, with their breasts swinging from side to side, he wouldn't move. He looked along the line of clerks, all with their mouths open, their eyes against the wire and their hands deep in their raincoat pockets. He said he couldn't decide which was more fascinating, the butches wetting themselves by pushing into each other or the blokes pushing their hard-ons up against the fence.

I'd allowed five minutes for walking round the fence, but I couldn't make Jake move. He was spoiling everything. It was like taking a dog for a walk who suddenly smells a bitch on heat.

'Come on Jake, I'm in charge, remember? You do what I say.'

'Oh, all right, Mam, but you are mingy.'

I hurried round the square and into a house. Jake said what was it, a private knocking shop. I said no, it was the Sir John Soane museum. Jake was amazed when we got inside and saw all the statues, furniture and paintings jammed together in such a small house. I had to explain the Rake's Progress to him twice. He thought it was marvellous. That would have been him, he said. He was turning over the folding paintings, slamming them against the wall so fiercely that I was scared he'd break them and we'd be chucked out.

'So what, I'll buy them another bloody lot. Don't be so bossy.'

'You can't. And anyway, this is a surprise. You don't do that sort of thing on Surprises.'

We went out and into the Inns of Court. Jake said all the barristers looked like actors dressed up. I said they were. He wanted to smash their faces in, they looked so smug. I said not on a Surprise. I showed him the vaulted arches where they'd recently shot some scenes for Tom Jones. He said what's Tom Jones.

We had a salt beef sandwich and a glass of lemon tea in a nosh bar in Chancery Lane. He hadn't had that sort of lunch since he'd left Soho. He said he was giving up the Mirabelle from then on. Three hour expense-account lunches were a waste of time. The thing about Jake was that he was an enthusiast. His enthusiasm was soon replaced and forgotten by the next enthusiasm, but at least when he said something, he meant it.

I'd intended to go into the silver vaults or to cut across Holborn to Grays Inn, but he'd ruined things by hanging around those girls. It was a mad dash to get a taxi, but I got him back, just on the stroke of two. I felt it had been ruined. He said it had been smashing. He'd have another surprise this evening. He'd cancel fucking Yolande. I could take him somewhere else. Having sat around for weeks doing nothing, I was now having the pleasure of a whole day in the life of Squire Sullivan.

'Now go and get fucked, I've got some meetings.'

The house was in the mews behind Marylebone High Street. It looked a dismal alleyway at first, just the back ends of houses and the fronts of large garages. Jake asked if we were slumming.

As I got nearer I could see that each door was painted like a work of art and covered with shiny brass sanctuary knockers. There were bits of tame vine being desperately encouraged to try hard and curl round the door. Even the smallest little window had a primrose yellow window box outside. Primrose yellow was very 1963.

The house we were looking for wasn't hard to find as it had a huge blue French number plate outside. They'd probably chosen it to be able to put up the nicest foreign looking number. The letter box was about three feet long and took up most of the bright purple door. It was big enough to have bodies posted through. I couldn't find anything so vulgar as a front door bell to press. I tried the sanctuary knocker but it had been glued down. Amongst the vine I found some Portuguese cow bells which were obviously for ringing, gaily, so I did.

Jake was going up and down the mews, leaving big sweaty fingers prints everywhere as he examined door knockers and chipped at the paint to see how good it was. 'I should have done this with our house in Thwaite. I could have got an extra thousand just with a purple door. "Charming bijou residence". All charm and no fucking room to reside.'

I could hear a quick flip-flopping of someone coming down inside. I hoped Michael didn't mind me bringing Jake. I suppose I'd invited myself, by chatting him up about his home and saying how smashing it sounded and how I'd love to see it. He'd said of course, come any time, in the way that public school types always do. When? He'd smiled in his usual charming way and said well this evening, just pop round, that's what everyone else does, have a drink and a bite, love to see you. Bring that clever girl friend if you like. I hadn't been able to get hold of Antonia and so here I was with Jake instead. I planned to stay only half an hour, and I'd got Jake's chauffeur lined up to come to the house at eight. We'd then go to the

Prospect of Whitby for a proper drink, to let Jake see a real London pub, and then to the Good Friends in the East End for dinner. He'd had enough culture for one day.

The door opened and standing there was a boy of about nineteen. He was wearing a pink shirt, pink canvas sailing shoes with rope soles, very tight white trousers and a striped butcher's apron. He was clutching his chest, to show he'd been rushing.

'It's always the same,' he panted. 'Rush, rush, rush. You find your way all right? Oh listen to me, you're here, so you must have done. Are you Tom?'

I said yes. I was about to introduce Jake, but he'd turned and was rushing back up the stairs.

'Well, I'm glad to see your friend is a gentleman. That's nice. Oh, that ratatouille. It'll be going all dry. Excuse me. Just come on up.'

At the top of the bare polished wooden stairs he stopped and told us again to follow and to excuse the mess.

'What's he on about?' said Jake. 'Where are we? Whose house is it? I'll give him bloody gentleman.'

'It's a surprise,' I said. I was beginning to think that perhaps it might be too much of a surprise all round. I'd found out about Michael, but I didn't know how much Jake knew.

We went upstairs and into a surprisingly large, light room, furnished with bright modern furniture, all very Heals and Habitat. The kitchen was at one end and there was a door into a bedroom at the other. I could just glimpse a double bed and a mass of cosy chintzy furnishings, the exact opposite of the living room. Michael came out of the bedroom. He was in a sky blue shirt, sky blue rope shoes with tight royal blue trousers. He was also wearing a butcher's apron.

Jake didn't take it in at first, that it was Michael. He was wandering round the room, goggling at the furniture. He'd never seen such way-out stuff before. For a second even I didn't realize it was Michael. I was quite unprepared for such a transformation. His casual clothes suited him, his body seemed freer, younger. He was barely thirty, but at work he always looked and acted middle-aged in his office uniform.

Michael stopped suddenly when he saw it was Jake. For a minute I thought he was going to rush back into the bedroom and to change back into his other persona. Then he smiled, forced himself to walk casually across the room.

'What sort of drink do you want, Jake?' he said. ' 'Fraid I haven't got any State Management Nut Brown.'

Jake turned as Michael spoke. 'Christ on a crutch! Are you in a competition or something?'

Michael looked at me instead of answering Jake. For a second I could see his fury at me, then he walked over to the kitchen.

'This is Kenneth,' he said over his back. 'He's very kindly come in to do the cooking.'

'Oh?' said Kenneth, raising his eyebrows. 'Charming.'

Michael bent over the pots with Kenneth and whispered something in his ear. Kenneth shrugged his shoulders.

'Cooking?' I said. 'Please don't bother about us. We're eating later.' I looked round desperately at the table. It was laid immaculately with thick straw mats and little bowls of flowers at intervals along the bare pine table. It was set for four. I'd expected to find at least a dozen people, all standing around chatting so that we'd hardly be noticed.

'Don't be silly. It's all prepared. I wouldn't hear of you not eating,' said Michael. 'Good gracious.'

'Not a bad little dump,' said Jake, looking round. 'I expected you'd live in some Victorian slum. Some fucking musty museum, like the Sir John Soane or somewhere. You been to the John Soane, then?'

'Dr. Johnstone's house, in Fleet Street?' said Kenneth. Michael glared at him. Kenneth bent over the pans again. 'I'm never away.'

'*Sir* John Soane,' said Jake. 'Christ, don't say you don't know where that is. You wanna get to know London, mate.' Kenneth was going to reply again, but Michael got in first.

'Yes, I've always meant to get there,' said Michael and asked Jake what he'd thought of it. Kenneth brought round some drinks. Michael watched carefully until Kenneth went back to silently cooking the meal.

'There'll be a slight delay,' said Michael. 'I hope you won't mind.' I said of course not. It was our fault for being early. Michael said no. It was his fault. I said no, it was mine.

Jake was banging the polished wooden floors to see how good they were as if he was a J.P. He said what a good idea. He should have done that when he was converting houses.

Cheaper than fitted carpets. He admired the ornaments and the framed paintings of Victorian pornography and Edwardian half-clad beauties. He was genuinely impressed and obviously liking it. There was a statue of a nude boy on a long plinth, and he slapped its bottom familiarly as he passed it. I could feel Michael relaxing more. He was chattering more easily to Jake, telling him where he'd got all the bits and pieces and what bargains they'd been.

'Nearly ready, chaps,' said Kenneth.

Jake went over to the kitchen and began fingering the gadgets and ornaments. He opened the pine cupboards and tried to shake some china hand warmers to see if they were real eggs.

'Yes, a nice bit of stuff you've got here.'

'Cheek,' said Kenneth. Michael smiled and fetched another bottle from the fridge. He took down from a wall a heavy carved cane, and opened it to reveal a corkscrew. He placed the bottle between his feet on the polished wooden floor to pull the cork out.

'Mind the floor, dear,' said Kenneth. 'I've just polished it this afternoon.'

'If you can't help me,' said Michael peevishly, 'then keep quiet. Is that ratatouille ready yet? We've been waiting hours.'

We got through two bottles of hock with the famous ratatouille and two bottles of Beaune with the Boeuf Bourguignon, by which time everyone was jollier – Jake visibly relishing Kenneth's description of his afternoon.

'And then he said, step in this closet and I'll try you for size. Not likely, dear, I said. Oh, they were devils. He'd already said I couldn't be a nun, so I wasn't going to let him have a free feel, was I?'

'Why wouldn't he let you be a nun?' I asked.

'He said it was the policy of the establishment. Bloody cheek. I fancied my little self as a nun. And Michael was panting to be a bishop, weren't you dear? I can just see him with gaiters and letting people kiss his ring.'

'So then what did you do?' I said.

'I said what about a Girl Guide. I told him my friend could go as a Boy Scout and we'd be a right pair. But he said no. That was also against the policy. So I stormed out, telling him where he could stick his policy.'

170

'No you didn't,' said Michael, butting in, obviously having heard the story already. 'He brought out a costume for you to try on, didn't he?'

'Look, who's telling this story, eh?' said Kenneth. 'I was there. You weren't. Yes, anyway, he said he had something he *knew* I'd love. Henry The Eighth! Can you just imagine it. *Me,* as Henry the Eighth? I ask you. What are you two going as, The Two Stooges?'

'Going where?' I said. Michael stopped laughing and glowered at Kenneth.

'Bertie's fancy dress party,' said Kenneth. 'It'll be a rave.'

Bertie was Jake's architect, the very smooth one who knew his way round every regulation.

'I haven't been fucking invited,' said Jake.

'But I thought *all* his friends were invited,' said Kenneth.

'Jake's not a particular friend of his,' said Michael, trying to explain it all amicably.

'You haven't got any friends, have you, Jake?' said Kenneth.

'I'm the fucking boss,' shouted Jake. 'I don't need friends.'

'You can always hire a friend,' continued Kenneth, deliberately ignoring Michael who was making faces at him to stop. 'More little lap dogs you can take round with you all the time.'

I edged downwards in my seat. I wasn't going to reply and I hoped Jake wouldn't. I didn't want him to protect me. I sensed that Kenneth was repeating what Michael had said privately. I'd always thought Michael had liked me, ever since our first lunch. Now I realized he never wanted me to come in as Jake's friend, paid or otherwise.

'You're quite right, cunt face,' said Jake to Kenneth, very quietly. 'I haven't got any friends. I never make any.'

'Well, you don't really,' I started. 'Once you're over twenty-one, you don't make new friends the way you do when you're young. Don't you think so, Michael? I don't have any friends now. Just acquaintances.'

'He's met me since he was twenty-one,' said Kenneth. 'A lot more than twenty-one. It's just not true. It depends on the sort of person you are.'

'I *never* had any fucking friends,' said Jake. 'I always said I didn't care, but I did.'

This was a huge admission and a real revelation for Jake himself. Everybody went quiet. Jake emptied his glass then got up and went to the door, crashing into the furniture. Michael bounced up to help him.

'Fucking sit down,' said Jake. 'I'm not bloody drunk.'

'I'd better be going as well,' I said, getting up.

'Sit down you,' said Jake. 'You fucking lap dog.'

He staggered down the stairs, missing most of them, slammed the door and lurched into the mews. I hoped his chauffeur was still there.

We all sat still, then Michael's face seemed to cave in and he started abjectly apologizing for what had happened. It was the worst thing Kenneth had ever done. He knew I was a real friend, the only one Jake had. Jake needed me desperately, though he would never admit it. How could Kenneth say such things. I said it was all my fault. I'd never forgive myself.

Kenneth very quietly cleared the table, not looking at me or Michael. Michael started again, but I said it was OK. Not to worry. Just forget it. I understood.

I didn't really understand. I knew seeing Michael in his natural habitat would be a surprise to Jake, but I didn't want it to turn out like that. Perhaps it had been brought home to him how selfish he'd been, never finding out about Michael, or bothering to get to know him. Bertie's party had shown him how really isolated he was.

I said I had to go. Neither of them protested. I dragged myself out, feeling very miserable. It started to rain and I hadn't a coat. I felt disgusted with myself. I was like a drowned rat when I got home. No, a rather wet pathetic lap dog.

Chapter Seventeen

A message from Jake summoned me to his flat. I hadn't seen much of him for a few weeks and I was glad of something to prove I still existed. I wished the summons could have been posted up on the office board for everyone to see.

Jones the butler showed me in and asked if I'd like a glass of hock and some canapés. There was no sign of Jake. I thought for a bit and then said what about a cup of tea and a fried egg sandwich. I'd not eaten since lunch and I was quite pleased with myself at doing a Jake.

'Certainly sir,' said Jones at once. Mr. Sullivan would not be long. He was taking a bath. I said who with, or even with whom, but Jones had glided out.

'You're getting very middle class,' I said when Jake at last appeared. He was wearing a long silk dressing gown. He'd combed back his wet hair in a middle parting and looked like a 1930s matinee idol.

'We're not all filthy working class buggers like you.'

He was admiring himself in the mirror, pulling stage faces. It was a change to see him jokey instead of aggressive.

'You know, that's the first bath I've ever had because I felt like having a bath rather than because I needed one.'

'You'll be having an au pair next,' I said.

'And what'll you be having, my good chap,' said Jake rubbing his hands and putting on the posh. 'Glass of canapés and a plate of hock, what! what? Where's that fucker, Jones?'

'I've had some tea.'

'Good show. I'll go and slip into something cool. Ask Jones for anything else you fancy. I want you to have a lovely evening.'

Jake's charm was ridiculous. His accent, when he was trying to be upper class, was worse. He had no ear for dialogue, just as he had no ear for so many other things. But all the same, a lovely evening might be lovely.

'Where's the fucking orgy, then?' said a loud Liverpool voice in the hall. I hadn't heard Jones letting anyone in. It was Ron, the Cambridge free-lance who did occasional things for the Express, the one who'd come in the aeroplane to Carlisle for Jake's party and ruined my exclusive.

'Doesn't say there's nobody in,' said Ron, coming into the room staring straight through me. I could see he was annoyed at finding me. Not as annoyed as I was.

'Christ,' said Jake, returning, still in his dressing gown. 'I thought I told Jones not to admit any bums.'

'We just thought we'd drop in to see you for half an hour,' said Ron,

'Well you've seen me. Get out,' said Jake. 'Hey, who's the *we*?'

'Chloe?' shouted Ron. 'What you doing out there? Don't start touching up Jones. He's married.'

Chloe entered and Jake and I turned round immedately, having expected from Ron's language that it would be one of his usual slags. Chloe was the height of elegance. She was so faultlessly dressed and so beautifully made up that she seemed to have a spotlight on her. On closer inspection she didn't have much of a figure, in fact she was decidedly thin, but she radiated style and glamour. She said hello, all round, and gave me and Jake, equally, a huge charming smile and a chance to admire her upper class manners and accent. She was one of those women who are so well turned out that they might be any age from fifteen to thirty-five. I put her at twenty-eight.

'So how's business, then,' said Ron, sitting down as if he owned the place. 'Everything's gear I hope, or have the Fraud Squad got you yet?'

'Just make yourself at home,' said Jake.

'I will,' said Ron knocking back the hock which Jones had served him.

'What about your grandmother then,' said Jake, smiling. Chloe beamed back, taking the remark as perhaps he meant it, that no one obviously so young could be anyone's grandmother. In another mood, he might have trodden on her. She was the sort of well-bred girl Jake maintained he hated, though I don't think he'd ever met one close up. 'What would you like, darling?'

'Oh, how terribly kind,' said Chloe.

'I'm a terribly kind bloke,' said Jake.

'Excuse me while I vomit,' said Ron. 'You know you're getting another blackhead.'

Jake rushed to the mirror to examine his face. His adolescent spots had recently come back again and he'd tried every patent medicine and Harley Street doctor without success. He usually drew attention to them first, to show he wasn't self conscious.

'Ever seen a spotty millionaire then, Chloe,' said Ron. Chloe was looking round the room, ignoring Ron. 'Doesn't Tom squeeze them for you, Jake? That's what he's for, isn't it?'

I quietly got myself a drink as I couldn't see a way of slipping out without being noticed. I'd always hated Ron who was trying his nastiest tonight to keep in with Jake whom I'm sure he really despised.

'Don't offer anyone else a drink, will you,' said Ron to me. Both Jake and Chloe were taking no notice of him.

'It's a sign of virility,' said Jake to himself in the mirror.

'Wanking, you mean,' said Ron. He poured out two glasses and took one to Chloe. He put it on a table beside her and put his hand on her thigh. Chloe picked up the glass and poured the contents over Ron's head. Jake almost fell over laughing. I decided it was perhaps worth staying a bit longer.

'What the fuck was that for?' said Ron.

'If you use that word once more, I'm going now,' said Chloe, nicely but firmly.

'I'll fucking swear as I want to.'

'That's the trouble. You do, and by doing so lose any effect it might have by stupid repetition. You think it's clever and aggressive and realistic. It simply becomes meaningless and, in the end, really rather boring.'

'If it's so boring, why are you commenting on it?'

'Because I hate to see you displaying your failures so openly,' said Chloe sweetly.

'What failures?'

'Your failure in self-expression. You have to resort to swearing because you are unable to attract attention in any other way. I can excuse Jake, just, as he obviously knows no better, but I expected better of you, with your education.'

'What absolute cock,' said Ron. 'Swearing is a way of enriching speech, not debasing it. Christ almighty, haven't you read Chaucer and Shakespeare? Shakespeare uses damn a hundred and forty-seven times. In his day that was tantamount to fuck. And what about the first scene of Comedy of Errors? What do you think "By my troth" means?'

'Whatever it means is completely beside the point, and you know it.'

'It means by my cock,' said Ron.

'What absolute lies,' said Chloe.

'Swearing is the perfect vehicle for all emotions, from disgust to elation. And it can be fucking funny. I think Jake here is at his wittiest when he's swearing.'

'Fuck off,' said Jake.

Jake was very impressed by Ron's performance and was making mental notes to trot out some of it as his own. I was also thinking of using it on Antonia. In her honesty, Chloe was a bit like Antonia, but there the comparison ended. Chloe carefully dispensed her honesty with a charming smile, giving everyone the benefit of her niceness and goodness. It was surprising that someone so attractive should also want to appear so good. Perhaps she *was* good. I found her sick-making.

'What does your friend do?' said Jake. 'When she's not charming for England?' Chloe smiled at this.

'She's my agent,' said Ron. 'She owns ten per cent of me. You can guess which part.'

'What are you writing, Ron?' I asked, surprised to hear myself. I thought I'd gone.

'I'm not writing. Chloe's selling. She's flogged the American rights, the Serbo-Croat rights, got an option on the film rights and I haven't written a word yet.'

'Sounds good,' I said flatly. Jake, back to his gentleman bit, had gone over to Chloe by a window to give her another drink and asked her if she'd like a Niblet, a cocktail stick or a glazed expression. Chloe had muttered some politeness about seeing the rest of the flat and Jake had escorted her away.

'Shouldn't you be doing something,' said Ron, helping himself to another drink. 'I mean, wiping the lavatory seats or something.'

'I can't. I've been lumbered with you. You know what it's like when awful people arrive, uninvited.'

'Well, you could leave now, couldn't you?' said Ron.

'What about you Jake?' said Chloe returning. She was in the middle of an Alpha Plus charm performance. 'I'm sure you could write an absolutely brilliant book, hmm? Won't you try. Just for me?' She uttered this last comment in a tone dripping with implications. 'Oh Jake, say you'll at least *try*. I'm so desperate to get people like you. You must have had many fascinating experiences.'

'What do I want to write a book for?'

'Money,' said Ron.

'Oh Ron, don't be so crude,' said Chloe, still gazing at Jake. 'Well, if you ever change your mind and suddenly have the desire . . . promise you'll come to me first, hmm?'

'Lie down beside me then,' said Jake. 'See what you think of my writing hand.'

'Promise?' said Chloe.

'Promise,' said Jake, smiling, or at least leering back. I was having the benefit of Chloe in profile. Her nose was small and neat and her chin slightly upturned, while her whole expression was bright and enquiring. Chloe after all, as she'd patently made clear, wasn't thick. Her breasts from the front, in her beautifully tailored suit, had seemed non-existent, but now in profile they were obviously there, protected inside, gift-wrapped and hermetically sealed. Her mouth was probably slightly big, but if you're going to have film star's teeth you can't have a diminutive rose-bud. But no, it was all pretty perfect really. I wondered if she was a lesbian.

Jake obviously didn't think so. He was now trying to grab her.

'There's a good boy,' said Chloe, backing away, but still fluttering. 'I must go with Ron to one of his boring parties. It'll be really bloody, but when you're so brilliant, you've got to go around and let everyone have a chance of seeing you, haven't you?'

She gave a huge smile, big enough to suck Jake right in. Jake smiled back, blowing her kisses. Chloe went out, going straight into a conversation with Ron about the film option being on certain conditions.

'Cock teaser, like all those posh prigs,' said Jake, the minute I got back into the room. 'I've met more of them than you've had hot crumpet.'

'I'm going,' I said. 'Let me know when you're having your next lovely evening. I'll make a point of staying at home.'

Maggie buzzed through to say that someone called Rupert Crudd-White had arrived to see Jake. 'Tell someone called Rupert Crudd-White to get fucked,' said Jake. He'd called me in to read out a piece in the Daily Sketch about himself, saying after every paragraph how awful it was. He'd read it three times so far, each time saying how awful it was.

'The Monday papers are always hard up for stories,' I said, 'especially the diaries.'

'Just watch it,' said Jake. 'It's everywhere, so they can't be all that hard up. I think I'll ring them and tell them this is all old news. I'm now going into a monastery. What do you think?'

'And really get the piss taken out of you,' I said, picking up the Sketch.

The other papers had smaller stories, mainly knocking the Sketch's story and taking the micky out of Jake, which is about all you can do with a follow-up story. In the Sketch, Jake's take-over bid for Buckingham Palace was the lead story in the diary, complete with a big picture.

The week before, some Labour MP, yet again, had been criticizing the upkeep of the Royal Family. As a variation on his usual theme, he'd added that Buckingham Palace could be used as a hostel for eight hundred of London's homeless instead of housing one small suburban family. This had passed almost unnoticed, until the Sketch had got dynamic, twenty-four-years-old property millionaire, Jake Sullivan, to announce his plan exclusively to them. Mr. Sullivan had sent a telegram to the Queen, so the paper said, offering five million quid for Buckingham Palace. The Royals could have one wing rent free for themselves – " "I'm a bloody Royalist at heart", says tough-talking, ex-lorry driver Jake' – and he would develop the rest, providing two thousand new homes for Londoners. They'd gone back to the Labour MP with Jake's plan and quoted him as saying that it certainly sounded a good idea and he was certainly going to look into it.

In the Express and Mail diaries, Jake was called a twenty-nine-year-old self-styled millionaire. They had a Buckingham

Palace press officer denying any knowledge of a telegram and when asked if he thought it was just a cheap publicity stunt, they had the Labour MP saying no comment.

Maggie rang again to say that Mr. Crudd-White was still waiting. Jake asked her if she'd read the Daily Sketch. Very haughtily she said no, certainly not, she'd never read it in her life. What about the Daily Express and Mail? Maggie said she couldn't stand the popular papers. She only read The Guardian. You're fired, said Jake.

Michael said yes, he'd been told about it. It sounded shoddy and rather vulgar. He thought Jake had better things to do with his time than ringing round cheap newspapers with a lot of lies. Jake almost had a tantrum at the suggestion that *he'd* rung any paper. And anyway, he was going into a monastery. Michael missed this last bit. He'd hung up.

I thought the story was a good laugh. It was an archetypal pseudo-Royal story. They were always great fun to write, as you could make it up as you went along, and always good to read as you knew from the beginning there wasn't a word of truth in it. But I was getting a bit bored by Jake going on about it. I said I couldn't see why he was so impressed. This got him furious again. Neither of us noticed that somebody had entered.

He was standing nervously at the door, smiling shyly and trying to catch Jake's eye. He was very plump and jolly-looking, in a floppy public school sort of way. He had floppy hair, a floppy soft collar turned up at the edge and a floppy Guards tie. It was that careful, upper class untidiness which could easily be mistaken for scruffiness, till you realized his tweed suit was hand made and that his shoes were very expensive and only needed cleaning with a suede brush. In his floppy right hand he was holding a floppy pork pie hat. He gave another nice smile, at me as well as Jake. He looked the sort who was nice all the time, to managing directors as well as office boys. Nice, absolutely harmless but probably, when you got to know him, completely boring.

Jake, without turning, and still speaking in the same furious tones, said over his shoulder OK Fatso, whoever you are, I'll give you two fucking minutes.

Rupert Crudd-White smiling shyly at Jake, picked up a faded brief case which he'd placed on the floor beside him. I could see it was real leather and had his initials, plus a faded coat of arms, on the side. He spent at least two minutes searching through it, trying to find what he wanted, apologizing all the time, saying how terribly, terribly sorry he was. I felt sorry for him. He'd be booted out before he'd got going. His name clicked, and I remembered he'd been the PR who'd once offered me a job, though I'd never met him. He looked much more affable in the flesh than he'd sounded on the phone.

Jake made two calls into the battery of telephones round his desk, to show how busy he was. Crudd-White at last got out a pile of tattered newspaper cuttings and placed them on Jake's desk.

'If you're gonna wipe your arse,' said Jake, 'do it outside, eh.'

Crudd-White smiled, but not at Jake. He hadn't appeared to take in his remark. It was a general good-will smile. He was turning over the cuttings and mumbling about how jolly well Jake had done, jolly well indeed.

'I'll say you have,' he went on. 'Good gracious, half of a page here! Jolly well done. Jolly well done. And here's another, almost as big. And what a splendid photograph. Amazing. It really is. Super. How well you've done. And all on your own.'

'I have got friends, you know,' said Jake, betraying at last that he was interested. Rupert Crudd-White had a copy of every cutting about Jake, from my crummy feature in the Sunday News to all that morning's stories. He was now holding them up as if they were papyrus.

'Christ, you haven't got today's shitty stories as well,' said Jake. 'I haven't had time to read all that crap.'

'Oh, they're not crap', said Rupert Crudd-White, pronouncing it crep, with a long 'e' and making it sound rather good. 'I think it's jolly good.'

'Waste of time, all of them,' said Jake, obviously pleased that Rupert disagreed. Rupert was now flicking through them, looking for something.

'Oh, didn't the Guardian do anything? Or the Financial Times? What a shame, such a jolly good story. It's a brilliant idea, if I may say so, developing Buck House. I'd have thought their city pages could have made something of it.'

'What do I want to get in them shitty papers for? Nobody reads them.'

'People who matter do, and people who matter, matter. Don't you think?'

'What's this shithouse on about,' said Jake, turning to me, pretending he didn't understand what Rupert had said.

'You've got this beautiful, dignified office,' said Rupert Crudd-White, gesturing with both floppy hands, 'in this beautiful, dignified building. All you need now is some dignified publicity . . .'

'Fuck the dignity,' said Jake, 'as long as they spell my name right. Now get out. You've had ten minutes.'

'Oh gosh,' said Rupert Crudd-White, 'and I haven't even started to tell you what I'd come for.' Perhaps he hadn't but he'd very cleverly moved on from saying how well Jake had done to suggesting he could be doing a lot better. He was packing up his cuttings, taking as long as he'd taken to unpack them.

'You're quite right of course,' he went on, as if agreeing with something Jake had just said. 'Quite right. When you've achieved something so marvellous on your own, as you have done, who needs publicity, either in the popular or the quality press? There's no point in *pretending* to be dignified.'

'Watch it Fatso,' said Jake. 'If you're insinuating me or my directors aren't dignified, I'll have you by the short hairs, if you have any.'

'And as you've done it, why should you want to go on and do other things. I quite agree. Why move on into new and different circles? That's always difficult, especially if you want to get a bit of power and influence as well. You're probably quite right to stay as you are . . .'

'Listen, clever guts. I haven't started yet. Now get out before I throw you out.'

'It's most awfully kind of you to put up with me. Now, where did I put . . . Ah, here it is. As I was saying, to move on you need the right sort of image to attract the right sort of backers and the right sort of contacts. It is amazing what a bright young Tory MP on one's board can do for one, just with a few words in the right places. Or even a couple of peers. It's amazing how people are impressed by such things. I can never really understand it.'

'Who's fucking impressed? I'm not,' said Jake.

'Of course you're not. I know that. But you know what other people are like ...' Rupert Crudd-White was giving a slobby smile, I thought, which was a mistake. He'd appeared so earnest and sincere so far. 'Especially shareholders ...'

'I've got a few partners,' said Jake, 'not shareholders. I'm in charge of everything. See?'

'Of course you are, but there might be a time when you might want to go completely public. Let me see now, on 15 October last year you said to a gentleman from the Daily Mirror, over a champagne cocktail with a Miss Wonder, that you were personally now worth two million. By the end of this year, if you put Seacrill Paradise on the market, I'd say you could easily make three million for yourself ...'

'How do you know what Seacrill Paradise is worth?'

'I don't. But I do know about you, Mr. Sullivan ...'

'Like fuck you do. By the end of this year, Paradise will be worth five million. Five million! In just two years. Do you know my father worked for thirty years and never made more than £10 a week? Down the mines for thirty years, till he was too weak to take his cock out in the lavatory and a pit pony kicked him to death. And me mother never got a penny pension either, except what I give her. That's bloody Tories for you, and bloody peers. Not that I care. I'm going into a monastery next month.'

'You're so right. It's all unfair. But I can't help admiring you for having done it. You've beaten them at their own game. You could beat them even more, you know, and still at their own game. That's how the big Government contracts are landed these days, by having the inside contacts. It's sad, but that's how it's done. However, I've obviously come to the wrong person. You're quite happy as you are, and why shouldn't you be? It's been a great pleasure to talk to you, Mr. Sullivan. I've heard so many good things about you ...'

'Don't treat me like a mongol, you creepy arsed bugger,' said Jake, advancing towards him. 'Go and ponce somewhere else.'

Rupert Crudd-White moved backwards, all humble smiles and thanks and apologies. As Jake opened the door for him and pushed him towards it, he pulled a large foolscap envelope from his briefcase, saying he was sorry he'd been carried away with talking to him. This was what he'd really come to give him. Jake threw it into a waste-paper basket then shoved him out and slammed the door after him. When he'd gone, Jake got the envelope out and read the contents at his desk.

'Christ, what a con. I've heard of rentaflunk, but rentadirector! It's diabolical.' Jake was between personas at the moment. The American bit had disappeared and he was now lapsing into cockney, but my next bet was Liverpool, that's if the Beatles stayed at the top.

He threw across the literature to me. Rupert Crudd-White's firm was called White Associates. Its list of directors took up about half a page. There were many well known peers, politicians, sportsmen, retired ambassadors and even a couple of Harley Street doctors. On other pages were the names of the firms which the company represented.

In a covering letter, Crudd-White explained how he could produce any two of these directors, for example a prominent politician and a prominent peer, to go on Jake's board. If they went on Jake's board, they wouldn't go on any others as that would devalue their currency.

Providing directors was only an ancilliary service. Their main work would be in handling all promotion, advertising, marketing, display, printing, press conferences, statements. They had a staff of forty-five executives for such purposes. As an extra promotional service, Rupert Crudd-White could personally handle Jake's personal publicity. He could ensure dignified publicity in the quality press as well as TV appearances, if so desired. All this for only £10,000 a year, all of it a legitimate expense. They had already had that agreed with the Inland Revenue.

When a PR is writing about PR you either laugh all the way through, or get taken right in. I laughed aloud when I'd finished it.

'As cons go,' I said, 'it's a very smart one. They once offered me a job. If I'd been more of a half-wit, I might have accepted.'

Jake rang for Michael. He showed him the literature and asked him what he thought. Michael said the notepaper was enough to show what sort of firm it was.

'They think it gives them a semblance of status. They're always keen on status. Just as every prostitute calls herself a model, every thief is an antique dealer and every lay-about is a company director.'

'You mean the currency has been devalued,' said Jake. I knew he'd fall for that phrase.

'Precisely,' said Michael.

'You're so precise you'll cut yourself one day. Right, as you're all in agreement, that's settled. I'll take them on for a year. Maggie!'

Michael left as Maggie came in. I wasn't sure if I was meant to leave. Jake went across to a bookcase lined with leather volumes. He pressed a button and they slid apart to reveal a huge cocktail cabinet. Jake poured himself a drink and studied himself in the mirror.

'I've never been on telly. I could show that David Frost and all the rest of them. Think they're so bloody smart. Nobody has yet grabbed one of them. If one tries it on me, I'll just have him by the balls. That'll make him shut up and listen to me. Pow, wow, wham!'

I left, leaving Jake still talking to himself.

Chapter Nineteen

I was at the back of the studio with Henry. Rupert was rushing around like a Royal flunkey, saying Mr. Sullivan would want a whisky and coke straight away, Mr. Sullivan wouldn't like that light, Mr. Sullivan would have to sit on the swivel chair, Mr. Sullivan mustn't be kept waiting. I said what a slob. Surely Jake must see what a slob Rupert was. Henry said yes, he was rather, ha ha ha.

Henry Hornsby was the so-called prominent Tory MP that Rupert had brought in. In six months I hadn't heard him come out with an opinion of his own. He agreed completely with what everyone said to him. He went around all the time as if he'd just had his Christmas dinner, belatedly beaming through his pebble glass spectacles, exuding a bloated goodwill to all men. How Henry ever summoned up enough energy to get up in the morning I didn't know. His only real activity seemed to be giving parties and bringing people together, which he did all the time, either at one of his many houses or at the home of one of his many well-connected relations.

I hadn't managed to tell Jake to his face how much of a slob I thought Rupert was. Jake seemed to be so thick with him, it might look as if I was jealous, so I limited myself to showing by my attitude how I disapproved. All that happened was that I became increasingly ignored and out of things. I felt Jake would eventually see through Rupert, but there seemed to be no sign of it yet. Rupert had done most of what he'd said he would do. Jake had got lots of mentions in the heavy city pages, which I had to admit had been of great help in his take-over bids. He'd leased one office block to the Minister of Pensions, thanks to Henry's contacts. And he had placed Jake on several TV programmes. I'd hoped that this would prove Rupert's undoing. I had only seen Jake fluent when it came to money or to bawdy invective. I couldn't see how he could keep his end up in any serious conversation. Somebody like Antonia, or even Chloe, could easily tear him to shreds in a proper argument.

His first programme had been pretty useless. It had been about young people from the North from different fields who'd made it in London. Jake had come across as stupid and conceited, simply boasting how clever he was and listing all the things he owned. Then in the general discussion afterwards, when all the young humble Northerners were given the chance to chat informally, Jake hadn't said a word. He said afterwards that no one had asked him anything.

Rupert explained that no one ever would. These chats were like competitions in which you got in front, regardless, and stayed there until someone forced you into the side. Three weeks later Rupert got Jake into another show, a fifteen minute chat programme when three ordinary people, not professional TV performers, talked about topics of the day. The two other supposedly ordinary people were an ex-actress and a journalist. They spent an hour beforehand while the producer got them to run through their impromptu chat. Jake had been useless in the run-through, knowing nothing about the impromptu subjects the producer had arranged for them to talk about, never mind having any opinions on them. On the programme itself he ignored completely all the prepared topics. Before anyone else could get a word in and before the chairman had finished saying that they were going to discuss first of all the rise in the bank rate, Jake had started an attack on the Tories. 'They're behind it all,' he said when the chairman gently tried to ask what the connection was. 'They're behind everything, so don't give me any more of your half cocked crap. I've met some of these bloody Tories and they can't pee straight, never mind think straight . . .'

When the chairman managed to wrestle a few seconds away from Jake, to say they were now going on to Russia's latest diplomatic note, Jake launched in turn into attacks on the aristocracy, the Church of England, the public schools, the Government and education. He shouted down anyone who tried to butt in. When he'd unloaded all his prejudices he started on about his sex life and then asked the others about theirs. The actress managed to get a few sentences in while Jake scratched himself. Then he jumped on one word, class, dragged it out of context and began again, forcing them to chase him and try to follow what he was saying before they could take over. As conversation, it didn't exist, but as entertainment it was a huge success. That had been six months ago.

Rupert was now rearranging the chairs once again. Jake imagined he had one profile better than the other. Now that he wore his hair so long, brushed straight forward in a Beatle cut, each side seemed the same to me. Rupert kept on looking at his watch, loudly cursing Jake's chauffeur, letting everyone know Jake had been held up at the House of Lords.

At last, Jake barged in, followed by Maggie carrying various notebooks and Jimmy carrying Jake's long leather coat, the sort Nazi dispatch riders used to wear. Jake was in jeans, gym shoes, and an old-fashioned faded vest with buttons down the middle. He did some press-ups in the middle of the studio while Rupert and Henry hovered round, oohing and aahing.

The studio technicians took no notice. They were busy doing the last rites which only they knew about, carried away by their own importance the way Willie Sullivan used to be when he got his slide rule out. They'd heard all about Jake

Sullivan and his exhibitionism and were determined *they* weren't going to show any interest in him.

Richard Cheam, who was going to do the big interview, was sitting on a stool in the corner while a make-up girl dabbed his brow and the director whispered in his ear. He was known for his smooth incisive nastiness. He had his well tailored jacket off and was sitting in his fashionably broad red braces. They looked very tight, pulling up his pants so high that they must have been constricting his crutch. Jake shouted 'Seconds out!' as he jumped up from his last press-up, clapped his hands loudly and told Maggie, Jimmy, Rupert and Henry to stop crowding him. 'Let's have you,' he shouted across to Richard Cheam. Cheam gave Jake his smooth incisive smile and a quick nod, and went on listening to the director.

Jake shoved his entourage away and beckoned me to follow him to the dressing room. I picked up my copy of the notes, knowing Jake had probably lost the top set.

The make-up man was short and bronzed with huge shoulders and biceps, about fifty but dressed like a teenager from West Side Story, with his hair combed carefully over his forehead in a Negro fringe. He smelt strongly of Old Spice.

'Christ, not you again,' said Jake. The make-up man danced round Jake like a fencer, dabbing drops of powder on Jake's face then bobbing back to get the full effect. He cocked his head on one side and froze in rapt concentration. He wasn't concentrating on Jake, he was watching himself in the mirror.

'Beautiful,' said Jake. 'Give us a kiss.'

Meanwhile I passed Jake the notes one by one, explaining what they were. I folded the newspaper cuttings for him and placed them in his trouser pockets, telling him where each one was.

'I don't think I'll use any of this shit tonight,' said Jake. 'He'll be expecting it. I might break down and cry. I haven't decided.'

'Why not?' I said. 'Or strip off naked and flash yourself to the viewers. You haven't done that either.'

'What do you think, sexy?' Jake shouted to the make-up man. 'Are you in the mood to see my lallies?'

Although Jake had become known on TV for his loud mouthedness, his preoccupation with sex, his vulgarity and

187

his refreshing honesty, he was always very careful never to blaspheme, or to be really obscene. He'd established himself as a son of the soil, as an uneducated ex-lorry driver, so he got away with his lack of logic, his bloodies and calling people stupid gits. He appeared to say the first thing which came into his head and didn't care about anyone. His invective and insults were made up on the spot, saying the sort of things to the interviewer's face which people at home in their own living rooms were saying anyway.

But ever since the first disastrous appearance, Jake had carefully prepared his attacks. He was a natural at jumping illogically all over the place, refusing to listen to anyone and coming out with hugely exaggerated generalizations. That was him in real life. But anyway, most viewers don't carefully follow the path of a conversation, but they pay attention when someone shouts, loses their temper, or threatens to start fighting. To make sure he could keep all this up and dominated the conversation, Jake realized he needed refuelling. This was my job. I had to amass the sort of information he could come out with, as irrefutable facts to silence people who were getting the better of him. Facts are always good ammunition, even when they've little to do with the subject. If you suddenly ask someone if they're familiar with the Silkin Act of 1947 or the 1953 Town and Country Planning Act you're bound to stop them short. I knew Jake so well and had heard his prejudices so many times that I knew the sort of things he could drag in, to help to prove his half-backed ideas.

I passed Jake the list of Prime Ministers who were adulterers, from Disraeli to Ramsay MacDonald and Lloyd George. I gave him a cutting from the Guardian which listed the names of schools with the most open scholarships to Oxford and Cambridge, starting with Manchester Grammar School. I gave him a brief resumé of what the critics had said about Inadmissible Evidence, the opening of which I'd gone to last night, comparing it with Luther. I knew he could make good use of the fact that Luther had been obsessed by his bowels. Jake usually managed a fart or a belch during a programme, which would give him an opportunity to ask Richard if he'd seen Luther and which Jake could say he had.

Part of my job was to go to all the important plays, films and exhibitions, then come back and give Jake enough off-beat potted opinions about them to keep him going in any thirty-second TV or press conversations. Now and again, as a surprise, I managed to drag Jake away from Rupert and take him with me, saying he *had* to see something himself, if he was going to talk about it. But not often.

I was still the Surprise Assistant, but now I had to make all my surprises of some use, instead of being simply abstract, artistic or emotional experiences, which were what I wanted to give Jake. Now they had to be ammunition he could use as a TV personality. I took him to the State opening of Parliament so that he could be speaking from experience when he said what a bloody farce it was. We went to the Badminton Horse Trials so he could see for himself the upper classes in their cavalry twill, moustaches and tweedy, headscarved awfulness. I took him to the Durham Miners' Gala so he could speak from the heart about the working man being natural, honest, upright and sick all over the place.

The TV director was now shouting for Jake. I gave him his last ammunition, some quotations from Cyril Connolly's 'Enemies of Promise', about homosexuality at public schools and how public school boys acted for ever as if they were still at school. I hoped he didn't get it mixed up with the open scholarships bits.

Cheam was sweating and looked more nervous than Jake. You wouldn't think he'd had about ten times as much experience of TV as Jake.

'They're always fucking nervous,' said Jake, so loudly that Cheam couldn't avoid overhearing. 'That's 'cos really they're useless. They know they're going to get found out at any minute. Bloody parasites. Never done a day's work in their lousy lives. TV personalities! What an abortion. Famous for being famous for fuck all.'

'Aren't you nervous then?' I asked Jake when he'd finished shouting.

'Give over. I've got all the money in the world I want, all the power I need, all the girls I can lay, so why should I give a fuck about TV? I'm just doing it for the giggle. As for that little git, all he can do is look smooth and give a few mums a quick thrill.'

But what Jake had missed out about himself was fame. He had money, power, sex, that was true. But, till he went on telly, no fame at all. Now he was recognized all over the place. His vanity couldn't get enough of that.

The producer sat Jake and Cheam on their respective chairs. They were on very high stools so that they seemed to soar above the backcloth of skyscrapers and office blocks, used to demonstrate that the latest profile subject was in the property business. There were two cameras right under their feet, looking up, ready to zoom in and close up on half an eyelid, or a left nostril. Jake scratched his balls, but failed to make the technicians pay any attention to him. Jake liked to have an audience, of any sort, to have some reaction round him. Me and the rest of his acolytes were too far away, huddled in the wings, to do any good, though we were smiling and laughing at his every move.

The producer told them to talk away to each other. Perhaps Richard could ask him a few questions, just to warm up and as a final check for sounds. Jake said get lost and went on scratching himself. Jake always refused any warm-up, preferring to come out with his insults, fresh and unexpected, the minute he'd clapped his eyes on the interviewer.

'Don't you find this terribly unreal, Jake?' said Cheam quickly, trying hard to be matey and friendly. Jake didn't answer. He moved on from scratching to picking his nose. 'Here we are surrounded by all this wonderful equipment and brilliant experts (a big smooth smile all round) and we imagine everyone cares what we're going to talk about. It's so pretentious, isn't it? Just like man himself, don't you think, Jake, hmm?'

'What you talking so quickly for?' said Jake. 'You farted or something?'

The technicians laughed this time. The producer said ten seconds. Everyone went quiet. The introduction music began and the titles could be seen coming up on the studio monitor. Exactly on cue Richard Cheam beamed a Richard Cheam smile to a camera in the far corner. He'd turned his back completely on Jake, knowing Jake wouldn't know which camera to look at. Jake sat still, knowing they always had the initiative at the beginning. The secret was to sit still, ignoring every camera, looking thoughtfully into space and saying nothing, even when they eventually spoke to you, until the very last minute. You must make them use up all their tricks first.

'Jake Sullivan used to be a labourer,' intoned Richard, quietly but solemnly. 'A labouring labourer, who got his hands dirty and his speech soiled. He was then a bus conductor and a lorry driver. After that he became an out of work bus conductor and an out of work lorry driver.'

He was reading from a teleprompter, which was unrolling in front of him like a telex machine, but doing it cleverly, keeping his eyes straight and his head up so that the viewer couldn't tell.

'Today he's a millionaire, many times over. He's done it in property and it's taken him only five short years. He's one of the new breed of working class tycoons, who've clambered to the top at a very early age, but despite all their tycoon wealth and power have still remained very much working class. Jake Sullivan is known in the City for his financial brain, his dynamic personality and his brilliantly successful property developments. Now he's becoming known to the man in the street for his refreshingly candid opinions and his outspoken attitudes to life. He is labouring in many fields these days, but he still retains, how shall I put it, the labourer's touch . . .'

He finished on a big smile. The teleprompter clicked off and he turned slowly back on his chair to face Jake, pausing dramatically, looking him very sincerely in the eye.

'Mr. Sullivan,' he said, suddenly going curt and formal. 'You know better than everyone else how well you've done. (Pause) What would you say I missed out?'

He was very pleased with the question. Jake could easily hang himself with it, either by coming on too strong and conceited, or by humming and haaing, don't-knowing and losing all the initiative.

Jake paused for a long time, as if stumped. Then he came to life, grinning with all his teeth. He sat forward, pulling himself together, trying to pretend he'd been day-dreaming and not listening to this pompous bore.

'What have you missed out about me?' said Jake, raising his eyebrows as he repeated Richard's question. 'You mean from that stuff you've been reading out on the teleprompter? Well, don't ask me, Mr. Cheese, ask the bloke that wrote it all out for you.'

Jake kept up his wide open smile, as if it was all a good-natured joke. He didn't mean it nastily to show him up, just a friendly quip. There was a loud clatter from the wings as Henry and Rupert fell over some cables in their delight. They were warned they would have to leave if there was any more noise. Richard Cheam was caught by the camera glancing down at some notes secreted between his knees. He'd planned to look at them while Jake messed about answering his first clever question.

'Mr. Sullivan,' he said, assembling his face to show how incisive he was going to be. 'Wouldn't you say there was something *immoral* about making three million pounds in four years?'

'Completely, Mr. Chimes, completely,' said Jake, looking humble. By chance he'd let Jake onto one of his oldest hobby horses. 'It's not only immoral, it's unfair, farcical and ridiculous. In fact it's bloody daylight robbery. I'd always thought so, long before I'd made it. But like most things in life, it's best to criticize from experience don't you think so, Mr. Cream?'

'So you admit you're immoral?'

'Yes, weren't you listening? Your notes have fallen on the floor, if that's what you're looking for. Listen, whack, my father worked in a lousy job for forty lousy years and never got more than eight lousy quid a week. *That's* what I call bloody immoral. Do you know that as a kid I never . . .'

'Yes, yes, Mr. Sullivan,' said Cheam, determined to take control and not let Jake wander off. 'Perhaps you'd tell us a few facts about yourself before we get on to that. Where were you born?'

Jake had to answer this properly. Cheam followed it sharply with another abrupt factual question, taking Jake smartly through his early life, not giving him a chance to score, pushing Jake to admit that his father was a white-collar worker, not a miner, that he grew up in the lovely Cumberland countryside, not the Gorbals as some newspapers had said, and that his parents actually *owned* their own house. Jake got very worried at that one, in case they'd found out what happened to that house, but Cheam jumped on to say wasn't it a fact that he'd only, in fact, been a lorry driver for a *week*, in fact? Jake nodded.

'It seems to me, Mr. Sullivan, that you come from a normal, happy, upper working class background. You weren't at all deprived. In fact, the only thing you seem to have been deprived of was being deprived. (Big self-congratulatory smile), I'm surprised, frankly, that you go on about your background so much.'

'The reason's simple. I happen to be grateful for it. Mind you, I didn't realize there was anything to be grateful for, till I met middle class phonies like you. I don't mean that personally, Richard old chap. You can't help it, poor sod. You've been shoved into an accent, into a set of attitudes and into a phony facade you can't get out of. You can never say what you really mean. Look at you now, all false smiles and apologetic grunts. It's impossible for you to be yourself. Honest, I feel sorry for you. (Scratching his balls). All those years of fagging or having blokes jumping on your backside at your lousy public schools, then you pretend for the rest of your life it was wonderful. What a drag. No wonder you're hung up.'

'You said earlier, Mr. Sullivan,' said Cheam, jumping in, 'that it's best to criticize from a position of experience, by actually knowing what you're talking about. How do *you* personally know about the public schools?'

'This bloke Cyril Connolly. You've heard of him haven't you? He went to Eton or Benenden or somewhere, didn't he? In that boring book he wrote, "Enemies of Promise" he talks about all that. Correct me if I'm wrong, but didn't he say that the public schools were . . .'

Cheam cut him sort, but Jake managed to get most of the quotation out, correctly as well, which was a surprise without getting out his notes.

'But you yourself Mr. Sullivan, what have you *personally* got against the public schools?'

'Nothing at all, as schools. They've got the best teachers, so I'm told. And the best schools get the best pupils, so I'm told. Well, you can't go wrong, can you?'

He paused, waiting for Cheam to jump in, pretending he didn't know what to say next.

'But I'm against education, personally. As long as you can read and write and add up, what more do you want? But let's *not* be personal, for a moment Mr. Chime. Let's think about others for a change. What do you think this lousy country's greatest natural resource is?'

'You tell me,' said Cheam, refusing to join any game.

'It's not coal. Last year the National Coal Board made a loss of £18.5 million. It's not North Sea Gas. You might as well forget that for at least another twenty years. It's not even land. The Forestry Commission owns most, then there's the Queen, the Countess of Sutherland, Cameron of Lochiel, the Grosvenor Estates and all the rest. Go on, make a guess. You're a clever bloke. You went to Oxford, didn't you?'

Jake had got away with his facts without being contradicted. I think he'd made most of them up.

'I can't, but I don't see what it's got to do . . .'

'Brains,' said Jake, tapping his head. 'They're our greatest natural resource. So what's the bloody use of picking out just a handful of them, because their bloody father's got a bit of money, and giving them the best education. *Everybody* should have the same chance. Eh? It's the fault of bloody people like you, supporting these bloody public schools. It's not bloody fair . . .'

'But life isn't fair, Mr. Sullivan.'

'Of course it isn't, you creep. I know that. Some of us were born handsomer than others. Some are cleverer. Some are witty. Some are talented. (Pause) What happened to you, smoothie chops? (Serious again) What I'm trying to say is that there are some things we can't do anything about. But some things we can. Like education and health. They should be equally available for all. But thanks to people like you supporting these bloody awful places . . .'

Jake was shouting, leaning forward, furious and shaking. It gave Cheam a chance to show how cool and collected he could be.

'I've been told you can be furiously angry in a matter of seconds, Mr. Sullivan. Is this always so, or is it a way of attracting attention, as some people have said, hmmm?'

Jake leaned right forward. He'd glanced in the monitor as Cheam was talking and saw they were now both in close-up, pores and all. With his right foot he kicked Cheam quickly but savagely in the balls. Then he leaned back, going suddenly soft and appealing.

'I know,' he said slowly. 'My mother always told me I was a show-off. I've tried to correct it. I've been spending every spare weekend for the last year in a monastery, meditating, praying, thinking or just keeping quiet. I'm a little better, but I still jump to the attack all the time. It can't be my background.

194

You've already told me how nice that was. (Winning smile) So it just must be me. I'm sorry, Mr. Cheam. You'll have to take me as I am, warts and all.'

Cheam was in agony. He'd managed to keep on his stool and out of the camera, but only just. There was nothing he could do. The producer had missed the kick as Jake's leg had been half hidden. He was waving to Cheam from the wings, indicating that he'd got Jake in a mood no one had seen before. He had to go on.

'You're swearing,' grunted Cheam. 'Not necessary, is it, really? Apart from showing off?'

'What swearing?' said Jake innocently, this time swinging round quickly with his left leg and kicking Cheam again. Cheam bent over with the pain, but managed to make out he was only coughing, then returned to the attack.

'And your viciousness. Physically attacking people. You must admit it. You have been rather nasty . . .'

Jake's soft gentle demeanour suddenly went. He leaned right forward this time and had grabbed Cheam by the lapels, dragging him bodily off his chair.

'Who says I'm nasty? Only when I lose my temper with little runts like you,' shouted Jake. 'I know your sort. Just 'cos you've been on the telly for a hundred years you think you can goad innocent people into making fools of themselves. Well, it won't work with me. So fuck off.' And Jake jumped down from his stool and marched off the set, pushing away the producer and assistant who were trying to restrain him.

The screen went blank in ten million homes. Jake went straight home, refusing to talk to anyone. Fifty reporters and photographers sat outside his flat all night. The next morning the Daily Express offered £500 for his life story, the Daily Mail offered him his own column and two publishers wanted him to do a book. The Oxford Union asked him to debate and he was put up for the rectorship of Edinburgh University. Jake said nothing.

At midday Rupert gave out a statement which said that Mr. Sullivan had sent a personal apology to Mr. Cheam. He had not used a four-letter word, as many newspapers had said. He had personally seen a re-run of the programme and what Mr. Sullivan had said was 'nick-off', a phrase used in normal speech in Cumberland and the North West. That was all.

Chapter Twenty

Now that Jake was famous, he was laying them in elegant drawing rooms instead of bedsitters, but the details seemed much the same. Jake was always fabulous. He gave them the best time they'd ever had. Jake was always being told this.

'Do you fuck?' was Jake's opening gambit. He was now specializing in rich young society wives of rich old middle aged men. They have nothing else to think about. In the afternoons, when the nannies are out with the kids, nothing else to do. There was one titled woman, married to an ex-MP, who had lemon tea, cucumber sandwiches and a warm bed all ready for him every afternoon at four o'clock. He'd picked her up at one of her famous ten-a-side dinner parties where he'd managed to insult every one there, most of all her husband. She specialized in up and coming, dynamic aggressive working class lovers, collecting them as her friends collected charities or china. He went to her house every afternoon for a week until Michael told him, when he'd been boasting about her at a board meeting, that she was known as the easiest lay in Debrett.

'Well, at least I know *you* haven't had a go at her,' said Jake. Michael walked out of the meeting before Jake could go on. But the minute he'd gone, Jake changed the subject.

I went round to his flat one night and found a man ringing the bell who was carrying the latest Super Eight cine camera. He said it was a present for Mr. Sullivan, purely a goodwill gesture. He did happen to have a photographer outside and he was hoping he could be photographed handing it over to Mr. Sullivan, just for the trade press, not the nationals. It wasn't a publicity stunt, oh my word, no.

Jake opened the door, pulled me in, held his hand out while the man presented the camera to him, greasing on about how his company hoped Mr. Sullivan would get many years of pleasure and perhaps Mr. Sullivan might ... but Jake had the door slammed while he was still talking.

I said he should give the camera back, he was compromising himself by accepting it.

'Get stuffed. It's blackmail, that's all it is. What you do with blackmail is accept the bribe but do nothing else. I accept everything. Everything. Have a peanut.'

He had a shelf full of twenty large size tins, another present from the manufacturers after he'd said on Juke Box Jury that he loved peanuts. 'What I actually said was penis, but nobody's sent me one yet.'

I hadn't been round to his flat for a few months. All his spare time had been spent recently with Rupert or Henry who'd been taking Jake round the society circles.

On his own he was still OK, but surrounded by people like Rupert, the worst in him was brought out. I suppose in a way I was jealous. They were providing the sort of attention he'd never had, just as I had been brought in to provide the child-like surprises he wasn't getting. He was awful to them all the time, telling them how much he hated and despised them, but he still let them do things for him, accepting everything, ungraciously and ungratefully.

'OK, so don't have any peanuts. Now, what else has arrived today? Oh, yeh, there's some more rubbish in the bedroom. Have a look, see if you fancy one.'

I opened his bedroom door slowly, knowing it would be something stupid. I could see two female forms stretched out on his circular bed. Neither of them moved. I came back and said I'd have a peanut after all.

'The one that wakens up first is yours, OK?' said Jake. 'Have a drink, or do you want some pot?'

'No thanks.'

'Still the same bloody prude.'

'That's right.'

'I hear Antonia's gone off to Mongolia with some Yid.'

'America, and he's Indian.'

Not that the details mattered. Antonia had decided to spend the summer vacation touring American campuses with some stupid OUDS productions of The Caucasian Chalk Circle. She was Grusha and this smooth Indian was the King. I'd wanted her to spend the summer with me in my posh flat. She said every time she came to it she felt like a call girl and, anyway, her father was bound to find out she was living with me. I said what if he finds out you're living with this Indian on your American tour? Very funny she said.

We'd agreed there was nothing sacred about sex, inside or outside marriage. All our contemporaries were sleeping around. We'd agreed it was pointless to wait until we were married, and the official starting gun went off, as if that meant anything. All the same, I was a bit late getting started. I'd missed out when Jake and the rest had been passing contraceptives round the class and fitting them on under the desks when we were fourteen. That would have been the best time, when it was either just a laugh, or a schoolboy dare. I'd been too stuck up.

I'd said to Antonia it was against my principles to pull those awful things on. In the end Antonia went to get fitted up. Fair's fair, equality of the sexes and all that. The minute she mentioned it in college, about a dozen girls, all fresh out of Cheltenham and Roedean, were rushing to give her addresses of little women whom mummy had taken them to when they were twelve. We picked one off Harley Street. She turned out to be not a little woman at all. She was enormous. She was called Ernie, at least it sounded like Ernie. She marched in, like a lesbian butcher, with arms bare and her moustache bristling. 'Knickers down' she shouted, walking along a row of little cubicles where Antonia and a lot of twelve-year-olds were crouching.

They all screamed back at college. They'd meant for her to go on the pill, not get a diaphragm. That was like being back in the Ark for Chrissake. Antonia said it was against her principles. The pill hadn't been tested long enough.

'It must be great to be faithful,' said Jake, turning up the volume on 'A Hard Day's Night', two of his TV sets and a tape recorder on which some Indian woman was huskily reading out choice bits from the Kama Sutra. 'She's an Indian you know,' he kept on saying. There had been complaints from neighbours about the noise Jake made, so he'd bought the flats on either side of him. He wanted me to have one but I'd refused. Jake used one as a corridor, walking through it, kicking the walls when he felt like some exercise. The other was turned into a cinema and a games room. There was a choice of games, all of the sort found in fair grounds, a row of one-armed bandits, two juke boxes, a roll-penny stall, What the Butler Saw, a Test your Strength machine and a rifle range. I envisaged him having to buy over the whole block when I heard the noise the rifle made, but after a week's constant use, he hadn't been in the games room since.

'Don't you ever fancy anyone else?' continued Jake. It was a change to hear him asking about my sex life rather than boasting about his own. 'I do all the time. I'm off them before I'm on them some times. By the time I get them in bed I'm mentally stripping someone else in my head so that I can manage it. It's just like a hot meal you know. Blokes happen to be able to eat a hot meal at all times of the day, when they suddenly feel like it, but women don't. Their organs are different, you know.'

'I know,' I said. 'I've seen the film.'

'Blokes get aroused quickly, then it's over. It doesn't mean a thing. You only get hung up when you make it important. Women's needs are different. They only have an orgasm now and again.'

'It's like being back in Sunday School this . . .'

'Women need love,' said Jake, determined to finish his home-spun thoughts. 'And men need sex, and if you don't shut up being fucking cheeky I'll thump you.'

When Jake made jokes, then it was jokes all round, but when Jake was being serious, no one had to mock him. I was embarrassed, that was the main reason for trying to be funny. I didn't want to hear what he was saying because I was beginning to think it was true. The day I'd suddenly stopped saying my prayers, I'd expected God to strike me down. He hadn't, not so I'd noticed anyway. Perhaps if I now stopped being faithful nothing would happen either. I'd be disbelieving in Santa Claus next.

'Sorry sir,' I said. 'I won't do it again.'

'Oh, do it again. Please,' said a voice from the doorway. It was one of the girls, clutching herself across the bosom, trying not to hide herself in a bath towel. She had a faint Scottish accent, but putting on the London posh.

'First on,' said Jake, pouring himself another drink. 'Let's have you. Look after him, eh, Rose? He's just come out of a monastery.'

'Super,' she said, disappearing toward another bedroom.

I hesitated for a moment. Jake was messing around with some new tapes, taking no notice of me. It was like being on the buses again. When the inspector told you to be at the Town

Hall you did absolutely nothing for ten seconds, to show you weren't going to be bossed around, then you ran like mad to get there in time. I stood up, yawned, looked at Jake who was still busy, then followed Rose to the bedroom.

I got undressed quickly and got into bed and lay there, wondering what Antonia was doing in Swathmore, Penn. Then I wondered if Jake had a secret camera in the ceiling, filming it all. Then I wondered if it was all a joke and he'd just leave me there for hours, in an empty flat. I'd already lost most of the excitement, lying there in the cold sheets.

Rose came through a side door, which I hadn't noticed, from what looked like a dressing room. She was naked, clutching a cheap plastic sponge bag instead of the towel. She gave me a disembodied smile, the sort window dressers give if you stare at them long enough through the window as they arrange the paper grass and cardboard flowers in their stockinged feet. The cheeks of her bottom were indented like old button-back chairs. They sagged and swayed and seemed very long as if they'd been stretched. She had three large moles down the middle of her back like little traffic lights. I made a note to keep away from them. I put my hand down slowly and felt a few invisible stubbles. She smiled, faintly, but at long range, moved not by me but by something which had happened at the back of her head. It was her first week on the counter at Woolworths in Sauchiehall Street and the manager had asked her to come to his office to check his stocks.

Rose gave a last shake, opened her eyes and looked at me through the shop window, as if surprised to see someone had been watching her outside. Wonderful, she said, you were just great. Have you seen my ciggies? I had them earlier. What's your name, pet?

'I wasn't great,' I said. 'I was useless.'

'Well, I didna expect you to be any better, pet.'

'I'm sorry.'

'Don't apologize. I don't care. It doesn't matter to me. It's your wife I feel sorry for. You can't give her much fun.'

She turned and was asleep, genuinely, in a minute. My longed for complete exhaustion wouldn't come. I didn't look like a married bloke, did I? Perhaps she said that to everyone. She hadn't meant it as an insult. Just an idle observation. A professional casually casting an eye over a struggling amateur.

I got out of bed, jumping up quickly, trying to throw ev[erything] into the past. I searched for my underpants. I hop[ed] Jake hadn't moved them, as a stupid joke. It would be just lik[e] him to appear from under the bed, or to wave down from a[?] one way mirror in the ceiling. I found them, covered in Rose's cigarette ash.

I went out quickly, determined to get home as soon as possible and to sleep. Jake was probably on his seventeenth performance by now and getting ready for another encore. He said Hi as I came into the main room. I hadn't seen him lying on the floor. He was turning over the pages of an advance copy of Keble Martin's Flora of the British Isles which I'd given him that morning. He was fascinated by himself being fascinated by it and obviously wanted me to listen to what he'd discovered.

'Haven't you been in . . . the . . .' I started.

'What? No, I went off the idea. Just a couple of scrubbers those two. I'd have to be really pissed to fancy them. How was Rose?'

'OK. She's a real goer. A right sexy little bit.'

'Like hell. She hates it, almost as much as she hates working. But she tries hard. Someone once told her that she must go on as if she has an orgasm every time, just to make the bloke feel good. Did this bloke really start work on this book in 1898? It's bloody amazing.'

'She's professional then, is she?'

'The drawings are fantastic. He did them as well, didn't he. Oh yeh, Rose. Very high class. But she's like all high class whores. All technique and no feeling.'

'What's wrong with that?' I said. If the technique was good and satisfying enough, I could see that having feelings could only complicate and mess things up. I was glad that Rose at least didn't pretend, before or after, that it was a big gooey love match.

'Do you know,' said Jake, closing his book and turning over on his back, 'who I had the best lays with?'

'Nobody.'

'Now, now buster, there's no need to be cynical, just 'cos you never got in.'

'I did.'

'Don't lie.'

Tell me then.'

'Beryl. Really. Those first few months were fantastic. I fancied her all the time, in every way. I couldn't get over the fact that she'd married me. That I'd got her. The bird I'd drooled over for so long.'

I didn't say anything. I wanted to get home.

'I envy you, you know,' continued Jake.

'Oh aye,' I said, expecting some smart follow-up, to wipe out what he'd given away by his Beryl admission.

'You and Antonia. It must be great to have a big steady thing and want nothing else. That's how it should be. You might not get it as often, but that's when you get the best fucks, when you're both in love.'

'I don't know,' I said, embarrassed. 'Look at all the smashing lays you've had. Different ones all the time. I thought that was what blokes needed, so you said.'

'They're all so bloody stupid. I can't bear the look of them, before or afterwards. I may be a sex maniac, but I wanna talk to them now and again for Christ's sake. Sit down and have a drink.'

'Thanks, but I've gotta go.'

I went to the door. He picked up his book again and flicked over the pages.

'I didn't think you would, you know,' said Jake. I didn't answer. 'You've let me down. But we've all got to go through it. To find out. That's the draggy thing about life.

'We used to have this mingy bit of roast beef every Sunday dinner. Lilly would give us so little I could hardly see it. She'd be keeping the rest for cold on Monday and soup on Tuesday and Christ knows what else. I vowed when I had any money I'd eat a whole roast, at once, all to me self. And I did. Now I know one slice, beautifully done, once a week, is best.

'Anyway,' he said as I went out. 'I'm getting married again. If you're doing nothing at lunch time tomorrow, come round and have some Babycham.'

Part Four

Chapter Twenty-one

Jake's second marriage was as unceremonious as his first. It was again a registry office ceremony and Michael was again best man. I was a bit hurt Jake hadn't asked me to Caxton Hall, but I suppose Michael looked good on those sort of occasions. I was more upset that I hadn't been told till the last minute.

I sat in his flat not knowing who his new wife was going to be. Nobody at the office, not even egregious Rupert, had any idea he was getting married again. I was very pleased Rupert didn't know, though it meant that just as I was getting close to Jake again, someone else must have come into his life. I'd bought a present, but I was keeping it inside my pocket, in case it was all a trick.

I could hear a lot of laughing and shouting outside. Ron Rogers entered, followed by Jake with his arm round Chloe. Jake had a carnation in the buttonhole of his brightly striped Ivy League blazer, the only sign that he had been to a wedding. He tried to pick up Chloe and carry her into the flat, but she playfully pushed him away and told him not to be so silly.

'Wincarnis or Babycham?' said Jake, giggling and pouring out champagne for everyone.

'Well, congratulations,' I said.

'Thank you Tom,' said Chloe, giving me her big smile. 'Darling, just a little for me.'

It was strange to hear Jake being called darling. Beryl now and again had called him sweetie and that had been ridiculous. Jake gave Chloe a kiss as he gave her a drink. She accepted both in passing and went into the kitchen to fetch the savouries. There was no sign of Jones, Jake's manservant. She looked quietly radiant as she handed them round. She'd thrown off some of the top layers of the really gooey charm and appeared naturally nice. She was in a lilac-coloured cotton suit with a simple broderie anglaise blouse underneath. It made her seem even thinner and more flat chested, but at the same time very demure and fragrant.

Jake had gone a bit softer. He hadn't belched or farted once since he'd come in. Perhaps they were going to be good for each other.

'How's it going lass?' said Jake in mock Carlisle. It sounded stupid, as it always does when somebody with a natural regional accent tries to put one on. It's almost as funny as a posh person imitating a posh accent.

'Grand, lad,' said Chloe. 'Just grand, lad.'

She gave a last look round to see everyone was happy, and then went into the bedroom. Michael and Ron had started a Cambridge conversation, out of embarrassment when Jake and Chloe had gone into their country bumpkin chat.

'Hey, you two best men,' said Jake. 'Stop yattering. It's my bloody day, isn't it?'

'It's always your day, Jake,' said Michael.

We stood around in silence. Jake was grinning and winking at me. Michael was awkward. Ron was searching hard for smart remarks, to goad Jake into being Jake.

'Have you booked the Savoy Grill?' asked Michael.

'I've changed my mind. Too vulgar. I want something a bit more private.'

'You mean *Chloe* said it was too vulgar,' said Ron.

'Do you want to be thumped?' said Jake, laughing, knowing he was going through an old routine. He was now the proud husband, proud that his wife was a strong personality.

Chloe reappeared in a well tailored tweed suit, heavy brogues and a high neck woollen jumper. We all piled into Jake's Rolls and drove to the Trattoria Terrazza where we were ushered into a private room.

'Whose side are you on?' said Jake to a waiter in a striped jersey. The meal was a strain at first. It was somehow topsy turvy, as if we were having Christmas Dinner in midsummer.

'I wanted to have a big do,' said Jake. 'With three hundred people, ten beat groups and naked girls jumping out of balloons. But Chloe was against it.'

'I've always hated balloons,' said Chloe, smiling at me.

Five was an odd, artificial number. I felt the oddest of all which Chloe seemed to realize and tried to chat to me, asking about Jake's childhood and was he as awful then as he is now. Jake kept butting in like a little boy, forcing everyone to listen to him, saying it was his day.

There was a commotion at the doorway and a middle aged bloke wearing an RAF moustache staggered in. The waiters tried to restrain him, saying it was a private party. Jake beckoned him in, offered him some champagne, said sit down, he was just having his Bar Mitzvah.

'I only want your autograph,' said the man, aggressively. 'Not for me, you understand. My silly wife has got it into her fat head that you're somebody called Jake Sullivan. Well, are you?'

'Not somebody called Jake Sullivan,' said Ron. 'A nobody called Jake Sullivan.'

Jake took the man's biro, asked him his wife's name and scribbled. 'Happy Chinese New Year Enid from Jake Sullivan' on a piece of paper. He gave the man a big smile, being extra nice because the man was so obnoxious.

'I don't know how you can put up with people like that,' said Ron. For once, I agreed with him.

'He was demanding your autograph, as if it was your duty,' I said.

'It is,' said Chloe, smiling round, almost as a challenge.

'What is his duty?' said Ron coldly.

'I think you're smashing,' said Jake, leaning over and kissing Chloe on the cheek. She moved him carefully back in his place, preening herself. 'Don't you think she's smashing, Tom?'

'Tom, didn't you hear me?' continued Jake. 'I said isn't she smashing?'

Chloe put her hand over Jake's mouth and shushed him. He pretended to nibble her hand, putting salt and pepper on and carving it.

'Jake is in the fortunate position where he now doesn't *have* to be nice to anyone,' said Chloe. 'It is therefore even more his duty to be nice to everyone.'

'What do you mean now?' I said. 'He's *never* tried to be nice to people.'

'Exactly,' said Ron. He wasn't such a bad bloke after all. 'I would say Jake is the nastiest bloke I've ever met.'

'If I wasn't so nice I'd plate you,' said Jake, loving being discussed to his face.

'I like him because he's nasty,' said Ron. 'The people I hate are all these phoney charmers.' Chloe smiled charmingly at this. 'If he had been nice, he would never have succeeded.

Have you ever met a nice millionaire? No, of course you haven't. Nice people aren't materialistic. They don't want to dominate, to prove anything or to work off grudges or inadequacies, that's why they're never millionaires.'

'Tell me about my inadequacies, Ron,' said Jake. 'Go on.'

'Beethoven was a nasty bit of work. He got VD and went deaf because of it. Tolstoy was a sex maniac. You wouldn't call that nice. Dickens was sleeping with his sister-in-law. Shakespeare was laying them all over the place. You wouldn't call that nice. No, nice people never did anything in this world.'

'What about Jesus?' said Chloe. I half thought this was a joke, but her face was serious, defying anyone to titter.

'Look what happened to him, for Christ's sake,' said Ron.

'Exactly,' said Chloe, timing it perfectly, bringing Ron to a halt as he listened to his last remark. The lunch was livening up. I was glad to be in the discussion for a change, though it was already beginning to jump all over the place, leaving me out.

'What Ron is twisting nice to mean is hypocritical,' said Chloe. 'As if someone who is nice is therefore false. Ron is a great believer in the virtue of vice and the vice of virtue.'

'That's put you in your place, Ron,' said Jake.

'Well I'm glad I'm not in your place,' said Ron. There was a moment's pause. I think Ron half regretted that remark. It was the nuptial lunch, after all. Jake was rising to thump Ron, but Chloe restrained him. You could almost see her 'enjoying a stimulating conversation'.

'To get back to the point,' she said. 'I meant it was Jake's duty to be civil and courteous to everyone, whatever he thinks about them. I don't mean he should pretend he thinks they're wonderful when he doesn't. That *is* being hypocritical, not nice.'

Chloe had been married before, which I found surprising. She'd gone to all the right schools, at home and abroad, the sort which are supposed to insulate you from any chancers on the make. In Switzerland she'd been made by a forty-year-old international chancer who was supposed to be teaching her French. She'd been eighteen. They were married for two years before she found out he was still chancing himself with other teenage girls. She'd come back to London, determined never to be taken in by men again and to carve out a career for herself, relying on no one. She'd started as a secretary to a literary agency; then set herself up on her own. She'd had a brief affair with Ron, which he now boasted about. She had really been using Ron. Through him, she'd made contact with all the Varsity and Footlights bright young men, signing them up before they'd left Cambridge. When you branch out on your own as an agent, you've got to be prepared to dig out new talent before anyone else has seen it. She'd started with a couple of romantic novelists, who had followed her from her first agency, impressed by her breeding and her efficiency, and for a year they were the only two who'd made any momey. Then one Cambridge bloke blossomed into a TV star and another a pop star. Only Ron hadn't actually done anything yet, though she had sold his famous unfinished masterpiece.

Marrying Jake meant that Chloe's agency was now secure. She had the money behind her to do what she liked. It probably made her more secure all round, as a person. All that measured charm must be covering up for something.

Why else had she married him? It's hard to say. Perhaps she loved him and that's all there was to it. Unlike poles attracting. Apart from the money, she was no doubt attracted by his image, the tough working class contemporary sort of hero which so many well bred girls were falling for. He was exciting, I suppose, if you like that sort of excitement. He was sexy. As for the things he wasn't, like Beryl, Chloe probably thought it was her duty to give him these things. She would knock him into shape. Right from the beginning, this was what she started to do.

Chloe hadn't told Jake they were going to the Lakes. He'd said he fancied honeymooning in the West Indies. She'd booked the Sharrow Bay hotel on Ullswater, which was just the sort of smart place she would know about. Jake loved the idea of her arranging things for him, especially something like going on a train with the plebs. He hadn't been on a train since he first came to London. Chloe had sacked Jones the morning they got married. Her next move was to make him get rid of some of his cars. She said they were pure ostentation.

'Let's go and see your mother,' said Chloe, jumping up brightly on the third day of their honeymoon.

'So that's the fiendish plot, is it?' said Jake. 'I might have known.'

'I can't understand why you try to keep her hidden from me. You know I'd love to see her.'

'I was just making it all up, that was the reason. I'm an orphan.'

'What?' said Chloe, worried for a moment. Perhaps he had lied to her.

'Yes,' said Jake sadly. 'It's because I'm always off and on . . .'

He leaned out of the bed and tried to grab Chloe and bring her back on the bed, but she shook him off.

'Oh come on. Don't be rotten.'

'I'm not being rotten. It would be silly to start that now. I'll be tired all day and we've too much to do.'

'I won't be tired.'

'You were tired last night,' said Chloe.

They got a hired car to Thwaite. Chloe was all for them walking into Penrith and getting a bus, but Jake said in that case he was definitely staying in bed. The house was empty. They sat outside for an hour, waiting for Jake's mother to arrive.

'She probably doesn't live here any more,' said Jake. 'I can't remember now if she died or not. We should have brought Tom. He remembers them sort of things.'

'*Those* sort of things,' corrected Chloe.

'Which? Where, what you on about?'

'Haven't you ever tried to contact her? You are frightful, Jake.'

'She refused to see me.'

Jake had intended to tell Chloe about the trick he pulled on his mother, when he sold her house. He'd always been guilty about it, but he didn't want her to say he was making a virtue out of admitting such an awful thing. He knew he should have done something positive about it years ago. Each morning of the honeymoon he'd been going to tell her, but she'd been so busy getting him up and out, organizing expeditions, walks, boat trips.

Lilly looked older and worn. Jake hardly recognized her. She was in the gate and through the front door before he realized. He had to knock at the door to be let in. His mother didn't know him either at first, she didn't associate him standing there on the front door step with this elegant lady.

'This is my wife, Mam.'

'My, you've grown tall, Beryl.'

'She's called Chloe, Mam,' said Jake pushing past her and into the house. He'd hoped she wouldn't be in. Chloe was thrilled. She was all set to charm the pants off Lilly. She saw herself being super friends with this simple peasant woman, really understanding her, which was obviously something Jake had never tried to do.

'Have you changed your name then?' said Lilly, going round picking clothes from a steaming clothes horse round the fire and shoving them in a cupboard. 'I've heard of people doing these funny things when they get to London . . .'

'No, she's my new wife. I got divorced from Beryl.'

'Oh, Jake,' said his mother, straightening up and looking at Jake then looking away again quickly. She'd got smaller since he'd last seen her. 'That wasn't nice.'

'No, it wasn't,' said Jake lamely, opening cupboards. 'Heh, this is a drying cupboard, you know. What you putting clothes round the fire for? You're not in Solway Terrace now.'

'Lovely girl, Beryl,' said Lilly.

'You never met her,' said Jake, staring out of the window, looking for Daft Jimmy.

'Didn't I? What name did you say this one was?'

'My name's Chloe,' said Chloe, going over to Lilly and trying to take her by the arm, to show she wasn't against touching such people. 'Please don't put everything away, Mrs. Sullivan. I want to see it as it is, and you. Come on now, my dear, sit down. I've heard so *much* about you.'

'Oh?' said Lilly, cocking her head on one side, suspiciously. She refused to sit down and went on clearing up. Chloe sat down on the battered couch, smiled up in the air, stretching her arms and breathing in the lovely home atmosphere. It does me good to get back to the roots.

'Oh, what a beautiful clock. Can I look at it?'

Chloe simpered, then jumped up like a young elf. Lilly looked at her as if she was a bit simple. Chloe read out the inscription on the clock, all about William Sullivan's colleagues at Armstrongs wanting to show their mark of respect on the occasion of his demise. She made it sound like the first part of a gay story on BBC Woman's Hour.

'Chloe?' said Lilly, flatly. 'Is it foreign? Everybody has these foreign names these days. I don't know what's wrong with the good old English names, like Sarah and Rebecca and Mary ...'

'They're Jewish,' said Jake.

'Oh, are you?' said Lilly, turning to Chloe. 'You don't look it. Of course they never do these days. False hair, false teeth, false noses. I don't know what the world's coming to. I really don't ...'

'Not that one again, eh Mam,' said Jake. 'Where've you been this aftie? We've been waiting hours for you.'

'Oh, listen to me going on. I haven't offered your wife a cup of tea. She must think I'm awful.'

'I certainly don't think that, Mrs. Sullivan,' said Chloe, beaming. 'Or may I call you Lilly?'

Lilly stopped dead in her tracks. It was as if Chloe had made some indecent suggestion. Nobody called her Lilly. Neighbours in Solway Terrace, whom she'd known all her life, had always called her Mrs. Sullivan. Even Willy had avoided anything so intimate and personal. He'd called her Mother, conjugating it according to the context, mainly Your Mother as he tended to talk about her in the third person, even when she was there.

Chloe got the message quickly and changed the subject hurriedly.

'And how's Cedric doing, Mrs. Sullivan?'

'Wonderful,' said Lilly, slowly softening. 'He's such a good son. I always knew he'd do well. He was never fast or clever, like the other one.' For a moment Chloe thought there was another child she didn't know about, then smiled as she realized this meant Jake. 'But oh what a lovely little boy he was. So good and happy, and so pretty. Not like the other one. Oh, I'd give anything to have him back now.'

'He's dead is he?' said Jake.

'Oh Jake, what a terrible thing to say,' said Lilly, genuinely hurt.

Chloe gave him a look, ordering him to behave better, which he ignored.

'Where is he, then?' said Jake. 'Hiding?'

'He's at Spadeadam during the week,' said Lilly. 'He's got a very good job. You know, yon rocket place. He's really deserved all his success.'

'I don't call working at Spadeadam a success,' said Jake.

'Not just that,' said Lilly, looking round in case anyone was watching at the windows. 'I'm not supposed to tell anyone. Promise you won't. Jake? Beryl? Ssh. Promise? He'd never forgive me.'

'Oh Mam,' said Jake. 'Come on, I'm wetting myself.'

'Well, on Saturday afternoon a Carlisle United scout came to watch the team. That meant Cedric, of course. He *is* the team. We've been expecting a knock at the door all week. Fact, when I saw the car I thought it was them, till I saw the girl . . .'

'That's wonderful, Mrs. Sullivan,' said Chloe. 'You must be very proud.'

'Fab gear,' said Jake, giving a heavy sigh and looking at his watch.

'It's the best thing that's happened to us since poor Willie passed away. If only he'd been here. He always hoped one of them would do well, and Cedric was his favourite.'

'What about me, Mam. Don't you think I've done well?'

'What? Carlisle United aren't after you are they?'

'I mean my job.'

'Your job. Oh yes. Very nice. Talking about jobs, have you heard about Tom Graham? You remember him? Grand lad. His Dad died in Wales, or was it Ireland. Down a pit, or was it in the war?'

'A Welsh pit, mother.'

'He was in your class at school wasn't he? Then he went on to university. Clever lad, though no cleverer than you could have been if you'd stuck in. I was talking to his Mam in the Co-op yesterday and she was saying he'd got this big job as assistant to the chairman of this big company. In London I think she said. He has done well. But his poor Mam. She looked very poorly to me . . .'

'Mam, you're raving,' said Jake, coming over beside her. He'd been standing behind her making funny faces, pretending to wind her up like a gramophone. 'It's me!'

'I know it is dear. It's very nice of you to come. Oh, I haven't made that tea yet. I'm wandering in my old age, I really am. I go up street all the time and never know what I'm going for.'

'Never mind the tea, Mam. We've got to go. We can only spare half an hour . . .' He ushered Chloe towards the door.

'Oh well, if that's how it is,' said his mother, rather sharply.

'Rush, rush, rush as usual. Only half an hour. I see. It took longer than that to have you, but I s'pose that doesn't mean anything.'

Chapter Twenty-two

When Jake came back from his honeymoon I said I was going. Jake said don't be daft. I said I'm not. Where's me cards.

What had I to give him? Chloe was such a culture vulture, far more clued up than me. She was at every first night and if there wasn't one in the West End, she made an expedition to Stratford or an evening out at Glyndebourne. She particularly loved Glyndebourne, dressing up to stun them all. Sammy had given him Soho. Ron had given him Cambridge. Rupert had given him society. Chloe would give him culture. So what hope was there for me.

I said I was thinking of TV. Jake said I'd be useless. I had no personality, unlike him. I said thanks. OK, he said, if I stayed with him another year, he'd buy me a nice literary magazine which I could run myself. I said oh yeh. He said it would have to make money, naturally. He wasn't an idiot. But first, for a year, I would become more of his personal assistant, seeing how business worked.

Perhaps another year would be fine. Antonia was now doing research. She could join me on the magazine when she finished if, of course, it ever materialized. I'd heard those sort of stories before.

Getting to know more about the business turned out to be interesting. His continuing success had surprised most people, but I'd been rather bored by it recently to pay much attention.

One of the inbuilt handicaps of meteoric success is that you can't keep it up. The curve is bound to start straightening out. If it suddenly starts straightening, at a moment when you've got all your capital tied up in new schemes and you can't get hold of it, then you can be in trouble. Shortage of liquidity, or something like that, is what the experts call it. Rumours go round, people lose confidence, backers draw out, shares drop and soon even the paper millions are down to paper hundreds.

The know-alls had been forecasting this about Jake since the beginning. He himself admitted the problem by once saying that if he stood still, then he might as well give up, because that was the same as going backwards.

The heads started nodding first of all in 1962 when capital gains tax began at last to be introduced. This would soon put Jake in his place, so everyone said. It did cut down some of his profits on each scheme, but Jake had so many new ones coming into action at the time that it didn't affect his overall profits too much. Instead of diversifying, looking for easy profits elsewhere, Jake decided that he knew property best. And anyway, whatever the temporary restrictions, land was a limited commodity and in the long run it was the thing to be in.

He consolidated what he had, concentrating personally on big schemes, and at the same time he went in for take-over bids. This needed the same flair. With property, you see a site which you consider underdeveloped and then you develop it. With takeovers, you see a business which you consider undervalued, then you develop it to its full value. In both cases, you needn't actually do any work yourself.

Jake's first take-over was for a string of fish shops. It had started when one fish shop happened to be in the way of a development scheme. In looking into its value, he found that its site was still down in the books at its pre-war valuation. It turned out the directors had no real idea of its present value and there were twenty shops in the chain, all in good situations in London and the suburbs, and all similarly grossly undervalued. He bought the whole lot for half a million. He then sold the freeholds of half of them to an insurance company for half a million, buying back long leases at modest rentals. This meant he ended up with a chain of fish shops which were making a good profit, and on which he could still raise plenty of money if he wanted, plus the half million he'd started with.

Other take-overs were harder. Once it was known he was interested, others tried to get in, the directors fought hard to keep him off and the price went up. But usually he still managed it.

213

There were more rumours that his end was nigh when a huge block he'd put up in Oxford Street remained empty for a year. He wanted a rent of £50,000 a year, which even the estate agents handling it said he'd never get. At the end of the year they said he should take £40,000, which had been the only offer, and one they thought very good. It was doing both his reputation and theirs harm, by lying empty. They'd never get £50,000. Jake said he wouldn't take £50,000 now anyway. The rent was now £55,000. And every month it remained empty, it had to go up another £5,000.

At the end of a further six months, when the asking rent was £80,000, there was an offer of £70,000. Jake agreed, giving in slightly. He was very pleased. I said it all seemed mad to me. He'd lost eighteen months rent.

'Haven't you learned anything, you schmuck? At a rent of £70,000 a year that lot is now worth a million quid to anyone who wants to buy it from me. At a rent of £40,000 a year it was only worth £600,000. It's the value of a property I'm interested in. The gain in total value in eighteen months has been £400,000. The loss in rents has been fuck all, say £60,000. Who wants fucking rents? All you do is pay tax on them.'

'But what about the upkeep?' I asked.

'What upkeep? You don't pay rates on empties. Christ, have you been asleep in that office of yours?'

The next big scare in the property world was in November 1964 when George Brown put a ban on any more office developments in London. There had been a lot of luxury blocks lying empty, while London's homeless increased, and every right-minded person naturally thought this was disgusting.

Many developers began to panic, caught half way in setting up new deals. But Jake was very lucky. It just so happened that he'd completed a batch of buildings. He had one particular one which had lain empty for nine months. It was his biggest so far and he was genuinely worried. There was so much cash tied up in it that he needed it back quickly for other schemes but the minute the ban on more buildings came into being, there was a scurry to buy up what was empty. People in the middle of plans with other developers drew out sharpish to buy up what was already there. Jake sold his block overnight, for his fancy asking price.

The Brown ban had the effect of shooting rents up, as the

supply was now limited. People like Jake, who was already doing well, did even better. He was able to ride the restrictions easily, taking in a lot of cash and having a go at more take-over bids of existing, but undervalued, properties, until the restrictions on building new ones were lessened.

By around 1966, when Jake married Chloe, and the height of the boom was over, he was looking for a really Big Scheme. Not to make himself safe. He'd already made more than enough money to get out for good if he wanted. But he'd always done something bigger and better all the time. It had been a gradation, all the way from Carlisle to London and from house conversions to skyscraper blocks. He was always bored with every scheme the minute it had succeeded and impatient to go on to something new and better and different.

The first thing which Chloe made Jake do when they got back from the honeymoon was shave under his arms.

'What do you think I am?' said Jake. 'A bloody poof?'

'I've always done it,' said Chloe. 'Since I was fifteen.'

'Don't, don't,' said Jake. 'You're ruining the mystery.'

They were sitting on the roof balcony of Jake's Park Lane flat having breakfast, prepared by Chloe; unsweetened orange juice and one Ryvita each. Jones had always made Jake two fried egg sandwiches every morning, the most disgusting thing Chloe had ever heard. It probably explained why Jake was far too fat and unhealthy. As well as smelly.

'I don't smell,' said Jake. 'Apart from the sweet smell of suck sex.'

'You do.'

'Have you noticed how sex has a fishy smell, like sardines? I wonder what fish fucking smell of?'

As he was talking, Jake tried to grab a second Ryvita but Chloe was too quick and had the packet wrapped up and out of his reach. Jake's language was getting back to normal again, but Chloe was more interested in his body at that moment. She'd get back to his language later.

'You'll find a new razor in your bathroom. I want you to use it every three days. The smell of your stale sweat last night was revolting.'

'Do you know that in South America stale sweat is the big thing? The blokes like their women to have a lot of it, especially under their arms. The more hair the better. It's like tits in Europe, bottoms in Africa and noses in Greenland. It's the big thing.'

'And I think you should shampoo your hair every day for a few weeks. It's become very greasy at the back. If you insist on wearing it that ridiculous length, then it *must* be kept clean.'

'Yes Mam, three bags full Mam. What time's the kit inspection?'

Chloe leaned over the table and kissed him. They embraced for about fifteen seconds, then Chloe said she had to rush. She had to be in her office.

Jake was working hard on his Big Scheme, but Chloe was working almost as hard on her business, and she had the flat to look after. A daily came in to clean, but apart from that Chloe did everything else. She said she didn't like having staff. She was too good to them she said, it meant she inevitably got involved in their personal problems. Staff always seemed to have personal problems. Anyway, it was her *duty* to look after her husband, Chloe would say as she let it out that she did everything. People would say how marvellous, you are clever, how efficient. Jake would say yes, he was getting her a paper round next.

'The thing about Chloe,' he told me one day, 'is that she is always gainfully employed.'

It was true. She never gossiped, never lazed, never let others do what she couldn't do herself. In fact you couldn't fault her on anything. She looked good, spoke good, thought good. On Sunday mornings she even went off and did welfare work in the East End, visiting the housebound elderly, while Jake lay in bed with The People and the News of the World.

But what chuffed Jake most of all was that he discovered she was in Debrett. She hadn't even told him before. Why should I, said Chloe.

It had come out one evening. I'd been invited round by Chloe for supper. That was another thing she did. Invited people round for meals. They were talking about children and Chloe said she only wanted two, a boy and a girl. How middle class, I said. It's not, said Chloe. The world's population will have doubled by the year 2000 and we'll all be starving. If only every family restricted themselves to two children there would be no population problem. And anyway, I'm not middle class. What are you then, I asked, expecting her to say upper working class or something smart like that. I had used middle class, as anyone would, as a term of contempt.

'Actually,' she replied, 'I'm upper class.'

This was when it came out that her grandmother was a Lady in her own right and her father, long since dead, had been an Hon. Jake couldn't get over it. He bought copies of Debrett and had them scattered all over his office, open at the right place, though Chloe refused to have any around the flat. She was against clutter and she had turned the flat into an austere, modernistic, neo-Brutalist creation. Plush sofas, thick pile carpets and thick pile wallpaper were definitely out. Out, too, were Jake's framed press cuttings and his chocolate box portrait of himself which were banished to the guest bedroom. Instead, on the stark white walls went stark white abstracts. What she hated most was clutter, in life and in art.

At her own work she got rid of two pieces of clutter she'd despised for a long time, her two elderly romantic novelists. With the security of marriage to Jake behind her and her bright young men at last making money, she could afford to let them go.

Chloe was sitting embroidering with her back to the TV. It was one of their frequent nights in. She refused to go to night clubs. Dinner parties, or cocktails, yes, where she could see and be seen by the people who mattered. But nobody who mattered ever went to a night club. Jake said he hoped nobody dropped in. It would be a queer shan if any of his friends found them just sitting, doing nothing. I'm not doing nothing, Chloe said. I'm embroidering.

'I feel like some chips,' said Jake. 'Fancy some?'

'No thank you. If you want your spots to come back and your stomach to become repulsive again, by all means, go and have some.'

'It was only repulsing you. Nobody else ever said I was fat.'

'Aren't I enough? You've already told me that all those big busted ladies didn't care about your looks, or your mind. They were just after your money.'

Jake came over and lay down at her feet, putting his hand up her leg.

'I thought it was chips you fancied?' said Chloe.

'I fancy you more.'

'Because you can't think of anything else to do. Why don't you read a good book, some Thackeray, Jane Austen or even D. H. Lawrence. I don't suppose you've ever read any of them.'

'I should be reading some files if it comes to reading. Do you want to hear about the Big Scheme?'

'No thanks. I'm taking up a hem.'

'Put it down and give us a kiss, eh? You know, I fancy you more and more all the time. Never happened before. Funny, isn't it?'

'Hilarious,' said Chloe. She peered over her reading glasses, gave him a quick smile, then went back to concentrating on her work.

'You're very sexy you know, despite having no breasts.'

Chloe didn't fall for that one. She smiled, knowing what sort of conversation he was hoping to have.

Jake threw down the TV Times and pretended to sulk, like a little boy.

'Look, put that lousy sewing down and go and make some hot chocolate. You've been at it all night.'

'It's your turn. I made it last night. And make it half and half. I hate it all milk.'

'Christ,' said Jake, 'all these bloody millions I've got and I've got to make me own supper. Heh, what's happened to those bottles of HP sauce I sent Tom to get?'

'I threw them out. My cooking doesn't require sauce.'

'I'll throw you out,' shouted Jake, going round the fridges, picking bits and pieces to eat. 'I know, let's go out and have a drink.'

'You mean you're bored.'

'I didn't say that,' said Jake knowing what sort of conversation Chloe was leading up to. 'OK, let's go to bed.'

'That's exactly what I have every intention of doing,' said Chloe, wrapping up her sewing. 'I've got a very heavy day tomorrow.'

'You always have,' said Jake. 'It's either that or a sore head, or back ache, or tooth ache, or I smell.'

'That's not fair.'

'Sorry,' said Jake, going over and kissing her. She accepted the kiss then pushed him away. She was putting on the sulks now.

'You can put your pyjamas on,' she said as they were getting into bed.

'Why?'

'You'll catch cold otherwise,' she said.

'All you think about is not-sex,' said Jake. 'Your mind is preoccupied, by not feeling like it, not wanting it, not going to give in. You're a not-sex maniac. You should see a not-sexologist. The cure will be to give up not having it. Come on, start now . . .'

'Stop it Jake,' said Chloe, pushing his hand away. 'I really am very tired.'

'Naturally.'

Chloe didn't reply to this one. She gave him a kiss, at long distance, on his forehead, then turned over. Jake lay on his back, looking up at the ceiling. He couldn't stand this going to bed early.

'Do you know what a First Class Covenant is?' he said after a pause.

'Huh,' grunted Chloe.

'It's what we call a really big tenant, like ICI or Shell or the Government. If you can get someone really big and solid like them to fill a building, then you can flog it to anyone.'

'Oh yes.'

'And the big insurance companies. They're also First Class Covenants. I was talking to a bloke today who told me that the Prudential has one million quid coming in every working *day*. A *day*! And they're not even the biggest insurance company.'

'Really,' said Chloe.

'They're desperate for something good to invest it in, now that the stock exchange is so dodgy.'

'Is it?'

'So of course, if they can buy a building which already has a First Class Covenant all set up to rent it, then they'd be very keen to buy it. Wouldn't they?'

'Of course.'

'Are you listening? This is the basis of my Big Scheme. Don't you want to hear about it?'

'Ugh.'

'Henry's found out that the Ministry of Defence, a *whole* Ministry, is looking for a new building. They've got bits and pieces all over London at the moment. They could do with about 100,000 square feet for a start. I think I know where I can lay my hands on that, and more. It'll take time, but I can do it.'

'You are clever, Jake,' said Chloe, half asleep.

'It's in Holborn. It's a huge area. Be the biggest development site in London if I get it. Could be 400,000 square feet. That part of Holborn is fetching a rent of £3 a square foot. The whole lot could bring in £1,200,000 a year. That's not peanuts.'

'Not peanuts,' Chloe repeated sleepily.

'If you're not going to listen, I'll shut up.' Jake was hurt, carried away by his Big Scheme and genuinely interested in explaining to Chloe how it worked.

'Honestly, I am,' said Chloe, turning over and managing a sleepy smile. 'It sounds fascinating.'

'I've already got two insurance companies lined up who would buy it from me.'

'How much would they have to pay you, darling?'

'Well, thirteen times the annual rent at least. That's how you usually work out what a property is worth. That comes to £15,000,000. But it'll be worth more by the time it's all ready."

'Good God, that's fantastic! But how much would it cost you to put it up?'

'I estimate I should do everything for five million including a million to buy up the site, piece by piece, using my own money for that. It'll probably cost about three and a half million to build. Then there's all the other expenses. Yeh, I think five million should do it.'

'So your profit will be ten million?'

'Yeh, not bad is it?'

'I can't contemplate it,' said Chloe, lying down in bed again. She couldn't either. The effort of forcing herself awake had been bad enough.

'Don't try,' said Jake. 'My little sexy one. Just cuddle up to Uncle Jake and he'll look after everything . . .'

'No you don't,' said Chloe, turning over and pulling the clothes tightly around herself. 'I was tired before, now I'm absolutely exhausted, listening to all that nonsense. Good night.'

Chapter Twenty-three

'Remember Rita, that coloured bird I used to have?'

Rupert nodded, his lower three chins folded in layers like the Michelin man.

'I'm thinking of bringing her back.'

'Super duper. Rather a dishy girl, I always thought.'

'Like hell. She was a right scrubber.'

'I suppose she was, actually,' said Rupert, still nodding intently.

'She wants to open a girls' hostel. Bring across a few foreign girls, help them to learn the habits and mores of English men. Mores. That's the word, isn't it Tom? I'm going to let her have that empty house in square thirteen,' continued Jake. 'OK, Jimmy?'

'Yes sir,' said Jimmy, fluttering his papers and looking over his half moon spectacles, trying to appear clued-up.

'I say,' said Rupert, slowly, feeling his way. 'You're not thinking of going into brothels, are you Jake?'

'Going into them. I can't keep out of them. I get discount all over London, and Green Shield stamps.'

'I mean owning them.'

'Certainly not. This highly respectable lady wants a ten-bedroom house so I'm letting her have it for six months, rent free.'

'But Jake, the publicity would be most harmful if it ever came out!'

'Listen Fatso, it takes the police time to close a brothel, I mean a girls' hostel. They've got to take it in turns hiding outside the windows, training their binoculars on the vital parts, photographing Mr. X in an intimate position. They can easily spin that out for a year. So tell her six months Jimmy,' continued Jake. 'Then she's out. That should suit our purpose.'

'I hope you don't mind me saying this,' said Henry. 'I'm just speaking off the top of my head, you understand. Shoot me down if you have to. But what exactly is our purpose, Jake old chap?'

It was a question everyone really would like to have asked. It was six months since Jake had first let out bits and pieces about his Big Scheme, but apart from Jake himself, no one yet knew the whole master-plan.

'What they do in brothels is fuck,' said Jake. 'That filthy Anglo-Saxon habit. A lot of nasty stick-in-the-muds think it lowers the tone. So they move out. Got it? We want to get square thirteen cleared, as quickly as possible, don't we? Any news of Cobblestone yet?'

'No sir,' said Jimmy. 'Still refuses to move. We've offered him everything, a new shop anywhere in London, the lot. He's been there all his life and he's not moving. He says he's only going out in a box.'

'That could be arranged,' said Jake.

'I hope you're joking,' said Michael.

'Rupert,' said Jake, 'I want you to go and see Cobblestone. Find out if he likes little boys, or little girls, or whips, leather or anything. And make sure nothing gets into the News or the Standard. I can just see those buggers making a big thing of the little shopkeeper holding out against the big nasty property giants.'

'Yes,' said Rupert. 'I'm sure we'll find a way of doing it amicably. Personally, I'm more worried about that convent school. They say they won't move because they've nowhere to move to.'

'Christ, that's the easiest of them all. Buy them a bloody new school.'

'Where?'

'Anywhere they like. Their slum is worth far more to us than any new school. What about Blake?'

'I sent his wife the new Triumph Herald as you said. That should be more than ample.'

'Shows how fucking much you know. I've sent him a new car every year, and I haven't asked him one favour yet. All he does is not stand in the way. Christ knows what he'll want when he hears what we want him to actually *help* with this time.'

I'd been quite surprised when I'd heard what Blake, an official in the council's planning office, was getting. Jake had told me it was nothing. Blake never did anything against the laws, just bent them slightly. All Jake was doing was keeping in with him, the way all businesses entertain and give presents to important contacts.

After the meeting, Rupert and I had a drink with Jake in

his private suite. Rupert knew about getting the Ministry to rent the big block, because he and Henry were looking after that side. But he didn't know that the scheme was four times the area he imagined, and was to take in three smaller blocks, a new shopping centre and an hotel. Rupert was safe, even if he did find out. He'd been given shares in the Jersey company so he'd make some money for himself, on the side, when the big sale took place.

'How much do you think we'll make altogether on the Big Scheme, Jake?'

'I don't know,' said Jake. 'If you mess around any more getting the site empty we won't make any.'

'As a guess, though, what do you think?'

'Listen, Fatso, I'm not interested in money, unlike you.'

'By the way, Henry has been telling me how to get a knighthood. It would help enormously if you had one, Jake. You'd get in Debrett, in your own right ...' Rupert was smirking. 'How about an OBE for a start? Henry can find out what sort of things the Government would like done at the moment ...'

'Christ, I'm not gonna help the Government, any Government, they're all a lot of dozy sods. They're just wasting my bloody money.'

I was glad he was still anti-Government. Most self-made people tend to be for the Government whatever they say. They want the conditions which made their success to continue as long as possible.

'They're all as stupid as each other, making Acts and regulations, then changing them and fucking around so they don't know where they are. Do you know that up until 1959 you could apply for planning permission for any bit of land you like – *without* owning it! Christ, they must have been mental.'

'You'd be helping yourself, Jake, if you got an OBE,' said Rupert.

'How about a PLP?' said Jake. 'Fancy a PLP. Are you a P.L. Fatso? Answer yes or no.'

'No,' said Rupert, not knowing what he was talking about.

'You're not a Proper Living Person! Ha ha. Now say yes.'

'Yes.'

Jake got up and threw himself against Rupert, knocking him to the floor then lying on him.

'That means you're a Public Leaning Post. See, you missed a lot by going to Eton, didn't he Tom? At Thwaite Primary they know all about PLPs.'

Rupert was having convulsions when Chloe entered, dressed in a billowing silk trouser suit. She smiled and gave a little sigh. Such silly boys. So this is what they do at their office. I might have known.

'It's a take-over,' said Jake, grabbing Rupert's arms. 'See Rupert, you should have kept your arms free. Always leave room to manoeuvre so that you can get out. Fluidity at all costs. Right, get up. Tomorrow I'll demonstrate a killing on the Stock Exchange. Coming darling?'

Jake got up, pulled his polo neck shirt straight, put his jacket on, brushed himself and took Chloe by the arm, leading her to the door.

'Evening dress, is it?' asked Jake.

'Of course,' said Chloe.

'That's good. I put a clean jock strap on this morning.'

Chapter Twenty-four

The Sunday papers were full of the Disaster. Terrible floods had cut off huge areas of the North West, particularly in the Lake District. Ullswater had burst its banks and completely submerged a village. At least fifty people were missing, feared drowned.

'Jake. Do you realize it just missed where we had our honeymoon,' said Chloe.

'What?' said Jake, showing interest in the news for the first time. 'Well, it'll bring the tourists flocking.'

'The Government now denies all responsibility,' said Chloe. 'They're blaming the Lake District authority. Isn't it typical? Having petty political rows while all those poor people are suffering. Over sixty are now dead, with ninety-five homeless.'

'Don't put the radio off,' said Jake, 'I want to hear Pick of the Pops.'

Next morning Rupert swept into Jake's office self-importantly fluttering papers and memos.

'Have you heard the latest?' he said.

'What, you've got shot of that shop?'

'No, no,' said Rupert huffily. 'The Disaster. A hundred people are camping on the hillsides. More rain is expected.'

'Not you as well. It's worse than the bloody Test scores.'

'I've been on to our Carlisle office.'

'You what?'

'Remember that house you bought at Ullswater all those years ago? It's empty again. It could house fifty people easily. The Carlisle office say they know where to get some cheap surplus blankets.'

'Have you joined the Boy Scouts or something?'

'I've arranged for you to hold a press conference at two. That should just catch the last editions of the evening papers, but leave enough for the TV news. We can give another statement out this evening for the morning.'

'What are you raving about?'

'The Jake Sullivan Memorial House. You can make it available to the nation in this hour of need. In your speech this afternoon you can call upon other right thinking businessmen to help in any way they can. I've been on to the Ministry. They jumped at the idea. It takes the attention away from them for a few hours. An Assistant Under-Secretary will be on the platform with you at the press conference.'

'What am I supposed to do? Give a song or tell dirty stories?'

'It should only cost about a thousand, which is nothing when you think what we'll get out of it.'

'You mean an OBE?' said Jake.

'At least,' said Rupert, smiling.

'And what do I do for a knighthood? Turn the house into a holiday home for one-legged Ministry officials?'

'I think you should keep the house afterwards. All the publicity is bound to put the price up . . .'

'No, I want to go on for a knighthood. Then I can piss all over the OBEs.'

'I'm glad you approve,' said Rupert. 'I must rush and give out the press conference details to the agencies . . .'

Jake couldn't help laughing, but nobody else did. Everyone was very serious and magnanimous in applauding Mr. Sullivan's generous and prompt gesture. It all went as Rupert planned.

'What made you think of it?' said Chloe that evening. 'Usually, you think of no one but yourself.'

'Well you're wrong for once, clever clogs. It happens to be my homeland. And when something affects my homeland, it hurts me right here.' Jake thumped his right breast.

'I only hope it doesn't backfire, that's all.'

All evening telegrams and messages poured in, offering free food, blankets, fires, gas stoves and clothes. A Carnaby Street hat boutique offered a free hat to every homeless lady.

'Fucking disgusting,' said Jake. 'Free hats at a time like this. Have people no principles? Turning it into a cheap publicity stunt. What are you doing tomorrow? Rupert's laid on a helicopter to take me up. Be good if you came as well. Make a better photograph.'

'I'm having nothing to do with it,' said Chloe.

The helicopter, naturally enough, took six chosen journalists and photographers up to Ullswater, as well as Jake and Rupert. He was photographed meeting the poor people, handing out blankets and soup to the fifty people he'd so generously accommodated in the house he'd so generously donated to the nation. Every paper said he'd *donated* it. A Manchester contractor, who flew up a team of workmen to do an emergency job, dividing the house into bed sitters for each family, obviously thought Jake no longer owned the house. Likewise a Newcastle paint firm who redecorated the whole house, outside and inside, for free. The house was of course just a loan. Jake was getting it publicized and improved for nothing.

'I think it's the meanest trick I've ever heard of,' said Chloe, that evening.

'What do you mean?'

'Rupert has been telling me, no, not telling, *boasting* to me how much the value of the house has gone up. He even says you might get a knighthood. I hope he's joking. I'd divorce you if you did.'

'Listen baby,' said Jake, getting angry. 'There were fifty families crouching in the mud. OK? Now they're all in nice heated little bedrooms. OK? Is that bad? Is that disgusting? No. So go and stuff yourself.'

It was Rupert who was concerned with making a profit on the house but Jake was too angry with Chloe to try to explain. He gathered up the evening papers and carefully re-read all about himself. After an hour of not talking, they went to bed, still not talking.

'Good news,' said Rupert, coming round to Jake's desk a few days later, brandishing the usual pile of papers.

'You're having a sex change,' said Jake.

'What? No. A prep school wants to pay £60,000 for the Ullswater House, all fittings included. I've said yes.'

'Then you're fired. I'm getting fed up with your mercenary attitude to everything. Why can't you do something worth-while for a change?'

Rupert smiled, thinking it was one of Jake's little jokes. He looked at me to join him in an indulgent pause, before he went on to elaborate his brilliant coup. I was reading Nudes of the World. Chloe had still never managed to get her hands on Jake's office literature.

'Take that fucking smirk off your face before I thump you!' said Jake.

Rupert changed his face immediately, going all concerned, somewhat belatedly picking up Jake's mood.

'Sorry, I was getting carried away. Of course we want to do something worthwhile. That was the whole point of the scheme, when I thought of it . . .' He let that sink in. 'But there is no reason to ignore the advantages which go with it, is there? Shall I say we want £70,000 . . .?'

'Get out!'

Jake leaped over his desk, but Rupert just escaped.

I'd checked up all the companies that Rupert had worked for. They were mostly one-man overnight sensations. Rupert had moved in with his prestige package deal, then just as smartly moved out, well before the crash came. There was a bloke who made a million selling ten thousand plots in the Bahamas. Rupert resigned before it became known to the public that he'd sold the same plots ten times over. Rupert always had his fat ear to the ground, so it was pretty obvious that Jake Sullivan must still be doing very well. Otherwise he wouldn't be so keen.

'Eight o'clock you said. It's now ten.'

'I'm sorry,' said Jake, coming into the flat and giving her a kiss. She moved away and went on reading a pile of manuscripts. 'I couldn't help it. This meeting went on for ever.'

'You know how to phone, don't you? In the whole year we've been married you've never been on time yet.'

'Just 'cos you do things by the clock, you think everyone's the same. One minute to piss, two and a half minutes to dress, twenty-three minutes for breakfast . . .'

'The meal's ruined. I came home an hour early to make it, not that you would care about that.'

'Christ!' shouted Jake. 'I've told you a million times to get a bloody cook. Nobody *asks* you to do the cooking.'

Jake stormed into the kitchen and after a lot of banging he came back with a mug of tea and a pile of cream crackers. He sat down in front of the TV and began to eat. He'd soon forgotten the row. From time to time he started to tell Chloe about the latest on the Big Scheme. She took no notice. He laughed and made funny faces at her. She went on reading.

'I've tried not to mention it before but I can't stand the noise of you eating,' she said suddenly in an exasperated voice, 'I've now reached screaming point.'

'How jolly decent of you,' said Jake, imitating her. 'Not telling me before. You are a brick. Christ, you'll be telling me you don't like the way I breathe next.'

'Well you might occasionally try to show a little consideration. I don't expect many of the social graces, God knows.'

'Oh shut up,' said Jake, throwing his mug against the wall, to show he didn't care. 'This is my house and I'll behave as I like.'

'You do think you're Andy Capp, don't you? What you really want is another empty-headed Beryl, to run after you and tell you all the time how wonderful you are.'

In bed Jake put his arm round her but she firmly shook him off.

'I dunno,' said Jake, leaning back. 'I don't know what's happened to my nuptial rights. You're always making out I'm some sort of beast. I haven't had it since Tuesday. Three whole nights ago.'

'I refuse to feel guilty, so don't try that one. I've told you, I just don't feel like it.'

'OK,' said Jake, 'So you haven't had an orgasm for a couple of months. It's not my fault.'

'Of course it is. You don't make the effort any more. You've no finesse or tenderness. In the old days you did make vague attempts to get me in the mood. Now you just want to bash ahead whenever you feel like it. It's pure masturbation. The number of times I've lain here in agony while you've dropped off to sleep after a couple of pathetic wriggles. You're the one who's not up to it, so don't try to blame me.'

'OK, I won't. Let's forget the past, eh. This might be your big night, girl. So come on, eh.'

'You've watched the telly. You've stopped thinking about your boring work. You've stopped eating your revolting biscuits. Now you think you'll have a lay. And why not? That's what you feel like. Well I'm different. Sex comes out of an evening of being together, not as a quick night-cap to get *you* off to sleep.'

'I can't bloody help it!' said Jake angrily. 'That's how all men are. Men want sex all the time and women don't. They just want love. It's not my fault.'

'God, not that rubbish again,' said Chloe. 'You're just so wrong. Women have a far greater capacity for sex, physical sex, than men. Men just aren't up to it, that's the trouble. And would you kindly mind leaving my nipples alone? I don't know which of your gutter women told you that was exciting. All you are doing is scratching me.'

'You've got a lovely bottom, you know,' said Jake gamely. 'Lovely and smooth. I wonder when it'll go all pock-marked and flabby? They should have bottom lifts, like face lifts.'

'For the last time, Jake,' said Chloe, very slowly, turning and sighing, with sleep already forming in the corner of her eyes. 'Will you stop it. I happen to make love with my mind as well as my body. You've failed on both counts. So go to sleep.'

'What a funny fella you are,' said Jake. 'I make love with my cock.'

'Exactly. Good night.'

At the top of the queue were three giggling school girls so busy nudging each other, spluttering through their hands and bursting out laughing at the remembrance of some incident that they didn't notice the shop keeper was impatiently waiting to serve them. He let the rest of the people in the shop know what he thought of them by pointing to his head and saying 'educated' in a loud stage whisper. He was short and stocky with thick greying hair, thin at the front but worn very long at the back. He had it swept back theatrically at the sides and was continually pushing it into place with both hands. He obviously loved his shop. He didn't look the sort who would sell out, not for any property developer. It was his stage. All his best gestures were straight out of The Seventh Veil; someone must have once told him he looked like James Mason.

'If you are quite finished, darlings,' he said very slowly and sinisterly, both hands on the counter, enunciating every word like a posh Boris Karloff. He paused. 'WHAT DO YOU WANT!' he suddenly shouted. Everyone in the shop jumped several inches.

'Oooh, you didn't arf give us a fright,' said the cheekiest looking school girl.

'I'll give you more than a fright in a minute,' said Mr. Cobblestone very quickly. 'My word I will. I know your sort. I know your sort very well indeed. Oh yes I do. I've met your type before.'

'Never seen him before, have you Sylv?' said the girl. 'Just give us three French rolls, please.'

'You lot should have been in the Western Desert!'

'Heh Sylv. What's the Western Desert got to do with French rolls?'

'Nothing,' said Mr. Cobblestone. 'Nothing at all. That was the trouble. There were no French rolls in the Western Desert. Or Tide. Or Omo, or New Zealand butter, or Rice Krispies, or Sugar Puffs, or Marmite, or Swiss Roll, or Coca Cola, or Tutie Fruitie, or streaky bacon.' He went round his shelves, declaiming each article with a lofty wave of his hand.

'Do you know what we had in the Western Desert?' he turned round and hissed at them. 'Do you? 'Orrible privation. A little bit of privation is just what you lot want . . .'

'What I want is a French roll,' said the cheeky one, turning to leave.

'The trouble with you lot,' he shouted up the street after them, 'is that you have no excitement left in your life! None! You've had it all too damned easy!'

Whatever their reply, Mr. Cobblestone didn't catch it. He came back into the shop all smiles, his duty done, another victory, ready for the next engagement.

'Twenty Senior Service, please,' I said quickly. I had no intention of being a feed for Mr. Cobblestone.

'Sorry!' he said, loudly and sharply, turning away and blowing on his fingers. 'No call for them.'

'I've just called,' I said.

'Too late. I've stopped listening.' He was straightening his tie and combing his hair, bending down slightly, looking intently into a non-existent mirror.

'OK then,' I said, smiling, indulging the fool. 'Twenty Players.'

'Come come sir. You told me you preferred Senior Service. You can't now take Players. Never take second best in this world, my good sir. I suggest you try the supermarket on the main road. It's rather shoddy, rather scruffy, rather nasty, incredibly vulgar, completely soulless, altogether common and in fact totally horrible. You'll like it. They sell anything to anybody. Good day to you sir, and may you never knowingly be dissatisfied. Next for shaving please!'

I stood at the doorway while he served two more people and when the shop was empty, I went back to him and gave him my card. Tom Graham, Personal Secretary to the Chairman, Sullivan and Co. I was rather proud of it. Mr. Cobblestone did a lot of face twitching, eyebrow raising and holding it up to the light.

'You've heard of Jake Sullivan,' I said.

'Yes, yes, yes, yes,' he said lying, smelling it for clues.

'He's just started making his new film. There's a perfect little part in it for you. Present yourself this evening at Shepperton studios. I can assure you you'll not be wasting your time. Good day to you.'

I was picking up his affectations. He thanked me with his

hands, tumbling them like a spin dryer, bowing to the floor, pushing back his theatrical hair and fixing me with his James Mason stare till I'd left his shop.

I was now in a terrible dilemma. I wanted to rush straight back to Jake with the great news, but I'd only popped into Cobblestone's shop, on the off chance, on the way to see Antonia. I'd promised to go and pick her up at the airport and I was already late.

She'd been away almost two months and I'd missed her desperately. Her letters had been very passionate. Saying how much she'd missed me. The usual stuff. But I just couldn't get Cobblestone out of my head and my own bit of quick thinking, which had surprised me most of all. I got to the airport just in time, got her bags in the car, then rushed back to phone Jake.

I should have waited a bit longer, instead of dashing about the minute I'd said hello to Antonia. But I was in such a hurry to tell Jake. There were huge queues at each phone. It was a judgment. I shouldn't have bothered.

'How was it then,' I said as we raced along the motorway into London. I'd got into a seventy mile an hour traffic jam, where you can't get out, slow down, swerve an inch either way, or take your mind off the road for one second.

'What's the hurry,' said Antonia.

'Nothing,' I said.

'Then slow down.'

'How was it then?'

'I said slow down.'

'So it was OK, then,' I said, hunched over the wheel, feeling the speed taking over and making me invincible. I couldn't crash. I was flying.

'I've got to pop into the office. I hope you don't mind. It's pretty important.'

'It always is.'

After all the slush and everlasting love of the letters, we were now back to petty bickering.

It would wait, my great news. What was the hurry. Jake probably wouldn't be pleased, or it wouldn't come off. Cromwell Road was like Silverstone, with tyres melting and fumes pouring as idiots did racing starts at every traffic light. Should I cut over to Kensington? Should I wait till after lunch?

232

'So how was it? I suppose you feel you've never been away, now that you're back to all this. Christ, look at that fool!'

'I'm looking at him,' said Antonia, looking at me. It was like playing football in the lotties at Thwaite. Having to come in for tea, but bolting it back in a panic, desperate to return as quickly as possible to the lads. My mother would be chuntering on, saying I'd make myself ill. I'd get back and the lads would have gone.

'You are smashing,' I said, dropping Antonia at the flat. 'I'm sorry, honest. It won't take long. We'll have lunch at your favourite restaurant as a treat. Wheelers. OK?'

'Rupert, you're a prick. What are you?'

'A prick,' said Rupert, smiling nervously.

'So he had no vices? He didn't like girls or boys? The only way would be to open a cut-price supermarket next door? Christ, what a lousy judge of human character you are. You can't see further than your fat arse. Go on, get out.'

'But Jake, what's happened? Is Cobblestone going?'

'Of course he bloody is. My Personal Assistant has arranged everything.'

It took Rupert a few seconds to work out who this was. I was deep in Whip Whip Hooray, but as Rupert turned in amazement to stare at me I raised my right hand, blew my nails and rubbed them on my jacket.

'Jimmy,' said Jake into the intercom. 'Go round to Cobblestone. Yes, I've just spoken to him on the phone. He'll sign a contract, for that film I've got money in. They need a shopkeeper. Ask him if he really isn't James Mason. That should please him. Buy the shop and promise him any help if he ever wants to go back into shopkeeping, though tell him he obviously won't. Not with his looks. OK?'

'Right, Tom. A little surprise?'

Ten minutes later we walked out into Piccadilly then across into St. James's Park and down to Buckingham Palace. We spent half an hour looking at the Queen's Gallery. It was the simplest surprise of all, being so near our office, but we'd never got round to doing it. We'd done very few surprises in the last year, since Chloe came along.

I couldn't have timed my little triumph better. I'd been a passenger for so long, contributing nothing except an attentive audience. I'd been dreading reminding Jake about his magazine idea. Now was the time. Antonia was back. She'd had her fling and was looking for a teaching job. It was a nice time to settle down and glide gently out of the mainstream of Jake's life.

'Yes, I'm rather chuffed,' said Jake as we went round the gallery. 'Cobblestone had been one of the little things bugging me.'

'Don't tell me you've got other problems.'

'Not really. Just these bloody insurance gits. They're so bloody stuffy. All they do is refer things to each other all the bloody day. Please sir, can I go to the lav, can I pick my nose, can I loan this bloke ten million. You know the sort. None of the fuckers will make a decision. Did the Queen paint all the pictures herself, then?'

'No, one of her corgis did them,' I said. 'But surely they're going to give you the money. It's to their advantage.'

'Of course they are. I just want them to hurry up. The Big Scheme depends on it. I'm spreading it a bit thin at the moment.'

'Spreading what?' I said, only half listening to him. 'Your money?'

'No, me sperm, what do you think.'

At exactly two-thirty we left the gallery and came back into the middle of the park. On a bench by the pond was a Fortnum and Mason red and yellow uniformed messenger, opening the straw hamper and laying out the champagne and the bucket of ice, the smoked salmon sandwiches and the chicken legs. He poured us out the first drink and then departed, hoping everything was to our liking.

'It's marvellous what you can get on the National Health these days,' I said.

Jake invited a couple of tramps to join us, asking them how they liked their champagne, one lump or two. In no time at all there was a crowd round us, nudging each other. People take on a special expression when they recognize someone recognizable like Jake. Their head stiffens and becomes locked, stuck at an angle, while their legs and body move on till they bump into someone and fall over. Then they go into reverse, like a film running backwards, and come back the way they've come to get a better look. They nudge their friends without disengaging their heads, talking sideways so they don't miss anything, waiting for the Someone to recognize them. They've seen the Person on TV in their own sitting rooms so they almost expect Him to recognize them in return.

When an unfamous person attracts attention in the street, either by being incredibly beautiful or dreadfully deformed, people stare just as much, but secretly and furtively, taking it in at a glance and continuing walking, giving nothing away. But someone who is known for being known is public property and therefore nothing can possibly be too rude or intrusive. There was a middle-aged lady in a plastic mac taking pictures of Jake's right ear, holding her light meter under his nostrils. Two boys were trying to pull his shoes off, a red headed girl was ruffling his hair and a very pucka man in a bowler hat had picked up Jake's jacket and was peering at the label.

Jake had been on TV a lot over the Disaster story, but I was still surprised he was so easily recognized. Jake loved it, which distressed me somehow. He was always affable, put up with everyone, made jokes, tickled ugly women under the chin, gave the V sign to workmen who waved at him and kissed babies. You should see him at home, I tried to tell people. They stared at me as if I'd escaped from somewhere.

'It's amazing isn't it?' said Jake as I dragged him away at last.

'Well you're so famous,' I said.

'That must be it,' said Jake, accepting it as the truth.

'Yeh, you're almost as famous as the blokes who read the weather forecast. They have to go out in pairs otherwise they get mobbed.'

It was a lovely summer's day and the sun had come out again and everyone was peeling off to lie on the grass and look silly in their white Marks and Spencer shirts and London white ankles. I suddenly felt very distant from Jake. I wasn't jealous of his face being known. I knew that happened to anyone who got on TV more than once or in the papers. He was the current good-for-a-quote millionaire who was in every ring-round feature. You know the sort. Pet aversions, Christmas presents, holidays, bad habits, embarrassing moments or some such other lousy topic which the features editor has thought up and some poor bloke has to stand up. So he rings round Lord Boothby, Kingsley Amis, the Duke of Bedford,

Stirling Moss, Sir Miles Thomas, Mary Quant and anyone else daft enough to answer the phone. Jake was now in this gang. There is always a first eleven of instantly accessible people who won't be rude enough to hang up. It didn't mean a thing. Jake thought it did.

He said wasn't it stupid, people staring at him, wasn't it mad, people must be daft or hard up, he certainly wouldn't do it, who was he anyway, he hadn't done that much, and so on, making it even clearer how much he loved it.

I went quiet and let him rant on. We cut through the back streets behind Piccadilly, heading for Carnaby Street. I kept slightly ahead, guiding him still without saying much.

'Heh, don't be daft,' he said putting his arm round my shoulder, pulling me round so I had to look him in the face. He pretended to hit me under the chin. 'You're stupid, you really are.' It was strange to be touched by him. We walked on. His arm was still round my shoulder. I walked slowly, so that it wouldn't fall off, but on a traffic island a surge of bodies, fleeting from sudden death, forced us apart.

There were six pairs of bell bottom trousers, all his size, and all ready with his name on when we got to Carnaby Street. I said have those kaftans, over there. They look like you. As they'd been laid out for him, they naturally fitted perfectly. The surprise was going well.

He was several months behind the times in wearing them, but it would suitably annoy people like Rupert at the next board meeting. As we came out of the shop, a girl linked Jake's arm. It was the red headed girl who'd been ruffling his hair in the park. If Jake was going to start playing up to the crowds again he'd spoil the whole surprise. I'd only had five minutes to tell Miss Moon what to do before we left the office, but she'd arranged everything perfectly.

We walked on with Jake ignoring the girl on his arm. We passed a sign saying 'To Let' and Jake stopped suddenly. It was a huge smelly warehouse. Jake kicked the door open and went in. If it wasn't girls it was business. The sooner I got onto my little magazine the better, though with all these hangers-on and interruptions, I wouldn't get a chance to mention it to him.

There was a man in a suede jacket taking notes while a youth went round with a measuring tape. Jake said how much. The man said they'd only put up the board that minute, give us a chance. How much, said Jake, going close so the man might recognize him. To you Mr. Sullivan, £120 a week. Jake said £100, take it or leave it.

We went out again and continued on our way. The girl had waited outside, but was soon attached to him again. Jake pretended he was Desperate Dan, asking where that pesky fly was which was bothering him, trying to flick her off, but not too hard. The suede man came racing after us and said OK, seeing who it was, £100 a week on a three year lease.

Jake took out a midget microphone from his top pocket as we walked along Regent Street. 'Miss Moon,' he said, speaking softly into it. 'I've just bought a property off Carnaby Street. Get Smithson to ring the agent. His name ...' He held out the microphone and the suede agent man breathlessly gave his name, office, and telephone number. 'I've agreed £100 a week for three years. Now fuck off. Not you, Miss Moon. This bloke's still hanging around. Thank you.'

The man moved off as Jake aimed a kick at him. The red headed girl was holding on for dear life, looking at Jake with gooey eyes.

'Ring JP the builder,' continued Jake into the microphone. 'You'll find him in Maggie's old address book. I want him to put hardboard partitions in, dividing the warehouse into fifty compartments, ten by ten. Then get the design department to work on a fifty foot long notice board with large gilt letters made of wood saying "Boutique Supermarket". Over and out. Roger. Cheers.'

'What else did Santa bring you for Christmas?' I said to Jake. The girl giggled.

'Listen son,' said Jake. 'I'm on a winning streak today. Thanks to you starting it off well. I won't forget you. How many boutiques have you counted since we left Carnaby Street?'

'I don't know,' I said, bored with him showing off. Even some half witted shop girl who followed him in the street had to be impressed.

'Thirteen,' said Jake. 'You don't keep your eyes open, do you? If you didn't worry about girls so much you might notice a few things. Listen, you can't get moving for boutiques at the moment. Every little art school pseud wants to open one and every deb wants to work in one. If I let those fifty out at £5 a week, plus rates, that will be £250 a week. Advertising, promotion, a doorman to keep an eye on things should come to no more than £50. So that's £100 a week profit. Yes? What were you saying Tom before we were interrupted?'

'We've come the wrong way. We're now in Oxford Street,' I said. 'Thanks to you messing about.' The girl was looking longingly at a rather nasty fur trimmed bikini in the window of a rather nasty departmental store.

'Not my size, darling,' said Jake looking at it.

'What's your size Jake?' said the girl in a very breathy whisper.

'Heh, you're not as daft as you look,' said Jake. 'What's your name?'

'Mary Jane,' said the girl.

'Where do you live?'

'In the grid.'

'What's your number?'

'Cucumber.'

'What's your station?'

'Eggs and bacon.'

We went into the shop and up the escalator for several floors with Mary Jane holding on to Jake like a suburban wife, up for the day with her car salesman husband. The women's department was huge, old fashioned and cadaverous, with alcoves and side turnings everywhere. Middle-aged assistants, huddling behind pillars, keeping out of the way, were locked in timeless gossip. They were all short and fat with heavy lurid make-up, cheap jangling jewellery and bad legs forced into tiny shoes. Jake chose lots of bikinis, beach robes and shift dresses for Mary Jane. He found the dopiest looking assistant of all. She was on her own sitting on a stool with watery eyes and her bad leg across her lap, massaging it frantically. She nodded wearily to a far corner when Jake asked if his wife could try these on.

Jake gave me a big wink and went into the changing rooms with Mary Jane. I watched the curtain close. There was a rustling of clothes and a bulging of the curtains as they got undressed. The curtains in the next cubicle parted and a woman in a dirty grey-white slip, a headscarf and smoking a cigarette stepped out. She'd got her hand on Jake's curtains and was pulling them apart before I could leap forward to stop her. Just as she stepped in, Jake's bare arms pushed a pile of creased clothes into her arms and elbowed her quickly out again. She muttered thanks, still in a trance-like state, and went back to her own cubicle, clutching her clothes. The sweat was lying on my brow.

Jake and Mary Jane were in the changing room for a good half hour before the dopy assistant lumbered towards me.

'Do those corsets fit your wife?' she said, her mouth half open. 'I better go in and see.'

'Swimming costumes,' I said hurriedly. 'She took six in, so she'll be hours yet. I wouldn't bother her. She's a bit funny about people watching her, you know?' I gave a big woman to woman smile. She said her son was funny that way as well. He wouldn't let her see him put his school gym shorts on. I said tell me more about your fascinating son. He turned out to be thirty-five and a stoker in the Merchant Navy where the problem of school gym shorts presumably wasn't as bad. She went off to get a photograph and I whistled for Jake. He came out alone, putting on his jacket. He took out a wad of notes, peeled some off and thrust them under the curtains, then we both left.

'She wants to get into films,' said Jake. 'We're one all so far. You fixed Cobblestone. I fixed Mary Jane. I'm starving. Come on. They'll give us something at Shepherd's Nosh.'

He meant Shepherds Bush and the BBC TV station. He hadn't mentioned he'd agreed to do an interview that afternoon. If anything else had turned up, he probably wouldn't. Jake was for ever letting press and TV people down, but they still seemed to want him.

It was to be a short ten minute piece with A Man In The News. Jake was out of it really by now, with the Disaster dying down. The interviewer turned out to be Richard Cheam, the Face to Face bloke. Jake hadn't met him since then, though he'd been on every other programme and come up against every other so-called TV star. I feared this would be Cheam's chance. With the worst of the tragedy over, he could accuse Jake of doing it all for publicity, yet not lose any audience sympathy. This was why they were doing him a few days late. I tried to point this out to Jake but he said mind your own business eh, just get me some coffee, that's all you have to do.

'I think I talk for most of the country,' said Cheam slobbily, beginning the interview, but with a slight glint, 'when I say how marvellous it was that you so quickly came forward and did what you could, regardless of expense. But there's just one little thing, perhaps I might be permitted to ask in passing. What incidentally was the expense?' He was holding up some notes, this time making no attempt to hide them.

'You tell me the answer, Richard,' said Jake smiling, 'because I don't know it. Some people are very good at doing clever little sums to find out exactly what other people are worth or what they spend. Me, I'm interested in action not money.'

'Yes, you've said that before,' said Richard, fluttering a wodge of newspaper cuttings in front of the cameras and glancing at his notes. 'For someone who's repeatedly said that making money was a farce and something you didn't care about, it's amazing what an incredibly small amount you did fork out, when you consider ... what you got in return ... (holding up cuttings) ... I might even be forgiven for thinking that you do *care* about publicity ... and money ...'

Jake got out a packet of cigarettes, pulling out at the same time a bundle of papers and notes. He lit up, looking completely unworried. Richard was going into a blow by blow exposé of Jake's stunt, demonstrating how he got so much for free, when two people in the studio audience jumped up, pointing to Jake.

I thought Jake must have dropped something on the floor, though studio audiences are usually too overcome and cowed by the occasion to dare to interrupt for anything so trivial. Then I looked again. Jake had lit his cigarette with a £5 note. He now lit another five of them, letting them burn in front of Richard's nose. He took another handful of fivers from his pocket, tore them in half and threw the bits to the studio audience who immediately rushed forward and started to scrabble for them while studio assistants vainly tried to push them back into their places like circus animals who'd forgotten their tame tricks.

I burst out laughing as I watched the chaos Jake's simple action was causing. Nobody else thought it was funny.

'You see Richard, money is only a symbol,' Jake was saying. 'So why should I care about it or value it for its own sake? You don't have to believe me if you don't want to ...'

Fivers and half fivers littered the studio floor. As the programme faded to an end, the studio audience were closing in on Jake again, fighting for the bits, while Jake showered Richard with fivers as if they were confetti. In the confusion, he'd managed to tear up Richard's notes and was scattering them too.

Jake came off the stage, put his arm round me and said let's go for a fried egg in the canteen. It was half empty when we got there. When Jake saw nobody of note was queuing up he said what about dinner? He was feeling even more on form and felt like a bit of style. We'd go to Parkes, or Wheelers or somewhere.

The mention of Wheelers did it. My God, I'd promised to meet Antonia there, at *lunch* time. Her big coming home treat! Christ! I'd forgotten all about it. It was almost seven o'clock now. I ran to the front entrance and rushed out, shouting after a cab, with Jake following.

We both got in. Jake put his arm round my shoulder again and told me not to worry. It was best to keep them waiting. You mustn't seem too keen. He would explain to Antonia that there had been an urgent board meeting which I had to be present at. I said no. I'd tell her.

There was a note on my typewriter when I got to my office. The note said very curtly that she was catching the afternoon train to Durham. She didn't know when she'd be back. She didn't know when she'd see me again. If ever.

I sat for half an hour, looking out of the window, then I went to see Jake. He was talking into two telephones and dictating messages into a dictaphone at the same time. Miss Moon was standing patiently in front of his desk, holding a letter.

'Your wife left this letter,' said Miss Moon when Jake at last put down one of the phones.

Jake tore it open. I could see it was about three pages of very small, very neat handwriting. Jake read it all, letting his phone go dead.

'She's left me,' said Jake, throwing the letter across to me.

'How thoughtless,' said Miss Moon. 'Will there be anything else?'

Most people had gone home. Miss Moon, as usual, had waited for Jake to reappear.

'She couldn't stand me eating,' said Jake, flatly.

'What did you eat, Mr. Sullivan?' asked Miss Moon.

'What?' said Jake staring at her. 'Me eating. That was what she couldn't stand.'

'How strange. Have you seen Tom Jones, Mr. Sullivan?'

'Not now. I don't want to see anyone.'

'I mean the film. They had a very good eating scene in that, Very erotic. That's the word isn't it Mr. Sullivan.'

'That's the word you're groping for Miss Moon. Now fuck off, for Chrissake.' Miss Moon scurried out.

'If that bloody bitch thinks she's going to get any money out of me . . .'

Part Five

Chapter Twenty-six

The Big Scheme *was* reality to Jake. It had always been abstract to me, but to Jake creating plans, hatching plots, signing
deals, working out site ratios, estimating profits and moving
round paper millions was his life's blood. So far it had taken
almost three years and entailed a hundred and fifty separate
deals.

I went to have a look at the site. They had begun building
the shops, hotel and two of the minor skyscrapers, though
to the man in the street it looked an isolated collection of
London's usual hotch-potched rebuilding. Until the main
building got going and all the flyovers and raised pavements
were connected, no one could see that it was part of one enormous scheme. It was even more important now than ever before that no one found out what was going on. It needed only
a few busybodies poking around, writing to newspapers and
complaining that it was too big, too ugly or just too much and
someone would be asking for an enquiry. Jake had a lot of
enemies who would love that. He dreaded most the Royal
Fine Arts Commission being asked to step in and give a judgment on the suitability of the design. That would hold things
up for years, just when all the parts were falling into place.

There was one panic, but Michael had solved it. An old
widow, from the same square that Cobblestone had lived in,
had come back to say that she'd sold her property illegally.
In moving out her stuff she'd discovered an ancient lease which
said her house could never be used for any commercial purpose. She was very sorry, but she wanted her house back. One
must respect the wishes of the dead. She'd spoken to a friend
on the Daily Telegraph who'd agreed she had no option. It
was the mention of the newspaper which caused the most
worry. Michael tried legal arguments saying that commercial
in Victorian days meant manufacturing which by definition
didn't apply to shops, but she stubbornly refused to be per-
suaded. In the end the plans had to be slightly altered, drop-

ping in a small block of luxury flats, which had been going elsewhere, in the middle of the row of shops, just where her house had been. 'Gentlemen's apartments' was what Michael called them. She agreed.

Jake had bought up every little bit of his huge site by now, except one little Government building. This was one of the many little scattered offices belonging to the Ministry of Defence, the Ministry which would eventually be moving into the big block. Michael and the legal department at Sullivan and Co. had never got round to doing the conveyancing, assuming it was a formality. They had been more pre-occupied with the difficult people like Cobblestone and the widow. Then overnight the Council announced a new road scheme, an enlarged one-way system which would entail the building of a big new roundabout. None of Jake's contacts, for all his boasting and presents, had tipped him off. The scheme would be right on the edge of Jake's site, the most important part, beside his main block. The Council announced that it would be issuing a compulsory order to buy the Ministry's office. They weren't actually building on it, but they'd need elbow room to clear the way for the roundabout. They'd also be buying up all the sites round the roundabout.

This was calamitous. Work on the main building hadn't started yet, but all the other projects were already under way and they couldn't move such a vast building around at this stage. For weeks Jake was in a fury, storming and raging. In the end he managed to solve it. It was perhaps the smartest single bit of property jiggling he ever did.

In the middle of his own worries, Jake found out that the Council had also run up against difficulties. The Ministry would sell their little building to the Council. They had to really, with a compulsory, though Jake had tried every bit of string pulling to stop them. But there was one owner, whose site the Council desperately needed as it was right in the way of the roundabout, who was refusing to sell. It was an old property developer of seventy, a whiz-kid from the 1930s London suburban shopping boom, who'd seen his empire crumble. He'd gone bankrupt twice and was about to do so again when his little tumble-down site, his last bit of property and the one in which he lived, suddenly became highly desirable. He told the Council he wanted half a million for it, which was almost ten times what the Council could possibly pay, or be allowed to pay. He'd go to every court and to the House of Lords to fight the order, for years if necessary. The Council knew these delays could spoil their plans. They were in such a hurry that through a mix-up between departments they sent him two orders to quit, or Notice to Treat, as it's officially known. The old tycoon had them. The Treats were slightly different. Which was the legal one? Well, that was the sort of thing rival lawyers could take a decade to argue about. The Council couldn't wait that long, yet they couldn't pay the half million. They were stuck.

Jake stepped in immediately when he heard. He had a series of informal discussions with the Council officials and said he'd get them out of their mess. He'd pay the old bloke half a million for his old block. Then he'd give it to the Council for free, as a present. The condition was that he would be allowed to buy the little Ministry site. They wouldn't compulsorily buy it. They'd also look favourably upon the plans which he had for its development. He already had Blake, in another department, helping him with things like site ratios. Now he had council chairmen and traffic officials all on his side, owing him a favour.

Jake had a struggle getting the half million pounds, having already exhausted all his credit getting the five million together for the site as a whole. In the end, he got it, but only at enormously high interest.

There was no holding him after that. He was all sweetness and charm. Nothing could now go wrong. Life was really beautiful, man. At long last, after three years of plotting and scheming, he owned every little piece of the site. Michael told him to be careful and not to shout too loud. It was still vital that no one heard anything.

I thought it was a good moment to tell him my plans. I had several, the most important of which was that I was getting married. I thought he might be annoyed at that, as he'd looked upon me as his personal property for so long.

'Great,' he said. 'I'll be best man of course.'

'I wasn't best man at yours,' I said. 'Fair dos.'

'You can be next time.'

'Seriously, Jake,' I said. 'It's just going to be a small do. Not even any parents. Antonia wants it that way. Her Dad'll go spare, but that's what she wants. We're not having *any* best man. We'll just go outside and stop some passer-by and ask him to sign the register.'

Antonia dreaded Jake being at the wedding. That was one of the conditions she'd imposed, if we were getting married. She was against marriage, personally. Only a romantic, slobby fool like me, scared of not conforming, was interested in marriage. I told Jake all this. He stopped joking around and said of course. He understood. He'd respect her wishes.

We were standing on the steps of St. Pancras Town Hall, which was what everyone still calls it, though it's officially Camden. I had my best suit on and a large carnation. My hair had been cut too short and I felt a real jerk. Antonia looked smashing in a crochet holey dress, also with a carnation. I was very thrilled and excited with myself. Getting married was an occasion, even on the Euston Road. I pulled Antonia quickly aside, cuddling her as I did so and she pretended to stop me. We'd been getting mixed up with another wedding, a huge gang of Africans who seemed to have about sixteen little kids already, all in pink puffed out party dresses, running up and down the steps and knocking the photographer over.

We moved inside and waited for our turn. It was like being at the doctor's, with people self-consciously whispering to each other and looking round, wondering what everybody had got, or, in this case, was going to get. Every bloke had had his hair cut too short.

'There's bound to be some official hanging around who can witness it,' said Antonia. We hadn't bothered to find out how many and what sort of witnesses you needed. It had been a joke about getting a passer-by.

'No, I'll go out in the street and stop someone,' I said.

'You'll probably get arrested,' said Antonia.

'I like the idea of someone crossing our path at random, yet being joined together for ever with us in the registrar's little book. When Ph.Ds at the University of Texas are doing research on our life in fifty years' time they'll all be arguing about the identity of the witness . . .'

'Stop blathering, and go and get someone then,' said Antonia. 'And your hair looks awful.'

I fought my way through another wedding party on the

steps, this time all Indians. We were the only coloured couple getting married that afternoon. I went into the street and banged straight into an idiot in a purple Little Lord Fauntleroy suit, with tights so tight that his balls were crammed all to the one side like Gourock. He had sticking-up fuzzy Jimi Hendrix hair. I thought it might be Tiny Tim. He grabbed me by the arm, twisting it so I shouted out, and took me back up the steps again, singing 'Congratulations', that Cliff Richard song. It was Jake.

Antonia was right at the top of the queue, just about to go in and get married on her own. She didn't realize it was Jake at first. I didn't say anything. All she was thinking about was our honeymoon in Albufeira. She wanted this farcical ceremony over as soon as possible. She started to protest as she saw Jake, but the Registrar was upon us, hushing us into reverence.

We came out and there was a fleet of chauffeur driven Rolls Royces with a fleet of meter maids hovering round. All of the cars had banners and streamers saying 'Just Married. Tom and Antonia. Love from Jake Sullivan.' Trust him to get his name on.

We were bundled into the first Rolls by Jake. He was dancing around the steps, shouting and singing, so pleased with his little surprise. He went round the meter maids and bundled two of them into a Rolls. They'd said they were going off duty and wouldn't mind a lift. Into another car he shoved a wedding party of West Indians. He'd found out they were going back to their evening shift on the Underground.

Jake took his Hendrix wig off in the car. Antonia said that if he didn't get us to London Airport in an hour's time she was suing. What for, said Jake. Everything, said Antonia.

'Give us a kiss,' said Jake. 'Don't get up-tight. Come on. Smile. Uncle Jake has arranged everything. There's a private aeroplane standing by at London Airport to take you to Faro, just as soon as you're ready, which won't be for a long time yet. OK Tommy lad, you give us a kiss.'

He tried to kiss both of us and in the struggle burst his purple tights. I thought it was all a joke. Jake was only trying to be kind, in his new policy of doing nice things for people. But Antonia was absolutely livid. I had to force myself to keep a stony face.

We arrived at the Riverside entrance to the Savoy and went up the steps and into the River Room. There were about a hundred people all sitting down at tables. The whole room was covered in streamers and balloons. I started to move out quickly, thinking we'd come to a private party. Then I recognized my Mum at the top table, with Antonia's parents on the other side of her. There were three empty chairs between them. Jake sat in the middle, putting us either side of him. There were boos from the next table, so instead Jake put us together in the middle and sat beside us. On this next table I noticed Miss Moon, Rupert, Michael, Henry, James Black and all the other people from Sullivan House. Jake had turned our wedding into a works social.

Then I noticed a long tall thin weedy bloke with specs and the suspicion of a drip on the end of his nose. Jake said it was Basil, a bloke we had been at school with. Jake had done a This is Your Life, dragging down from Cumberland all the boring friends and relations I'd grown up with. Miss Moon must have had a terrible job digging them all out.

Jake stood up to toast us and everyone cheered. Antonia's Mum cried and so did mine. They were having a great time. I felt quite guilty that we'd intended to have a nothing wedding and deprive them of all the fun. Once the meal was under way and everyone was tucking in and enjoying themselves, even Antonia seemed quite pleased. Jake had got rid of his silly outfit and was now in a psychedelic shirt and hippy beads and looked almost respectable. He obviously wanted us and everyone else to have a good time.

Jake gave a little speech at the end of the meal. Since he became a TV star, you couldn't stop him making little speeches. He pretended he was my father, remembering little things about my childhood, and then said yes, after a lot of thought, he had agreed to give me away, as this month's free offer. Antonia's parents thought Jake was the nicest, most natural and unassuming young man they'd met for a long time. They couldn't see what she had against him.

The minute Jake sat down a curtain at the end of the room fell apart and there on a stage was the Cumberland Barn Dance group, flushed in the face and shanned at being at the Savoy Hotel instead of the Aspatria Farm Labourers' Institute. Everybody was soon dancing eightsome reels.

Jake had planned it well, knowing that the party was all ages and that an old time dance, which everyone could join in, was the best way to get rid of any inhibitions. Next came a beat group, then a Palm Court type orchestra, then an Irish family playing Irish instruments, which was the sort of music Antonia had always liked. I didn't know how Jake found that out. In between there were conjurors for the kids and an MC telling not too blue jokes for the grown up kids.

It was nine o'clock before I realized it. The room seemed to be getting more crowded instead of thinning out. I noticed a few reporters had arrived, and a couple of TV teams. They must have heard the noise of the knees-up. I hoped Jake would tell them to go away. He went across, but he seemed to be plying them with drinks.

Jake jumped up again after the next dance and called for silence. This time he had to tell everyone that it wasn't just a big day in his life – he'd forgotten us by now – but a big day in the life of the whole family of Sullivan and Co. and all its associated companies. He was now going to announce, for the first time to the whole world, its biggest project ever, something which would revolutionize the face of London.

I caught Michael's eye. He was shaking his head, sadly, as Jake got more and more carried away. This must be the Big Scheme. Michael had always said it should never be announced at all, until the opening day.

Rupert was in a frenzy, rushing round the press and TV people, shoving glossy brochures into their hands. There were now about fifty press people. I noticed that they'd arrived carrying tickets and handouts.

There was more drum rolling and onto the stage was wheeled a huge trolley, covered in tinsel. It was unveiled to loud cheers. It was a wedding cake. We hadn't been completely forgotten. It was in the shape of the main block of Jake's Big Scheme. Balloons cascaded down and everyone cheered. Then suddenly at the other end of the room, the wall started dividing in two, moving aside like the beginning of Cinerama. On a dais, which took up the whole length of the wall, was a complete model of the whole of Jake's Big Scheme. It was beautifully carved in balsa wood, with trees and shrubs, model cars on the fly-overs and little wooden figures on the raised pavements. The press and TV people rushed forward to get a close look. Jake said loudly, in answer to a question, that the model cost £2,000 and contained seven hundred light bulbs.

Antonia and I tried to get out, but the crowds held us back. Jake hadn't finished yet. There was more trumpeting and drum rolling. Jake waved his hands over his head like a triumphant boxer. When there was silence, he went all quiet and humble, saying he'd never been one of those, perhaps unfortunately, who'd made any secret about how much money he made. All his friends knew how much he despised money. In fact, probably most of the world knew it by now. (Smiles all round, most of all from Jake.) That little offering there, he said, pointing to the gigantic model, is worth almost twenty million pounds. (Gasps.) He didn't mind talking about his profit – no, sorry, *our* profit. (Arms outstretched.) His firm was a co-operative family firm and where he'd be without his trusted colleagues he didn't know. (Cynical smiles from all his trusted colleagues.)

Our profit, he continued, would be no less than ten million pounds. (Prolonged gasps.) But he had decided (long pause) that it was time he started *constructively* giving his money away. (Even longer pause from Jake. People moved on the edge of their seats. Was he going to throw all of it in the air, now . . .?) Jake coughed, raised his hands for complete silence, and went on in deep reverential tones to say that from today he was setting up the Sullivan Foundation. Five million pounds was going into it, all of it to be given away.

There was a hush, then clapping broke out, started by Rupert in the far corner. He was going round giving out more brochures. The press hardly looked at them. They were all rushing forward to ask Jake questions.

Antonia grabbed my hand. If I wanted to stay, I could, but she wasn't staying one second longer. I said of course I was coming. I'd never seen a more revolting ceremony in all my little life.

'I'm glad,' said Antonia, as we hurried out of the door and down the stairs. 'It's taken long enough, God knows. You *have* given your notice in, have you?'

This was the condition she'd imposed if we were to get married. I said yes. Thank God for that, she said. You've come to your senses at last.

Over the microphone, which Jake had somehow got hold

of, I could hear him blubbering on, half crying, that it was the happiest day of his life.

I suppose it was.

Chapter Twenty-seven

'Give us a chance,' I said. 'I've only been there once.'

'Well ask somebody,' said Antonia. 'Don't be so stubborn.'

'Hang on, I'll find it. Don't be so impatient.'

I had the A to Z on my knee, but the car light wouldn't go on. It was a big 1947 Riley that I'd bought for £100 and nothing worked. I had kissed good-bye to my smart Mini, as well as my flat and smart salary, when I left Sullivan and Co.

Eventually, I caught sight of the mews we were looking for, and drove up to the house. She hadn't wanted to come and I knew that if things went wrong they'd be all my fault and she'd say well, I didn't want to come, it's all your fault, and so on. All our arguments are about who started the argument. We'd argued constantly for seven years, since the very minute we met.

I looked for the dangling rope bell, but it had gone. I banged the sanctuary knocker and tried to look through the window. The window boxes had now been painted Thames green. Very 1969. I couldn't see in. All the shutters were up.

Antonia liked Michael. She'd got on well with him one lunch time he'd been trying to get her to join Jake's magazine. It had never materialized of course. I could have hung on for years with Jake still promising it.

Michael was still working with Jake, but Antonia had vowed she would have nothing ever to do with Jake again in any way which was why she hadn't wanted to come tonight. But I wanted to see Michael, to hear all the gossip. I wanted to see Jake as well, but I wouldn't be able to do that, not for a long time, unless I did it without telling Antonia.

The first month after I'd left I'd kept completely away from the sort of places I'd meet them. I hadn't a job. It would be too embarrassing to admit I was out of work and living on Antonia's salary. She'd said I should teach like her. I'd be useless, I'd said. She agreed. Someone as feeble as me would never have any discipline. I fancied going back to journalism, but eventually, through an Oxford friend of Antonia's, I'd got a job as a Government Information Officer. I wasn't established, but if it worked out, I might be by the end of the year. I wanted to tell Michael all this. He'd be quite impressed.

'He did say tonight?' said Antonia, when I banged again and got no reply. 'Be typical of you to have got the wrong day.'

'Of course,' I said, but now wondering. I'd met Michael outside the Garrick Club in Covent Garden last week. He'd said come for dinner, a week tonight, he had lots to tell me. I saw him put it in his diary as he walked off towards Leicester Square. Bring Antonia, *not* Jake this time, he said, looking back and laughing. He was wearing his long dark overcoat and a blue and white spotted silk neckerchief.

'Save the details. You're not in the Boy Scouts,' said Antonia wearily. 'Did *you* put it in your diary?' I got it out. I had. Michael must be inside. I banged again. I couldn't understand why all the upstairs shutters were closed. As I banged a bloke came out of the house opposite. He said Michael was in. He'd noticed him coming home yesterday lunch time, which he'd thought was funny. He'd seen Michael's light on in the middle of the night and he definitely hadn't gone out since. He'd worried all day. He looked a really nosy bloke, but I was beginning to be worried too.

I said where's Kenneth. He'd never heard of Kenneth. He said Michael lives alone, giving a little knowing nod to his head.

He went across to his house and came back with a large heavy spanner which he jammed in Michael's door and started to lever it open. Antonia said she was going. We were just being stupid. Michael would have the police on us for breaking and entering. The door opened quite easily and the bloke bounded up the stairs. Michael's bedroom door was locked, but it opened easily when we pushed it hard. Michael was lying peacefully asleep in bed. He was on his side, facing us, looking very calm. We'd caused about ten quids' worth of damage, all for nothing. I was turning to go when the bloke went to the other side of the bed and picked up eight little bottles from a side table, all empty. He shook Michael. Nothing happened. He went into the living room and rang for the police.

So I was involved once again in the affairs of Sullivan and Co., despite myself. The police saw me three times and I had to go over and over what I knew about him, how definite the dinner arrangement had been, did I know of any rows.

I gathered that Jake, foolishly, told them about a row between Michael and himself, after our nuptials at the Savoy. By midnight he'd been dead drunk and when Michael said he had been absolutely foolish to unveil the plans, Jake had told him to fuck off. What was he doing at a wedding anyway, a pansy like him? They'd had a furious row and a great drunken gang of people had witnessed the encounter. They laughed and jeered when Michael turned and left, with Jake blowing kisses after him.

The police put two and two together and got five. How long had he and Mr. Stein been intimate friends? Had they had many quarrels? Mr. Sullivan wasn't married either, was he? Jake denied vehemently all the inferences, but he admitted that their quarrel might have had something to do with it. What else could it be?

This was partly Jake's usual conceit. He knew so little about Michael and his private life, but he naturally thought he was the biggest thing in everyone's life.

Rupert tried to keep it out of the papers. The stories were very carefully written, as no one knew what exactly had happened, but one reporter, who'd witnessed the Savoy row with Michael, rang up Jake about it. Instead of threatening to sue if it was mentioned, Jake discussed the possibility of it having some connection with Michael's death. Once that was out, everybody started re-telling old stories about Jake, bringing out his violent side. In two days the papers were inferring murder. Rupert was very worried that the Providential, the insurance company putting up all the money to buy the Big Scheme, might get alarmed by hints of scandal and draw out. They were a very old fashioned, highly moral firm.

I ran into James Black, the Scottish ex-RSM, in Soho one morning. He took me into a bar and confided his theory about

Michael's death based on inside information. Michael was jealous, dead jealous of Jake. Always had been. He'd been in at the beginning and been very important. But, well, he'd got left miles behind. Now that Jake was the most successful, most brilliant, best known businessman in Britain, he couldn't stand it any longer. So Michael had done himself in. Jealousy, that was it. Simple. I knew this was all a pack of lies, but I couldn't be bothered arguing with James. I said it hadn't even been proved yet it was suicide so wasn't he jumping to conclusions?

Without telling Antonia, I decided to go and see Kenneth. He said he hadn't heard about Michael's death, but wasn't surprised. The police hadn't got to him yet. He was amazed when I mentioned they might. He hadn't lived with Michael for at least a year, so he didn't see why they should – all very nonchalant and off hand.

He said he'd never really liked Michael. 'I can't stand these queers who can't stand being queer.'

According to Kenneth, Michael had worried about this all the time he'd lived with him, never really reconciled to his nature, or learning to live with it. And it was a very funny nature, mark my words, said Kenneth. Michael was the sort of female queer who preferred very butch boys, who *weren't* queer. This was one of the reasons he'd been attracted to Jake in the first place.

All that leather and Teddy Boy gear and aggressiveness had really sent him. He always went for this type, picking up dockers or seamen, bringing them home and trying to lay them. It rarely worked and Michael usually ended up by being beaten. 'He loved that as well, darling, being a masochist.'

No wonder Michael was on sleeping pills, continued Kenneth. The doctor had always let him have more than he should have, just to keep an eye on him and stop him getting them on the black market.

Michael was also a frustrated artist, said Kenneth. He hated being a businessman. He had casefuls of poetry which he'd written. Very pretentious. That was another reason he went off him.

So Michael's death had really nothing to do with Jake at all? Kenneth said do you mind. It had *everything* to do with Jake.

'Christ, that's why I walked out. It was Jake, Jake, Jake, all bloody night long. That's all he ever talked about and thought about. Jake drove him mad. Michael hated being trodden on by him, yet he loved it. He couldn't do without him. In the end I packed me little bags and went. Anything else you want to know, dear?'

'No thanks. You've been great.'

I couldn't resist telling Jake. It was showing off really. No it wasn't. I just wanted to discuss it with someone, to go over what Kenneth had said. I couldn't tell Antonia.

I rang Jake. I didn't tell him about Michael loving him, but I did go into the awful life Michael had led, being beaten up by labourers and all that. Jake was completely silent. It was all a revelation to him. I don't think he'd really taken it in that Michael was queer.

It was like a gangster's funeral. There were so many hearses piled high with flowers and wreaths and insignia from Sullivan and Co. that the police had to divert people away from Finchley Road. It was standing room only at Golders Green crematorium. Jake had been furious that no synagogue would lay on a big service of commemoration. Michael had never been to a synagogue in his life. But it was Jake which put most of them off. In every conversation with the rabbis he went on about having the funeral first thing in the morning so they'd catch every edition of the Evening Standard.

'Me oldest mate,' said Jake as we filed out of the chapel. He was dabbing his eyes, but not so that he couldn't see where the reporters were and managed to move, solemnly and in deep distress, towards them.

'What a lousy life. And I didn't know. So much for my friends. You were right Tom. I just think only of myself. It was my fault. I should have got to know him better. Do you think I could have helped him?'

I muttered about not thinking so. Michael should have seen a psychiatrist when he was fifteen.

'Not now lads, please,' said Jake, as the reporters approached, 'Have some bloody consideration for a change.'

Jake moved off to speak to several of the leading mourners, especially some minor starlets, looking very dramatic in black, he'd dragged up from somewhere. He comforted one of them waving away the photographers from getting too close.

'Christ what a crowd,' said Jake, coming back to talk to me. 'He was a great bloke. He really was. You've no idea how much I miss him. Really. I've just got all those shitty creeps like Rupert now. Tom, when are you coming back then . . .?'

'You remember the Sullivan Foundation I mentioned at that Savoy shambles?' Jake was conducting another one-man meeting.

'It was a very good party, sir, if I may say so,' said Jimmy.

'Shuttup you bastard,' said Jake furiously. 'It was fucking awful.' The argument with Michael afterwards had now clouded Jake's memory of the party for ever. 'I didn't tell you any details at the time. I've now decided what the Foundation will do with its money. What's more it's not going to have five million, but ten million. *Every* penny we make from the Big Scheme is going into the Foundation. What is the most important natural resource this country has?' said Jake turning on Henry.

'Natural gas,' said Henry. He'd just been put on an All-Party committee on natural gas, which Rupert was hoping would be useful when future contracts were given out.

'Brains,' said Rupert. Most people had heard Jake ask this question before and thought they knew what was coming.

'Exactly,' said Jake. 'And fortunately, this country is not short of brains, only of a way of using them. So I'm going to the root of the trouble. I'm beginning a University. Geniuses like me don't need education,' continued Jake, after he'd given a suitable pause for this to sink in. 'But most people do. We need technologists, scientists, teachers, the lot. And they have to go to University. OK?'

'Where?' asked Rupert.

'Where what?' said Jake.

'Where's this marvellous University going to be?'

'Carlisle,' said Jake. 'My home town of course. They've wanted it for years. They've got a Cathedral, a Castle, but never a University. And me old Mum always said I should help my own folks first, bless her lousy heart.'

'Will it be called the University of Carlisle, or Jake Sullivan University?' said James.

'Thank you James,' said Jake. 'If you just sit tight, I'll pass my arse over to you. There's no need to stand up. You can lick it sitting down.'

'It sounds marvellous,' said Henry, thinking of the honorary degrees he'd be bound to get.

'The ten million will set it up,' Jake went on, ignoring Henry. 'And I'm going to make over to the University every share I possess in Sullivan and Co., Paradise and all the other firms I control. This will give them an income which they can use to run things.'

'But you wouldn't lose control of the firm, would you Jake?' said James, all consternation. 'I mean, it wouldn't be the same if *you* weren't absolute boss.'

'Don't worry your little fat arse,' said Jake. 'I'll still tuck you up at night. I'll still be chairman, if everyone wants me. All that's happened is that at last I've found something really worth doing with all the loot.' There was a long pause, while Jake looked very sincere. Everyone else, though panic stricken at these plans being unfolded before their eyes, tried to pretend they were all equally sincere.

'After all, you can't fuck money. I'm going off to Carlisle for the weekend to have a look at a site. So you can now all fuck off.'

On the drive up to Carlisle in Jake's psychedelic Rolls, Rupert telephoned on the car telephone. Surely Jake must have been kidding about giving *all* the ten million profits to this University. No, said Jake, positively all. What about my little share, whined Rupert, the stuff stashed away in Jersey, with all the other secret shares? All gone, said Jake. I've re-sold them all back to the company. Nobody is making anything on the side. Rupert started to protest, saying it had been dishonest. He'd been taken in on false pretences. Oh shut up, you fat slob, said Jake. You're fired. To his surprise, Rupert said fine. That suited him.

Jake was going down Botchergate, the main street into Carlisle, when he saw a newspaper poster announcing a big property scandal. It was the Sunday Times, one of the papers Chloe had always tried to get him to read. He left his Rolls outside, half on the pavement, blocking the way, with the engine still running, just as J.P. used to do.

It was the whole of an Insight investigation. Three pages

devoted to photostats of confidential documents, private letters, estimates, plus graphs showing the numbers and heights of buildings allowed in central London in the last year. It made it clear how strange it was that the enormously high ones had all gone up in one particular area by one particular firm.

The article was on payola in the property business. It revealed all about directorships, presents and outright bribes given to councillors and council planning officials. There was a lot of stuff from a couple of property tycoons who'd gone bankrupt, telling how they'd always given bribes, but not enough to survive – compared with what the really big boys in the business gave.

Jake stood in the doorway, stopping customers getting in or out, shouting and swearing. He called the shop keeper a fucking bastard when he was asked to move. He started kicking the door down, venting his fury. The shop keeper said he was going for the police. Suddenly Jake stopped and raced across the road into the Citadel Station, the station he'd left from all those years previously.

'London immediately,' he shouted at the ticket barrier. 'I'm Jake Sullivan! At bloody once. First fucking class. Come on!'

He was in luck. The best express train of the day was just arriving. He forgot his Rolls, still ticking over, blocking the pavement for Carlisle's Sunday morning strollers.

Jake knew that the hints about one big property tycoon meant him. But where had they got the information from? It was too bloody ironic. After all the years of petty fiddling, cutting corners, pulling strings, pushing people around to make himself a millionaire. Just at this moment when he'd decided to go straight and do something worthwhile with his money.

Chapter Twenty-eight

'Never liked the chap myself.'

'Which chap?'

'Sullivan, of course. That chappie who was exposed in the Observer. Or was it the Telegraph?'

'How do you know it was him it referred to?'

'Come off it. Who else could it be?'

'Well, you did pretty well out of him, boasting how you put your clients on to this good thing.'

'That was our junior partner. He spent six months under-covering the Seacrill Paradise affair. Yes, we did get in pretty sharpish there, before the prices went up. But we're getting out pretty sharpish as well. My word yes.'

'He'll get out of it, I bet. These fellas always do.'

'But the damage is done. That's what matters.'

Over in Sullivan House Jimmy Black was going round mutter-ing that it was worse than the Blitz. Then at least you knew who the enemy was. Now, everyone had a rumour ready to thrust in.

Jake spent most of his time laughing hysterically, refusing to allow anyone to say it was the end. He'd personally strangle the next bugger who relayed any more gossip. All we've got to do is smile and keep quiet. You'll see. In a few weeks the whole thing will have been forgotten. No one takes any notice of these rubbishy newspaper stories. The next person he caught not smiling in the corridor was going to be sacked.

He was right about the newspapers. The following week In-sight were exposing another art forgery, using what looked like the same graphs as the property scandal. There was no mention of Sullivan and Co. nor any other property firm.

Privately, Jake didn't think it was at all a laugh. Miss Moon had never seen him so neurotic. He began to stay in the office for days, refusing even to wave out of the window at the secre-tary in the opposite building he'd formerly made obscene sig-nals to. He maintained she was watching him. He could see her binoculars gleaming. They had a telephoto lens trained on him. He was changing his office.

'It's a fucking plot. I know it. They're ganging up against me. Miss Moon, ring some private detectives at once. And close that door when I tell you. Christ Almighty. Is that new office ready yet?'

'You only mentioned it this morning, Mr. Sullivan. I'm unable to do everything at once. I can't get hold of the carpenters.'

'Don't stand there twitting on! Have you got these detectives? I've told you once already.'

The detectives were commanded to follow Rupert, Jake's Number One enemy. He was convinced Rupert was behind the Sunday Times story, that he'd sold them the information. He'd do anything for money and revenge at being cut out of the Big Scheme. They had to follow Rupert everywhere, open his letters, listen to his calls.

'Rupert? Is that you, you fat fucker?' said Jake, making his fifth call of the evening. 'I'm coming round to get you. Now! Are you listening? It's no use hiding. You can't hide. Ever. I know exactly where you are. And I know exactly what I'm going to do to you . . .'

Rupert in turn hired a bodyguard and got his solicitors to write to Jake threatening that they would take out an injunction restraining Jake unless the threats ceased.

Jake needed an audience to let off steam and have someone to react against. Michael and I had done this. The faithful Jimmy wasn't much good. Everything that Jake did was marvellous. As Mr. Sullivan had predicted, the rumours and gossip had done no harm. The name of Sullivan and Co. had never actually come out. The Big Scheme was going perfectly. The rats who'd left the ship would live to regret it. The Sullivan Foundation and the University of Carlisle would live for ever.

'Oh shut up, you slob. You bore me. Get out! Miss Moon get rid of him before I hit him.'

Jake closed all the doors, pulled the curtains, hung up all the phones. When Miss Moon returned he had his head in his hands.

'I'm sorry, Miss Moon.'

'Don't apologize, Mr. Sullivan. I understand.'

'You know something? Money and sex don't really matter

in this world. People is what people need. I've got no people left.'

'Can I go now, Mr. Sullivan.'

'Get out! I don't need you. I don't need anybody!'

Jake continued threatening Rupert, then gave up. Rupert was obviously too scared to pull any fast ones or sell any information about Jake. Rupert didn't really know much anyway. But Chloe. Jake had told her everything. Chloe now became Number One.

'A malicious bitch, a really nasty, slimy bitch. I should never have trusted her.'

'I was always of that opinion myself, sir,' said Jimmy.

'Then why the fuck didn't you tell me!'

Jake rang his solicitor to send in a writ for the return of stolen property.

'What property? You must itemize each object exactly.'

'Itemize? What are you going on about? Didn't you see those documents in the Sunday Times. She stole every fucking one of them!'

'Hello shit house.'

'Yes,' I said, nervously. I was wondering when Jake would get round to accusing me.

'I want you to come round at once. I've got some more papers here you might like to sell.'

'Thanks, Jake. I'm giving them up.'

'That's how you got back into journalism, isn't it? I might have known. You bugger.'

'I just happen to be a Government official now, that's all, Jake.

'Don't try to be clever with me. I know you fucking journalists. I should never have trusted you. And after all I did for you, you little runt. Paying for your bloody wedding as well. No wonder you resigned eh. When you'd got what you wanted. You've had it now, though.'

'That's right. Antonia's got me tea ready. I'll have to rush. See you.'

Jake probably reached his depths when he came to the conclusion that it had been Michael after all. No wonder he'd committed suicide. He'd passed on the information to the newspaper, then committed suicide out of guilt. Jake said he'd never *really* liked him. A cold, superior, stuck up prick. That's all Michael was. Not his type at all.

There had been a lot of delays over the inquest on Michael's death, but when the coroner eventually reported, the official verdict was accidental death. It wasn't suicide. Michael had simply taken an overdose of sleeping pills by mistake, allied to an equally high dose of anti-depressants.

'What rubbish,' said Jake, back in the office. 'Typical, psychologist claptrap. I never saw Michael depressed in all my life. A lot of rubbish.'

'If *you* never saw him depressed, Mr. Sullivan,' said Miss Moon, 'you can't have known him very well.'

'What did you say? Who do you think you're talking to. He was the closest friend I ever had. The best. Come on, explain your bloody self, woman.'

'There's nothing to explain. If you didn't see him depressed, then that's it. Incidentally, Mr. Sullivan. I might as well tell you now. I'm leaving.'

Jake got up and advanced towards her. Miss Moon didn't move. He took her by the shoulders and shook her. She said nothing. Jake sat down, mopping his brow.

'I'm sorry. Stay a bit longer. You know what's been going on. That lousy newspaper. It's been a lousy time for everyone, we're over it now. I'll give you more money. Is that what you want?'

'No. I've got a little bit saved. I'm going abroad. I would like to leave in the next week or so, when you've got a replacement.'

'Have a drink.'

'No thanks.'

'Where did you get the money from? It wasn't you was it, flogging secrets?'

'I have a few investments. I've been rather lucky.'

'Tell me more,' said Jake sneering.

'Bolton Textiles. You know, the paper panties firm. I had quite a bit in them. I told Mr. Michael to do the same. He did, but he took it out too soon. Silly boy. He was in one of his usual money panics.'

'I didn't know he had money troubles?'

'All the time. These dreadful boys he picked up were always

blackmailing him. Going off with his things. He must have paid a fortune to get back what they stole from his house.'

'Get me Tom.'

'I tried him earlier. He's not at home. If you don't mind, I'd like to go now.'

I went round to Kenneth's flat as soon as Jake had rung me. Kenneth had gone. The neighbours had no idea where. Abroad, that was all. He'd left a few weeks ago. Checking at the local shop I discovered Kenneth had gone the day after I'd been to see him.

'What do you think, Antonia?'

'I don't think anything.' She was marking examination papers and didn't look up as I burst into the flat.

'It *was* suicide. Michael was being blackmailed by Kenneth. He'd stolen some stuff from Michael and wanted money from him. That's what happens when queers fall out.'

'Who's Kenneth,' said Antonia.

'Give over. You remember. His little friend.'

'I don't. And I don't care. Would you mind keeping quiet?'

'Hey, perhaps it was those documents that appeared in the paper? They were what Kenneth had stolen. When Michael couldn't pay up any more, he flogged them to the paper. Do you think I should go to the police?'

'I think you should keep quiet.'

'I'll go and see Jake. That's the best thing.'

'I'll never forgive you. There is no need to see him, or to have anything to do with Sullivan and Co. again.'

I went up in the lift at Sullivan House. There were few people about. Not like the old days when I worked there. It was pretty early. I was popping in for a few minutes on the way to work to have a word with Jake. Antonia would never know.

I went straight into Jake's suite, not bothering to go through his offices. I didn't have to keep in with anyone. He was standing with the letter in his hand.

'They've backed out.'

'Who have,' I said.

'They couldn't even come and tell me, or even ring. The fuckers.'

Jake sat down quietly, passing me the letter. The Providential, the insurance company putting up the money for the Big Scheme, had changed their plans. They were going to invest their ten million elsewhere. No reasons were given.

'You'll get some other insurance firm, won't you? The Scheme is still as worth buying as it ever was. Isn't it?'

'That's not the bloody point. They've bolshied on me.'

'Why?'

'Christ, don't ask me.'

Jake was staring into space. I was waiting for an explosion, but it was as if Jake had been waiting for this letter. Obviously it was the rumours that had done it. They were a very stuffy, traditional insurance firm. Any hint of scandal and they started running. With Sullivan, ever since the Insight exposure, there had been fresh gossip every day in the City, stories of blackmail, corruption and suicides. Admittedly, there had been nothing else in the newspapers, but there had been nothing to deny all the gossip.

'Don't you worry, son,' said Jake getting up. 'I'll do all the worrying. It's the most bloody marvellous Scheme I've ever done. Not just me. *Anybody* has ever done. There's been nothing like it in London before. Of course I'll sell it. What are you doing here anyway? I never invited you. Get out.'

'I was just passing, that was all . . .'

'What I'll do is put the price up at once. I now want eleven million for it. Not ten. I'll show those fuckers.'

I hadn't managed to tell Jake that Kenneth was at the bottom of the Michael suicide, and perhaps at the bottom of a lot more too. But it was just as well. In El Vino's in Fleet Street that lunch time I heard that the Insight people had dug up all the information themselves. Nobody had come forward and sold them any documents. It was their usual massive team of reporters who had managed to get people to part with the information.

It stood to reason, really. Kenneth wouldn't have been mad enough to try any more blackmail or passing stolen documents, not after Michael's death.

'I bought an Evening Standard. On page two, the first City page, there were two short stories, side by side. One said that the Providential had changed its mind about the proposed deal with Sullivan and Co. They'd not wasted much time giving out that news. They wanted shot of any connection with Jake as soon as possible. An anonymous spokesman for the Providential was quoted as saying that they now considered the deal 'unsatisfactory'. An anonymous Sullivan official said 'no comment'.

The other story was beautifully positioned beside it, hinting to those people in the know at mysterious connections, yet doing it in such a way that no one could sue. It said simply that Robert Blake, one of the GLC's leading planning officials, had resigned suddenly. No reasons were given.

The juxtaposition wouldn't be wasted on Jake, or on a lot of other people. Blake had been Jake's personal contact for years.

Jake had never actually seen him before, which was surprising. Through their years of contact, Jake had always got Jimmy or Rupert to do the dealing. They'd done the lunching and fêting and presented his wife with the new Triumph Heralds, or whatever it was. Jake had stuck to late night telephone calls, going through to him at his stock broker Tudor house in Esher, knowing that important decisions had to be made by the next morning. Jake was good at being menacing, joking about past presents, hinting at future pressures.

It took him some time to find Blake's house. It was on one of those private estates which are arranged like a massive Hampton Court maze, houses hidden well away behind huge hedges, with no numbers and few names to identify them, the sort which Russian spies or famous pop singers always seem to live in.

Jake drove his car across the lawn missing the front drive and main entrance. He ran to the back of Blake's house, crashing in through the rear French windows.

The first surprise was that Blake was about six foot six, well built, bearded and tough looking. Jake had always imagined him a weedy little clerk with rimless specs and shiny trousers. But Jake didn't stop to think twice. All he wanted was to get him.

'You bastard.'

'You've broken that window,' said Blake, ignoring Jake and going to inspect the damage.

'I might have known you were at the bottom of it all. I should have expected a runt like you to be taking bribes from

every fucker, and selling the information to bloody newspapers.'

'Why didn't you come in through the door? I've a good
mind to throw you straight out.'

'Just try it, come on. That's exactly what I want, you two-
timing git.'

'If you're going to stay, sit down and calm down. If you
keep control of yourself, nothing else will happen. I resigned
on medical grounds. That's all. I didn't tell anything to any
newspaper. The first thing I knew was what I read in Insight.
That immediately made the Council start its own investigation.
They haven't reported yet. They might never find anything
else. I waited a few weeks till things had quietened, then I got
my doctor to say I must stop work and go to a warmer clim-
ate . . .'

'You bloody liar!'

Jake lashed out at Blake with his foot. He caught Blake on
his hip, but Blake managed to grab Jake's leg and they fell to
the ground. Jake fell on top and had Blake round the neck
when a manservant entered the room and pulled Jake away.
With Blake's help, the two of them threw Jake out.

'Oh hello Jake,' I said. There was a long pause from the other
end. 'Fancy you ringing. I tried to get you last night. Where
were you?'

'Half killing Blake.'

'Oh yeh. Better than watching tele I suppose . . .'

There was another long pause. Perhaps I shouldn't have
joked.

'So, how is it going, then?'

'It isn't. It's coming down.'

'What is? London Bridge?' There was silence. 'Or knickers?'
Jake still didn't laugh.

'You're joking!'

'A bloke from the Council came round this morning. Nice
little bloke. Just a clerk. Rimless specs. He said the whole building has to come down. Apparently I haven't got some minor
permission. Silly isn't it. Blake had promised me he had it all
cut and dried. He told me that himself last year. He said we
could go ahead and build. Everything was in order. But, there
you go.'

I didn't know what to reply.

'Bit of a fucking shame, isn't it. That's the end of Sullivan and Co.'

'Don't be daft. It doesn't mean that.'

'Oh yes it does. Everything was tied up in it. I've no other money. Not that I care. Just hard luck on those uneducated people in Carlisle. They've had their fucking University, this time round anyways.'

'Jake, there's no need to over-dramatize it . . .'

'You what,' said Jake not listening to me. 'So, if you want to see everything falling down, come round next week some time. I'll probably get J.P. to do the demolition. Be a good laugh. See you.'

Jake didn't wait a week. When he hung up on me he drove round to J.P.'s yard, got out a bulldozer and drove it through the West End to Holborn.

He'd driven through a pile of scaffolding and was charging down the workmen's huts, screaming and shouting to the delight of a large crowd, when the police arrived.

The charge was bodily assault. That was the first charge. Blake, who'd been arrested as the result of Council investigations, had lodged a complaint against Jake. This charge was soon dropped when the proper case against Jake came up. It lasted five weeks at the Old Bailey. It was for bribery and corruption. Jake got three years.

Chapter Twenty-nine

It was November 1970. I was thirty, exactly. I was trying to remember who else had the same birthday as me, but I couldn't remember. It's a sign of getting ancient, when you stash away in your head such trivialities as people with birthdays near yours. Another sign is always likening every new person you meet to some old person from your past. The bloke selling newspapers outside the Angel Islington had worried me for days. That long body with the drip on his nose reminded me of someone I knew. But who?

I went to Upper Street and cut across to the Caledonian Road. There seemed to be a series of high walls. I got behind one, but there were others I couldn't find the gate to. The main one appeared to be boarded up. I went left and came into a block of what looked like Gorbals tenements. Now who was it I knew who used to live in the Gorbals? That would worry me all day.

I knocked at one door and three kids rushed out, saying if I was the Club man their Mam was out. They didn't have wives and families in prisons, not the last time I went to the films anyway. I thanked them kindly and retraced my way to the main road.

Pentonville Prison had always sounded quite attractive. Not like Dartmoor, the Scrubs and Strangeways. I liked the sound of it, the way I liked the sound of Angel Islington. Being brought up on Monopoly all those years had made it very homely.

I was shown into an Assistant Governor's office. He was watching me watching an enormous white mug, the giant size that workmen have on labouring sites. He took it away and put it in a drawer. I hadn't even been looking at it, just resting my eyes. I turned with a smile and found myself reading a cyclostyled news sheet, upside down. It was the prisoners' house magazine, written and duplicated by themselves. He jumped across the table and put that away, locking the drawer this time.

I was doing a bit of free lance journalism. Like being a policeman, people always think journalists are going to put things down and bring them out later in evidence. He must have found out I was here as a journalist, though I hadn't told him. I was sure all visitors didn't do their visiting in the Assistant Governor's office. I was officially visiting a friend. At least he used to be last time I saw him. I was also here to do a bit of work, a piece for a colour supplement series called Where Are They Now. Even so-called posh papers have people thinking up corny ideas. You could do Where Are They Now articles every week these days. People get built up so quickly and then fall down even quicker that in a week people start saying, I wonder what happened to old so and so, he used never to be out of the papers?

It was now almost a year since Jake Sullivan had made a line. This was so long ago that in writing the piece I'd have to have a long intro, setting him up and informing all the ignorant millions about him, before going on to say that now he's down and out.

Jake probably wasn't. Though he lost millions on the Big Scheme and the firm was ruined, I'd always suspected he'd got a bit stashed away in Switzerland. He could probably have carried on the firm and started even more deals even with his Big Scheme knocked down, if the Council hadn't carried on their enquiries even further.

Jake came on strong and cocky, as usual, clapping his hands together and rubbing them.

'Let's have you, Tommy lad. What's new?'

'Not much,' I said. 'You ain't missed nothing. Balance of payments just the same. No change in the bank rate. Antonia's having a baby.'

'Curses,' said Jake. 'That's not gonna help my stocks and shares, is it? And another mouth to feed. Well, there's always the Moon.'

The Assistant Governor was sitting at his desk, pretending to read his Daily Telegraph. Jake was walking round and round the room, making faces behind him. Not nasty ones. Just playing silly buggers.

Jake looked slightly thinner, but much fitter and healthier. He had an anonymous blue boiler suit on. I'd been hoping for upturned arrows and had been practising jokes about no entry, one way only and make sure your exit is clear before entering the box.

'You're looking well,' I said.

'It's the caviar and the smoked salmon. I've had heartburn ever since I entered this place.'

The Assistant Governor smiled thinly, turning back to the page he'd just read. I'd have preferred Jake to be silent and sullen. He would have been stronger somehow. Making jokes so bravely was a bit sad. I didn't like the position of him humouring me, by being cheerful. I'd much preferred it when it was me humouring him.

'Don't take any notice of him,' said Jake. 'He just lives here.

He's got a non-speaking part today, unless of course I say F-U-C-K or S-H-I-T. Before I come out I'll have to take correspondence classes in swearing again. I'll have forgotten everything. So how's the little woman?'

'Enormous,' I said.

'I've got this great idea,' said Jake before I'd even started to tell him about Antonia. 'I'm making a take-over bid for Pentonville. It's a natural. I'm also after Holloway, Wandsworth, Brixton and Wormwood Scrubs. Do you realize all of them have got fabulous positions, all within a few miles of Piccadilly? It's bloody ridiculous – sorry, sir, it just came out.

'Five prisons in the middle of London! They should be in the north of Scotland or somewhere cheap like that. I could build five fantastic blocks on the sites then build them five new prisons somewhere for nothing, out of the profits.'

'Sounds great,' I said.

'It's more than great. I'd be a public benefactor and really get me OBE. This is the worst prison I've ever been in, ask anyone, even our non-speaking friend there. They're all the same. All built last century and should have been knocked down fifty years ago. Have you read the Mountbatten Report?'

'Eh, not recently,' I said. 'Anyway, after you've done all that, what are you gonna do?'

'Well for an encore, I'll do the London hospitals. There's no need for them to be where they are either. Look at Charing Cross Hospital, have you ever seen a dafter place for a hospital? It's falling down, yet the site's worth at least a million.'

There was a knock at the door and a warder, I mean prison officer, brought in three cups of tea. They must definitely suspect I was a journalist. I thought about mentioning I wanted to write an article, but I'd be put straight out. It was too late now. You have to get special permission first from the Home Office to get into any prison as a journalist, then they have to see what you want to write. I couldn't be bothered with all these petty regulations. It was petty regulations of course which Jake hadn't been bothered with either.

'Seriously,' I said. 'You'll be out in just over another year, what are you gonna do?'

'Not property anyway, probably not even money. I've done all that scene. If I can do it once, I can do it again, so why bother. I'm just lucky I got all the scene over with quickly. It must be a real drag if it takes till you're sixty to make your pile, and *then* lose it. What a come-down.

'But me, well, I haven't done nothing yet, have I? All I've done is get to square one. I started behind. Now I'm level. I don't have to prove anything any more. I can do what I like.'

'Such as?' I said. I needed a few definite ideas for the sake of my piece.

'I dunno. Underwater wrestling. Sky diving. You can write whatever you like.'

The Assistant Governor turned round and looked at me.

'I've written to your mother this week,' I said hurriedly. 'I'll keep it for next week's letter. Do you want anything next time I come, bread and dripping, jug of water, or does Jimmy bring you such luxuries?'

'You're joking. He went off with Miss Moon. Jimmy wasn't as stupid as we thought. Miss Moon's got thousands stashed away.'

'And what about you ...' I said slowly, watching to see if the Assistant Governor was listening.

'I'll do all right,' said Jake, smiling. 'But you could do me one favour and get me some things.'

The Assistant Governor was now all ears.

'A big gnarled stick,' said Jake. 'The sort that gnarled Boy Scouts have. A see-through compass. A good pair of walking boots. A couple of pairs of shorts, shirts and some unisex under pants. Just get them ready for me on the day I come out, OK?'

'Are you opening a shop?'

'Give over. I'm walking round the world. See some reality for a change, some real people. What else is there in life? I'll probably pop into Switzerland first, look up a few old numbers, that sort of thing ...'

'Well,' I said getting up. 'Great to see you. I'll tell them all in Thwaite you're in grand fettle.'

'If it's a girl,' said Jake as I was leaving the office, 'Call her Jake, eh. And a happy birthday. See you.'

I was going past the Angel Islington when I remembered it was also Jake's birthday. I'd forgotten his. He remembered mine. Nice to have friends. Who wants money or sex.